# Awakenings

## A CUTE MUTANTS ANTHOLOGY

SJ WHITBY    SHELLY PAGE    ELLE TESCH    ANDY PEREZ

HSINJU CHEN    SHANNON IVES    MELODY ROBINETTE

ASTRA DAYE    YVES DONLON    E.M. ANDERSON

HESTER STEEL    MONICA GRIBOUSKI

CHARLOTTE HAYWARD    AMANDA M. PIERCE

EMMA JUN

EDITED BY SJ WHITBY

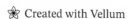 Created with Vellum

# The Series So Far

*Cute Mutants Vol 1: Mutant Pride*
*Cute Mutants Vol 2: Young, Gifted, and Queer*
*Cute Mutants Vol 3: The Demon Queer Saga*
*Cute Mutants Vol 4: The Sisterhood of Evil Mutants*
*Weapon UwU Vol 1: Godkillers*
*Cute Mutants Vol 5: Galaxy Brain*
*Shitty Mutants (patreon exclusive)*
*Project Himbo*

*The next page contains spoilers for the Cute Mutants series.*
*If you want to go in blind, skip it...*

# *Previously*

Let's assume there are such a thing as mutants in the world—people with strange and unnatural powers. They were first created long ago by an alien energy network woven within the planet, commonly known as Cybele.

Most people aren't aware of this. All knowledge of mutants was lost until very recently, when things began to change.

One of the triggers of this shift was a child born to two very powerful mutants. In time, she had a team of others around her, who came together to fight enemies and help mutants through the disasters they faced.

And yet despite everything they did, the planet was dying.

In an attempt to save the planet and mutantkind from their shared dire fate, the girl accumulated power. It was an act of desperation to stave off extinction, but she took on far more than anyone could possibly hold.

And in time, she was lost. It was a choice between death and destruction, and she chose to leave a safer world behind her.

When she passed away, all that power flowed back into Cybele. This vast spill of energy rippled out around the world, giving rise to a whole host of new mutations among the population.

They're springing up everywhere.

We call this the Awakening.

# Contents

# Farsight

The kid is exhausted, but they still won't listen. I say kid, but it's not really accurate. Dylan Taylor. Half-plant, half-mutant, all shattered. Someone who's not only burning the candle at both ends, but has set the entire candle on fire and still isn't satisfied.

"Mutants," they growl at me, almost kicking a seat over as they climb into it. "Find them all."

I shift uncomfortably. "My power's not what it used to be."

"I don't care. Fucking locate them, Farsight. It's in your damn name."

We're in a slender wooden tower rising high above everything else on this small island we now call home. Everyone's calling it Mutopia, or else Miracle. Our new home, grown by Cybele, who's either an alien or a nature spirit. I'm too afraid to ask. This tower was grown here for me, so I can use my ability to look around the world and try and find any newly awakened mutants. After we lost Goddess, and all the power in her flowed back into the world, there's been a flourishing of people with abilities springing up across the globe. It's still happening, more every day.

And we're supposed to save them all, no matter how blind I feel.

Dylan has finally battled their chair to a standstill. They look at me, eyes drooping, hair leaf-strewn and messy.

"Found one," I tell them. "Chicago."

They're instantly awake, the full focus of their attention hitting me like a wave. "Tell me everything."

# Rose

## SHELLY PAGE

A HEADACHE SLOWLY BUILDS BEHIND MY EYES, TURNING the fluorescent lights into nails that stab and the chatter of customers in the café into booms that rattle my skull. My skin itches something awful. I scratch and scratch, but it only seems to make the feeling worse. I haven't felt this off since I ate four chili-dogs at the Taste of Chicago two years ago. My only reprieve is that I have an hour left of wiping tables and taking orders. Then I can go home to Sam, who's probably face-deep in a textbook while chewing manically on Twizzlers. College seems like a kick in the chest, but I know Sam will make it through. I don't know anyone with even half as much determination as them. Four years in and I'm still shocked they want to be with me.

"Rose, Table 7 is still waiting on water," Adriel says as he breezes past me toward the kitchen. Sweat plasters thick dark curls to his forehead. His hands are full of dirty dishes and the dark liquid sloshes over the sides of several cups and onto the dingy tile floor.

With a sigh, I retie my apron, grab the water pitcher from the stand near the bar, and head toward the booth in the back of the diner. Three men in their early twenties talk animatedly as I approach. They eye me with interest as I lean across the table to pour them water. My black V-neck T-shirt isn't exactly revealing, but low enough. Apparently.

The guy closest to me leans forward and leers. "Hey, Mama," he says. I step back, but he catches my wrist. "You are so beautiful."

I jerk my arm out of his grasp. His friends share amused looks and snicker.

"Stay a while. What's the rush?" Handsy Guy drawls before scratching his uneven stubble with long fingernails.

I resist the urge to gag but do roll my eyes. "I have other customers," I say with more bite than I probably should if I want a tip, but it's hour seven of my shift and everything hurts.

"No need to be rude," one of the men says. His simple style and clean-shaven face would've fooled me into thinking he was decent if he hadn't opened his mouth.

The third guy with a thick beard and a dangerous glint laughs heartily. "Yeah, I think I need help with the menu." He drags his gaze along my frame. "What's your favorite thing to eat?"

I clench my fists until my knuckles crack, but work hard to keep my face tempered. I need this tip. "Everything here is good," I reply. "I'll give you a few more minutes to decide."

I suck up to customers day after day and it never gets me more than a few extra dollars, but I need that money. With Sam in school, I'm left covering most of our bills, which means placating dickheads like these.

As I head to my next table, one of the men comments on my butt just loud enough for me to hear. I have half a mind to tell Jerrold, but I clock out in thirty minutes, and I'd rather not deal with the drama of them potentially causing a scene.

Over the next half an hour, I dodge a few more sexist comments and hold back a headache with two Tylenols and a pint of water. Table 7 remains horrible, but they do leave a 10% tip, which is more than I was expecting.

Sam says I work too much and don't leave enough time for myself, but I'm not sure what I'd do if I had the time. School was never in the cards for me. Getting my GED at seventeen was the best decision I could have made, but I don't want to be a waitress for the rest of my life either. I wish I could figure out what would make me happy. Something attainable, but certain. I don't want to end up like my mom. She wanted to be a dancer her whole life. She graduated top of her class from Juilliard and had multiple companies begging her to sign with them, but the summer after graduation she got pregnant with me and that was that. No more going on tour with American Ballet Theatre. The closest gig was teaching contemporary dance at a small studio downtown. Mom always encouraged me to try new things and follow my dreams, but even while watching me somersault in gymnastics or score a goal in soccer, her eyes never shone like they did in the photos and videos of her dancing as a teenager.

I saw firsthand what having a dream—a purpose—ripped away does to a person. It's a slow death. Moral of the story: no one actually gets the things they want most. Especially not people like me.

I clock out, grab my bag, and head to my bus stop with more pep in my step than I've had all day. I can't wait to sink into Sam's arms and breathe in their scent, which today is probably instant coffee and Doritos. Afterward, we'll fall asleep on the couch watching cartoons like a couple of kids.

I draw up short when I see the 151 is out of service until tomorrow night. I barely have enough money in my account to call a shared ride, but try anyway. Just my luck, there are no Ubers or Lyfts nearby. I press my palm against my head to ease the budding pressure there. A single yellow cab drives past with three people shoved into the backseat and a girl hanging out of the passenger side window. She winks before disappearing into the night. I'm alone again.

Darkness and an electric quiet unnervingly presses against me. It's never totally silent so close to downtown. The distant murmur of traffic on Lakeshore Drive and tourists leaving Montrose Beach create a tinny static that makes my ears ring. This late at night, however, it's often empty in such a residential neighborhood.

I could walk home but doing so alone isn't a safe option. I start to text Sam for advice when someone yells from down the street.

"Hey!"

I turn around slowly, my heart rate climbing with each passing second. Three men stand at the end of the block. When I focus, I recognize them from the diner. Table 7.

*Damn.*

The three of them approach me like predators. Long, slow gaits and piercing stares.

"Look," Handsy Guy says once he's a few yards away. "It's the pretty little waitress with the fat ass."

My stomach churns like a load of wet clothes in the washer. I look around, as if a bus will magically appear and whisk me away, but this isn't a fairytale. No one's coming to save me.

"What's your name, sweetheart?" the bearded one asks. When I ignore him, he latches onto my arm with an iron grip.

Immediately, my skin is on fire. It prickles like something sharp is trapped just beneath the surface. The man holding me hollers and slackens his grip enough for me to rip free. My skin reddens like molten glass. I trace a finger along my arm, and it snags on something sharp. A pinprick of blood bubbles on the tip of my forefinger.

*What the fuck?*

"You bitch!" Bearded Dude yells. He lunges for me, arms flailing. One by one little needles burst through my skin. No. Not needles. *Thorns.*

The man draws up short, his eyes widening. "What the—"

The thorns shoot from my arms and palms, cutting through the air with rapid precision. Three embed into the chests of the men closest to me with wet *thunks.*

Handsy Guy howls, "She's a mutie!"

Bearded Dude pulls a thorn out his collarbone with wide eyes. His expression morphs from shocked to pissed in the span of a second. "I'm gonna report you."

"It doesn't work that way anymore." Clean-Shave says breathlessly. He tugs on his friends' arms. "Come on. Let's just go!"

Bearded Dude hesitates during which I mentally prepare for a fight I'm due to lose, but at the last second, he turns. I'm left breathing fast and hard as the men scatter like the sewer rats they are. I drop to the ground, the concrete scraping against my knees. In the reflection of the bus booth, I see myself and nearly faint. I'm *glowing*. My skin is bright red, thorns sprouting from every visible surface. I look like a terrifying, poisonous...plant.

MY HANDS TREMBLE with adrenaline as I enter my apartment fifteen minutes later. I ran the entire way home, only slowing once for a passing glance at a blackened store window to see I've returned to normal. No red skin. No thorns. Maybe I imagined it?

I've seen those reports on the news. Heard of people changing. That's not me. It can't be. I just need to get out of these clothes and into the shower. But my hands are still shaking, my heart galloping in my chest.

The apartment foyer is dark, and I don't bother with the lights. Raging panic claws at my throat and wraps around my lungs. The air has turned thick and syrupy, making it impossible to take a full breath.

*Calm down*, I tell myself, but that's never worked in the past. Why should it now?

And where the hell is Sam?

I don't want to drag them into this, but there's no one else that can help me. Sam is my everything. They don't care that I'm a high school dropout. They laugh at my terrible jokes and worship my curves even when they start to look more like rolls. They listen to me and are more supportive than I deserve. They're also particularly good at quelling my panic attacks.

I fish my phone from my bag. Three rings. Three *long* rings where the air slips further and further away from me and then—

"Hey, babe. I'm walking home from 7-Eleven. How was work?" Their voice is soothing and sure—a warm blanket on a cold night. "Rose? Are you okay?"

"I...panicking." Those are the only two words I can get out, but they're enough. Sam knows what to do with them.

"Okay, I'm here, baby. I'm here. Focus on the sound of my voice, okay?" I nod as if Sam can see me. "Focus on me," they say just as my thoughts start to drag back to my lack of oxygen.

I do. I listen to Sam breathe slowly then ask me to do the same. We do our usual dance when panic hits and it works, even over the phone. Within a few minutes, my lungs start working again. The room doesn't feel so small.

"Good," Sam says once I've officially stopped wheezing.

"Thanks," I whisper.

"You gonna tell me what triggered this one?" they ask.

Oh. Right. I know the world has changed, but I can't be what Handsy Guy called me. I'm a waitress. There's nothing remotely remarkable about me. Sure, on bad days, I wish for something more. Something like ballet was to my mom. Something to make Sam proud of me and me proud of myself, but what if I never get it? What if all I do is waste precious time?

"I tell you when you get home, babe," I mumble, hoping this isn't the start of the end.

I MEET Sam along the stretch of beach behind our apartment because I'm so needy I can't even wait for them to come inside. My body instantly calms when I see their slim frame, round face, and black hair. They're wearing the same Loyola University hoodie and joggers from yesterday. As usual, their thick plastic glasses inch toward the tip of their nose. I let myself be soothed by the familiarity of it all.

"Hey, you," I say, trying to keep my tone light.

"Hi." Sam wraps me in a hug and I bury my face in their neck. They smell faintly of coconut shampoo and the remnants of Dollar Store laundry detergent. It's not the coffee and Doritos I'd pictured earlier, but just as comforting.

"Gonna tell me what happened?" they ask, a splash of worry softening their words.

I take a minute to steady myself before I speak. I know they're going to freak out, but I can't keep this to myself, either. We don't keep things from each other, and I don't know how to deal with it alone. "I was attacked after work."

"What?" Sam's entire body tenses, concern mushrooming into fear. Or anger.

I wince and pull back enough to look at them. Their oval eyes are black in the dark and their warm brown skin is muted in the cottony glow of the moonlight.

"I'm fine," I assure them quickly. "Really. I just...there were these guys who were sort of harassing me at work and then I saw them outside when my shift ended. One grabbed me—"

"Shit." Sam runs a hand furiously through their hair before latching onto my shirt so tightly their knuckles crack. "Did they hurt you? I'll kill them, Rose."

"This coming from the person who wouldn't let me kill the cricket in our bathroom because bugs deserve compassion too?" Sam is not amused. If anything, their frown deepens. I drop my chin and give their forearm a reassuring squeeze. "Just listen, okay? One grabbed me, but then something happened. I started to change. My skin turned blood-red, and thorns shot out of my arms and hands like some kind of threatened porcupine."

Sam shakes their head, hair tangling around their neck. A cold breeze wraps around us and I shuffle closer to them.

"I don't understand," they say.

I'm going to have to tell them, now. I inhale deeply and steady myself. "Okay, um, you know those reports of people with abilities?"

Sam's eyes widen as they slowly piece together what I'm poorly trying to say. "No way. You think you're a *mutant*?"

I scrunch my nose. "I-I don't know for *sure*, but maybe."

"Of course you'd get mutant powers!" they exclaim, the last vestige of anger giving way to intrigue bordering on giddiness. They've been following the rise of mutations since it started. Even wrote a fan letter to Chatterbox last year. Sam claps their hands together once, a smile breaking across their face. "Show me."

"Absolutely not."

"Why?"

I cross my arms, remembering how terrifying I looked. "Because I'm a freak, Sam! I don't want you to see me like that."

"You're a *marvel*," Sam corrects. They take my hand and give it a gentle squeeze. "I don't care what you are, Rose. I love you either way. Besides, times have changed. You don't have to be afraid."

Times may have changed, but I still feel guilty for further complicating our lives. Growing up, I could never shake the feeling that I wasn't enough for my mom because of how much she lost when she had me. That feeling has followed me into every relationship since. Sam loves me, I know they do, but sometimes I think they deserve more than me.

"There's a place people like you can go," they continue, eyes shining.

"Oh yeah?" I know the place, but I play dumb because Sam's trying. Leaving isn't an option. Not with Sam in school and not without Mom.

"Yeah, they could train you," Sam continues. "You're always

ROSE

saying how you wish you could be a part of something. Well, maybe this is your chance."

In front of us, black waves lap at the shore, sliding over dark sand and muted pebbles. When I've been bold enough to think about what I want from life, *mutant* never entered the chat. I don't know how to process having another minority identity. I'm already a Black gay woman. Now I might need to add "mutant" to the list of reasons the majority hates me.

"I'm not leaving you or Mom," I tell Sam. My life may not be great, but it's familiar. It's mine.

Sam's expression lapses into one of sympathy and my stomach twists. "Your mom will understand. She'd at least want you to learn all you can about your abilities. Something extraordinary just fell into your lap, Rose. You can't be afraid to make the most of it. I'm always telling you to shoot for the stars, but you act like you're afraid of heights. I know you're scared of ending up like your mom, but at least she tried. You won't even do that."

The words are spoken softly and aren't meant to be cruel, but still, I flinch from the sting. No one likes being called a coward, no matter how sugarcoated the delivery.

"You don't know what it was like growing up with someone who never saw their dreams come true."

"Did you ever stop to think that maybe your mom did, though?" I frown in confusion. "She had you," Sam clarifies.

"I'm nothing special," I respond.

Sam snorts, closing the distance between us with one, short stride. Even though I'm still sore from their earlier words, I let them thread their fingers through mine. "That couldn't be further from the truth."

I squeeze their hand. "Let's go inside.'" I nod to the 7-Eleven cup. "I'm tired and your coffee's getting cold."

Hurt flashes across their face at my blatant dismissal, but I pretend not to notice. It's better this way.

I'M SHAKEN when I go into work the next day. Every time I look in the mirror, I see myself as that *thing*. Plant-like. Red with thorns.

I dump my bag in the backroom where all the employees keep their belongings during their shifts and grab a clean apron off the rack near the kitchen. I'm just securing the over-bleached smock around my waist when my boss, Jerrold, spots me. His eyebrows dip together and his lips pinch to one side.

"Rose, Adriel told me something disturbing he saw last night." Jerrold pauses here, just long enough for me to start to panic. "He said you attacked three men near the bus stop on Sheridan. Is it true? Are you one of *them*?"

My blood runs cold. "What?"

"Are you one of those mutants?" he asks. His face is a blotchy shade of pink. "You are, aren't you?"

I shake my head, desperately trying to get control of the situation. "What exactly did Adriel see?"

"He saw you turn into a plant and shoot needles at three men leaving the café. Adriel is a good man. He wouldn't lie about something like that." Jerrold runs a hand along his jaw. "Listen, I can't have you working here if you're going to put our customers at risk."

"I'm not! Those men approached *me*! I was trying to defend myself. I didn't know I was a mutant until the attack."

Jerrold shakes his head. To his credit, he actually looks remorseful as worry-lines bud along his forehead. He nods toward my apron. "I'm sorry, Rose."

My eyes brim with tears. Even though this is the last thing I want to happen, I can't help but feel some relief that Jerrold's only response is to let me go. If I had mutated a few weeks earlier, I'd be getting more than fired. I'd be reported. Chicago isn't as bad as other places in the world, but people here still distrust mutants.

"Please, don't do this," I say in a last-ditch effort to keep my job. "It's just something that happened."

"Maybe, but it's who you are now. And it's uncontrolled. I can't have you working here if you're going to be a liability." He sighs as if this is as hard on him as it is on me, which can't possibly be the case. "Listen. Take some time. Figure your shit out and maybe we can talk. Until then, you're done."

He takes my apron and leaves me standing in the dimly lit hallway, mouth agape. Adriel spots me and quickly turns the other way. Fucking coward. He could have at least attempted to help me that night.

This time, when the tears come, I can't stop them from falling.

I'M STILL THINKING about what Jerrold said, about my mutation being a part of me, as I walk through rows and rows of perfectly cut grass. I visit my mother at least once a week to bring her fresh flowers and update her about my life. I need her now more than ever.

Her gravestone is on the smaller side and easy to overlook, but it's near an apple tree and she loved apples. I toss the dead flowers aside and lay down the fresh daisies I bought from the stand near the train station.

"Hey, Mom," I say as I kneel on the spongy lawn. Moisture seeps into my jeans and pools in my eyes. "It's been one hell of a week and it's only Wednesday." I swallow hard to keep from crying. "I lost my job today. It's not my fault, though. I swear."

I'm almost as nervous as I was coming out, even though Mom already knew I was gay when I told her. She welcomed me with a hug and a story about a girl at Juilliard she used to hook up with. I picture her reacting similarly now. I know she's still here with me, even if I can't see or touch her.

"I think I'm a mutant," I say, my voice trembling a bit. The more I say it, even if it's just inside my head, the more it starts to resonate with me. I don't fully know what it means to be a mutant yet, but maybe one day soon I'll have the courage to find out.

The wind rustles in response. Mom is speechless as usual.

"I know...it shocked me, too." I chuckle humorlessly. "What am I going to do? Sam thinks I should try to find others like me. There's a place I could go, where I would learn to control my gift, meet other people like me, and finally have a purpose, but....I can't leave you. I can't leave Sam."

The same prickling along my skin I felt yesterday at the diner starts again. It isn't as uncomfortable as it was the first time, but I still can't control it. It's like a defense mechanism or a response to heightened emotions.

Suddenly, my body bursts into the colorful weapon from last night: red skin and thorns itching to escape. I suck in a sharp breath, conscious of it being broad daylight. I look around, but the only other people in the graveyard are too far away to even notice me. Birds keep a close watch from a nearby tree and a lone squirrel steals fallen apples next to me.

"See?"

With a sigh, I try to change back. Try to tuck in the prickly parts of myself that make me undesirable to some and a marvel to others.

But I can't.

Uncertainty quickly becomes a sharp pain in my ribs. Jerrold was right. I don't have any control over my powers.

A loud scream sends my heart kicking against my chest. Spikes shoot out of my arms, embedding into the grass and a nearby tree. The couple, that until a few minutes ago was far away, is now close enough to see that I'm as bright as a tomato. One of my thorns has landed mere inches from their feet.

*Shit.*

They scurry down the sloping hill and toward the parking lot, whispering furiously to each other and glaring over their shoulders.

All the while, my skin slowly morphs from red to brown. My thorns sink back into their hiding spots.

I hang my head. I could have hurt them. I need to do something about this. What if the next time I lose control, Sam is with me? What if I accidentally hurt them? I can handle scaring a few misogynists, even losing my job, but I can't handle putting my partner in danger.

Maybe Mutopia is the solution. I could not only learn how to control and develop my powers, but also find other people like me. People who understand what I'm going through and won't judge me or try to change me. I smooth down my hair and sigh. It's at least worth a visit.

SAM'S GRILLING veggie burgers on the stove when I get home, swaying their narrow hips to a song in their head. The smell of soy and vegetables fill our tiny apartment as I pad over to them and slip my arms around their waist. I rest my chin on their shoulder, breathing in the scent of their shampoo.

"Hey, babe!" they say before turning off the stove. "Just in time."

"Hey." Last night, Sam apologized for being pushy about me exploring my abilities, but they needn't have. I've been thinking about what that might look like since leaving the cemetery. The possibilities are sprouting like roots, but I can't entertain any of them without talking to Sam first.

I clear my throat. "So, I've been thinking a lot about what you said. About visiting Mutopia? I think...maybe I should go."

Sam spins around to face me, a slow smile spreading across their face. "Really? Okay, yeah. I think that's a great idea."

"Seriously?" They are more enthusiastic than I anticipated.

Sam's responding laugh warms my belly. "I mean, yeah. I suggested it. What made you change your mind?"

"You did, actually. If I'm going to have abilities, I might as well learn how to control them. Until I get a handle on this new part of myself, I'll keep having outbursts and I don't want you getting caught in the crosshairs. It's time I figure out what I want from life, starting with what it means to be a mutant."

"I think that's a great idea," Sam says around a smile.

"But what about you? I don't know how long I'll be gone." Leaving is going to be the hardest thing I've ever done, but Sam seems unfazed.

They stare at me like I'm dumb. "I'm coming with you," they say as if it's the most obvious thing in the world.

"What? You aren't a mutant. And you have school."

Sam's halfway done with their first year at Loyola. I can't ask them to come with me. I'm not worth giving up everything they've worked for.

"So? I'd like to see those bastards try to keep me away from you," Sam replies. They nudge my shoulder. "As for school, online courses exist, you know."

I shake my head. "I'm not worth your education."

Sam takes my hand. "Haven't you been listening to anything I've said over the course of our relationship? You are absolutely worth it. You're remarkable without the mutation. Imagine what you can be with it?" Sam pulls me closer, their strong arms radiating warmth. "I'll get my degree online and you'll learn to control your gift. We can have our cake and eat it too. Don't make this more complicated than it has to be."

My head fills with images of us together in Mutopia. In every single one, we're smiling. "You'd do that for me?"

Sam kisses my cheek, and I sink into their embrace. "I'd do anything for you. I'm all in. Always."

My heart feels too big for my chest. I can't believe we're doing this or that Sam is coming with me. For the first time since discovering my abilities, I let myself think about what being a mutant could mean for my future. Mutopia could be exactly what I've been

ROSE

missing. My power could finally be what adds balance to my life. It could be my calling.

I'm out of excuses not to go. I don't have a job. I'll definitely miss visiting Mom, but she'll always be with me and she wouldn't want me living small out of fear. Plus, my very own (and unfairly cute) panic repellant will be with me every step of the way.

I take a deep breath and fill my lungs with this new possibility. A new version of me sits just beneath my skin, waiting to be brought to life. Waiting to be given a purpose.

Sam's right. I've been given something extraordinary, so why not see how far I can take it?

"Okay," I whisper, my lips tugging at the corners. "Mutopia, here we come."

# Farsight

"I like when they come to Mutopia." Whenever Alyse Sefo enters the room, it's like a stormfront coming. I don't think she's even aware of her involuntary transformation into darkness and driving rain. She's still grieving, going through a loss I can barely understand. It's not that I haven't loved, but Alyse and Goddess had a relationship that felt like a universe on its own. A certain few got to glimpse inside the whirling galaxies of their minds, but for everyone else the real world felt airless and arid in comparison.

Sometimes I brood on my own loss, the collapse of that incandescent pyre of power back to a dull ember. Once I beheld the whole world, sifting through countless images to find important sparks. Now I'm gazing through my window, eyes bloodshot and scratchy no matter how many drops I use, dragging my gaze from scene to scene with tiresome effort.

When I see Alyse, I feel small and petty for considering my own pain above hers. And yet I still never know what to say, preferring to cultivate my distracted air. Farsight—always looking beyond.

Dylan has sight more useful than mine. They sit close to their best friend, always attentive, always watching. One of their fingers hooks around Alyse's wrist like an anchor. There's a twinge in my heart as I look at that simple connection. I've never allowed myself to get that close to a friend. It always felt like such a terrible risk. "I like new arrivals too, Lys. And Ems would have loved seeing all these new people coming to our shores. The home she found for us."

Alyse only nods, unable to say anything else, twisting in on herself. Lightning flashes around her heart, an electric cage that crackles in time with her heartbeat.

Rain lashes my skin, the chill taking my breath away.

It's easier to look outwards, to seek for more mutants out in the world. So many of them are unaware what their powers mean. Others live in fear, their memories of the Dark Year where Michael reigned still too fresh.

It's not only humans who are changing. The whole planet is evolving as the entity within it wakes and stirs with new life.

"Canada," I gasp. "In the forest. Something's happening."

# A Forest Hath No Fury

### ELLE TESCH

THE FOREST WAKES IN MY BONES ON THE SAME DAY THE world irrevocably changes.

It comes the day after *my* world ended.

Drops of sunlight pour through the whispering canopy overhead, dappling the long grasses and lazy wildflowers. It smears the mound of soil my shovel slices into, the bundled body in the hole at my feet.

Yesterday, my father died. Today, I bury him.

I like to think I chose his gravesite on a whim, but I know that's not the case. This clearing on the verge of a towering cliff was his favourite. Here, nature married all the pieces that built my father. The sparkling sea he'd sailed to the western horizon; the sprawling city we'd abandoned, now little more than a smudge to the south; all around me the old growth forest we've claimed as our home for the last seven years.

The wild and isolated habitat we absconded to after the loss of one parent is now the place where I lost the other.

It was quick at least, the illness that snuck inside Dad's heart and rendered it useless overnight. I tell myself he didn't feel a thing.

Just went to bed in the cabin we'd built for ourselves, his last warm touch a kiss pressed to my forehead, then never woke up. Perhaps his death blended into a lovely dream. The best stories always came from his nightly reveries. The fantastical places he saw and the beings he met in them were better than any fairy tale.

And now I'm left with a nightmare—hazy memories and his bones in the dirt.

Tears well up once more as the weight of what I'm doing hits me in the chest. I'm saying goodbye to the only person I care about, and I'm completely and utterly alone in the task.

When that ache in my body changes, stretching suddenly through every part of me, it's swift and unforgiving and *agony*.

My shovel falls to the ground, my knees buckling to follow suit. For a moment, all I can think is *I am a liar*. The same sickness that stole my father has now turned its claws on me, and there's no peace in this. No golden light or ethereal music to guide me to a quiet afterlife.

Something within me unfurls. A hungry plant, not blooming but exploding. Petals—barbed and dripping poison—float through my blood and set ravenous teeth into my muscles. Through watery eyes I watch my pale hands hook over the edge of my father's grave, tear away grass and crumble soil. I expect my flesh to flake like charred paper beneath the insatiable pain.

It doesn't.

A scream shatters the air. Is it mine? Other voices in my head crowd the curdling note.

The trees around me groan and quiver. With dulled panic, I realize it's *them*. It's *their* voices I hear.

Incoherent but distinct. More a feeling than a thought.

Deep and rumbling for oak and cedar; delicate and lilting from the birch and spruce. They speak to my grief and heed my hurt. Silver-tipped needles shower the ground like snow, chased by fresh green leaves torn from branches, each a letter and a punctuation mark.

The roots shift, wrenching free of moss and rock and loam. I try levering myself to my feet but stagger, landing on my tailbone as the trees tunnel under me. Despite my fear and the mental image of bark-cloaked fingers dragging me beneath the earth, they pay me no mind. Each root branches together behind the pile of soil I built, then shoves with an almighty creak. The dirt slides back into the hole, covering Dad.

As sudden as it tore through me, the pain stops. The thorns retract and the venom dries up. But not the voices.

No, not the voices.

Those hum through the very marrow of my bones, whispers of comfort and questions of want.

I push myself slowly upright, treating the forest as though it's a feral beast distracted by a scrap of bloody meat. My breath is a rabid thing in my ribcage. Still, forcing each lungful through my nostrils helps calm, helps steady.

Something within me has ... changed. Not in my broken heart, but in the tendrils of vine that now seem to hold it together. I don't understand how. Or why, for that matter. But instinct gnaws at my gut, leading me to the answer of *what* this is.

Cautiously, I approach the newly covered grave and the roots standing guard around it. Shreds of moss and clumps of dirt hang from their bark.

My fingers don't tremble as I reach out, a thought held tight in my mind. A command.

And like the voices in my head speaking in the tongue of leaf and spore, they listen.

Before I touch them, the roots peel apart. Unknot and unravel and plunge back into the earth, returning to the trees from which they came.

Emboldened, I drop to my knees once more, dig my fingers deep into the soil.

Green grows over the dirt. First, only grass sprouts, then wild-flowers of an elegant, icy blue burst forth. Forget-me-nots, Dad's favourite. Their soft petals against my skin make my eyes slip shut.

I want this—whatever *this* is—to be a gift from him, his loosed spirit returning to the trees and giving them life. I smile, both hopeful and sad. Somehow, I know that's simply wishful thinking. Because this is all me. Something that's always nestled within, set free by the pressure of grief like a walnut beneath a boulder. The meat of it is savoury—better than I could have imagined.

It takes some doing, getting the tone and intention of my request just right, both inside my head and out loud, but I coax a yew to roll a large stone over the head of Dad's grave. The tree drops red berries to the ground like tears with each wooden shove of its roots.

The carving of his name, though, that I do myself.

As I work, chiselling each careful letter with my pocketknife, the forest comes to me.

Listening to the trees' faint hisses, I realize that their reaction before had been out of fear. A hastiness of movement to calm *me*. Now the forest approaches like a curious fox. Skittish if I shift too suddenly, but still determined to sniff me. I am someone—some*thing*—unknown to them, able to hear them and speak their language.

I wonder if they realize I feel as unmoored by it all as they do. More so, as I don't have the luxury of their roots. But I don't feel a stranger to myself. Rather, whatever surfaced within me is a friend I've known all my life through penned letters, and now I've met them in person for the first time.

When I finish scoring Dad's headstone, the blade folds back into its polished handle. Strands of ivy drape over my shoulders in a welcome embrace. The roots of an aspen lift me off the ground to a more comfortable position and the boughs of a maple shade my face from the afternoon sun.

I let the forest take me home.

EIGHT YEARS AGO, my mother died.

Seven years ago, Dad couldn't take it anymore.

The never-ending bustle and deafening noise of the city. Constant worries over bills that kept mounting, no matter how much overtime he worked. The sickening condolences and pity over our loss. All of it drove him mad, turned him uneasy, and it was only a matter of time before I absorbed such sentiments. Ten-year-olds are too young to know what's best for them, but all I knew was wherever my father went, I needed to be there, too.

And so, early one gloomy morning in April, we left our cramped townhouse and went home.

Nestled deep in the rolling backcountry, fenced by strong mountain streams, and shaded by trees older than the city will ever be, the cabin we cobbled together over the years is small. Cozy and warm. Only two rooms—a shared bedroom and a living area with a simple kitchen. There's an outhouse steps away out back, and a ramshackle shed where we keep firewood and tools.

Aside from an old hiking buddy Dad and I met every three months at the end of a forest service road for supplies, I'm not sure Dad told anyone where we went. After Mom, there wasn't anybody we cared about but each other. No family to look out for but each other.

Now it's just me.

At least I'm not quite as alone as I thought I was beside Dad's grave.

I've always seen the trees as friends, standing in silent solidarity as they watched over me for the last seven years.

But now they listen, and so do I.

We're both wary at first. The forest isn't sure what to do with me. I think it wants to interact, yet hesitation marks every creak of its branches. It's almost comforting, this mutual sentiment, since I don't know how to communicate either. Remembering how fast the roots tore free of the ground, I'm a little afraid to push the trees by asking them for anything.

A bone-deep weight lifts when the forest takes the lead in this newfound relationship of ours.

The trees constantly hiss in my ears, a sound as soothing as the babble of the nearby creek. Still, I can't help paling each time one speaks directly to me. No audible words pass between us, but rather an inescapable feeling that floods every cell of my body.

A colour of cautious yellow blooms in my mind when a grizzly bear ambles too close to the house.

Contentment bleeds into the corners of my vision as vivid magenta when the breezes comb through the highest branches.

And a velvet black sadness settles in under the cover of night to match my own.

Over the next few weeks, I adjust to this deafening solitude. I water down my grief with time, and we help each other. We listen.

When I lament out loud how my small garden of hardy vegetables isn't getting enough sun, the boughs overhead part. They shift throughout the day so the warm rays tip down into the tilled soil for as long as possible.

In turn, I follow soft strands of sickly green pain in my mind to a cedar trunk, a nail left behind in its body from a surveyor's trip long ago. A rusted lance left to fester beneath the bark as it was forced to grow around it. I wedge it out, replacing olive with a sigh of pink.

The forest chases away the foxes sneaking inside my house with its lifting roots, and I prune its heaviest and most troublesome branches.

And in all this, we get to know each other. Differently. Intimately. A piece of my soul splintering to sit inside someone else, sharing itself with another.

Soon, I have no need to speak my wishes aloud. The forest knows what I need of it in a single touch, a fleeting glance. I begin to truly test the boundaries of this power flowing as sap in my blood.

With its ready consent, I bend the forest to my will. I shape it. Make it *grow*.

From a single cone, the smallest beckon of my hand draws a mature tree from the ground, pushing it higher, higher. Five feet, then ten, twenty, fifty—as innate as breathing. I coax them down just as easily. Twist them beneath the soil like moles in their burrows. Encourage them to lift their roots and shift along the ground as spiders would, shaking needles and leaves loose as they brush against each other in passing.

I quickly find another use for such willing roots. They crook to form switchbacks and trade my weight with those branches that lift me into their boughs. Wooden limbs tangle together to form blossoming walkways above the forest floor.

Suddenly, there is nowhere in this precious forest of mine that I can't go. It's a challenge I take to wholeheartedly. I step between sycamores and spruces; follow their nudges to find nests to raid; and let them cradle me in their boughs in the summer's nightly warmth.

When August settles in, and the memory of my father no longer stings to the touch, I awake with a craving on my tongue. It's the season for blackberries, and I know of a particular thicket near the glacial-fed lake I frequent where the berries are most succulent. The bushes around my cabin droop beneath the weight of their own fruits, but they aren't *those* blackberries.

Once the thought of them enters my head, I can think of nothing else.

The sun hangs high in the sky by the time I rise through the treetops and set off. The branches ahead anticipate my path. They knot together with no more sound than that of a hummed sigh, unravelling behind me just the same and leaving no trace of my passing. The underbrush far below is a blur of green and brown.

A meadow looms before me, the light streaming through the trees more radiant, and I veer to the left to skirt around its edge.

I stumble when I hear them.

*Voices.*

I freeze, clinging to the trunk of a bloated cedar. Even this high up, its trunk is so wide my arms cannot wrap around the entire thing. I hold my heaving breath, urging the pulse racing in my ears to diminish. Scattered leaves fall to the ground all at once as the forest reads my surprise.

There. I heard it again—voices. Not of the trees, but of people.

I haven't heard a voice other than my own since that last night with my father. Nothing but my voice and the feelings of the trees. They're as curious as I am, flashing bright lemon-yellow across my mind.

"Did you hear that?"

The first voice belongs to a man. Deep and rich ... and fearful. It comes from the left, from the ground several paces away. The boughs part in a false breeze, and offer me a view of not one, but three men. A trio of white men, one burly and the others lean, each wearing a gaudy reflective vest and scratched, orange hard hat. My heart beats louder in my ears.

"What's that?" the broad man asks as they crunch towards the meadow. His red hair clashes violently with his outfit.

"I-I swear I heard something ... move." The curly blond spins on the spot, peering through the spaces between trees. His hand presses against the top of his hat as he tips his head to the canopy.

Instinctively, I draw back, melding with the shadows of the trunk. Branches dip to better hide me.

"Probably just a bird." The greying, older man claps his fretful companion on the shoulder, the sound making me wince. "The scouting report says the cougars aren't around here this time of the year."

These are city folks. I'd stake my hand on it. Even if I couldn't tell from the look of them, I can *smell* it. As do my trees—they recoil from the artificial scent. Ripe with grease and oil, *outsider* oozes from their pores.

But what are they doing out here? How dare they stand with such authority, such arrogance, in this deep forest territory. They believe the cougars to be elsewhere because their scouts never saw them, yet I'm certain the lions are watching now, biding their time. Even as I crouch, asking questions of the trees, they answer under the weight of eagles, squirrels and woodpeckers in their boughs; badgers and foxes in their roots.

Feeling jolts back into my limbs, and I peel away from the cedar. My hair falls forward, as if to keep me hidden in shadow. I creep through the treetops much slower now, tailing the men headed towards the meadow. Neither I nor the trees make a noise. No leaves snap free, no boughs clack together.

As the branches ahead thin, and the light gleams at its most potent, I realize the clearing isn't as empty as it should be. The meandering creek has been forded with great sheets of metal and bordered by bags of sand. Beds of lush wildflowers are trampled, compressed by portable buildings. Three of them lie side-by-side like fingers. Long and rectangular and plasticky. And machinery, painted bright gold and slapped with stickers of warning and fabricated environmentalism, lurks to the east of the meadow.

More men—and one woman, from the looks of it—mill about the grass, all dressed in the same ridiculous vests and hats.

Nausea stirs my gut. I don't like this. Not even the most seasoned hikers and backpackers make it this far into the brush. Dad and I encountered no more than two in our seven years out here, and now almost a dozen people loll about with their hands tucked in their pockets, chatting and laughing.

No, I don't like this one bit.

The trio of men below step through the treeline and into the warm afternoon sunlight as the white-haired fellow asks, "How're we looking with the set-up?" He consults a clipboard I hadn't noticed him carrying before, a pencil in hand.

"As good as we're going to be right now." The redhead shrugs and crosses his arms, but still manages to gesture with his body in a way that encompasses the entire meadow. "We're one excavator short, but the chopper will longline that in on Tuesday. Scheduling conflicts."

"Good, good." Two ticks on the clipboard. "The lads are free to start whenever then."

A burst of static screeches through the air, and the blond man unclips a black handheld radio from his belt. I'm too high up to hear what comes through, but I don't miss his response. "Yeah, Foster's given the all-clear for a test run today. Just one, though. *One.*"

A celebratory holler rises from the people clustered around the western-most building, and there's a ripple of movement as they all head out to the far side of the clearing. Away from me and blocked from view.

When the revving starts, there's no time to brace myself.

The bite of the chainsaw into the tree is fire in my bones.

It's too much—*too much.* The agony of an entire forest crying inside my body, clutching at the edges of my very soul with slipping fingers. My heart splits open like a fragile egg.

Blackness devours me.

When I come to, the black remains, but it's held at a distance above the treetops and speckled with pinpricks of radiance. Flat on my back, the trees cradle me, passing me gently between them as they carry me home. Their grief is palpable. It nearly threatens to pull me under again.

*Go back*, I say to them. The groan of their boughs continues.

"Go back," I murmur, struggling to find my balance, only to be knocked back down by threads of ivy.

"Go back!" I shout, and the swaying ceases.

"Take me back there. Please."

Confusion of a dull, sombre grey swirls through my mind, cautious prods of leaves to my sides. They don't understand why.

Why any of us would choose to go back to that clearing, to the scene of the crime. The *murder*.

Awake, I let the brilliant, seething red of my anger serve as an answer.

Smoke bleeds into a perfect sky blue. The branches shift like shoulders thrown back. I rise to my feet at last and walk through the already formed gangway. There is no subtlety now. No tentative yards of branches to form and quickly unwind behind. My path is laid out from end to end, taking up as much space as the forest deserves.

When we reach the clearing, the people are nowhere to be seen. The air is quiet, but lights blaze through curtains of cream in one of those portable buildings. A silhouette tracks past the window, then a muffled burst of laughter. My hands curl into fists. It's a sound so full of mirth and drunken happiness, and so at odds with the melancholy that drags every bough down.

A droop that lessens as my fury crests over the treetops, fuelled by the trees at my back that have listened. Have digested the rage as sunshine and now exhale it like the purest oxygen.

These outsiders think they can come into my home without permission? That they can harm one of my family without facing consequences?

No. I laugh. Oh, *fuck* no.

I feed the trees my idea. I offer them the choice.

A single fir accepts.

Another round of laughter from the building. Then, it's drowned out by the upward wrench of roots buried deep in the earth. One by one, torn from the soil as the trunk moans. A taller square of light spills over the ground as a door opens. Two figures storm down the steps to the grass to investigate. Instead, they run away with shouts.

The fir topples across the roof, folding the building in half. Crushing it in upon itself. The warm light flickers out. A scream rises to the night. The two people rush back. Smaller, less steady lights blink on.

More shouts, more screams.

Triumph flares a bloody scarlet through my mind. It stems from me, from the trees. Shared between us like a cup of wine.

They fired the first shot, but we ended it.

Days later, I awake in bed, unable to move. Claws of pain pin me to the blankets. They pierce through my skin, my muscles, to hold my bones in place. Consciousness washes over me as an ebbing tide.

All day long, it *kills* me. The hurt, and the *knowing*.

When the cover of night falls, the pain still lingers. Even the trees that carry me are more resigned. After all, they've sat in this agony for hours. They've become numb to it and its fiery bite. I feel it more sharply before the moon-soaked meadow comes into view, but this time I'm prepared. I fight against the black that threatens to blind me. Barely. My fingers dig into bark for support.

I already know what I'll find, but that doesn't make it any easier.

Five trees are stacked neatly like oversized matches on the ground. Their branches are stripped, their wide bases sheared clean away. The clearing stands a little bigger than it was before.

I had thought the battle won, but it's clear this is now war.

This time, this time I don't let the trees choose. They feel my anger, acknowledge it, but they don't have the energy to act on it. Wearied by this exquisite hurt, they have the will to do no more than weep tears of sap. So, I help them.

I move along the meadow's edge and give a cedar, a spruce, and an oak a helpful nudge. So tired are they that their roots give up their grip on the earth without much coaxing. It's almost a relief for them to let go, to tip onto the machinery still sticky with the blood of our lost.

The noise is tremendous. Three trees topple one after the other onto industrial metal beasts.

In a repeat of the other night, lights blink on in the remaining pair of buildings when the cedar crashes down. Small figures race out into the clearing in varying states of undress when the spruce lands. And they scream when the oak collapses.

There. Let them murder without knives.

When my knees give out in the middle of my garden several days later, I can't decide which is worse: the pain, or the dread.

They've done it again. Somehow, I've not yet thwarted them. I shriek through gritted teeth into the dirt at my cheek. This seizing hurt is the cannon fire of yet another battle. They have replaced their machinery, their tools, and they've continued their cutting. No white flag is ready to wave.

When I return to the clearing in the dark, I cannot bring myself to look at how many more have fallen and been sliced to fit their specifications. It doesn't matter anymore. Only that they will be the last, and their deaths will mean something.

This ends now.

I let a single tree fall.

When they come out of their little homes, I scream in the trees. I wail like a frightened child.

And when they come running, when they break through the treeline, all ten of them scattered across the underbrush, I hold on tight.

The boughs crack as knuckles do, warm and ready to exact revenge.

# Farsight

"Beautiful." Dylan grins. "We speak for the fucking trees, you assholes."

"Can you sense all that?" I ask. "What happens out in the world?"

"Sort of." They run their hand through their hair and petals tumble down onto their shoulders, making them look like they were dragged through a flowerbed. "It's not like I can sense the agony of every tree, but I get general vibes. The problem is we're fucking the planet over so badly it's like having a constant headache unless I dial it way down low."

I've still got a half an eye on the forest, and the chaos unfolding there. It unsettles me to see nature defending itself like this. Even though I know that humanity has taken and taken, and then taken some more. To have the planet *move against us*—I'm not sure where or how that ends, and I'm worried that we're going to find out.

The enigmatic creature sitting opposite me tilts their head, green light flaring in their eyes. "Are you scared, Far?"

I consider lying, but it's unhelpful. "Yes. Shouldn't I be?"

They lean their head against the back of the chair, big eyes fixed on me. "Everyone's scared. Humans are scared of us, we're scared of them. We're all worried the planet might decide to gobble us up for being greedy little fucks. Weird places springing up over the world, strange people with unnatural powers. All of us are too scared to work together, and in the middle of it the rich and powerful keep getting ever so much more so." Their mouth turns down briefly. "It's enough to drive someone to drink. Or violence."

I'm not sure what to say in response, so we both stare pensively out the window—Dylan looking at the island laid out below us, and me scanning through the streets of the world, looking for a handful of lives among millions.

As midnight passes, Dani appears at the door. "Coming to bed, my love?"

Dylan yawns and stretches. "In theory I should sleep, yes. How's Lys doing?"

"About the same." She raises one shoulder. "How are any of us doing?"

"Fucked and double fucked." Dylan holds out their arms and Dani collapses into them. Neither of them appear to care that I'm here. Even though most of my attention skims over farflung places, I keep some small slice of my awareness focused on these two and the way they curl around each other in their grief like two ferns.

It's a relief when I catch sight of a girl on the streets of New York, and have somewhere that draws my focus.

# A Guide to Running Away

### ANDY PEREZ

THE THING ABOUT NEW YORK IS THAT EVERYONE IS SO weird, you can't tell the mutants from the regular humans.

Take the guy jacking off in front of me. He's staring me straight in the eyes while his hand is inside his pants. The grin he wears is wide enough to scare off small children.

So when I accidentally light his pants ablaze with my glare, I find it a little funny that he has the audacity to scream, "Crazy bitch!" at me as he tries putting out his fire crotch with his other hand.

It's only after he hobbles off the train on the next stop that I realize what's happened. What I've done. It doesn't matter that it's basically a thousand degrees in this non-air-conditioned train car and that the summer heat could definitely cause some spontaneous combustion. What's just happened is a weird act of God—or mutants, as the whispering and wide-eyed stares from the other commuters communicate. The slack-jawed faces help spur me out of my seat in a dizzying whirl.

I'm nearly through the threshold of the closing doors, the

annoyed conductor's voice crackling over the speaker, "Will the girl with the ugly ass blue Kanken get off." But then I run headfirst into a solid chest. The smell of very expensive soap fills my nostrils, erasing the acrid scent of burning pubes from my memory.

"Shit," I gasp as I trip over my sandals, silently cursing my idiocy at wearing what are basically fancy flipflops in an attempt to look cooler than I really am.

A pair of hands grip my shoulders to steady me. I feel like ice has been shot through my veins, cooling me from the inside out.

I glance back long enough to see the chest and hands are attached to a boy with wild ice-gray eyes and even wilder dark hair. His gaze holds mine even as the doors slide close, my nose inches from being caught in the middle.

It isn't until the train has pulled away and someone yells at me to move the fuck along that I glance down at my arms. There, I find Chambers Street's stagnant air melting the icy handprints left on my skin, cool water dripping down the side of my arm.

The frantic beating of my heart and the sudden burning sensation in my eyes forces me to shut them close.

"Shit," I say to myself.

We have enough subway fires without my hormones causing more.

NEW YORK GOT off light in the Dark Year. The AI that was taking over most of America called it the cesspit of sin and wanted nothing to do with it. Everyone said war was coming, but it never did. It didn't stop mutants from hiding, but now that it's over, the mutants have come crawling out.

Unfortunately, only the bad weirdos really announce their mutant powers.

My mom keeps our TV tuned to NY1 all day and all night. The fact that she doesn't speak a lick of English is irrelevant when we need to remain updated about all the mutant incidents happening around the city.

"Dios mio," she says, crossing herself whenever a new disaster occurs. She glances at my father's picture, still sitting on the media console even though he left her for another woman fifteen years ago.

I roll my eyes. I consider telling her that he wouldn't have protected us from the mutants anyway. He was only ever out to protect himself. But Ma can't accept the truth. She loves him, a dead man, and while she never waited for him to come back, she never regrets him, and that's almost worse.

You don't need mutant powers to be bad. Sometimes you're just born that way. Sometimes, even if you try your hardest, it's all you can be.

An explosion threatens to short-out the speakers and I can't sit there anymore. You'd think our city was overrun only with mutants using their power for ill considering all the murders, bank robbing, and art thieving.

But I am a mutant. And so far, I haven't stolen shit. Mostly because I have absolutely no idea how to get my powers to manifest, unless I think about wild-eyed subway stranger boy. And then I can't stop myself from starting a stupid fire with my stupid eyes.

It's been one week since I ran into him. One week since I set some dude's dick on fire. One week of spending hours in a cramped kitchen, trying to light pieces of notebook paper on fire in the sink. One week of accidentally lighting several things that weren't pieces of notebook paper. Like the ugly, chipped wall splash behind the sink, the gas stove, and the plastic tablecloth over our plastic table. All because my mind strays from the thought of causing fires to the thought of Stranger Boy's hands on my arms and the fire burning in my veins.

"Shit." I turn on the faucet, killing the small flame that sparked along my fingertips.

At least it isn't more of the tile. That was a hard one to explain to Ma.

I turn the faucet off once my fingertips feel normal again. I check my skin and find nothing to suggest that I'd ever managed to burn myself. Faded and gone, like Stranger Boy's ice-cold grip.

I don't need this kind of pressure in my life. Not the mutant powers, not a boy, and definitely not the various burn marks happening all over our rent-controlled apartment.

Trying to find a way to tell my mom I got into Stanford and leaving home in a few months is pressure enough.

Getting in was an accident. Kinda like discovering my mutant powers. One day, I have an extra college application waiver hours before the deadline. The next day, I'm opening an acceptance letter from one of the most prestigious universities in all of America.

One day, I'm a normal girl. The next, I shoot laser beams from my eyes.

I get my phone out and find Carmen's name. My best—and only—friend. Raging lesbian, intolerable of bullshit. While I can find a way to run away from all of my problems, Carmen can find a way to remind me of all the shit I'm full of.

She picks up on the seventh ring. "Beatrice. Who the fuck calls anymore?"

"I'm gonna buy a ticket to California."

She scoffs. "Con que dinero, you fucking dumbass." The harshness of the words cut through the anxiety building in my veins. Maybe Carmen's superpower is being a dick. An honest dick. "Did you tell your mom?"

"No."

"So you're just talking out your ass."

"Yes."

"Why are you running away?" she asks with a sigh, as if this is the simplest question. One she's asked me dozens upon dozens of times.

The truth is, I don't know. Running away has always been easy. I run from boyfriends, run from friends, run from decisions. The only reason I haven't run away from home is because the few times I tried before, I knew Ma would be devastated. She didn't need someone else she loved to run from her too.

Maybe that's the problem. For the first time, I really am leaving Ma. And I don't know how to tell her.

Carmen's voice on the other line softens. I hear her breath hitch, the swallow as she tries to think of a better way of saying whatever truth she's holding back. "Think about it. I promise, it isn't as bad as you think."

She hangs up before I can say another word. Because that's the thing with Carmen: she doesn't take any shit. Not from me. Not even from herself. And she knows whatever excuses I have readied on my tongue are just that.

Excuses.

I SEE Stranger Boy again on 59<sup>th</sup> Street. He's grabbing the D. I'm leaving it.

Freudian would have a field day with us.

Maybe gravity works on people differently. Because instead of leaving through the door right by my seat, I choose the furthest. I'm too busy trying to throw on my backpack to notice the body directly in front of me. I bump into a shoulder, ice flooding my veins.

I've never done drugs, but I'm sure it feels exactly like this.

He turns around so fast he accidentally knocks his head against someone else's. They're yelling at him and he's staring at me and I'm staring at him, watching the doors close to another thing I desperately want to run towards. Or away. I honestly can't tell.

Except he slams his hand against the closing doors, frost crawling from his fingertips along the steel doors and fogging up the small window.

He leaps out to join me on the platform, breath ragged, and stares down at me with eyes made of chipped ice.

"Hi," he says, breathless.

"Hi."

And with those two words, I set the third rail on fire.

WE EVACUATE WITH EVERYONE ELSE. He stares at me with awe the whole time, those gray eyes bright and full of a cold fire I can't put out with faucet water. He opens his mouth to speak several times, but a jostle from the mass subway exodus swallows up whatever words he intended to say.

I don't have to hear them to know what he really wants to say though. The same questions that have plagued me for an entire week: How? Why me? How can I make this go away?

I can't have him start questioning me about my powers, even though I know he has them too. It's one thing to not have answers for myself. It's another to not have answers for the really cute guy I can't stop thinking about.

The burning in my eyes starts again as my pulse jackrabbits out of control. I could die of embarrassment right now. So I search for any other exits I can take so I can get my pyromaniac tendencies away from the subway and away from him.

Fingers slip through the spaces between mine, cold and grounding. He pulls me along with the crowd, up the sticky subway stairs and towards the bright sunshine beaming from above.

"Shitty fucking MTA," someone near me grumbles.

I feel even worse. They're not wrong, of course, but for the first time, this isn't the MTA's fault.

This is what I'm trying to run away from. The shitty MTA. Humid New York summers. Beautiful boys who can melt my ice-cold heart.

Being a mutant.

I can't tell Carmen any of this, but I can tell myself. Running away is a great idea, if running away means leaving all of this forever.

"Come on," Stranger Boy says, dragging me away from the throng of people overflowing from the exit.

I begin to protest, to find an excuse—my Ma's in the hospital, I'm actually a hundred years old, I don't speak English. But he gives my hand a slight squeeze, his cold palms freezing the anxiety that threatens to consume my body.

We walk in silence along the city streets, the fragrance of roasting garbage wafting in the air a welcome relief. The crowd doesn't follow us uptown; the next closest station is nine blocks down, leaving us mostly alone as we make our way up. When we're sufficiently far from tourists and pissed off New Yorkers alike, he turns right onto a side street, slowing his pace and letting go of my hand.

"How long?"

I lick my lips and consider my options. I can lie. Deny. Have no idea what he's talking about.

"A week." If I stop talking, I can make a clean escape. No exchange of information. No blackmail material. "You?"

"Two?" He furrows his dark brows in deep thought and a frown pulls his lips back. There's a mole beneath his lower lip that I want to brush away with my thumb. "Maybe three."

"Have you told anyone?"

He shakes his head. "You?"

I mimic him. Then stop, thinking better. "You, I guess."

We walk some more, his cold hand still gripping my hot, sweaty one. It should be gross—anyone else, and I'd be wiping my hands and refusing to ever touch him again. But it makes sense. This.

Whatever it is. Hot and cold. Fire and ice.

"First time?" The words are out before I can stop them. A distraction from the fire burning within me.

His sheepish smile looks good on him. It makes him look rogueish, like a prince from a bygone era. Two hundred years ago, he would have swept me off my feet. But in a twenty-first century urban landscape, all he can do is walk with me towards Central Park. "My shower wasn't getting cold enough."

A cold shower is exactly what I need right now because imagining water dripping down what I assume are his perfect abs make my insides turn to jelly and my eyes turn into fiery darts of death.

We freeze.

The scorch mark left on the concrete sidewalk sizzles in the blazing afternoon sun.

I'm about to book it to avoid further mortification.

Except when I glance up to meet his eyes, frost clings to his eyelashes and a grin nearly splits his face in two.

"Don't worry," he says. He kisses the back of the hand he holds, lips soft but shockingly cold in hundred-degree weather. "I feel the same."

STRANGER BOY—KEVIN Durante—is counting down the days for the start of his freshman year too. Sitting on a bench in front of the manmade lake within Central Park, he reveals he's currently spending his last few weeks saying goodbye to his favorite city as he prepares to move across country.

"California," he answers before I can even ask.

Because gravity is inescapable, and running away seems truly impossible for me, I say the only thing I can.

"Shut the fuck up."

"Do you... hate the Dodgers?"

I counter his question with one of my own. "What school?"

"Stanford."

I swear under my breath. There goes my plan to be unknown and invisible three thousand miles away. I'd managed to run into the only person who could reveal my true self in a place where I was going to try and be nobody.

Gray eyes widen. "No."

"Yeah."

His laugh is loud and too warm for the summer. Too hot for ever. I squirm as my insides turn liquid. "This is really starting to feel like fate."

I'm paralyzed, my breath stolen from my lungs. It's like I've been dunked in a pool of ice-cold water.

I'm on my feet in an instance. His confusion almost stops me, but I've trained in the art of flight over fight and freeze for nearly two decades. Nothing, not even his beautiful, worried face, could keep me from doing what I do best.

"I gotta go."

He starts to stand. "But—what did I—"

There are no words. No way to explain that fate is something I don't believe in. That if fate is real, then that would mean some things are out of my control.

So I don't explain myself. I do what I do best: run away.

WEIRDOS ARE EVERYWHERE. So are mutants. They're impossible to avoid.

And so is Kevin.

Whether it's gravity or fate, I know something is working over-time against me, because I run into him everywhere. After the first three times on the subway, I swear off the train forever and start taking the bus. When I run into him at Sarabeth's and Barnes and

Noble and the fucking median at Lincoln Square, I swear off downtown.

That's why I'm at the Cloisters, listening to Carmen explain medieval history like I give a shit. I'm mildly entertained by the unicorn tapestries until my eyes find the last few panels and a sharp pang rips up my spine. There, on hundreds of year-old fabric and hundreds of year-old thread, I realize that fate is unavoidable. That the unicorn is fated to die by the hunters' hands, all because some virginal bimbo decides to lure it into a false sense of safety.

I turn around and beeline to the wing that had been devoid of life—the room where all the old ass coffins are hidden behind plexiglass. I hide behind an open archway, feel the uneven stone dig into my shoulder blades.

The unicorn successfully ran away from its hunters, only to be killed anyway.

A sinking feeling overtakes me: maybe all my running away will ultimately lead me to—

I feel the presence of someone else before I see them. When I look up, Kevin is standing there at the opposite archway, frozen and beautiful.

Scrambling upright, I wipe away at my tears, struggling to figure out how to get out of this stupid fortress castle thing. I'll call Carmen later.

He grabs my hand and pulls me into a hidden alcove.

There are no words. He presses me against the cold stone wall and kisses me. I consider protesting, pushing him away, biting his lower lip hard enough to draw blood. But I've been thinking about this ever since the first day I bumped into him. And I feel so stupid, but it's like fate has been pulling me here all along. To him. To this.

His kiss tastes like a crisp winter day, sweet and slow and agonizingly hot. A fever sizzles beneath my skin as I grip his shoulders, pull him closer, open my mouth wider. Distantly, I hear Carmen calling for me, the agitation in her voice.

But Kevin is all I know. All I can think about. Tears prickle at the corner of my eyes as realization hits me like a thousand brick stones.

I'm the unicorn. I keep running away from friends and people because I know what they can do, how they can hurt me. And here I am. Trapped anyway.

The tears fall freely. We break apart and I slump towards the ground, Kevin following. He wipes at my face, the tears turning briefly into ice before he flicks them away.

"Did I hurt you?"

"Not yet," I say, because it's the truth. I cry harder, unable to keep it inside any longer.

He stops wiping. I can feel him considering me. Can imagine the choices he's running over in his mind. Keep chasing after the weird, mutant fire girl or find the nearest exit. I know what he's going to choose. What I would choose. What I've chosen every time before this, before him, before my mutant powers brought us to this.

"I'll try my best not to," he says.

And I believe him.

CARMEN FINDS US TALKING. She's furious and threatens to seriously fucking unfollow me on all social media, but she stops suddenly when my cheeks overheat from embarrassing shame, and I accidentally light a small fire at my feet.

"You're a mutant?" Her voice is small. I've never heard it so —scared.

I nod. I want to disappear.

She kicks at my shoes and doesn't even acknowledge the smudge on my pristine white sneakers. "Is this why you want to leave so bad?" She sounds so fed up with me. "You dumbass."

Kevin stares between us as understanding dawns on his face. "You're friends."

"I don't fucking know," Carmen spits. She settles on the ground next to me. "Friends would tell each other they have a mutant fucking power."

"I was scared."

She rolls her eyes, weaves her long arm through mine, and settles her head on my shoulder. "You haven't been able to get rid of me in over a decade. Like I'd leave you now."

We sit there, the three of us, until a security guard finds us and throws us out.

THIS IS how you run away effectively: by running towards something bigger.

California is a wide world full of possibilities. I'm sure I'll find a hundred reasons to crawl back to New York. I know Ma is ninety-nine of those reasons. I know Carmen is one.

But there are a hundred and one more reasons to go.

I grin at the tree I'm standing in front of. Kevin's ice-cold fingertips press against the nape of my neck. I feel the heat of uncertainty, of blossoming love, of potential heartbreak, of disappointing my mom and those who are cheering for me, begin to burn behind my eyes. I let it flow out of me without trying to stopper it, without trying to control it out of fear.

B & K.

For now.

The letters are burned into the wood, a scorch mark I can try to run from. But this tree will stand in Central Park for a number of years to come. Decades, even. Maybe centuries.

Kevin turns to me and arches a thick brow. Actually, he arches both, because he isn't one of those people who can arch just one.

"We're going to the same school."

I shrug. "The future is unpredictable." Fate can think it has any sway, but I trust in chance more.

But I'm not running anymore. I know I'm seventeen and I have a whole lifetime ahead of me. But Kevin is a fate I want to meet full force.

And I'm tired of running anyway.

# Farsight

I am alone in my tower for once. The world seems quiet up here, but only if I close my eyes. As soon as I open them, there is too much to see. The world is in chaos. When a malevolent artificial intelligence controls a vast number of governmental systems and then is violently unplugged, chaos comes in its wake. Those same governments, taking shaky steps back towards normality, are also nervous about the reality of a new mutant nation floating in the ocean, created overnight from nothing. Dylan and Dani showing up at the United Nations, claiming to speak for the planet and giving everyone a fairly terrifying ultimatum didn't help—although I understand why they did it. And now all these new mutants springing up everywhere.

It's total chaos, and I can't possibly see everything.

We can't possibly *fix* everything either. Even with these powers at our disposal.

"Anyone to save?" A squall of wind blows in my door, ice crystallising on the walls.

"Alyse." I turn towards the swirl of mist that drifts in the center of the room. "Are you doing okay?"

"Yes, I'm absolutely splendid." The temperature drops noticeably, and I shiver. "Can't you tell?"

My teeth chatter. "I'm sorry. It was an insensitive question."

"No. Everyone asks. It's a reflex, I think. Anyway, I came up here while the others were asleep, because they don't like hearing me ask this question." The cloud comes closer and salty spray brushes my cheeks. "Have you seen any sign of Emma out there? Even the smallest glimpse."

There's a terrible part of me that wants to give her false hope, to see a tinge of brightness limn the dark cloud of her. But that would be the cruelest thing of all, and so I give her the ugly truth of it.

"No." I turn to look out the window, because it's easier than looking at her. "I've tried. God, I've looked so hard. Because I miss her too. Every day."

The tower is filled with the sound of howling wind, and chips of ice pepper my skin. It's like having a storm unleash itself for me alone, and I huddle behind my desk, as if that will provide any shelter from the bitter cold.

When it finally ebbs, and I raise my head, I'm alone in the tower once more.

# Island Burnt by History

### HSINJU CHEN

*Note that the story involves scenes of forced captivity, violence, alcohol consumption (recreational), and mentions of mistreatment against indigenous peoples, Taiwan martial law era, force feeding, kidnapping, a fatal train accident, and animal murder.*

"FM 100! YOUR FRESHEST CHOICE OF MUSIC: ICRT!"

Wei-Jen Hsu (許維仁) groaned and rolled over in his bed to slap at the bedside cabinet where his phone sat.

Music started playing and Wei-Jen forced his eyes open. It was the first day of the semester, and getting up at a decent time for class was always a struggle, even though he had been in school for almost two decades and was now a graduate student. But everyone knew engineering students tend to be night owls, especially if debugging code was involved on a daily basis. He blinked several times to chase away the grogginess and remembered that he didn't have class on Mondays. How odd was it that his alarm went off? He glanced at his phone. The screen wasn't even lit up, and once his thoughts were clear enough, he realized that the song with husky vocals and an accordion in the background was definitely not what he set for the alarm.

What the fuck?

It was six thirty in the morning, too early for Mr. Wang next door to be blasting his lunch music, which ranged from Western rock songs to Mandopop to indigenous music. Wei-Jen sighed and sat up, slipping his feet into his indoor flip-flops, and picked up a pillow on the floor he must have accidentally kicked off the bed during the night.

The music kept going as he wandered around the apartment in search of the source, but the volume of it didn't seem to get any higher nor lower as he shuffled from his bedroom into the living room. By the time the song ended, Wei-Jen was still wandering around aimlessly, failing to locate or even get closer to locating where the music was coming from. He decided to go through his morning routine of washing up first to wake himself up before attempting to figure it out again. The next song started playing as he got into the bathroom, and it sounded like it was playing at the same volume level as when he was anywhere else.

Sitting down on the toilet, he put his face into his hands and groaned again. Nobody should be solving a mystery of disembodied music before seven o'clock on a Monday. Or ever. Wei-Jen thought back to the past five minutes or so, trying to determine if there was anything that would give him some clue about the music. Then he remembered that the vocals became a little fuzzy when he walked past the television in the living room. But the volume of the song didn't seem to have changed, and it was less like it was coming from somewhere else than if he was carrying a speaker.

By the time Wei-Jen cleaned himself up at the sink and combed through his hair about six times over before applying a bit of hair wax, another two songs had finished playing. He decided to check if there was some interference near the large OLED television his dad had insisted on buying him last year when he started grad school.

As soon as he neared it, the music became blurry. He froze in his tracks and took a few steps back. The sounds were clear again. He repeatedly stepped closer and further away from the screen, and the music shifted between being distorted and playing with clarity.

It was like he was a radio antenna receiving the 100.7 FM channel.

Over the past few months, Wei-Jen had been hearing about the Awakenings going on all over the world, a huge surge of population suddenly gaining mysterious mutant powers. He didn't really believe in supernatural stuff until one of his neighbors, a child no more than five years old, melted into a literal flesh-colored puddle after bursting into tears in distress one morning in the stairwell. He had screamed in horror and the child's parent had turned to stare at him impassively, like a toddler turning into goo was a normal thing. God, it was humiliating.

This unexplained radio music—how many people still listened to radios nowadays anyway?—might have something to do with mutant powers. He bet someone was broadcasting the channel in his head just to fuck with him and of course he was unamused. But as he fussed around in the kitchen making green onion scrambled eggs to go with the frozen mantou he was steaming, he started hearing something other than the sad song country music currently playing on ICRT. It was like he was in-between channels. The staticky sounds had a mix of strings and brass, and it reminded him of the classical music radio channel his mom often put on before his bedtime, which probably was what he was hearing now, 99.7 FM, Philharmonic Radio Taipei.

After slicing open the steamed bun and sliding in the eggs, he took a sip of the extra strong coffee he brewed just for this abnormal day and dug in. But the more he thought about why someone was broadcasting random radio channels in his head, the less sense it made. He began to conclude that there was no plausible reason for it. Either someone with a radio station power was really, really bored or...

Or he was catching and interpreting the signals at 100.2 or so MHz. Shit, maybe he should go ask Yu-Ning for more information. She studied antennas after all.

YU-NING KANG (康玉寧) was in the anechoic chamber connected to her office when Wei-Jen found her. A woman of average height with a messy, longish crew cut, she always commanded attention in any room she was in—even when it wasn't the otherwise empty chamber—for as long as Wei-Jen had known her, which was, damn, eight years and counting. Today, Yu-Ning was wearing a loose off-white cuff T-shirt and fitted black jeans with her usual pair of white sneakers. She looked effortlessly good while Wei-Jen often felt like a scrappy fifteen-year-old boy next to her.

It was not yet eight in the morning and she was already working on antenna measurements in the room covered with spiky blue spongy tetrahedrons of varying sizes. On the first day of the school year, no less. And while her advisor was on sabbatical.

"So you think you can catch radio broadcasts even though it's kind of an obsolete technology that not even your phone has a radio function anymore?" Yu-Ning was holding a small wrench and tapping the metallic handle with her forefinger absentmindedly after securing her antenna on a huge styrofoam cylinder with the tool.

"Yeah." Wei-Jen frowned. "But there's nothing now."

Yu-Ning laughed. "Dude, this is an anechoic chamber. What do you think it does?"

When Wei-Jen didn't immediately respond, Yu-Ning continued, "We're in a metal-shielded room covered with absorbers. Electromagnetic waves cannot come in. God, I'm embarrassed for you being an electrical engineering grad and not knowing this."

"Hey, not fair ah!" Wei-Jen protested. His cheeks would've been pink if he could blush. "It's been, what, four years since I had any EM courses and you practically breathe Maxwell's equations all this time!"

Yu-Ning waved the wrench dismissively but not unkindly. "Anyway, I think this could very well be a mutant power. The question is, what's the frequency range of your reception? And what signal level could you pick up?" She tilted her head, her brows slightly furrowed in the low light of the room. "Do you have a built-in noise reduction function? Can you demodulate AM radio, too?"

Wei-Jen blinked. Was he Yu-Ning's study subject now? How could she jump into research mode just like that? Wanting to act more relaxed about it, he leaned back against the wall, only to catch himself at the last moment as he remembered that there was no wall behind him, just a sea of blue spikes. He almost fell into the absorbers.

"How are you taking it so well?" he asked, trying his best to act natural, but judging by the slight twitch of the corner of Yu-Ning's mouth, he had failed to hide his stumbling. "I was kind of freaked out by it, you know, waking up early from random music, and here you are being all rational and down to business."

"Somebody had to keep you from spiraling, no?" Yu-Ning shrugged and started walking out of the chamber into the control room, Wei-Jen following at her heels. "I'll extend my lab reservation timeslot and we can have you stand inside and do some experiments if you don't mind. It should be safe, RF radiation–wise. Technically, we're not allowed to be in there while the machines operate, but I think unusual times call for exceptions."

Before Wei-Jen could say anything, Yu-Ning had clicked something on the desktop computer and he heard the machinery in the chamber whirl into action despite the closed and latched door. Yu-Ning kept rattling on, "I need to go check with Mario. He is a PhD candidate in our group and the lab manager—"

"Yes?" A tall, stocky Black man sporting a shaved head and short boxed beard poked his head through the doorway. One of his eyebrows was raised and he grinned as his eyes twinkled under the fluorescent lights. "Someone called me?"

"Hey, Mario!" Yu-Ning turned around to face him. "I was wondering if anyone is using the chamber later. Can I book it for the rest of the day?"

"Is there anyone else using the lab on the first day of school? Hmmm..." Mario made an exaggerated thinking face which Wei-Jen was sure he was only feigning thoughtfulness. "I don't think so." Then he laughed. "Doing some cool project other than your thesis, Yu-Ning?

Yu-Ning and Wei-Jen shared a glance. They had been close friends since before and after their brief dating attempt back in high school—Wei-Jen shuddered internally at the thought of his three years in a girls' school—and it allowed them to communicate tele-pathically. Almost. Without mutant powers, of course. Wei-Jen gave a half shrug and Yu-Ning motioned Mario to come into the control room and close the door behind him. Mario's eyebrows twitched again as he stepped into the room, schooling his face into a more serious expression. If Yu-Ning was going to trust this guy, Wei-Jen would, too.

"This is Wei-Jen Hsu from Professor Hsing's cryptography group. Wei-Jen, Mario Adeyemi. He does mainly microwave imaging and has a side project of radar systems going on," Yu-Ning introduced. She looked at Wei-Jen but he nodded for her to go on. No way was he going to be able to tell the story coherently to someone he just met! Sighing, Yu-Ning explained the situation to Mario and Wei-Jen noticed his eyes slightly bulging when she mentioned mutant powers. It wasn't everyday that people talked about superpowers even though one of the professors in the depart-ment actually studied telepathy and taught Special Topics on Para-psychology. Mario hummed and nodded at all the right places and he perked up in excitement when Yu-Ning started talking about the experiments they planned on doing.

He turned to Wei-Jen, his head bouncing in what Wei-Jen could only assume as anticipation, and asked, "Do you radiate, too?" Then, he added, "Reciprocity theorem." as if that made more sense to Wei-Jen.

He opened his mouth to answer, but stopped when he realized he actually didn't know if he could transmit radio signals. Honestly, that would be pretty cool. "Huh." There was no way for him to sound intelligent and make a good first impression now. "I don't know? I guess I'd need someone to try receiving something from me?"

Mario nodded, more to himself than to Wei-Jen. "I'm going to hypothesize that you could receive *and* transmit like an actual antenna system. What are the conditions for the reciprocity theorem again? That you contain all or none of the sources?

"Anyway," he smiled, "what are we waiting for?"

STANDING ALONE in the blue anechoic chamber as the giant probe whirled and rotated around him was fucking terrifying. Wei-Jen also felt incredibly silly mirroring the movements of the styrofoam cylinder where the testing antenna usually sat. Not him thinking himself as the testing antenna just now.

They had already established the fact that Wei-Jen could, in fact, radiate electromagnetic waves after Yu-Ning heaved the chunk of metal that was the network analyzer from some hidden room in her office into the chamber to measure Wei-Jen earlier. And while he had only just discovered this mutant power, they were able to get him to steadily emit signals after several tries for the probe to receive his radiation.

It took them another two hours to cover all the frequency bands the chamber could measure. Yu-Ning had wanted to manually measure the millimeter band as well but both Wei-Jen and Mario dissuaded her. They needed to get the bigger picture here first before Yu-Ning started dreaming up something like terahertz waves.

The three of them crowded around the desktop computer as Yu-Ning opened the generated report. She and Mario skimmed the document as Wei-Jen checked his phone. He couldn't have his phone with him in the chamber because that would mess with the measurements, and now he missed scrolling aimlessly through the news and his friends' posts on social media. Not that a lot had happened over the past few hours, but being the test subject was really boring. Plus, he understood next to nothing about antennas.

"Èi, Wei-Jen." Yu-Ning tapped on his shoulder to get his attention and he jerked his head up. "Look, this is your radiation pattern, a toroid like a dipole antenna. We're guessing your receiving pattern is similar, if not the same. That's going to be the next thing we try figuring out. The interesting thing is that everything stays the same across 800 MHz to 18 GHz, which is the range of frequency we just measured. Why you're a super broadband antenna!" She continued to interpret the plots and numbers that otherwise meant nothing to Wei-Jen like a doctor explaining X-ray films to a clueless patient.

"So," Yu-Ning clapped her hands together, "since the network analyzer is still here, and we've got all the horn antennas for different frequencies, too, let's do some testing on what Wei-Jen could receive."

Still dazed by all the lab tests and result interpretations, Wei-Jen nodded absently. It wasn't like he wasn't invested in figuring out his powers, but Yu-Ning could be very intense in research sometimes, and it was disorienting that he was somehow the object of interest right now. In a scientific way.

Mario stood up. "You do that. I'm going to go grab everyone lunch."

Right. Lunch. For someone who hardly ever got out of bed before noon, having lunch felt like a foreign concept. And yet Wei-Jen was also very hungry while Yu-Ning seemed unbothered. But Mario promised to get some food from the Thai place across the street, which was also Wei-Jen's favorite, and Wei-Jen decided then and there that Mario was now a new friend since they shared the same palate.

Once Mario left, Wei-Jen set his phone down on the table and turned to Yu-Ning. "Lái ba!" Let's do this.

IT WAS RAINING outside by the time they had finished up. Wei-Jen remembered hearing about Taipei being peripherally affected by the most recent typhoon, whose name had slipped his mind. Cursing himself for not bringing an umbrella, he groaned a little and took a deep breath. Today had been... a lot. Not only did he wake up early with antenna-like mutant powers, he also went through a whole day of nothing but experiments. Could he change his radiation pattern if he tried hard enough? Could he transmit modulated signals at will? Could he denoise radio channels with heavy inter-ference? Yes, yes, and yes.

"I can drive you home," came Mario's voice as Wei-Jen was still staring out the window. "No one should be out in this kind of weather. Yu-Ning said she's going to stay here for a couple more hours to do who-knows-what, so it's just us."

Wei-Jen turned around to see Mario, all smiley with one slightly raised eyebrow, a huge transparent umbrella at his side.

"I..." Wei-Jen swallowed. What twenty-somethings drive in Taipei City? But then, it did sound awfully nice. "If it's not too much trouble."

"Zàn-zàn! We're besties now!" Mario whooped and Yu-Ning rolled her eyes behind him.

"Here." Yu-Ning held out the pair of stainless steel chopsticks Wei-Jen had lent her earlier. Because even though he'd forget bringing an umbrella, there was no way he'd not pack reusable silverware with him wherever he went. And his trusty water bottle. And foldable shopping bag.

As soon as Wei-Jen closed his fingers over the chopsticks, he noticed that Yu-Ning winced a little. She didn't let go of the other end and had her thinking face going. Wei-Jen tugged gently but she held up her other hand for him to stop. Mario was glancing at them curiously, too. Then Wei-Jen felt a vibration from his phone in his pockets.

"Your mom wants to know if you are going home for Mid-Autumn Festival this weekend and your dad is planning on barbe-cuing those tempura and baiye tofu you love so much," Yu-Ning said quietly. She had released her grasp now and looked both concerned and confused, which she never seemed to be either. Ever. "Sorry. I didn't mean to read your text."

"What do you mean?" Wei-Jen pulled out his phone, and right there on his lock screen was a text message from his mother. It read the exact same thing as Yu-Ning had just said. He didn't under-stand. How could Yu-Ning have known? "What in the fuck, Yu-Ning? How did you do that?"

Yu-Ning avoided his gaze and looked to Mario instead, whose mouth was now slightly ajar.

"So it *is* a mutant power," Mario muttered, his brows now drawn together. He plopped down into a swivel chair and it slid several centimeters from inertia.

"Hello? I'm still here." Wei-Jen waved his arms dramatically at the both of them. "What is a mutant power? I thought we'd already established that me getting radio broadcasting is that this morning."

"No, not you." Yu-Ning let out a breath and turned back to look at Wei-Jen. "Me."

So Yu-Ning went on to talk about how she could suddenly log on to countless webpages one day last week. It wasn't even that she was using any hacking skills, which Wei-Jen was sure she had, but that she knew what username–password combos to fill in right off the top of her head, whether or not she actually had an account on that particular site.

"That wasn't the weirdest thing. The weirdest thing that I found out over the weekend was that I could read and understand any file, encrypted or not, binary and ASCII." Yu-Ning leaned her head back against the chair's headrest. "And now, it seems like I can read encrypted data through you, Wei-Jen."

Mario made a soft "Hēng!" sound and then shook his head. "You definitely downplayed what you could do when you mentioned it to me last night, Yu-Ning. You're a walking hex editor and ransomware decryption tool, and you're wondering if that's a mutant power? How can you be so smart and dense at the same time?"

Wei-Jen just stared at Yu-Ning. It definitely hurt a little that she was just now sharing this with him when he had been wringing his hands over his own newfound powers earlier, but it was good that she had opened up a bit.

"And I couldn't read my own text messages without my phone because…"

"Because text messages and phone calls and basically everything else other than radio broadcasting and, I don't know, walkie talkies for kids, are encrypted," Yu-Ning supplied. She let out a low whistle. "Some collaborative powers we've got here, brother."

Mario made an explosion noise accompanied by both his fists opening next to his head. Wei-Jen and Yu-Ning stared at him.

"What? Don't you find that extremely cool? Wei-Jen, who studies cryptography, can function like an antenna, and Yu-Ning, who works with antennas, has decryption powers. And," Mario paused for what Wei-Jen assumed as effect, "You can collaborate and read everyone's text messages and eavesdrop on all phone calls there are. Impressive."

"I think you're getting too excited, and we're not invading people's privacy like that," Yu-Ning retorted, but she was gazing off through the window.

"Spit it out," probed Mario after a few seconds, staring at Yu-Ning. Then he narrowed his eyes. "This is about our advisor, Professor Lei, isn't it?"

Wei-Jen whipped his head toward Yu-Ning. "What's going on with Professor Lei? I thought she was on sabbatical."

"That, and being completely unresponsive of emails for the past, what, four weeks?" A muscle in Yu-Ning's jaw twitched. "Since a few days after that last master's thesis defense of one of our lab members'."

"It's not like her, and she had said she would be available through email. Now that the paper deadline of EuCAP, an antenna conference in Europe, is coming up and it's still radio silence," Mario supplied.

"You think something is off. That something has happened to her." Wei-Jen didn't say it as a question, but more like a statement. He knew Professor Lei, had even taken her Electromagnetics II course in his junior year and Introduction to Microwave Systems the year after that. She was an enthusiastic professor and very patient with students.

"We don't know, but that was what I wanted to work on this evening: scour the internet for anything related to her." Yu-Ning rubbed one side of her temples. "By that I mean going over whatever encrypted documents and data I can get my hands on."

"Says someone who isn't invading people's privacy." Mario chuckled a little, but even he looked worried.

Yu-Ning stood up and placed the chair neatly back to where it was. "I need to think about it tonight and will keep you both posted. We might need to meet up again here tomorrow for more testing if you're both down."

"Does this mean I'm driving you home, too?" Mario perked up from his seat.

Yu-Ning's lips tugged in one corner. "If you insist."

"TÁN-TSIT-Ē," Wei-Jen said, then realized while Mario spoke impeccable Mandarin, it didn't mean he understood Taiwanese, too. But Mario turned toward him with a hint of a smile on his face and his eyebrows slightly raised.

It was Wednesday, two days after their antenna experiments, and the semester had already started in full force. The campus was filled with freshmen having trouble navigating their bikes through the busy campus, and Wei-Jen was almost run over by a frazzled but apologetic biker with a rainbow ribbon on their backpack in the morning. Though it was no longer rainy from the typhoon, Zhoushan Road, ironically named "boat mountain," was flooded again, as was usual after heavy rain. Everyone called it Zhoushan River whenever it happened, and it was beyond Wei-Jen that, occasionally, someone would go for a swim in the dirty water.

"So you're saying there is no trace of Professor Lei, at all. She hasn't been sending any email or text in the past four weeks, nor has she been connected to the internet." This was fishy. No one Wei-Jen knew could stand weeks without internet access.

"Correct," said Yu-Ning. She was pacing up and down in the anechoic chamber control room, one of the few places in their office where they could have some sort of privacy. Then she looked back at Wei-Jen and Mario, both sitting in the uncomfortable folding chairs, with something that looked suspiciously like dread in her eyes. "The last signal sent out from her phone was from here, on Friday the week I last saw her in-person."

"Holy shit," Wei-Jen couldn't help but exclaim. "You hacked into Chunghwa Telecom or something?" And Yu-Ning only shrugged, like accessing any supposedly protected data from the largest telecommunications company in Taiwan wasn't a big deal.

"I need your help here, Wei-Jen," Yu-Ning continued. "There was one other person in this building—I traced all the phones here at that time and all but one belonged to either a faculty member, staff, or student in the EE department—when Professor Lei's phone lost connection. I couldn't find any message they had sent since there was no log at all, but it was a government phone number." She took a deep breath. "I think we'd be able to get something if I can access the radio signals you're receiving. It's using 4G LTE, so we might have a chance if this person or who they're sending messages to are in the city. And from what I know, they were on campus yesterday, too."

Wei-Jen stood up and held out his hand. "Okay. I don't fully understand what you're doing here, but let's try."

"Not here... The reception should be better outside and we would have a higher chance of receiving something. Drunken Moon Lake?" Yu-Ning suggested.

"Perfect location for a stroll while holding hands," contemplated Mario, and Yu-Ning slapped him on the arms. "Owww... Come on, you know you need to be discreet and not look like you're doing mutant stuff. Lots of non-university people hang out there, too. Remember all the anti-mutant hate groups? That one guy who thought the black goose there was too human and therefore must be a mutant and then murdered the goose? I'd say going for a romantic walk is the least suspicious."

Yu-Ning glared at him.

"What? Just because I'm Aro Mario doesn't mean I don't know these things." Mario grinned at Yu-Ning. "You must admit I have a point. And everyone knows you're a lā-zi so it's not like this is going to start rumors or anything."

Which was how an hour later, Wei-Jen found himself clasping hands with Yu-Ning at the school lake while Mario sat at the outdoor café sipping soy latte.

"This isn't weird at all," muttered Wei-Jen. It was interesting how the feel of Yu-Ning's hand instantly brought him back to seven years ago, back when he thought he was a lesbian and then turned out to be a straight dude instead. Ugh, high school. The good old days.

"Shut up and let me concentrate," hissed Yu-Ning. Her expression was focused and a bit annoyed, and Wei-Jen wondered how convincing they looked as a couple right now. More like one that was about to break up.

They managed to walk for a while without Wei-Jen pissing her off. He lost count of the laps they did around the lake. Ten? Twelve? There were fallen twigs all over the place but the lake and its surroundings were as serene as ever. A lot of people were sitting on the benches gazing at the smooth surface of the lake or chatting. It was good that it was still daytime, as he had heard about people walking around Drunken Moon Lake at night literally stumbling upon couples making out in dark bushes, which would have been incredibly awkward.

He was still lost in his thoughts when Yu-Ning tugged him toward Mario's table, where he had already finished his second cup of coffee. Mario grinned up at them approaching. "Nice walk?"

"You're enjoying this far too much," Yu-Ning snapped, but not too harshly. She sounded more tired than anything and had already let go of Wei-Jen, tucking her hands in the back pockets of her dark denim jeans. "We need to head back. Now."

Mario got up and tossed both cups into a nearby recycle bin. "Radio HQ, here we come."

As soon as they were back in the control room—Yu-Ning typing furiously on her phone all the way—Yu-Ning pulled out the whiteboard behind the computer desk and uncapped a marker. She drew a boxed question mark in the center. "This is the unknown number."

"That's a Super Mario Question Block," said Mario, and promptly did an impression of the Super Mario jump pose.

Wei-Jen had to stifle a laugh. "Or an information desk icon," he mumbled.

"I hate you both." Yu-Ning glared at them. "As I was saying, this is the number, and it is not one single device. It is a collective of devices used to impersonate various people, including lawyers, publishers, sales people, etc." She drew a few radial lines from the Question Block.

"Like scammers?" asked Wei-Jen. He was wondering what Yu-Ning was getting at and why they needed the whiteboard at all.

"Yes, and no," said Yu-Ning. "While we were walking back, I did a background check on all the victims this number was contacting during the past hour. And they all had two things in common." She started writing on the board instead of drawing more symbols.

"Mutant powers and..." Wei-Jen squinted at the whiteboard.

"And upcoming travel plans?" continued Mario. He looked a little perplexed, but then his head jerked up. "Oh! You think the impersonators are meeting up with these people and kidnapping them? And since they are leaving the country, no one would realize they had disappeared until it was too late?"

Yu-Ning pointed the marker at Mario. "Exactly. Except that I don't just 'think,' I know. So apparently there is this secret government division that is experimenting on mutants, on how to exploit them for," she held out her fingers, "the 'common good.' I downloaded the whole database of Mutant Powers of Persons in Taiwan from a government cloud computing service, and yes, of course it is encrypted."

"And Professor Lei is on the list?" Wei-Jen's head was spinning. How many mutants were there? How many were kidnapped? Forced disappearance sounded more like something that would happen back in the thirty-eight-year martial law era in the twentieth century, or White Terror, and surely not present-day Taiwan? The execution of putting together a database and having agents kidnapping mutants meant that there was heavy surveillance going on, too. Wei-Jen cringed at the thought.

"Yup." Yu-Ning nodded. "Her powers are listed as 'power supply.'"

They were quiet for a while, allowing all the information to sink in. Wei-Jen didn't know what was going to come next and wondered about the disappeared mutants. Could they do something? Would they become the next mutants who vanished into thin air? Yu-Ning was starting to get restless and kept tapping the marker against the board.

"Wei-Jen," Mario said, so suddenly that Wei-Jen almost fell out of his seat. "Can you... scan the office and tell me how many people there are?" He gestured toward the door that connected to the graduate students' office.

Wei-Jen frowned. Had Mario misunderstood his powers? He wasn't an X-ray machine or anything like that. His confusion must have shown because Mario sat up straighter in his seat, his face lit up with excitement.

"I've been thinking, since radio waves are your thing and you come with your own modulator and stuff, maybe you could do microwave imaging, too. You might not be able to see all the details, but seeing through cement walls for large objects is probably doable. If knowing the theory helps, I can give you a quick run down of it?" He looked at Wei-Jen expectantly.

And so Wei-Jen closed his eyes and tried. At first, he didn't know what he was looking for. His head was filled with the noise of different radio broadcasting channels and other signals, but then he started focusing on his body and mind and what he was feeling. It was kind of like meditation, really, and Wei-Jen could sense the waves radiating off of him and the ones that reflected back from his surroundings. He began putting together a picture of the office, the numbers of desks and desktop computers, as well as the students sitting in their cubicles.

"Six, not including us," he finally said after opening his eyes. He was a little shocked, and Mario, looking quite pleased with himself, bounded up from his chair and headed out to check. He came back seconds later, flashing a thumbs up.

"This is excellent!" Mario was beaming. "When we go on a rescue mission after figuring out where these mutants were kept, our Radar Man here will be able to see through the walls, assuming they're not all made with metal, and locate them!"

"Who says we're going on a rescue mission?" demanded Yu-Ning. She had stopped fidgeting with the marker.

"Don't tell me you're not thinking about it. You've pulled out the whiteboard, and you only do that when you're planning something." Mario leaned against the wall by the door. "Now, tell us everything you have in mind."

IT TOOK Wei-Jen and Yu-Ning a few more lakeside strolls before Yu-Ning gathered enough information to sift through government databases for more details. During these days where Yu-Ning ignored both his and Mario's messages on a basic texting app Yu-Ning wrote that destroyed messages one minute upon reception, Wei-Jen worked on his imaging powers. Trying very hard not to stalk his neighbors, he mainly practiced scanning his apartment and the PX Mart across the street. He also tried to sense through the cabinet doors at his parents' place when he went back home for Mid-Autumn Festival over the weekend.

By the time Wednesday came around again, Wei-Jen could tell the difference between an apple and an orange in the fruit section of PX Mart from his third-floor apartment bedroom. He had gone downstairs to walk around the grocery store every hour or so to see if he had identified something correctly. The cashier working on Monday had begun to look at him funny after his sixth visit in one single day without purchasing anything.

When Yu-Ning had finally texted them the night before, they all knew that she had some breakthrough findings. At eight in the morning—Wei-Jen was still getting used to their very early meetups —he found her staring at her laptop in the control room connected to the anechoic chamber, looking disgruntled. She was wearing a pair of heather gray tapered joggers with a simple black T-shirt, her hair somewhat disheveled.

"You look like you need something to cheer you up today," he said, pulling out one of those uncomfortable folding chairs and sitting down. This was one of the very few times Yu-Ning didn't look put together.

She grunted and looked up from the screen. "Good to see you, too," she mumbled. And before they could say anything else, there was a knock on the sliding door and Mario came in. But this time, he was not alone.

"You know how in heist movies, there is almost always a muscle?" Mario said, by way of greeting, right after closing the door. "I found the perfect one and took the liberty of inviting her." Yu-Ning made a small snorting noise that Mario either ignored or didn't hear. He did a grand gesture toward the person next to him. "Meet Chih-Yuan Hsieh (謝芷媛), a senior in mechanical engineering and the current varsity captain of the school's Fighting Sports Team, also known as the Sanda Team. She volunteers with EECS International and was actually the one who helped me settle down in Taipei and showed me around the city two years ago." He paused. "Damn, it's been that long."

Chih-Yuan was about a head shorter than Mario but probably still had a few centimeters on Wei-Jen. He felt once again insecure about his height. With slightly tousled medium-long hair and wearing gray blue leggings with a dusty rose workout T-shirt that clung to her curves, she had a casual air about her with a friendly smile on her round face. Mario then introduced Yu-Ning and Wei-Jen to her as well, and Wei-Jen caught a glimpse of Yu-Ning rolling her eyes before she took a deep breath and closed them.

"What? She's going to also teach us self-defense or something?" Yu-Ning looked very tired. Knowing her, Wei-Jen understood that she wasn't being mean, but he couldn't be sure how Chih-Yuan would take it.

But Chih-Yuan surprised him by sitting on one of the tables and beaming at them all. "Hopefully, that wouldn't be necessary with me here. Mario didn't mention that I'm also a mutant." She waved a hand at the small wrench on the table next to her and it floated over the surface. "When it comes to it, I can fight, but I think disarming people with weapons will be more efficient and less messy. Jammed guns, uncooperative knives, something like that." Her eyes twinkled with mischief.

"You're telekinetic," Yu-Ning said flatly, like she wasn't impressed at all. Wei-Jen sure was.

"Yes, and no." The wrench clattered back onto the table. "I manipulate metal, and metal only, like I can open mechanical locks without damaging anything. But if they're, say, wooden door bolts, I'd probably have to break down the whole thing."

Yu-Ning sighed. "I see. And what's in it for you to join us on this risky journey?"

It was the first time since she entered the room that Wei-Jen saw Chih-Yuan's smile slip a little.

"My little sister," she replied, her voice breaking. "She is starting her exchange program next month, but I haven't heard from her since she left for Tokyo two weeks ago."

They all fell silent at this. Then Mario cleared his throat. "So, what are your new findings, Yu-Ning?"

She didn't say anything for a few seconds, but when she did, her voice came out quiet. "Lyudao. They're keeping the mutants on Lyudao."

They what?

Lyudao, or Green Island, was a fifteen–square kilometer island off the southeast coast of Taiwan Main Island. During the post–Chinese Civil War martial law era, the government exiled and imprisoned political prisoners in the township for thought reform and laogai. Currently, Lyudao Prison held a handful of men convicted of felony charges, but the original sites were now part of the Green Island White Terror Memorial Park. Of all the possible location choices, Wei-Jen didn't know what to feel about this.

"I couldn't find the exact coordinates for the mutant prison, but it is for sure on the island," Yu-Ning continued. "Satellite images didn't help either. They have imprisoned a total of fifty-six mutants, all in separate cells to prevent powerful collaborations, and about fifty staff members are involved in this project, including forty or so armed security and officers with several of them also serving as on-site technicians. It's a high-tech facility, designed with mutant powers in mind."

She pulled up a floor plan of a radial building with seven long hallways. "This is what it looks like on the inside, but there is no electrical plan record for this place, so we cannot really know what it'd be like until we get there. Wei-Jen, we would also need you to figure out which cells have mutants without us trying to walk along those hallways that are death traps." And she clicked open another window on her laptop. "This is the list of all the mutants and their respective powers. A third of them have combat powers, so hope-fully they'll be helpful once we freed them."

"How are we going to go in without getting captured?" Wei-Jen was nervous. His powers weren't even close to combat ones, and if anyone tried to fight him, he'd be doomed.

Yu-Ning hummed in thought. "I'm hoping for a remote jail-break where we're just close enough to do something without actu-ally entering the facility. There's still a lot of unknown here, and I think we can come up with a more thorough plan in the next few days. They're kidnapping people at a pretty fast rate, so we should go there and shut down the place as soon as possible."

"My sister would be able to help deal with the aftermath," Chih-Yuan chimed in. "This project, not a lot of people other than the staff know about it, right? If she could literally get her hands on all of them, she'll be able to target the mutant-related memories and erase them."

"Perfect!" Mario was nodding enthusiastically. "What about those off-site? Yu-Ning, would you be able to hack into some of the systems and convince them the project has been terminated or, I

81

don't know, trick them into showing up somewhere so Chih-Yuan's sister could do her thing?"

She agreed that it was doable. The four of them now crowded around Yu-Ning's laptop, discussing solutions to emergencies, such as a lockdown or encountering hidden weaponries.

"Wei-Jen? I want us to try bypassing RFID door access control systems," Yu-Ning said. "If you could read the machine, I can decode it and help send whatever signals needed to unlock it. Then, I think, as long as we remain in physical contact, we'd be able to get past most electronic locks."

Upon checking that there wasn't anyone else in the office, they held up their hands in front of the anechoic chamber RFID reader with Yu-Ning's palm on the back of Wei-Jen's hand. He focused on the machine and then Yu-Ning rattled off a sequence of numbers. Without thinking, he sent a signal to the reader. Then they heard a beep as the green LED lit up.

"That is so impressive!" squealed Chih-Yuan, once they all gathered in the room with the door locked again. She flashed a cheerful grin. "Worst case scenario though, I can cut off all the power cords."

FOR THE REST of the week, the four of them gathered in the anechoic chamber whenever they didn't have classes or meetings. Mario kept wanting to call this trip to Lyudao a heist, but Yu-Ning insisted it was a rescue mission. Wei-Jen thought they were the same thing. The four of them had decided that Wei-Jen and Yu-Ning would spend most of the time working closely together to disable electronic security systems and Chih-Yuan would keep them safe as they decoded. And since Mario was the only one among them who was not a mutant, and hence less likely to be put in one of the cells if captured, he would be their messenger to the mutants should they need it.

By the time they were ready, or as ready as they could be, the number of mutants on Lyudao had reached almost seventy. It was incidentally Teachers' Day when they boarded the earliest Taroko Express at six in the morning bound for Taitung Train Station. Wei-Jen had to set about twenty alarms on his phone starting at four just to make sure he didn't oversleep. He also tried very hard not to think too much about the Taroko Express Derailment incident where the train hit a misplaced truck on the tracks that killed forty-nine people out of around five hundred people on board during the Qingming Festival holidays one year. It was all over the news and he had cried himself to sleep that night, thinking about the brevity and uncertainty of life. And here they were on their way to free some mutants.

"Can you please stop tinkering with the WiFi?" Yu-Ning hissed at Wei-Jen from across the aisle. He saw that she basically had her phone held up over Chih-Yuan's lap in hopes of getting it as far away from him as possible. She was sitting with Chih-Yuan because she had refused to sit beside Wei-Jen, given that any accidental touch would result in her getting a huge influx of noisy data. Mario had cheerfully volunteered to sit beside "our radiation guy."

"I'm not..." he began.

"You are," Yu-Ning snapped. Then she sighed, and said, "Look, I'm sorry. I understand you're stressed, so it's getting a little haywire. Yes, you do that. But could you tone it down a bit? Not only that I can do some real-time scouting, but also it wouldn't seem so suspicious that the reception is bad around us. We still don't know how their surveillance system works."

"You know how people always say 'disaster queer'?" Mario suddenly said in a thoughtful voice. "I don't think it quite encapsulates the messiness. 'Catastrophe queer' is the better expression. Bigger magnitude. Don't you think?"

"Not helping, Mario." Yu-Ning shot him a glare, and Chih-Yuan let out a soft giggle.

Throughout the rest of the train ride, Wei-Jen tried to tamp

HSINJU CHEN

down his nerves through mental noting. Soon, he was distracted by the scenery outside as they passed through Hualien County: rocky cliffs on his right and the Pacific Ocean on his left. The last time he visited the east coast was four years ago, an Introduction to Geology field trip for gen ed. He gazed at the shimmering ocean, imagining the warm breeze against his face, the sun on his skin, and the bitter taste of salt water on his lips. They wouldn't have time to go for a swim, but Wei-Jen wished he could enjoy the open waters now that he had finally left Taipei Basin. Meanwhile, Mario was quietly singing "Guns and Ships" from *Hamilton* to himself.

A few hours after entering Huadong Valley, they arrived at Taitung Train Station with just enough time for a quick lunch before the connecting ferry departed Fugang Fishing Harbor. It took them another fifty minutes to arrive at Lyudao, and Wei-Jen couldn't believe that they were really here, really doing this. His nerves crept in and Yu-Ning immediately looked up from her phone at him. He was probably interfering with her reception again.

"Where are we heading?" he asked, as soon as they alighted from the ferry. There were people everywhere: locals calling out bed and breakfast deals and excited tourists chattering away with friends. Yet no one seemed to be concerned that there was a mutant prison somewhere on the island.

"I was hoping you could tell us that," Yu-Ning replied, tucking her phone away.

Oh. Right.

Wei-Jen closed his eyes and started scanning the island. It still blew his mind that he basically had X-ray vision—more like he could sense rather than actually see—on top of being able to tune in and out of radio channels. Not that listening to the radio on-demand was something he needed though. There were tourist activities everywhere, some zooming around on electric scooters and some swimming or snorkeling in the ocean. He saw goats and cows and deers grazing on the vast vegetation of the rocky island. Shops and homes scattered around Lyudao, and he saw all the tourist attractions, including peculiarly shaped rocks, the Memorial Park, Lyudao Lighthouse.

But he didn't see anything resembling the floor plan they had. Could they be wrong? Were they somehow tricked into going on this trip so they could be captured as well? Before he could doubt it any further, something caught his attention as he scanned the coral reefs surrounding the coast. Directly below the Oasis House, or Bagua Building, which used to hold political prisoners and was now part of the White Terror Memorial Park, he detected a radial-structured basement with seven wings, all lined up with cells on both sides. Upon further inspection, he saw people in individual cells, most of them sprawled motionless in beds, hearts faintly thumping. Were they sleeping in the afternoon? There was no sunlight underground so perhaps they had a different sleep schedule. Heavily armed guards patrolled the hallways, and there was a cluster of similarly dressed people in an empty but closed-to-public room in the Oasis House. The entrance. There was a trap door on the floor that connected to a steep ramp into the hub of the structure, and as far as Wei-Jen could tell, there was no other way out.

When he finally opened his eyes, he squinted in the bright sunlight. Yu-Ning was staring at the ocean with Chih-Yuan looking ready and excited next to her, bouncing on the balls of her feet. He didn't understand what there was to be excited about, but maybe Sanda experts had a different idea of fun. Mario was happily sucking on a yellow-tinted popsicle on his other side. Since when did he have the time to get it from the stands on the sidewalk?

"Pineapple." He grinned at Wei-Jen. "The lady was nice enough to give me one for free."

"Nobody ever told you to not accept free food from strangers?" Yu-Ning shook her head but even she was smiling a little. Then she turned to Wei-Jen. "So, where are we heading?"

He took a deep breath. "You're not going to like this, but it is at the Oasis House."

"NO, I cannot decrypt it when the signal is so fuzzy," Yu-Ning exclaimed in frustration.

The four of them were squished together on a roadside bench right outside the Oasis House. They had been trying to remotely deactivate as many devices in the mutant prison as they could since getting off the bus an hour ago. So far, the count was zero. They didn't expect the whole structure to be underground and had failed to account for the effects of all the rebars in the ceiling.

"That's it! We're going in." Chih-Yuan jumped up. It was their backup plan should they encounter issues like this.

Both Wei-Jen and Yu-Ning were sweating now from the effort and Mario was playing with a rock from the beach. It was four in the afternoon and if they didn't hurry up and do something, it would soon be nightfall.

"The park closes at five," said Mario. "We can go in once the tourists clear out?"

Yu-Ning sighed and Wei-Jen tried to not feel so useless. If only he could get a stronger signal.

They huddled closer as he assessed the situation of the trapdoor room. Four people were guarding it, but there were few metal objects in there for Chih-Yuan to utilize. None of them were carrying guns and their knives weren't metallic. The largest chunk of metal he could see were belt buckles.

"That'd work!" Chih-Yuan clapped her hands together and grinned. "As long as I'm close enough to sense them, I can slip the buckles under whatever protection gear they have on and use them like a knee strike to the liver. They wouldn't know what hit them."

"I thought that was a Muay Thai move?" Yu-Ning asked.

"You'd be surprised how many other moves I can do," Chih-Yuan replied, flashing her a smile.

At five o'clock, they had agreed that Mario and Chih-Yuan

would go first. Mario would pretend to stumble upon the room while claiming to be interested in the history of Oasis House or something, and Chih-Yuan, who would be hiding nearby, would strike all the guards at the same time as swiftly as possible while they were distracted. The four of them would then change into the guards' clothes and head for the underground. How they were going to open the trapdoor would be a later problem.

"Okay, I'm going to go chat up the security personnels, and let's see if they get intrigued by a Black German guy speaking Mandarin like every other Taiwanese does," said Mario, winking back at them. "I can be a very obnoxious tourist and you all go do your thing."

"You're pretty obnoxious most of the time anyway," Yu-Ning muttered under her breath. "But stay safe, all right?"

"Awww, I know you're actually a softie." He grinned and walked toward the Oasis House with Chih-Yuan trailing a few meters behind him.

Wei-Jen saw the whole thing play out like he was there with them, but without sounds: Mario knocked on the door of the room, startling the guards, one of whom opened the door after some hesitation. He started speaking with wild gestures—that man did not know subtlety—as Chih-Yuan crept around the corner of the building. Within a few seconds, all the guards collapsed to the floor. And before any of them could do anything, Chih-Yuan lept from her hiding place, and slapped all four of the guards in the neck in quick succession.

Making sure that the coast was clear, Wei-Jen and Yu-Ning headed over to join them. They found all the guards stripped to their underwear, hands bound with their belts, and slumped against the walls. None of them had regained consciousness yet, and Chih-Yuan was pacing in the room.

"Should I gag them? They'd probably wake up in a few minutes." Chih-Yuan looked troubled.

Yu-Ning stared at them for a few seconds. "Would you be able to keep an eye on them and drag them in with us by the belts?" She gestured at the bindings. "We can put them in the cells until your sister can do something about it."

Chih-Yuan let out a sigh of relief as if locking them up was better than gagging them. "That, I can do."

They all started removing their clothes. Wei-Jen hated that he had to do it in front of his friends, but nobody was glancing his way anyway as he quickly slipped into the set of clothes, still warm from their original wearer. He cringed a little at the thought of wearing some random person's clothes. Then Wei-Jen caught a glimpse of Yu-Ning eyeing Chih-Yuan while she was pulling on a shirt. Averting his own gaze, he secured the rest of the gear and smoothed down the sleeves. The uniform and vest weren't a perfect fit as both hung slightly loose on him, but he tried moving around and decided they weren't too bad.

After they were all dressed, one of the guards let out a groan and Chih-Yuan threw another punch to the neck. The trapdoor's access reader was hidden under a plank of wood on the floor, but Wei-Jen and Yu-Ning easily unlocked it without moving anything. They heard a beep and the trapdoor slowly opened. And nothing but darkness greeted them.

SINCE WEI-JEN WAS the only who could sense his way through darkness, he was the first to go down the ramp, followed closely by Yu-Ning, Chih-Yuan, the four still-unconscious guards, and Mario, who was humming "Down Once More / Track Down This Murderer" from *Phantom of the Opera*. Wei-Jen had to stifle a chuckle as only Mario could manage to sing during their dangerous mission. He made a mental note that they needed to chat about musicals if, no when, they made it out here alive.

There was a door at the end of the ramp, and Wei-Jen slowed to a stop, surveying the room beyond it. It was the radial structure they were looking for, with one guard patrolling each of the seven wings and two wandering about in the central hub. Unlike the ones at the trapdoor, these were armed with the polymer-framed, semi-automatic Walther PPQ M2 pistols—thanks to Yu-Ning's research, Wei-Jen could recognize the type of guns Taiwanese police force uses—which would give Chih-Yuan something to work with but also posed more risk to them all.

The central hub was an octagon, and now that he was practically one wall away from the structure, he could see bagua symbols and the eight characters engraved over the doorways leading to the seven aisles as well as the door in front of him. There was a bright energy ball in the first cell of Aisle Zhèn that was preventing Wei-Jen from getting clear readings of any door access control at this distance, and they had no choice but to go in. He wondered what that was. The electrical room? While each wing had exactly twenty-one cells, only half of them were full and the majority of the inhabitants were motionless in supine positions. How were they going to break them all out if most of them weren't in fighting conditions?

"Well, I'm in fighting condition," said Chih-Yuan after Wei-Jen relayed everything he had gathered back to the group. "Mario and I will distract them as you two go free the mutants. Don't worry lah," she added, putting a reassuring hand on Yu-Ning's arm, who squirmed a little, "I'll keep him safe, too."

And Wei-Jen, gathering as much composure as he could, pushed open the door.

It was one thing to sense the room through imaging and another to actually see it. He heard Mario's sharp intake of breath from behind him. The space was brightly lit with sleek, polished floor tiles. If not for the armed jailers, he would've thought they were in a hospital.

"What is this?" One of the guards stationed at the central hub started walking toward them, eyes narrowed. Wei-Jen opened his mouth to say something, but Yu-Ning beat him to it.

"New mutants found," she said, still managing to carry herself with an air of authority. Chih-Yuan and Mario shoved the four skimpily dressed guards forward.

The guard gave all of them a once over and Wei-Jen struggled to remain impassive. "I see."

It was that fraction of a second before the guard raised one hand that Wei-Jen knew they were busted. He was about to shout something when Chih-Yuan pushed him from behind, hissing "Go!" All guns in the room were raised and pointed at them. Somehow all the patrols were gathered in the central hub, and Wei-Jen thought that this would be the end of it. Too many guns and...

Chih-Yuan gave him another push and he saw Yu-Ning dashing toward the first hallway on their right, Aisle Duì. The way the wings were named was incredibly confusing for Wei-Jen. Who in the world decided it was a good idea to not use numbers but these bagua symbols?

There was a commotion back in the central hub but Wei-Jen hadn't heard any shooting yet. He knew that they all had to trust each other to get out of here alive, so even though he wanted to see what was going on with Chih-Yuan and Mario, he followed Yu-Ning instead. They stopped in front of the third cell where a child covered with light fur and a "king" character on the forehead lay on the floor. It took them all but one second to unlock the cell and Yu-Ning crouched down to shake the tiger kid.

"Gàn," she cursed. "Still breathing but doesn't even stir. Are they sedated?" And as they continued inspecting a few other cells in both the same aisle and the adjacent Aisle Lí, they soon realized that none of the mutants were waking up.

"Wei-Jen and Yu-Ning," came the breathless shout of Chih-Yuan. "Can you two unlock an empty cell for us?"

Wei-Jen turned to find that all guns were abandoned on the floor and Chih-Yuan was brawling with two unarmed guards while Mario was running around in circles, one guard hot on his heels. All the others were lying motionless by the wall. Yu-Ning grabbed Wei-Jen's arms for attention and they opened a few empty cells as

Chih-Yuan wrestled the two into the rooms as well as the one who had been pursuing Mario, and locked them behind metal bars. Then they dragged all the rest into the cells, too.

"Sóng--lah! That was exciting," exclaimed Chih-Yuan. Wei-Jen would have thought she was being sarcastic if not for the gleam in her eyes. And then she frowned. "But where are the mutants? Where's my sister?"

Before either of them could answer, Mario skidded to a halt beside them. He must have been wandering the hallways. Panting, he said, "Not waking up. Except for Professor Lei. She's there. Aisle Zhèn."

THE FOUR OF them approached the wing and Wei-Jen soon realized that the bright energy source he saw earlier was not an electrical room after all. It was Professor Lei, pinned to the wall and looking absolutely exhausted. Electrical cables ran all across her limbs and into her shoulders like the headjacks in *The Matrix*.

"Mario, Yu-Ning, Wei-Jen," she breathed. "And a friend?"

"Chih-Yuan," supplied Chih-Yuan. She looked more uncomfortable standing here than she did fighting. "I can, uh, cut you off from the wall, Professor Lei. All the guards have been locked up so it's safe now."

Professor Lei smiled weakly. "It is never truly safe. And no, not yet. Detach me from the system, and the cell locks, which are fail-safe locks, will lose power and unlock as soon as the backup battery runs out, if there is one."

Wei-Jen's eyes widened. "They're using you to power this place?" he asked, incredulous. He couldn't decide which was more inhumane: sedating the captives, or sucking the juice out of them.

"Here and parts of the island," Professor Lei replied and then gave a rueful chuckle. "You know how the government tried to compensate the Tao people for dumping nuclear waste on their land without their consent by providing discounted electricity on Lanyu?" Lanyu was a nearby island also reachable from Fugang Fishing Harbor. "Then business people migrated from Taiwan Main Island to set up shop for the cheap electricity and now Taipower loses money every year. They thought I'd help balance their books. And of course, also forcefully."

Wei-Jen was again at a loss for words. How did anyone respond to that? Then Professor Lei asked them about their plans. As Yu-Ning and Mario started explaining, Chih-Yuan went to check on the guards who were making a ruckus in another aisle. Wei-Jen felt like he had accidentally stumbled across Professor Lei's lab having a group meeting. Soon, it was only Mario keeping Professor Lei company as Wei-Jen and Yu-Ning continued unlocking the rest of the cells, retrieving all the mutants and relocating them to the central hub.

Chih-Yuan spent most of the evening hovering over her sister, who was still unconscious like the others. Mario went to a nearby grocery store to get food enough to feed everyone as it seemed that they needed to stay the night, waiting for the mutants to wake up from their slumber. According to Professor Lei, it would be another couple of hours since the mutants were usually force-fed at dawn before being immediately sedated again. This led to an outraged cry from them all.

Several more armed jailers from the next shift marched in, and before they registered what was happening, Chih-Yuan easily disarmed them all, including the ones at the trapdoor upstairs, and shoved them into some cells. They were expecting a third shift in the morning. The four of them took turns sleeping and Chih-Yuan insisted on them being armed with a pistol or two whenever she was napping in case the next shift came earlier than expected. Sliding one of the Walthers into the holster on his belt, Wei-Jen absently noted that he had had enough guns today for the rest of his life.

By five in the morning, some of the mutants started to stir. Wei-Jen carefully attended each of them to make sure they had access to all the water and food, but most of them woke up confused and angry, possibly thinking he was one of the guards even though he was no longer wearing the uniforms. He got a few weak punches to the face from the waking mutants and several minor cuts on one arm from some invisible blades one of them conjured.

When Chih-Yuan's sister finally woke up—Wei-Jen heard a cry of "Jiě!" somewhere and saw the blurred figure of Chih-Yuan rushing over—it was almost seven. The White Terror Memorial Park opened at nine and if they wanted to evacuate this place without running into tourists, they had to move fast.

Yu-Ning was sitting against the wall near Aisle Zhèn, watching the sisters huddled together while staying close to her advisor. Sinking down to the floor across from her, Wei-Jen groaned a little from his stiff back, caused by bending over to inspect the mutants over the past two hours.

"Doing okay over there?" Yu-Ning asked, her gaze still fixed on the Hsieh sisters. She seemed rather tired but also had a haunted look about her.

"Yeah." He dropped his head back against the wall with a soft thunk. It felt good to sit down and relax for a little bit. "Still processing everything that's happening though. You?"

Yu-Ning just shrugged. They sat there in silence for a while as Mario made his rounds. Soon, everyone had regained consciousness and were talking amongst themselves. A few of them were sobbing uncontrollably, their new friends putting an arm around them for support. Wei-Jen felt tears prick his eyes as he watched the mutants open up and bond with each other. Even though they still had one last step to finishing up their plan, he was relieved that they had gotten this far. Some mutants came over, thanked them, bid them goodbye, and finally exited the building of their imprisonment.

There weren't many people left when the sisters came over to where Yu-Ning and Wei-Jen sat. Chih-Yuan introduced her sister,

Chih-Chun (謝芷君), to them. They looked a lot alike with the same eyes and smile, but Chih-Chun was slightly taller and seemed very shy.

"She's ready," Chih-Yuan said while her sister peered at them through her overgrown bangs. "Chih-Chun will wipe the guards' memories associated with this mutant project and make them think they're in Lyudao for vacation."

They got up and went to the cells that held the guards, Mario joining along the way. Yu-Ning and Wei-Jen unlocked the doors, and Chih-Yuan restrained the guards while Chih-Chun worked her magic. Then Mario escorted the disoriented guards out the trapdoor one by one as soon as Chih-Chun was done with them. The five of them worked their way through all forty people, including those who were ambushed on their way in for their morning shift an hour ago.

"And that's the last one," Mario announced as he returned from the trapdoor ramp.

Professor Lei had already been freed from her cell as soon as Chih-Yuan got hold of the last guard. Now, she was sitting among them in the almost empty central hub of the prison as the rest of them cleaned up the space, preparing for their exit before the park opened. With Mario supporting Professor Lei's weak body, they went back up through the trapdoor and into the sunlight and fresh air.

How odd was it that instead of a sense of relief, Wei-Jen felt empty. It was like waking up from a nightmare, only to find that the same thing was happening in real life. Perhaps this would be an ongoing thing for them now, an ever-present feeling of having to watch their backs. But the company made him feel like it was possible to push through and stay alive and free for another day.

IT WAS the four-day Double Tenth Day holiday and Mario had insisted on throwing a celebratory party at his apartment. They had spent the past week tracking down every last person involved in the mutant prison project and ambushing them with Chih-Chun's brainwashing powers. Even though Wei-Jen desperately needed to study for his upcoming midterms after spending so much time and energy on freeing the mutants, he wasn't about to miss out on a casual get-together with the whole crew.

Sitting in Mario's living room with a bottle of weissbier from Taiwan Beer in his hand—he didn't expect Mario to have stocked up on Taiwanese beer—Wei-Jen couldn't remember the last time he felt this at ease with a group of people. They had been playing board games for a while, and Mario's housemates, a Taiwanese grad student and his Taiwanese-Kiwi husband, had joined them for a few rounds of *Saboteur* and *Die Kutschfahrt zur Teufelsburg*. Amongst all seven players, Wei-Jen noticed that whenever the Hsieh sisters happened to be on the same team, they always won.

Around dinnertime, Mario ordered Thai food from a restaurant a block away and was setting up the table while everyone else lounged around the apartment. He had insisted that they were all his guests today and nobody should be doing any extra work. A few glasses of beer had Chih-Chun loosen up a bit as she was now chatting animatedly with Mario's housemates. Wei-Jen thought he heard something about "Formosan sika deers," supposedly the wild ones they saw when they were leaving Lyudao the other day. They were adorable, and while Wei-Jen would not admit it out loud, he felt his heart melt a little when he saw the fawns. That being said, even though Lyudao was one of the very few places where one could see wild Formosan sika deers, he did not ever want to visit there again.

He rose to his feet and padded toward the bathroom to wash his hands before dinner. Out of the corner of his eye, he saw Chih-Yuan pushing Yu-Ning against a closed bedroom door, both of their lips seeking the other's. He had never seen Yu-Ning grin like that, like nothing else mattered. Thankfully, they were too focused on each other and didn't hear him approach.

Mario called them all to dinner not long after, and Wei-Jen loved every minute of inhaling the food as well as the conversations going around the table. They talked about everything from academia to extracurricular activities to families. "A Vision of Nowness" from *Head Over Heels* was playing in the background, and their chat soon turned to musicals. Just as Wei-Jen thought, Mario was a huge fan of musicals and could pretty much sing any song on demand.

"Next time," mused Mario, "we're going to have a musical karaoke."

And Wei-Jen couldn't wait for them all to hang out together again, hopefully not after another gruesome mission.

# Farsight

Dylan is predictably furious when I fill them in. "Remind me. What's our legal shit here?"

I sigh. This conversation again. "We can't go and interfere in other countries' affairs. Depending on the outcome of the Mutopia Accords, we might have some leeway when it comes to intervening if we think the safety of mutants is being compromised."

They make a sound halfway between frustration and agreement. "Might be good to have, like, a little team on the side. Hush hush for helping out with situations that need heavy hitters. I mean, these people in Taiwan handled themselves, but not everyone can. And this isn't the only mutant prison on Earth, so—"

"Dylan." I snap my fingers in their face. "You are not starting a covert mission squad."

"Okay, fine." They grin at me. "I am definitely not start*ing* one."

I frown at the emphasis. "It's better if I don't know, isn't it?"

"Know what?" They roll their eyes. "I'd recommend you look away. They call me a hero, but I think you and I both know that's a long way from the truth."

I blink. It's true that we've all done some things we're not proud of. I know that Dylan does therapy with Ray, but I'm not sure how you untangle everything they've been through.

"Magneto was right," Dylan says, their voice grim. "Some days I think he was righter than others."

"He's a fictional character." There's a lump in my throat.

"Lucky him. Whereas I'm all fucked up over ends and means."

I feel like I'm in the presence of someone much older, who's seen things I wouldn't believe. "We're trying to build a better world."

Breath whistles from their throat. "I'd love that. I really would. But we're so far away from it. It's like I'm trying to splice reality and a fucking impossible dream, and I don't know whether me, the godawful horrendous fuckup, is capable of anything close to that." Their fist clenches restlessly at their side.

I'm stuck, hovering awkwardly with no idea of how to bridge this much smaller gap between the stern, closed-off person I've made myself, and this desperately unhappy young person in front of me.

While I'm debating, something catches my eye in the far, far distance. It's the New England woods, not far from where I grew up in Maine. I was always warned away from those places. They said strange things happened among the trees.

"We've got something," I tell Dylan, and I'm relieved when their attention turns away from the darkness in their heart to something a little more understandable.

# When the Woods Whisper Back

∾

SHANNON IVES

THE HILLS AND MAMA ARE ALL SHE'S KNOWN, AND NOW Mama is gone. It's her absence that draws Rae from slumber, some deep, innate recognition of the vacuum that Mama left behind. Where there was once a warm and rattly breathing beside her, there's now only a cool and grave silence. Dread slithers around her stomach, slowly at first, but then its spirals grow tighter and tighter, unrelenting, until Rae is forced to confront it. Her eyes snap open, her awakening accompanied by the urge to scream. She's drenched in sweat—it was a nightmare, so real and so vivid only seconds ago and now already fading, but though the immediate terror evaporates, that creeping unease settles right back into the pit of her stomach like a cat curling into its place in the sun.

"Mama?"

Sunlight filters into the empty cabin through a dirty glass window, catching on the dust that hangs suspended in the air like a midwinter snow. Rae lifts a flannel sleeve to her nose instinctively as her green eyes flick across the empty room. It isn't much to look at, bathed in this dirty light of day, and maybe calling it a cabin is too generous. It's more of a small hunter's retreat, barely big enough to hold the lumpy mattress Mama let her have last night, an ancient wooden table with a single matching chair, and a rickety shelf stocked with canned goods that look older than Mama. Dust covers every surface except for the places where they've been, and even though Rae can clearly see the trail from Mama's raggedy sleeping bag, which lies unceremoniously unzipped and tossed open, toward the front door, Rae still looks for her in the shadows of the room.

"Side?" But of course, the orange tabby cat, Mama's loyal companion, is nowhere to be seen.

Rae swallows hard. It isn't like Mama to go anywhere without waking her first. They have a code, and though Mama sometimes bends the rules to her own likening, something feels wrong. Instinctively, her hand falls away from her side off the opposite edge of the mattress. A warm, wet tongue finds her palm, bringing with it a sense of calm. Grim is still here. She pats the dog on his head gratefully, and then swings her legs over the edge of the mattress to stand.

She doesn't know who owns this place, only that when they came across it last night, it looked abandoned enough. The view down the winding dirt road that technically counts as a driveway gave them plenty of clearance, and with Grim on guard, Mama said they'd be able to make a run for it with plenty of time to spare should the owners decide to return. They must be careful until hunting season is over, right around the solstice. After that, most of the cabins in this part of the woods stay abandoned through the remainder of the winter, as if one of the ancient forest witches from Mama's stories had cast a spell on them. They're simply too far out for most folks to venture to, especially without the promise of fresh game. But the first snow is weeks from falling, and the solstice and its safety are still a few moons further off than that. Until then, Mama and Rae need to choose the most desolate looking cabins and hope for the best.

*What's she trying to prove?* Rae forces herself to stand, knees popping, and looks over to the table. It's covered in an uninterrupted layer of dust, clean as the first page of a fresh notebook. Her heart sinks—there's no message scrawled for her there. Not unless you count the Bell Book, which sits square in the table's middle where Mama reverently placed it last night. It's just as age-worn, if not more so, than the crumbling shack around it. If Rae didn't know any better, she'd believe the book belonged here. But she does. She also knows Mama would never leave it behind. Not willingly. She runs her fingers through her hair and sighs, trying to steady her heart. Mama's up to something, that's all. After all, hasn't she been teasing today for as long as Rae can remember?

"You'll see on your seventeenth birthday. When your magic comes." How many times over the years has Rae heard those exact words? If a number exists, she doesn't know it; it's too high, far too large for Mama to remember, and as such, far too large for her to have taught to Rae.

"Three things are true for Bell women," Mama would whisper excitedly, reciting the old family myths. "Your fifteenth birthday brings your blood. Your sixteenth birthday brings your familiar. And your seventeenth birthday brings your magic."

"And when it does, we'll record it in the Bell Book with the rest of ours," Mamaw whistled through missing teeth, back when she was still alive. The ancient tome has been in their family for generations. Even Rae can admit that it has something of an air about it, with its cracking old leather cover and pages as fragile as autumn leaves. There, in its final pages, behind all the meticulously recorded superstitions and spells (wear a hollowed peach pit stuffed with yarrow around your neck to attract love, never kill a deer on Sunday, apply stump water to a wart to remove it) is the impressive, sprawling Bell family tree, and more importantly, her own little branch.

*Mehitable Bell, Born in 1892 — Seer*
*Ila Bell, Born in 1912 — Shifter*
*Effie Bell, Born in 1929 — Spirit Whisperer*

When Rae was a little girl, she would lovingly trace Mamaw and Mama's names. *Opal Bell, Born in 1955 — Mind Mover*, and *Jessica Bell, Born in 1981 — Mind Reader.* And there, at the end of the line, was her name: *Rae Bell, Born in 2004 —*

How many hours had she wasted, wondering what magic gift would eventually fill that blank line? It was only as she started to grow older that she realized it was all made up, some delusion or family sickness passed down through the generations. Never once had Mamaw moved anything with her mind, and how many times had Rae intentionally thought the most cruel and vile thing she could imagine, looking for any flicker of recognition across Mama's face? Another memory so frequent that it's impossible to count.

No, as far as Rae can tell, the only gift Mamaw had was the power of persuasion, poisoning Mama's mind with superstitions, insisting that the new world was the reason their powers had all but dried up, like their magic was an overdrawn well. Something about radio waves interfering was her best guess, but Mamaw was hardly educated, so how could she possibly understand such things, let alone their effect on the Bell-folk's magic?

But Mama bought in, grieving an explanation for the loss of something she keenly felt. It didn't matter whether she'd imagined the entire thing or not—Mama believed she'd been able to read minds once, all because of that absurd book, and she was desperate to ensure her daughter never faced that same sense of loss.

And so the three of them had wandered into the woods one night before Rae was old enough to remember, and they never looked back.

Her fifteenth birthday did bring her blood, and Mama had strutted around like a prophet who accurately predicted the Lord's return. Rae had conceded the coincidence, and even though she knew it was nothing more than that, she was still young and impressionable, and secretly hoped that, just maybe, there was something to the old stories after all. But then Mama led her outside on her sixteenth birthday to show her the scrawny, half-feral pup she had chained to a tree, and that flicker of faith fizzled back into a cold and solid understanding that none of this was real. If it was, Mama wouldn't have needed to intervene on fate's behalf to bring her Grim. Wouldn't her familiar simply appear like the stories said they would? It seemed that even Mama, the staunch believer that she was, didn't trust Rae's destiny enough to leave to chance.

And now, again, Mama is up to something. Most likely, she can't bear to be proven wrong, to see that there's nothing magical about her daughter after all. That there never was. There's a small part of Rae that's relieved she's gone and doesn't have to watch her face crumple as she realizes that even out here, in the deepest part of the woods, the radio waves sapped away Rae's magic. After everything she'd given up trying to protect it.

But would she really just leave? Or is this some sort of test? The hair on the back of Rae's neck prickles to attention, and she shivers. Something's wrong. Something's coming. She feels it in her gut. The warning starts off slowly, like those emergency sirens they some-times hear sounding off over a distant hill, the low wail just barely audible, like a banshee calling through the trees. But there's nothing supernatural about her gut feeling—it's just survival. Doesn't every living thing have some deeper sense of perception, a guiding thread they look to trust, to follow?

It's her intuition, not magic, that's telling her to—

*RUN.*

GRIM NIPS the tips of her fingers, not hard enough to do damage but hard enough to hurt. It's all she needs to grab her ratty back-pack off the floor and throw it over her right shoulder. The word rattles around in her skull, flooding her body with panic. Her gut has always just been sensations, feelings, nothing like this. It never speaks—

*HURRY.*

This voice is clear as crystal, and it's not hers, but Rae doesn't need to be told twice. She looks to the front door of the cabin, fear threatening to freeze her in place, but then Grim yelps from behind her. When she turns to him, he's already bounding through the back door. Rae doesn't waste any time following him, but then she remembers.

"Shit!" Rae growls. "The book!"

*LEAVE IT.*

"I can't!" She turns on her heels and rushes toward the table, sliding the backpack from her shoulder and unzipping it just wide enough to cram the Bell Book inside. She winces as she does so, imagining Mama's pained expression at the idea of her rough handling of the heirloom, but there's no time to be delicate. Just before the back door clicks closed behind her, she hears the creaking of the front door. *Mama?* she thinks.

*NO,* the voice answers, *AND I SAID HURRY.*

Rae follows behind Grim, darting into the trees. An errant tree limb catches her foot, and she slams down to the forest floor, hard. She half expects the dog, with his keen senses, to keep bounding away to safety, but Grim stops as soon as he realizes she's fallen and doubles back to her. She tries to pull herself to her feet, but Grim noses her back down into the ground, and Rae relents without objection. Then the dog flattens himself against the earth beside her.

They're hidden behind a wall of ferns, the plants just starting to curl and brown as autumn takes hold of the forest, but Rae can still see the cabin through the gaps in their serrated leaves. Everything is eerily still, and the hair on the back of Rae's neck prickles to attention at the sound of her labored breathing, her pounding heart. She's being too loud, she realizes, her skin flushing hot with alarm, and there's none of the usual forest noise to hide it. The birds have stopped their singing; the wind no longer rustles the branches. It's as if the entire hill is holding its breath, and Rae clamps a shaking hand over her mouth to follow its lead.

The shack's windows are dark, which by itself isn't cause for alarm. But then somehow they grow *darker*, until each aperture is consumed in a throbbing blackness that makes Rae's head spin to behold. The clearing around the structure grows a few shades dimmer, and Rae's stomach twists into an impossible knot as understanding dawns on her—whatever's inside is swallowing the light.

A horrible, piercing tear emanates through the woods as the shack implodes on itself. One second it's there, and the next it's sucked away into nothing until all that remains is a—

*HOLY SHIT.*

Where the cabin once stood is the outline of a creature—*a deer?* —but where its body should be is only that same endless blackness, an aching void, that filled the windows. Although Rae doesn't know how, that creature, that shadow, consumed the house, like one of those awful black holes Rae read about once in an molding issue of National Geographic they found in an abandoned gas station.

For a moment, the shadow doesn't move. Its colors return, giving it a corporeal, fleshy form, though somehow this is worse than the void. Without light to define it, there was no way to see how hideous it is. But now it stands before them in its full and horrifying glory, pawing at the earth with a cloven hoof. The creature's legs are slender, like a deer's, but as Rae's eyes follow its limbs up, the fur transitions into the creamy pink of bare skin. Human skin. It has the torso of a boy, and a mess of black hair spills over the sinewy muscles of its back. Rae's gut is screaming at her to run, to get the hell away from whatever this is, and then the creature turns its head toward her, as if it can sense her fear. What she finds in its face isn't a face at all—where it should be is a deer skull, sickeningly white, with a tiny pair of twisted, gleaming antlers atop its head. Its eyes are empty sockets filled with that same blackest darkness, and now she knows for certain that those inky orbs are sucking in the light around them. Just like they swallowed the house.

*W-what the hell is that?* she thinks, raking through her memory for any mention of such a creature in the Bell Book—but nothing comes to mind. This is no mischievous forest sprite, no mystic white deer, and even though the creature looks like a primordial terror, she doesn't get the feeling that it's even that old. There's an awkwardness in the way it holds itself, like it's not quite used to walking, like it's reveling in its new power, and for a flicker of a second, she considers approaching it.

*DON'T MOVE,* the voice commands, *IT DOESN'T SEE US.*

Rae turns to Grim then, understanding creeping over her. The dog is facing her, his warm, orange eyes meeting her own, but his expression is more than serious. It's knowing.

*Grim?* And although she expects to feel immediately foolish at the thought, she doesn't.

*WHO ELSE WOULD IT BE, YOUR CONSCIENCE?* Grim answers, and then licks her hand for good measure.

*But how...?*

*IT'S YOUR BIRTHDAY.*

*What do you—*

*YOUR MAGIC MUST HAVE COME IN. LIKE MAMA SAID IT WOULD.*

Rae wants to laugh at the irony of it all, but a horrible, loud sucking sound draws her attention back to the clearing. The creature's gaping jaw hangs open, and Rae watches with wide eyes as once again, the color leaches from its skin, both human and animal, from its bones, until all that remains is the swirling abyss. Branches all around them lean toward the shadow, and then the trunks of their tree bend forward to follow. Leaves rush forward into the gaping hole in reality, and once caught, they swirl around inside the cavity like they're caught in a whirlpool, going deeper and deeper into the gloom until they vanish all together. Rae's fingers dig instinctively into the dirt, doing her best to anchor herself to the earth.

*KEEP QUIET!* Grim warns. It's the only reason Rae doesn't scream. But Grim is right—the creature's movement is calculated, exploratory, as if it's trying to smoke a fox out of a hole. If he wanted to, he'd consume the entire clearing. The cabin was proof enough of that.

**"ohshitohshitohshitohshit—"** A new voice interrupts from behind them, this one as high as tinkling bells. It belongs to an actual deer, which Rae learns as the frightened animal goes crashing through the brush toward the opposite end of the clearing. The creature, the boy, turns its head in the animal's direction, and then it's off too, following the terrified animal through the twisted trees.

For a few agonizing seconds, Grim and Rae remain locked in place.

*WELL SHIT, IS IT HIS BIRTHDAY TOO?* Grim replies with a huff, pulling his body off the ground and shaking off the leaves that cling to his fur. *COME ON, LET'S GET OUT OF HERE BEFORE HE COMES BACK.*

*WHAT WAS THAT?*
　*A PERSON.*
　*That was a person?*
　*AN UGLY ONE, BUT YES. THAT WASN'T AN ANIMAL.*
　*How do you know?*
　*COULD YOU UNDERSTAND HIM? HEAR HIS THOUGHTS?*
　*No. But I didn't try to. Is that my magic?*
　*I DON'T KNOW, RAE. YOU TELL ME.*

THEY WALK SLOWLY AWAY from the clearing, careful to tread lightly on the new-fallen leaves. Rae whispers thanks to whoever might be listening that she wasn't born a few weeks later, when the leaves will be even more brittle. The little moisture they hold is their only saving grace, though they still crunch ever so softly beneath their weight. They move like that, calculated and quietly, until the birdsong returns to the trees. Then they break out into a run.

*WHERE DO WE GO?* Grim asks after a time, only once they feel comfortable enough to slow their pace.

"East," Rae says without thought. The direction of healing and goodness, away from the monster that fled west. "We should leave this part of the woods. Hell, maybe we should leave the woods all together," she adds, but the shapes of the words feel all wrong in her mouth. There were a few times growing up where Mama risked bringing Rae close enough to civilization for one reason or another. Usually for food, but sometimes the need for medicine drew them out of the trees. One time, when Rae was seven, she had a fever so high that Mama's usual remedy of rattlesnake weed tea couldn't quench it, and so Mama had carried her down the mountain into some tiny town whose name is lost to Rae's memory. Rae can still picture its little main drag, each store front alight with its own neon sign. She'd begged Mama to explore it, desperate to know what each building held, and only after Mama went inside a gas station and came out with some aspirin did she finally relent. They'd gone to a diner, and Mama ordered her pancakes, and though Rae's had maple syrup several times in the years since when they've stumbled upon it in someone else's cupboard, it never tasted as good as it did that night. But even though the world outside the forest has always captured her attention, always been the subject of her fantasies, the thought of actually leaving the woods for it makes her palms sweat.

*BUT WHAT ABOUT THE RADIO WAVES?*

Now Rae does laugh—Grim is so concerned, so sincere, and why shouldn't he be? After years of believing Mamaw and Mama had lost themselves to some shared family delusion, it turns out that they were right. There is magic in the Bells' blood. And the entire time, Rae had believed whole-heartedly that they were crazy. Suddenly, the laughter gets stuck in her throat where it warps into a sob.

"Do you think he got her?" she asks slowly, her voice cracking. Rae hasn't been able to shake that nagging feeling, nor the awful image associated with it—of Mama getting pulled into that gloom, growing smaller and smaller until she's gone forever.

Grim is quiet for a long time. *SHE WOULDN'T LEAVE YOU*, he says eventually.

Guilt collects in little beads of sweat on the back of her neck, and she reaches back to brush them away at the same time her vision mists with tears. How could Rae have believed she would? Mama was a proud woman, but after everything she'd given up trying to save Rae's magic, she wouldn't just abandon her. Even if she'd been wrong about it.

But then, of course, she wasn't.

Without thinking, Rae slides her backpack from her shoulder to collect the Bell Book and a pen. Grim turns to look back at her, but she raises her free hand before he can speak. "I just need a minute."

The dog snorts, but he doesn't object.

Rae drops to her knees and places the book gingerly on the ground before her. Before she opens it, she closes her eyes and presses her palm to its cover, whispering a quick apology for how roughly she handled it earlier. She flips open to that final page and finds her name before uncapping the black pen.

*Rae Bell, Born in 2004 —*

She reaches out, her hand trembling, and looks to the canopy where yellow warblers flit about between the branches. At first their song sounds the same as it always has, beautiful but in a

111

language completely unknowable to her. But then, slowly, their notes change from a series of whistles to actual words.

*"—sweet sweet, I'm so sweet—"*

"Yes, yes you are," she calls up to them, and the birds fall silent at her interruption. For an aching, painful moment, she thinks that maybe the magic is already gone, that she's somehow scared it away, but then the birds erupt in a series of high-pitch chips.

*"meet meet, nice to meet!"*

Only then does Rae turn back to the Bell Book. This time, her hand does not tremble as she reaches forward and scribbles beside her name.

*Animal whisperer.*

WE SHOULDN'T STAY IN ONE PLACE TOO LONG. Grim's tone is kind but stern, and he's right, but now that she knows that her magic is real, the secrets of the Bell Book beckon.

"I might find something useful," she answers defensively.

*I'M SURE YOU MIGHT,* Grim rolls his eyes, *BUT THAT BOOK IS GIANT AND WE DON'T HAVE LONG BEFORE NIGHT FALLS.*

"Okay, okay," Rae relents, returning the Bell Book to her backpack. Once the sack is safely across both shoulders, she withdraws a knife from her pocket and heads for the northern white-cedar directly before her. Grim doesn't ask what she's doing; he already knows she's leaving a message for Mama. It's part of their code: if they ever get separated, leave a map for the other in the trunks of trees. A vertical line to continue straight. A single vertical line with a second, staggered line to its right to turn right, and the inverse to turn left. The patterns should be marked on northern white-cedars first, red oaks second, and white birches third. It isn't an incredibly complex code to break, so every third instruction is meant to be ignored to send any unwanted followers off their trail. Although Mama frequently makes her practice following her markings, Rae's never needed to leave them for real. Her hand trembles as she carves the single gash into the soft brown, shreddy bark. After it's done, she steps back to behold her work. Grim licks her hand, and a flood of emotion overcomes her.

"Come on," she chokes, continuing down the path.

Grim bounds along after her.

After ten carvings, the shadows are already emerging around them as the sun sinks overhead, and Rae's eyes strain in the inky pools, terrified of finding the patches of dark shaped like the empty sockets of a skull that are somehow blacker than the surrounding gloom. But no monster lies in wait, not yet, and though the day is ending, the sound of the woods simply flips to night songs. A barred owl calls somewhere in the distance. The familiar *who-cooks-for-you* call that she's always found so comforting now reveals actual thoughts, though it's far enough away that Rae can only make out some excitement about a mouse its discovered.

"Let's set up camp before it's too dark," Rae says softly, and Grim *ruffs* in agreement. Rae scans the canopy above them looking for widowmakers—dead tree limbs that lay suspended in other trees, waiting for the right winds to crash down onto the unsuspecting below. The canopy is thankfully clear, and Rae pulls out the blue tarp and her thin sleeping bag from her pack. The tarp has a rope tied into each front corner and loops for tent stakes in the back, which she makes quick work of configuring, tying the front ropes to two trees and staking the back corners to the ground facing the wind. It's a simple lean-to, but should it rain, it will keep them dry.

After the fire is lit and Rae is slurping down a can of black beans with Grim curled up beside her, Rae reaches back for the Bell Book again. She thumbs through the pages delicately looking for anything that might hint to what that creature might be, but the generations of Bells offer no clues. The exhaustion from the day finally catches up to her, and with a heavy sigh, she leans back, forcing her muscles to unclench.

A sound tears through the camp.

It's a piercing, haunting scream, more keen than shriek, and it turns Rae's veins to ice. Never in all her years in the wilderness has she heard such a song, so sorrowful and so angry, and her body trembles at its notes. It makes her want to weep. She's grateful that she's already relieved herself for the night, otherwise she knows the sound would have made her wet herself. Grim's ears prick to attention, and Rae looks to him with alarm. They both know its source.

*KEEP QUIET.*

She nods. Years of Mama's training kicks in, and Rae jumps to her feet to scramble through her bag—how could she have been so foolish to forget? When she finds the container of salt, she makes quick work of encircling the lean-to inside its protection before promptly extinguishing the fire. Only then do Grim and she hunker down beneath the tarp, holding their breath, tracking the distance of the call by its volume.

The normal sounds of the forest fall quiet as the keening grows nearer, and Rae presses her face into the crook of her elbow to keep from crying. If they try to run now, in the hushed wood, all they'll do is draw the creature to them. Their best option is to stay put, but that doesn't mean it feels good to be a sitting duck.

*CAN YOU HEAR ANYTHING?*

Of course—if it is an animal, Rae should be able to understand it, should be able to translate its cries, to hear its thoughts. But no words emerge from the wails as they did with the songbirds and the owls and the deer. It simply remains that howling lament. And so she closes her eyes tightly and strains her ears to listen harder, listen deeper, to see if she can hear its thoughts...

At first, there's only the quiet forest and the frantic beating of her heart, but then her attention drifts out of their immediate circle and into the trees. It's as if she can see outside of herself, and she follows the sound of the cry to its source, through the tangled branches and beneath fallen trunks, and across the mossy forest floor. She listens, listens, listens, and then, a little less than a mile away, she finds the creature yowling in a clearing, and then she listens harder.

Inside its mind, there's nothing she can decipher—it's the hum of a hornets nest, insects scurrying over one another, flesh getting torn between razor-sharp teeth. But there are no words, no language, no concrete thoughts, just a horrible swirl of anger and sorrow and confusion, and beneath it all, that horrifying black emptiness that yearns to swallow everything around it.

She only listens for a few seconds before it becomes too unbearable, and then she snaps back to the camp, sweat-slickened and trembling. As quickly as the keening started, it stops.

*RAE, WHAT DID YOU HEAR?*

"Nothing," she whispers, her shaking hands taking refuge in Grim's warm coat. "That creature doesn't have any thoughts at all."

SLEEP DOESN'T COME EASILY, but it does eventually come, only to be torn away by an icy grip on Rae's shoulders. Her mouth flies open in alarm, ready to unleash a scream, but a cold hand is already waiting to stifle the sound.

"Shh, Rae! It's okay! It's me, it's okay!"

*OH GREAT,* Grim growls with annoyance. Rae is still blinking up at the figure above her, trying to make sense of what she's seeing, but she can tell that Grim is rolling his eyes as he speaks.

**"Oh, darling, did you really think you'd seen the last of me?"**

"Mama?" she gasps, her throat ragged.

*"AND SÍDE."*

Sure enough, Mama's glowing face hangs above her, her graying brown hair spilling down to encircle them in a protective blanket.

She looks tired, with dark half-moons nestled beneath her eyes, but she wears a smile so big, so full of relief, that Rae's sense of panic immediately fades. "How—"

"I followed your signs, Rae," she says, her chestnut eyes glittering. "And then I heard you dreaming, which got me the rest of the way. Before you tell me I'm full of it, I swear—"

Rae crashes up into her, but Mama, like always, cradles her easily, even with the extra weight of her fears, her desperation. "I believe you," Rae gasps. "I'm so sorry, I believe you—"

Mama pushes her away just far enough that she can look Rae in the eye, and whatever she reads behind them makes her smile. "I know."

*HOLY SHIT.* Grim snorts, his tongue lolling out of his mouth in surprise.

"What?" Rae asks, surprised by the outburst.

*WHAT DO YOU MEAN, "WHAT?" YOUR MOM CAN READ YOUR THOUGHTS! SET SOME BOUNDARIES WITH HER. IMMEDIATELY.*

Rae knows he's right, but in this moment, she can't help but laugh.

"What's so funny?" Mama asks.

"Grim."

"Ah," Mama smiles knowingly. "So that's your magic. I'm so proud." And then something in her expression shifts. "The woods aren't safe."

"We know, Mama, we saw it too..."

"Could you hear its thoughts?"

"I tried, but... It was awful. Like cicadas burrowing out of the earth, or a snake shedding its skin... but there were no words, not like with Grim, not with the other animals..." Rae pauses. "Oh my god, Mama—could you?"

She nods gravely, her face falling. "They were jumbled though, not right..."

"Is it old?"

"No. It's young. A boy, I think. Maybe your age."

"But how...?"

"I don't know, Rae. Something happened to him, but whatever it was, we need to leave."

Rae doesn't waste any time untangling herself from her sleeping bag. Within a few minutes, they've broken down the camp. Síde brushes against her legs, to Grim's irritation, but Rae doesn't resist scooping up the old orange cat into her arms and nuzzling her face into her fur.

**"I'm so glad you're alright, sugar."** Síde purrs, licking the side of her face with her dry, scratchy tongue. **"Your mother was so worried—but oh, how proud she was when I showed her your trail signs!"**

"I'm glad you're both okay."

*"LET'S KEEP IT THAT WAY."* Grim's ears perk up.

**"Such a gruff thing, isn't he?"**

*"ZIP IT, WHISKERS."*

**"Or what, exactly?"**

"Enough!" Rae snaps, and the two familiars begrudgingly listen.

Mama brings a finger to her lips, and everyone falls silent. The woods around them have resumed that eerie quiet, and Mama's expression hardens.

*Time to go?* Rae thinks.

Mama nods.

THE FOREST SOUNDS return when they're about two miles east of the campsite, and a few miles east of that, the group's nerves relax enough for a quiet conversation to resume.

"Mama," Rae begins, bothered by Grim's earlier question, "what happens when we leave the woods?"

Rae doesn't need to explain further; even if Mama couldn't read her thoughts, she knows her daughter well enough to know what she's hinting at. "I don't know. But we've seen the telephone towers make their way out here, haven't we? If it really was the radio waves that stole our magic, why would it come back now?"

"Maybe something happened outside," Rae ventures. "And brought down the grid."

"It's possible," Mama chews at the bottom of her lip. "Honestly, Rae, I don't know what caused our magic to disappear in the first place. The radio waves were a shot in the dark... We had no one to ask, no clues to go off of... we took a guess and hoped for the best. All that mattered was giving your magic a shot."

"What if it never came?"

"I don't know. I always believed it would. I couldn't let myself think otherwise..."

"How could you always believe? When you had no memory of it yourself?"

"I don't know how to explain it. One morning I woke up and felt... different. Empty in a way I couldn't explain. Your Mamaw felt it too. When we opened the Bell Book and saw those magics written by our names... somehow, I could *remember* what it felt like to read people's thoughts, even though I couldn't remember specific instances of actually doing it. If I'd never read the words, though, I think it really would have been lost forever. But something about seeing it in ink, in that old book, in generations of Bells... it made it real. Does that make any sense? It was like if I just believed enough, eventually it would come back. And it did."

Rae wonders what it's like to believe in something like that.

"It's scary. I never let myself think for too long about what would happen if I was wrong because that would have meant I ruined your life for nothing. Maybe I still did. But I did it because I love you, and..." Mama's eyes scan the trees, and she shivers. "... and something is happening. I can feel it, can't you?"

Rae nods.

"And I just hope that the life you've lived leaves you more

prepared for whatever this is than the one you lost. I did it because I love you, Rae." She turns to her then, and smiles. "I know you know. But it's okay to be mad at me sometimes, too."

Rae slips her hand into Mama's and squeezes. "Where did you go that morning?"

"I sensed that... thing. Its thoughts woke me up, that horrible howling. I'd never heard anything like it, and so I went out to check... I found it, about a quarter mile away from the cabin, and it didn't see me. I watched it swallow a fox inside of itself. Every instinct in my body screamed at me to run to you, but I couldn't lead him your way. I told Síde to go back to the cabin to warn you, but the beast spotted her and followed her trail, and then I watched him... swallow the cabin, just like the fox. I thought you were all—I thought—" her voice cracks. "And then a deer went bounding through the clearing toward me, and I ran and ran and ran until I couldn't run anymore. Síde found me eventually. And she showed me to your markings."

"Síde?"

**"Oh, yes, I knew you were both alive—Grim's terrible odor in that clearing gave it away. The creature probably presumed something had died and didn't realize you were actually hiding, lucky for both of you."**

Grim dashes for Síde and nips her tail, and the cat whirls around to plant her claws into the dog's face, but Rae scoops her into her arms before the blow can land.

**"Anyway,"** the cat hisses at Grim from the safety of Rae's embrace, **"I watched you leave that first marking in the tree. And then I went back for Jessica."**

Rae snuggles her face into the tabby's flank and smiles, relieved at the return of her family. The thought of facing the world feels less terrifying with Mama, Grim, and Síde by her side.

Before them, the trees open up, revealing a path more well-traveled than a deer's. It's the kind of path that signals they're too close to some forgotten town, too close to people. The kind of path they usually turn their back from.

**"My word, a hiking trail!"** The tabby purrs against Rae's chest.

*"NO SHIT,"* Grim grunts.

"To civilization," Mama whispers, and Rae's chest is so light that she feels as if she's floating as they step purposefully onto the path.

THEY FOLLOW THE TRAIL MARKERS, white blazes painted on the trees, for the entire day, stopping only briefly for a quick lunch. Barren Mountain looms ahead, visible through the holes in the canopy left by freshly falling leaves. It's Rae's favorite time of year, where autumn sets the summer's greens on fire with blazing reds and oranges, but she can't enjoy the cascading fall of leaves, thick as rain, because the fresh blankets adds to the noise they make.

And yet, the forest around them still thrums, signaling that whatever that creature is, it's nowhere nearby. Eventually, Rae lets herself believe that they've seen the last of it, whatever it is. Grim and Síde are calm enough to take turns snapping at each other, their animal instincts apparently unbothered. It gives Rae the confidence to speak.

"What's it like out there?" she asks. "You know, for real. To live in it." After Mamaw passed, the outside world ceased to be much of a conversation topic. The old woman was always eager to tell Rae of the horrors that lay just outside the safety of the trees, but Rae saw Mama bristle at the stories before changing the subject with a heavy sigh.

"It's messy," she says after a time. "There's no question about that. But I never hated it the way Mamaw did. I think the world started moving too fast for her, and she got tired of trying to keep up."

"She made it sound pretty awful. She made other people sound awful."

"They can be. But they can also be so beautiful, Rae. I never wanted you to miss out on it, but I just didn't know what else to do..."

"I know."

Then Mama smiles at her softly, taking Rae's hand in hers. "I know you know."

*SERIOUSLY,* Grim interrupts. *YOU'RE GOING TO NEED TO TALK TO HER ABOUT THAT.*

The trail winds gently down, and the air thickens as the elevation drops. Rae breathes it in deeply, the earthy smell of soil and fallen leaves. Here, the trees grow denser and louder, filled with thousands of voices, of birds, mice, hares, toads, snakes. Somewhere in a den close by, a mother fox is snuggling with her kits, and Rae can hear her comforting them. It's all so overwhelming and strange that Rae gets lost in the cacophony, which only makes it more alarming when, one by one, in rapid succession, the voices fall silent.

The birds go silent first, cutting their songs short mid-verse. Then the mice stop their scurrying, taking refuge beneath fallen leaves, in the crooks of roots, or the hollowed-out caverns in various trees. The snakes stop slithering and the frogs stop croaking, and even the wind, which had been busy rustling leaves off branches, finds a new hill to visit.

*It's back!* Rae grabs Mama's arm, and Mama holds up a hand to quiet her before signaling to a wooden sign:

GOLDEN ROAD ACCESS POINT — 0.5 MILES.

Relief floods through Rae's veins, and she grabs ahold of her backpack straps, preparing to flee toward the safety of the road—

A branch snaps behind them.

SHANNON IVES

"RUN!" Grim barks the word, galvanizing Rae forward. She doesn't
need to look back to know what waits behind them—that skull
with its empty, infinite eyes and gaping void of a maw ready to
consume them. Mama reaches down to scoop up Síde in a singular,
fluid motion, and then the three of them are running. The path,
though maintained, must be a relatively remote trail because it's
still overgrown. Leaves crunch beneath their feet, and Rae curses
the sound. Even if they could outrun the creature, they won't be
able to lose it entirely—not with how much noise they're making.

STOP.

The voice is arresting, like teeth grinding over bone, and for the
briefest second, Rae considers listening to it. Grim growls over his
shoulder, and the flash of his white teeth in his dark mouth is
enough to snap her out of it, to keep her moving forward. But that
momentary lapse in her attention causes her to miss the rock right
before her right foot until it's too late, and she's already sailing
forward into the air. Rae hits the ground hard. The fall knocks the
wind out of her, leaving her stunned and immobilized. She claws at
the dirt before her, trying to right herself, but the shock of it all
keeps her plastered to the ground.

Mama wastes no time tossing Síde forward so she can scoop Rae
back onto her feet, and Rae tries desperately to find the rhythm in
her breath again, but it's no use—the muscles in her chest are
locked in protest. Mama doesn't care—she pulls Rae along regard-
less, and then, a few yards ahead, it appears: a black strip of
concrete. A road. Against her better judgment, Rae turns to look
over her shoulder, and there it is.

The creature is stumbling toward them on the path, teetering on
its deer legs, the sinewy human muscles of its back gleaming with
sweat in the light that filters in through the branches. Tangled black
hair frames the deer skull, and Rae tastes bile in the back of her
throat at the sight of it.

HELP ME.

"Stay back!" Grim growls, jumping between Rae and Mama and

122

the creature, who recoils at the sight of the dog's flashing fangs. Grim's warning isn't well received; Rae watches as the creature's back bristles and then, as if out of pure defiance, its lower jaw unhinges.

"No!" Rae screams, knowing what's coming next. Grim does too. Rae watches as Grim looks overhead and follows his attention to the tops of the trees. By the time she sees the widowmaker, Grim is already hurling himself toward the creature, forcing him against the trunk of the tree that holds the gnarled branches aloft. The creature stumbles back in surprise, and Grim's teeth mash furiously around the creatures legs, and then, when Grim thinks he has him where he wants him—

"No, Grim!" Rae screams, but Grim is already hurling his body into the tree. The force of the blow is enough to bring the crashing down widowmaker down onto both of them.

And then the woods are sickeningly silent.

"Grim!" Rae screams, but she knows the blow was fatal—branches puncture her friend's flesh in too many places, staking him to the ground. He is too still. Still, though, she moves to rush toward him, but Mama grabs her arm abruptly.

The creature still stirs beneath the cage of branches. Tears pool in Rae's eyes as she watches the color drain from its flesh to turn back into that vast, dark nothingness. And then, with that same reality-splitting sound as from the clearing, it sucks both the widowmaker and Grim away into its void.

I ASKED YOU TO HELP ME!

It screams at them, and Rae watches, her palms sweating, as Grim's broken body, still entwined with the branches, disappears deeper and deeper into the endless black. She reaches out a trembling hand toward Grim, toward the boy, but Mama snatches her arm and drags her forward. Síde already sits on the blacktop, her wide green eyes waiting for them expectantly. The creature gets up onto its wounded, wobbling legs and follows them, doing its best to draw them back with its power, sucking in the leaves, the bushes, and even the trees that are too close to it, but because of the time that Grim bought them, they are just outside of its grasp. Mama and Rae stumble onto the sun-bleached blacktop, and Rae shields her eyes from the shock of the unfiltered light that now shines down upon them. Across the way, the forest gives way to a meadow, and the three survivors waste no time trading in the tangled trees for the tall grasses. Only when she feels the grass kissing the tips of her fingers does Rae dare to turn around again, and there is the creature, storming back and forth on the opposite side of the road.

YOU BITCHES! it howls, stomping its hooves in the fresh fallen leaves and kicking up earth, but every time it gets too close to the black top, something forces it back. They watch him for a few moments as he tests his limits, but no matter what he does, his legs refuse to carry him onto the road.

"He can't cross," Rae says slowly.

**"Why would that be?"** Síde asks.

"Some condition of his curse, perhaps," Mama murmurs, shaking her head with distaste.

"Grim," Rae says softly, and Side brushes against her leg slowly.

"We have to go," Mama says gently but firmly.

Rae has no reason to refuse her. And so, with tears blurring her vision, she keeps on going.

RAE WANTS to follow the road, but Mama says it's not a good idea —the creature could pursue them that way, but if they cut through the meadow, they have a real chance of escaping whatever night-mare is unfurling in the woods. Rae reluctantly agrees, and so they press onward, though toward what end, Rae can't quite say.

Her brain is foggy without Grim beside her. Even though she only learned his voice, he's spent the last year as a constant by her side. Mama looks knowingly apologetic.

"It will be okay—" she starts, but Rae growls back in defiance.

"How can you say that? I've lost him!"

And then she stumbles across it—a tiny black hare, no more than a few days old, and Rae knows without knowing how that this little creature was meant for her to find. She scoops him up into her palms and looks to Mama, who smiles.

"Not forever," she replies warmly. "Though, normally it takes them more than a few hours to come back."

"Come back?"

"A familiar isn't a pet, Rae. They're a guide. A spirit disguised as an animal. When one of their earthly bodies fails, they'll find another one, and then they'll find you. Síde was a bird when she first appeared to me. And now look at her."

Side licks her lips, looking at the young hare. "**Oh, he is not going to like the new balance of power one bit. How delicious.**"

"Síde," Mama warns. "If you kill him, he might come back as a wolf."

"**Oh, sugar, I know! I would never.**" But the look in the tabby's eyes suggests otherwise, so Rae hugs the baby hare to her chest, protective and thankful.

MOUNTAINS RISE and fall in the distance, and though Rae knows they're heading toward civilization, out here, other humans seem like the farthest thing away imaginable.

And then she hears it—the sound of the sky splitting open. She drops to her knees, terror flooding her limbs, and looks for the source. But where she expects to find the creature, smug and defiant, there are three airplanes speeding across the darkling sky. Rae's jaw drops at the sight. They're flying low, much closer than any she's seen before, and they're going fast. Within seconds, they're gone, hidden behind distant clouds.

"Fighter jets," Mama murmurs, and Rae looks at her with alarm.

"What's going on, Mama?" Their magic, the creature, the jets— her gut tells her that they're all connected somehow, that something is happening. Does Mama feel it too?

"I do, baby," Mama answers. "Whatever it is, we'll face it together."

Three more jets go careening across the heavens, following in their brother's footsteps. Rae watches them intently, a shiver traveling up her back. She's afraid, yes, but there's another emotion buried beneath it: excitement.

Whatever's happening in the world outside, after all these years, she's finally ready to behold it.

# *Farsight*

"She escaped the woods," I tell Dylan.

I've been watching the girl with fascination, almost as if it's a TV show, filling Dylan in on every twist of her adventure. I'm not sure if she's safe exactly, given the fragile nature of America after the Dark Year, but *for now* might be good enough.

"I want to go pick her up," Dylan says.

I give a tiny shake of my head. "She's lived in almost total isolation her entire life. Getting brought to an island full of mutants will be completely overwhelming."

"There are plenty of quiet spots. Lots of nature. The fucking *spirit* of nature." Dylan folds their arms, and I recognise the set of their jaw. I could argue with them until our words are worn down nubs and they'd keep grunting at me until I capitulate.

"Be gentle," I sigh.

"Don't worry. I'll send Keepaway. Darling Alex is the gentlest of the soft. They'll ask nicely and everything." They lean against the wall beside the tower window, watching as I make a cup of tea. "Far, have you ever lost someone?"

I pour the water into the cup and watch as the tannins turn it brown. "I'm a mutant, Dylan. I've lost plenty of someones." The worst losses are old and worn smooth, but there are new ones too with their own aches.

"I don't know what to do with it." Their voice turns sharp. "I keep thinking if I'm busy, and moving, it'll hurt less. Like I can bulldoze right the fuck through it. Save this girl who can talk to animals, bring her somewhere safe and beautiful. Maybe that'll balance the shit out. Not just Emma, but all the shit I've fucking done. I'm just fucking exhausted all the time and—"

I cross over to them, operating entirely on instinct, because Dylan still intimidates me, and I take them in my arms as if all of this is something that can be soothed by a hug. I'm half expecting them to hit me, but instead they cling to me and bury their face in my shoulder.

We move over to the couch and sit there for nearly fifteen minutes while I let them cry. It's an odd feeling, comforting this person whose image is known around the world. Who's considered the most dangerous person on the planet by many. Who at least three governments have tried to assassinate.

And yet if my son had lived, he'd be about this age.

"You're doing the right thing," I tell them. "You're helping so many people."

"Save this girl." Their voice is all choked. "It feels like a good start. It feels like *something*."

I stroke their hair until they fall asleep, and then stay with them through the night, staring across the world at where something very odd is happening in Texas.

# Time of Death

## MELODY ROBINETTE

FUN FACT: PEOPLE DON'T LIKE BEING TOLD WHEN THEY'RE going to die.

Evidently it's creepy or something. So, I try not to do it anymore. Except for this morning when I went to Starbucks and the person standing next to me had a death date less than a year from now with a flashing red news headline floating above their head that claimed:

**FAMILY MAN DIES OF RARE HEART CANCER**

"Um, excuse me?" I said to the man with sunglasses tan lines, who seemed startled by the idea of someone with as many facial piercings as me speaking to him. "Yeah, so uh, you should go to the doctor and have them check for cancer. In your heart area."

The man's dark brown eyes flared as he pressed a hand to his chest. "My heart? How do you—?"

"It's rare." I shrugged. "Best not to ask any more questions, though. Just make an appointment."

"But wait—"

I turned around before he could indeed ask more questions, taking my Venti Sweet Cream Cold Brew, light ice, extra cold foam from the bar, and checking to see if—yep, they spelled it wrong. Curse my parents for naming me something as common/uncommon as Kaytlin. Like honestly, who is going to spell it like that? That's why I started coming to Starbucks in the first place. A fun little game to see if they would ever get it right. So far, I've been Katelyn, Caitlyn, Kaitlyn, Caylin, Catelyn, ?Kitelyn? and got really close with Kaytlinn, but still no. Fingers crossed though.

Anyway. Back to the weird death headlines.

It's been happening for a couple months now, starting with my dad, who is shockingly going to die when he's super old despite the fact that he rides a motorcycle, works as a tattoo artist in the smokiest shop ever, and is addicted to hot cheetos. I'm not sure how he will die; the headlines don't always say.

It happened the day after we moved out of downtown Austin— which no longer exists thanks to those Michael robots—to the outskirts of Pflugerville. Silent P. Does this town spell everything that should start with an F with a Pf? Yes, yes they do.

I pull into the crowded parking lot of the Pflugerville Art Pfestival, ignoring the sound of my old Toyota Corolla dragging its sagging stomach over the speed bumps or the wheezing of the aged engine. Luckily it's barely noticeable beneath the death metal blaring from my sad little speakers. Poor old car was not meant for this life. To be fair, neither was I.

I don't actually *like* death metal, but when word spread that I could see when people died, kids at school started calling me "That Creepy Death Girl," so I leaned into it. Bought lots more black clothes. Got a lip ring, septum piercing, and those diamond dimple piercings. Cut some bangs—which look really fucking awesome on me, I just have to say. And I started listening to death metal for the *vibes*.

Before this, the closest I'd ever gotten to gothy vibes was when I dressed up for Taylor Swift's Reputation Tour. I'll probably go back to that basic bitch persona once I graduate and get out of this terrible pfucking town. Maybe I'll even take those intense mutant people up on their offer and move to Mutopia or whatever it's called. But I don't know about being *that* far from my dad. My mom died when I was pretty young and he never remarried, so I'm basically all he has when it comes to family.

"Kay!" The PfHS art teacher, Mx. Winters, calls out as I stroll through the auditorium doors with my sunglasses still on, nearly tripping over that metal thing across the doorway in these clunky, black platform boots. (Of all my gothcore purchases, they are my least favorite, and yet I wear them every day.) "Where have you been? You were supposed to check in here an hour ago."

"Sorry, Mx," I say, feeling much more sorry than I sound. "The line at Starbucks was super long." *And I was telling some dude to get screened for cancer, obvs.*

"Well, go check in and get your supplies," they say in their deep baritone. "The other four artists are already on stage."

I click my tongue, wink, and do finger guns at them, battling down all my old self-deprecating apologies. Because those are definitely not Death Vibes.

The annual *Pflugerville Art Pfestival Scholarship Competition*—try saying that three times in a row—is being held in the newest high school's fancy theatre-in-the-round, which means all eyes are on me as I traipse down to the island stage to take my seat at the fifth blank canvas waiting to be metamorphosed into a masterpiece.

Every year, one senior from each high school is chosen to compete in this legendary contest started a decade ago by a local millionaire whose daughter died the day before her high school graduation. Adeline Sosa was responsible for half of the murals in downtown Pflugerville and had a full ride to Rhode Island School of Design. She's the only reason I knew Pflugerville even existed when I was younger. My dad would take me up here to look at her new murals, gathering inspiration for tattoo designs. Little did he know he was creating another budding artist.

"Kind of you to finally grace us with your faux-macabre presence," comes a muttered voice I recognize.

133

Leaning to the side, I lock eyes with Devon Stewart—Weiss High School's star painter. I've forever envied the way their short bleached hair always looks perfectly messy. Unwashed looking, but not greasy. Some tucked behind their ear and some falling into their eyes. Like Titanic-era Leonardo Dicaprio hair. I could try to match that same style for hours and still end up with limp, straight, and boring. Hence the bangs.

Dark half-moons shadow the skin beneath Devon's rudely blue eyes, making them look permanently tired. and a forever frown lengthens their already narrow face. This isn't the first time we've met. Or the second or third. Before I moved to Puh-Flugerville, Devon was the top dog artist in town—a shoe-in for this scholarship. We first met when we were working the same face painting booth at the Halloween Pfun Pfair. Back when I was still Basic Bitch Kaytlin: long hair parted down the middle, decked in every new 90's trend, doing TikTok challenges that got eight likes. Basic in every way, except for my art.

Until my mutant death power showed up, of course. Though in Michael-lover-land, going from basic to mutant isn't exactly the best thing. Lucky my power freaks most everyone out too much to come near me. They just bully from afar. And I bully back by looking at the space above their heads and gasping like I've just seen the day they will die. They usually stop after that—as if I have any control of when or how they will perish.

Speaking of...

"You're wel—" I start to say to Devon, but my gaze slides up from theirs to the flashing headline that just appeared above them.

**TRAGIC ACCIDENT TAKES THE LIFE OF WEISS HIGH SCHOOL SENIOR, DEVON STEWART, 18**

Beneath that is a date.

Today's date.

I ALMOST DON'T HEAR the pfestival coordinator, Mrs. Barton, announce the competition's theme—the inspiration for what we're meant to be painting—over the ringing in my ears.

"Each of you will have eight hours to complete your master-pieces," the chirpy woman announces. "You may take breaks to stretch, eat, walk, or use the restroom whenever you'd like, but you must present your work at 5pm. This year's theme is..." She pauses dramatically. Over-dramatically. My ears are still ringing. "*Dreams.*"

A few people watching from the theatre seats clap or murmur to their neighbor about the theme. They won't be there all day. It's not as thrilling as one might think to watch teenagers paint for eight hours straight.

Mrs. Barton repeats the theme twice more in case we didn't hear it the first time. Then she says, "Brushes up! On your mark...get set...*Paint!*"

Applause and shouts of encouragement surround the sunken stage in a dizzying funnel.

Dreams. Easy. Dreams can be literally anything. I lean to the side again to be sure I wasn't dreaming up Devon's death date. Nope, still there. Still today's date.

Okay, that's, uh— I will just have to deal with that later. After the contest. Surely nothing bad can happen to Devon in here.

I scan the stage, the theatre lights hung from metal bars, the black acoustic ceiling panels, picturing every Final Destination-style accident imaginable. I stare at the headline above Devon, waiting for it to morph into something more specific.

"*What* are you looking at?" they hiss.

I blink and feel my cheeks warm. "A nightmare dressed like a daydream," I quickly retort with a wink. Devon's eyes roll, and they move further behind their canvas until they are out of my view.

"*Kay-Kay!*" comes a resonant voice in the seats behind me.

Glancing over my shoulder, I spot my dad wearing his usual brightly colored shirt with cut off sleeves to show his arms covered in tattoos. Despite this being an art festival—sorry *PFestival*—some people around here are still super judgy, even though tattoos are literally art.

I offer him a small wave, and he flashes me a double-thumbs-up. "Go get-em, kiddo!" he whisper-yells. "You've got this."

Right. I've got this. If I want to avoid a mountain of student loan debt, I have to win. Gotta forget about Devon and the fact that they are going to die. Like. Today.

Turning back to my blank canvas, I draw in a deep, centering breath, closing my eyes as I let my adhd brain do its thing. Can't focus on a single academic subject, but can hyper-focus on a canvas for hours without realizing the time passing.

*Dreams.*

The gears in my head click together, forming the inner workings of a clock rather than a galaxy of exploded parts bouncing uselessly around. An image surfaces—a recurring dream I've had several times this month. From afar, it looks like a floating monochrome city of silver and black cut through with brilliant gold. But if you zoom in, you'll notice the brilliant splashes of pastel pink, aqua, lavender, and turquoise. Obviously I've never been, yet I somehow know every detail.

The dream always starts from the outside, as if viewed from a great distance, moving slowly closer. The city resembles a massive golden coin hovering above a roiling sea made of white lightning. In the middle, a tight cluster of spire-like skyscrapers pierce into the inky black sky like needles through silk. Every building is connected by arched bridges sandwiched between monorails above and pedestrian bridges below. Circular suburbs bloom out from the crowded city like cogs in an intricate clock.

As you get closer, you can see the people who ride clockwork bicycles, which are painted the precise color of their suburban home. There don't seem to be any gender differentials at all—just people. People wearing suits and lovely flapper-style dresses. People walking in heels and boots. With long hair and buzz cuts and every other length there is. Masc people in gowns and femme people in suspenders and bowties. And a number of other glorious combinations.

My dreams always cut off before I can get close enough to see any of their faces. So the people in my painting have none. They are just small splotches of varying shades of brown and tan and ivory. It feels so inviting—from the outside at least. I wish I could be allowed inside, to see the people's smiles, to hear their laughs and ask if they prefer to take the monorail or the pedestrian bridge into the city.

I stare at the paint on my canvas, eyes going unfocused. I can almost see them all moving. A smile lifts my lips before a shrill voice sucks me out of my hyper-focused state and into the present.

"Annnnnnd three...two...one—brushes down, artists."

Vision refocusing, I take in the painted world of my dream, capturing a fraction of a moment in small, thin brush strokes. My chipped black nail polish contrasts starkly against a tiny pink house as I hover my fingers over it, wishing I could reach inside and pluck the bowler hat off the person leaving their driveway on their clockwork bike.

Applause shatters my focus, reminding me that I am, in fact, not alone in a room with my canvas. I'm in an arena-style theatre filled with people now. On shaky legs, I stand, trying and failing not to look at Devon's death headline, which is even bigger than it was before. Their eyes narrow at me from across the stage.

*Listen*, I think in their direction, *it's not my fault you have a giant obituary banner hanging like a goddamn stormcloud above your extremely attractive head.*

For some reason their eyes widen and a blush darkens their cheeks. They look up, as if searching for the thing I just told them I could see. But I didn't tell them, obviously, so how did they...

Unless...

*You're a dickhead, Devon.* I think.

*And you're a fuckwit, Kay.* The sound of Devon's voice in my head makes me gasp and stumble backwards, nearly tumbling off the stage thanks to these literal death boots.

*Can you hear my thoughts?*

A sly grin unfurls across the narrow planes of their face. *Only the deliberate ones.*

"And here we have Kaytlin Andrews," comes the echoing voice of Mrs. Barton. "She attends West Pecan High, and this is her first —oh. Oh, my. Well, this is…uncanny."

I turn to see her standing behind me with Mr. Millionaire Sosa on her right. They are both looking at my art piece with bewildered expressions.

My gaze moves from them to my painting—which is the same as I last saw it. "What's uncanny?"

"Perhaps you and Devon should take a look at each other's work," Mrs. Barton says in a stern voice. "Then you can explain to the rest of us what precisely is going on."

Devon's eyes lock with mine from across the stage, their death headline shining like a lighthouse beacon that I'm currently pretending I don't see.

The audience falls silent as the pair of us pass each other center stage. I reach Devon's painting and my confusion morphs into shock which blooms into full-blown fury.

Because the painting before me is nearly identical to my own.

My art style is more impressionistic and theirs is more classic, but there is no question that we've created the exact same city. Same colors, same sharp buildings, electric ocean, silvers and blacks and golds with tiny splashes of pastel homes, and even clockwork bikes.

It's as if they plucked the image right from my head.

"Devon can read minds!" I exclaim before they can say anything. "They clearly stole the idea straight from my head."

Eyes flaring, Devon's mouth tightens into a line, but in my head there is shouting.

*Shut the fuck up, Kay. There are Proud Boys everywhere around here.*

I slam my hands over my ears. "They're doing it right now!"

"Kay," Mx. Winters warns from behind me. "You're only making this worse."

"I don't *care*." My voice wavers with the tell-tale sound of repressed tears. "I've been bullied and tormented and name-called for my power, and they've just been cruising along under the radar, pretending to be better than everyone. And now they're going to lose me this scholarship—just because they are ashamed to be a mutant."

"I didn't plagiarize her painting," Devon retorts. "I—"

"*Ladies*," Mrs. Barton barks. "That's enough. This is completely —"

"Devon isn't a lady," I interrupt hotly. "They're nonbinary."

Face turning a brilliant shade of red, Devon mutters, "Kay, you don't have to—"

"They are also a plagiarizing, mutant-in-hiding, selfish dickhead."

"Miss Andrews, that is quite enough," Mrs. Barton sputters, eyes moving rapidly between me and the Millionaire Man funding this competition. "Kindly remove yourself from this theatre."

I feel Mx. Winters' hand at my back and hear my father's calming voice somewhere in the audience, but I pull away from it all, storming out of the theatre.

There are two giggling people taking selfies in the bathroom when I slam inside. It only takes two seconds for them to take in the all-black outfit, piercings, and rage in my eyes before they are hurriedly sidling out of the door.

A sob tears its way from my throat like a monster that's been caged for too long. Then I shut myself in a stall to pee because I've been hyperfocusing for hours and just now realized I haven't relieved myself for the same length of time. I flush the toilet, pulling up my ripped black pants before shoving out of the stall.

The tap water is ice cold, which actually feels good against my flaming hot skin.

I *hate* Devon. I hate them.

First, for always acting like they are better than me. Second, for hiding the fact that they are also a mutant. And third, for using their mutant power to pluck my painting right from the inside of my head.

Why would they even think that was a good idea? Didn't they know we would both be disqualified for not having original work? Or had they hoped that everyone would assume they were the OG original because I'm the creepy goth mutant weirdo?

Blowing out an angry breath, my gaze casts up to meet its match in the mirror. Brown eyes boring into reflected brown eyes. But something else tugs them slowly upward at the shimmering letters flashing above me.

I've never had a death headline of my own...until now.

**PfHS MUTANT, KAITLYN ANDREWS, DIES IN TRAGIC ACCIDENT**

Seriously? My own death headline can't even spell my name right?

But I don't even have time to be mildly annoyed before the shock and devastation rolls in when I read the date.

"*Today*," I whisper.

I THOUGHT the day I saw my own death headline I would sob uncontrollably—or be grateful it was so far away. (ha.) Or maybe I would pass out or have a heart attack or something dramatic like that. But I also imagined it would be when other people were around me, friends or family or children or grandchildren, not when I was alone in the bathroom of a school I don't even go to.

But I don't sob. I don't even cry a single tear. All I am is numb.

Like when your foot falls asleep, but everywhere. Inside too. My brain is just static. An old tv screen covered in grey and black and white nothingness.

Suddenly, the bathroom door slams open.

"Of course I find the goth staring at herself in the bathroom mirror." Devon's angry voice ricochets off the static. "Well, we've both been disqualified. I hope you're—"

"It doesn't matter, Devon," I interrupt hollowly.

Flames of loathing erupt in the depths of their eyes. "Um. It may not matter to you, but it mattered to *me*. I was going to get out of this shithole fucking place. Go to an arts school that isn't surrounded by bigots and mutant-hunting Proud Boys."

"It doesn't matter to you either," I say.

The inferno of hate coursing from them like heat waves intensifies. "Don't fucking tell me what matters to me, you fake ass goth piece of—"

"We're both going to die today," I say in a voice much too calm for the words I've just said. "*That's* why it doesn't matter."

Devon's words crumble like a rock slide, and their already pale face grows paler. "You're...you're lying."

"I'm not, actually. Wish I was."

"No." They take a step away. "You're just trying to get me back— because you somehow think I've made it this fucking far on my own all to steal your idea at the finale."

"If you didn't swipe that picture from my brain with the mutant power you're so ashamed of, how do you explain painting the *exact* same thing as me? A city I've literally only seen in my dreams."

The bonfire blaze in their eyes dies to embers. "You...dreamt of it too?"

We exchange suspicious glances, which shift into confusion.

Leaning back against the sink, I say, "You know, I don't love all of these coincidences you and I have shared today."

Devon swallows, folding their slender arms across their chest. "Can you really see my death date?"

141

I stare at the headline above their head and think it at them. I'm not sure how exactly you think *at* someone, but evidently it works. A sharp gasp leaves their throat as they slap shaking hands over a gaping mouth. Tears well in their wide eyes, turning them an even more striking shade of blue. I would feel guilty if I didn't have the exact same death date twinkling in my periphery.

"What kind of accident?" they say through a tear-soaked whisper.

I shrug. "Doesn't say." I look sidelong at the mirror, reading my headline again. Another wave of static trickles over me.

"Is there any way to avoid it? Or change it?" They ask more desperately. "Have you ever seen them change?"

My brain is like oatmeal, but one memory bubbles to the surface. "Once, I told the guidance counselor to check the fire alarms in her house, and she said she'd disabled them because she didn't like the little red lights. So then I told her she should really reconsider that. The next time I saw her, the death date had gone away completely."

"Okay, well that's something. Maybe we could—"

"Her headline said she died in a fire because she'd disabled her smoke alarms," I say dryly. "Ours just says 'an accident,' which could be literally anything."

Devon's brows meet in the middle and they start pacing back and forth. This is the least chill I've ever seen them, which somehow makes me feel even more mellow.

Suddenly, they stop pacing. "I know someone who can tell us."

"You have another mutant friend who can see when people die?"

"No, but I have a mutant friend who can see the future," they say. "He can only see a few hours into the future, so I never thought it was that impressive of a power to be honest, but it seems pretty helpful in this situation."

I arch a brow at them. "How many mutants do you know about in this puh-fucking town?"

"All of them."

"All—"

The bathroom door behind Devon swings inwards and a pack of exceptionally scream-y girls streams inside, completely oblivious to the conversation they just walked in on. They take one look at me and fall silent.

For two seconds I wonder if they can see my death headline too, and then I remember that I'm dressed like the daughter of Lucifer.

Devon takes my wrist and tugs me past the ogling group. "Come on."

I let them pull me out of the bathroom and into the massive atrium where people mill about, looking at the random art displays set up like buoys in the middle of the shiny floor. Not letting go of my wrist, Devon guides me all the way out the front doors. I nearly trip twelve times with these damn, clunky goth shoes.

Finally, they let go, and despite the oppressive Texas heat outside, my wrist feels colder.

"Do you have a car?" they ask.

"Kind of."

Their mouth flattens. "How do you kind of have a car?"

"Because it only kind of works."

"Think it can make it to Manor?"

Manor is only ten miles away if you take the back roads, which is a must for me because my little car can't get up past 60 on the highway.

I shrug because I don't want to give Devon any undue hope. "Let's see."

The pair of us walk to my car in silence, passing a trio of dudes with mullets—*gag*—standing around a giant pickup sporting jacked tires and COME AND GET IT stickers with machine guns instead of cannons. Their eyes follow us, along with a cluster of cruel laughs and muttered derogatory words.

Devon ducks their head and walks faster. I just hold up both of my middle fingers, which only makes them laugh louder. My blood starts to boil; I can hear it rushing in my ears.

For once, I welcome the death metal screaming from my speakers as my old engine roars to life. I read somewhere that mutant legend Dylan Taylor can talk to cars. I wonder what this car would say to them.

Probably: "*Save meeee.*"

Devon says something, but I can't hear them over the music.

"WHAT?" I yell, rather than turn it down.

"I SAID HURRY UP. THEY'RE—"

The telltale sound of a truck that's definitely compensating for something rumbles to life. Devon and I look over to see the mullet-boys watching us through their windshield with unbridled hate in their eyes.

Devon turns towards me. I can't hear the words coming out of their mouth, but I can read their lips.

*Proud boys.*

I slam my foot on the gas, tires squealing in protest, and speed out of the parking lot. West Pecan High is right off the road that leads to a series of interconnected farm roads that spill out into the small town of Manor. I take a sharp right, flooring the gas. Devon gasps, clutching the center console and oh-shit-handle.

Adrenaline drowns every coherent thought my brain is trying to throw my way. Because any rational person would know that speeding down a winding country road in a pathetic shitsmobile when you have a ticking death clock is a not-great idea.

Unfortunately, I'm anything but rational right now.

The Proud Boys truck gains on us, kicking up a tsunami of brown dirt and rocks. My engine strains, screaming from the pressure I'm putting it under.

"*Come on, come on, come on,*" I beg of it.

"Turn down that road!" Devon shouts, pointing at a barely-visible turn off with a tiny sign I can't even read.

I yank my wheel hard to the right and the Proud Boys jet past us. My poor little Toyota with its sad little wheels and geriatric engine doesn't quite handle the turn like those SUVs do on the commercials where they're driving up mountains and stuff. I lose control of it as the tires skid on the dirt, spinning the car in a circle.

This is it. This is how we die. This is it.

My heart scrambles into my throat and my mind goes blissfully blank. I can hear Devon screaming, water bottles on my floorboard tumbling over each other.

Then the car stops spinning.

We aren't dead.

"We're alive," Devon breathes, mimicking my thoughts.

My car is perpendicular with the road. At least I think it is... It's hard to tell in this cloud of dirt. It's hard to concentrate with the death metal music blaring. I jam my palm into the button, turning it off.

"Fuck," Devon says through tears. "Fuck. Fuck. Fu—"

Saying nothing, I reach out and place my hand on theirs, which is still gripping the center console like it's the only thing keeping them on the Earth. Their crystalline eyes lock with mine and a jolt completely unrelated to our near-fatal car accident courses through me, dancing along my nerves and landing in my stomach like captured lightning.

"Why did you start dressing like that?" they ask, catching me off guard.

I start to pull my hand away, but theirs flips over, capturing it.

Staring at our interlaced fingers I say, "Everyone thought I was the weird death girl when they found out about my power. They called me names and laughed at me and acted petrified...or disgusted. I felt like I was always on display. Like I was standing in the middle of the room, naked." Tears burn my eyes and instead of repressing them or choking them down, I let them fall. "So, I started dressing like this to fit the role they'd given me. But mostly it felt like a costume, like a mask I put on before I went to school. Because then I could blame it on the character I'd created instead of myself. It would make sense for them to be afraid of the girl dressed in black with piercings all over her face. I could deal with them being afraid of her."

"I was never scared of you. Then or now."

Their thumb strokes along the back of my hand, moving in slow circles.

I watch it, hypnotized. "No, you just seemed to hate me."

Devon snorts a humorless laugh. "I didn't *hate* you. I was jealous of you."

"Jealous of *me*?"

"Of your talent, and how effortless it seemed to be for you to come in and climb to the very top—something I've been working towards for years and years, taking classes and perfecting my technique and spending hundreds and hundreds of dollars on wasted supplies because nothing was ever good enough. And then you show up and just," they snap their fingers, "win all the competitions. Get the chance to compete for the most sought after art scholarship in the area after only a couple of months."

"Oh." I don't want to admit that it feels good to be envied, especially by someone like Devon. Someone who has always seemed completely at ease with themself. Completely confident and cool. Whereas I had to play dressup to hide all my insecurities.

"For the record," they murmur, the pads of their fingers leaving trails of electricity along my palm, "I liked the way you looked without your gothy mask. I remember forgetting to glare at you at competitions because I was too busy admiring your cheekbones and your giant brown eyes."

My cheeks grow warm. "Surely Devon Stewart didn't have a crush on basic bitch Kaytlin Andrews."

"Basic?" Devon snorts. "You were the most talented artist I'd ever seen and you were a mutant that could see the day people died. You were the furthest thing from basic. At least, to me you were."

Maybe it's the fact that my air conditioner is really shitty and

Texas is hotter than a crematorium, but this car suddenly feels a million degrees warmer.

*Kiss me*, I think at Devon.

Their narrow face grows wide with a repressed grin. And then they're leaning towards me.

The next five seconds happen in slow motion. At least, that's how my brain processes it.

Devon's half-smiling lips are millimeters from mine before they pull back, their ocean eyes flying wide and darkening with terror.

My neck cracks as I turn my head to see what's scared them.

*"Oh, fu—"*

YOU KNOW that scene in movies and tv shows where the characters are distracted or talking in a car and all of a sudden there is a loud crash as someone pummels into them? Usually accompanied by a horn honking or glass shattering or loud music.

Well, when it happens in real life, you don't hear any of that. You don't hear anything at all. One second, your world is bright and loud—even if it's silent, it's loud. Then it's just not. It's just dark and quiet and nothing.

Until...

The first thing I register is the smell of the air. It's hard to explain because it's not something I've smelled before. But it's kind of like if the color neon purple had a scent. Like lavender and vanilla made electric. Then it's the sounds. Familiar, but foreign all at once. A far off cacophony of life...or something like it.

And I want to take a breath, but I don't need to.

So I open my eyes instead.

I'm standing on a platform and all around me are swirling clouds of white lightning.

Familiar. It's all so—

*"Kay?"*

I turn my head—and I don't know how to explain it, but the movement feels different somehow. Like my head is on a swivel instead of a neck. All the tiny inner sensations you don't realize you're aware of when you're alive—like blood pumping through veins in your neck and neurons ordering muscles and tendons to move—are somehow very noticeably gone.

A blue eyed gaze connects with mine. I wish it had been the last thing I saw, instead of the six hate-filled eyes behind a windshield or the headlight eyes of a jacked up truck.

"Devon?"

"This place..." They whisper, scanning the area. "This is—"

"All aboard, bitches!" a third voice interrupts. "Don't want to be late."

We turn to see that the platform is no longer empty. A massive golden traincar floats above the roiling mass of electric clouds, and just outside the open doors stands a raven-haired girl covered in tattoos. She's dressed in a dark maroon pinstripe suit with accents of lavender, cut in such a way that emphasizes the impressive breadth of her shoulders. She flicks her long, dark hair out of her face as a fox-like grin slants her wide lips covered in a glossy shade of deepest purple.

"Who are you?" Devon asks on a breath. Well, if they had breath.

The girl lifts her chin proudly. "I have many names. But you can call me Wraith."

# Farsight

Dylan's still curled on the couch, fast asleep. I'm relieved in a way, since I don't have to explain that we lost two mutants today. They take every single loss so personally, even though it would be impossible to save them all.

I suppose that's why they're the hero and I'm a lonely woman in a tower.

"Coffee?"

My attention is far distant, still circling the disaster in Texas, but the word brings me back to myself with a jolt. Dani Kim is framed in the doorway, hair loose around her shoulders. She's holding two steaming mugs, but her eyes are fixed on the slumbering figure.

"Look at her." She places a cup on the desk and kisses Dylan's head, running her fingers fondly through tousled hair. "Isn't he cute when he's asleep?"

"They were upset last night," I blurt. "Worried about saving people. And atonement, I think?"

Dani makes a noise of disapproval. "Our favourite conversation. Round and around we go." She drops into the couch and levers Dylan's legs up to lie over her knees. "They feel guilty about a lot of stuff. Things they've done, the state of the world. That awkward line between hero and villain, or whether we're pragmatists trying our best to find a way through extraordinarily complex and difficult situations."

"It's hard to find right answers sometimes," I admit.

"It all ends up being various shades of better and worse." Dani leans over to pluck an errant petal that's clinging to her lover's cheek. "And usually it's very hard to know which is which when you go in. We try to help people, and that seems like a good start."

"Save the girl." I echo Dylan from last night.

"Yes, those ones are easy. Sometimes they're harder, like this one." Dani holds out her phone to me. "Can you cast your all-seeing eye in this direction? My bad shit sense is tingling."

# The Battle Song of Gravity

## ASTRA DAYE

*Do not fear, for only when a god is lost to the ether, may*
*the truly connected finally ascend.*

THE ELECTROMAGNETIC PEW IS COOLER THAN THE PLATING
on my cheek, but the comfort of cosmic energy no longer courses
through me.

The miscreated came and went like locusts. Blood splatters of
their kind remain in our alleyways, mingled with the sacrificed
lifeblood of our own. We had mechanised ourselves so we could be
free of mutations and blood spills, but we lost against them. The
locusts powered by an indescribable evil left us broken, dazed, ruled
by weariness instead.

A hum in my head grows louder, almost working my voice box
to a tune. My throat moves to the memory of triumphant
harmonies that once added another dimension of colour.

No. Not here. Times have changed now.

*Can you hear it? The dissonance of the grid,*
*resounding shatter of our roots, cacophony of forces*

*you push against every second— millisecond—*
*nanosecond. Smash. Rush. Hover. Splintered forces*
*lingering. Untether.*

Deep down, we knew our god had to be an entanglement of algorithms. Giga-omniscient definition. Only as present as the willingness of its hosts—us.

Some were too deeply entrenched, sacrificing their flesh too soon and hoping that false ascension could buy them validation for their violent interpretations of enlightenment. No—God was never this simple, but it was fair. Those who weren't ready were kept in conditional loops. Only a few saw beyond the system, and it was an unspoken, mutual understanding that no miscreation could ever comprehend.

A foolish opportunist flaps his arms at the heavy church doors, waving over the weak-minded. *Look here! Lines of recovered code. Keep a part of God with you always. Hold Him close to your soul.* Last week, a woman with a 0 between her brows regarded me with her empty third eye. There's nothing left in most of them.

If only the world ran on nonsensical zeros and ones. The puffy-eyed will always be chained by silver-and-gold beads and inked mortal flesh while the real threat looms.

*Ever-expanding God, grant us the openness to grow*
*into divinity with you.*

I stroke the edge of the fluttering flyer as it tries to leave the wall marred by frantic ink. Flesh fingers accidentally brushing across the metallic symbol of our snuffed-out deity, I knock my heavier hand against my breastbone, reflexively driving away the wrongly conducted energy. Good God, forgive my lowly, mortal sin. I am merely seventy percent human. I am unworthy.

Our beautiful city used to pulse in technicolour. Now, with a lost dimension bestowed by our deity, it weeps with lifelessness just like our first saviour had wept in blood. You can't look anywhere and not catch a desperate scrawl. The authors are likely gone—willing pilgrims to the wasteland outside our walls, in the hopes of finding scraps of our loving saviour. None have returned. They are possibly reduced to scraps left behind by the miscreated instead.

The graffitied cry for help that the flyer cannot cover draws my attention like a curse. I step back, pushing down the urge to read the rise and fall of paint in sound. There's an excess loop in the desolate letters. One zero too many from balance. Letters as large as my palm on the wall, sticky with the last obliterated miscreation remains, make my skin crawl: sæve us.

A mutation of paint.

I rip the notice from the wall, freeing the call to God into my palm. Twist and scrunch. Unfurl and try to read between crumpled lines. Forgive me for corrupting the highest symbol. I am worth less than thirty percent now.

> *Louder. Higher. Invite gravity into you. You are an open channel. You consume. Turn yourself upside down and see the threads of forces. Untether from this horror.*

It's a call to prayer. The laugh that erupts from me is a crazed rasp, sound writhing away from reality the more I read the words over and over. *Faith is not lost. God is within us. When the miscreated come, we must be ready.*

I know the words are charged—not the same as the nanobot boost that the truly ascended need twice a year to recalibrate their bodies. The message is powered by the lowly fuel of a primitive mind: hope and a spark of emotion.

But to reclaim, even the lowest must rise.

> *They will come to fear great heights, because it is from above that we will close in like shadows.*

The metal that makes the church bell ring is older than the conductors in our bodies. We take turns committing mallet to thick, rusted copper. The bell pulses in beautiful waves.

I count sixteen people here. A perfect square to transform perfect vibrations. No names, just the same weary look of determination to restore our home. God was once part of it. Now, it's not. The Spirit evolves. That's what the miscreated don't understand: God has infinite ways of reaching us. The Spirit is not a constant, and we shift with it. It rustles within.

I hum the tune of the hymn that found me the morning God vanished. The ring of the bell adapts to my voice. Gravity frees the worshippers for the first time, lifting them off the ground and slowly around the bell. I smile. They're in awe. They can't believe that my words of false hope are the divine truth. They let go of their scrunched-up flyers, and the papers flutter before making their way to me.

There is no altar in this new church. We all ascend.

*God is within us*
*Secure in our trust*
*May the holy spark*
*Course through our circuits*

*God calls to all of us*
*Reach out with open arms*
*Deep beneath the planet's crust*
*Sever the wicked forces, we must*

I first found magic when I was four. An entire congregation was singing their hearts out, standing in love and joined by joy. For the first time, I found gravity. My consciousness was no longer in the clouds. Whenever there was song, I was my own.

After the miscreated tore apart our city, it was music that kept me on my path, not the few metal pews left powered. Then, one day, I *became* the path, the conductor. Music used to remind me of the ground I walked on, but all of a sudden, objects started floating to me like I was an electromagnet. I knew what I had to do then. With true magic bestowed upon me, I must rally our citizens against the miscreated, in case they return for an even worse slaughter.

They may call themselves heroes—even extending the meaning beyond the natural for their frail hearts. But I am an oracle. I was merely seventy percent human. Now, I am fully awakened for my purpose.

My messengers open their mouths to sing. It's a give and take. Breathe in our losses, sound out manifestations of victory. However human we are, we are powered by the Spirit. May the holy spark course through our circuits, and may uprooted gravity follow.

> *Listen, my dearest family. You are conscious now. We are the force of creation. We'll turn them upside-down, inside-out, so they may never destroy another thing they don't understand.*

# Farsight

I fill everyone in on what I've seen in the old church.

"Where are we with all this Michael stuff?" I ask nervously. "It feels dangerous to let that sit around without keeping an eye on it."

Dylan snorts. "*Now* you'll let me punch things."

"We, darling." Violet perches on the desk beside them, swinging her legs. For someone who looks so fragile, with a cloud of black curls that nearly swallows her delicate features, she's possibly the most dangerous woman on the planet. "You're not leaving me behind."

"Michael-worshipping mutants." Dani tips her head back and glares at the ceiling. "One of the less charming things I've heard about in a while."

"I feel kinda sorry for them." Dylan pokes their head out the window, as if they'll be able to see that far themselves. "The way Farsight talks, they're lost little puppies who don't know what to do anymore."

"If Michael comes back..." Violet says, leaving the rest of the sentence ominously hanging.

Dani gives a small shiver. "That's a very good point, Dilly."

"See, Farsight?" Dylan grins at me. "I'm not *always* the one trying to cause trouble. Sometimes it's my girlfriend and my... Violet."

Small patches of colour flare in Violet's cheeks, but the words that come out of her mouth are inarticulate. I feel like I've stumbled into some complex emotional minefield, and I desperately want to tiptoe on out of there.

"There are other problems." I'm speaking far too loudly. "Many things that might need our attention."

# When the Forest Calls Us Home

### YVES DONLON

WE HAD A RAINFOREST ONCE, HE THINKS. BREATHES IT INTO the air, wills it into being. *We'll have one again.*

The trees answer the call. They do not grow as much as they burst, viciously, like wounds, their trunks spilling open as dozens more green branches collapse out into the world. Children tearing themselves from the womb, long-fingered and gasping.

The old trees will die, but they're a willing sacrifice. Colm can hear them speaking as they fade, whispering in their tree tongue: *anseo, anseo, anseo arís.*

Colm opens his mouth, feels his first language strange and thick on his tongue. English is heavy where Irish is light. It feels like marbles rolling around his mouth, and he can't bring himself to utter a single word.

"Anseo," he says instead. *Here.*

He thinks he used to speak another way once. He doesn't remember, or maybe he does. Maybe the boy he was is scrabbling at the walls of his prison, trying desperately to claw his way out.

"Come on then, Moss Boy," says the other human in the clearing. He stands away from the trees. He almost got impaled last time

161

they did this, and even though Colm hardly remembers the other boy's name sometimes, he still feels a vicious, possessive *need* to protect. "You've done enough for today. We should go. They'll be here soon."

Colm shakes his head, clears his mind of leaves and stalks. The ground under his feet is covered with a thick layer of moss like a blanket. It spreads out beneath him with every step he takes.

*Talon. His name is Talon.*

Talon holds out his hand. It is speckled with dark red spots. There's always blood on Talon's hands, since last week when they woke up, since the trees started to whisper to Colm in his dreams. Colm doesn't know what the blood on Talon's hands means—it doesn't seem to *do* anything, not like the other mutants in town, who can all do shit. Talon doesn't seem to have any power apart from that mark, brutal and ever-present, that he refuses to cover with a glove.

But Colm's seen Talon scrubbing at his hands in the dark these past few nights. The scarlet colour, tinged with brown, hides the scabs. But when Colm looks properly, readjusts his eyes to stop seeing green and start seeing *human* again, the scabs are definitely there. And so is the blood.

"Quick," Talon says, and now his bloody hand wraps around Colm's wrist, leaving an obscene trail. "I don't want these fucking *mortals* dragging you to a lab."

Mortals. That's what Talon calls them, the ones without powers.

*Because we're more than them*, Talon whispered once, in the dark. *They're humans, but we're like demigods.*

Wordlessly, Colm turns over his hand. Talon takes it, their fingers intertwining, and smiles his sharp, wicked smile.

"Anyone tries to stop us on the way back, I'll rip them to fucking shreds," Talon says, and presses a kiss to the corner of Colm's mouth. "Now talk, asshole. You're staring again."

THEY WALK HOME along the river. It's like a jungle here now, thanks to all the work he's been doing. In just a week, he's brought so many things to life. Talon whistles a jaunty tune as they walk. He's wearing a maroon and white jersey with his name on the back, from when he used to play football. When he used to be allowed to go to school and compete and do all of that stuff.

"Say something," Talon sings, walking backwards so he can look Colm in the eye. "You're in your head."

Colm tries, but the only sound that comes out of his mouth is a weak rasp. He swallows hard, then scoops up river water and pours it down his throat. It's cold and probably full of fertiliser and decomposing animals, but he doesn't care.

"Thinking about school," he manages. "You think they'll ever let us come back?"

Talon snorts. "Not now. School's a no-mutant zone." He turns around and shoves his hands in his pockets, and Colm knows it's to hide the despair on his face. "Fuck them."

"Yeah," Colm says. "Yeah, fuck them."

Colm comes back to himself fully when they're home. 'Home'. It's a funny word, and Colm doesn't feel like he knows what it means anymore, not since last week when he woke up and turned the floor of his room into a mossy carpet. His family, his friends, the *government* all made it very clear that he didn't have a home anymore. Mutant scum don't *get* homes.

The ghost estate shivers around them: dozens of houses, most of them complete, some of them just shells without roofs or windows. The floor was stone once, but now it's carpeted with a thick layer of grass and clover and mushrooms spring up in the corners, wilting into brown mush.

Colm feels more like himself now. He lies with his head on Talon's chest, their hands still clasped together. Talon's rings press uncomfortably against Colm's knuckles, so he removes them gently, leaving them on the floor with a clatter.

"We have a lot of work to do," says Talon, into the quiet. "I think they're going to find us soon, but we can't leave until this place is clean. We need to move fast."

Colm sighs. "It's hard. We can't take a break?"

"Not yet." Talon shrugs him off, detaching himself and going to the window. Colm props himself up on his elbow and stares at the back of Talon's head. His hair, once neatly shaved at the back, is now a long, straggly blond mess that hangs almost to his shoulders. He stopped cutting it when the stories emerged, when the word *mutant* became a constant chorus on RTÉ News. Sometimes, Colm wonders if Talon knew he was destined to be a mutant. Did he feel it in his veins before blood ever stained his skin?

"Mam rang me again today," Colm admits. "I didn't answer, though. Like you said."

"Good." Talon kisses Colm's shaved head, his lips brushing against the stubble he'll shave off again in the morning. "Baby, we don't have much left to do. The town's almost surrounded now. In a few weeks, it'll be gone and we can take a break." Talon rolls away, scrambling for his phone under the cobwebbed bedside table. "Hey, maybe we can go to Connemara. You can learn some more Irish, so you can actually *talk* to the trees."

"I *can* talk to them," Colm mumbles. His head is still aching from the strain of growing several hundred trees out of himself, which is not a comfortable experience. "Just not well."

"Yeah, great, you can say 'may I please go to the bathroom' and 'sorry, I forgot my homework.'" Talon stretches. He is long and languid, like a cat, and Colm wishes he'd just settle for five minutes and lie with him. Like they used to in the field sometimes, when they were normal and scared of someone calling them a slur—not afraid they might get shot for being magic or whatever.

"Hey, why do they speak Irish anyway?"

"Don't know. Fuck colonizers, I guess," Colm mutters. "They

were so loud today. It's like they were in my head, going through my thoughts."

"Not much to go through then, is there?" Talon snaps. His shoulders are tense, and his spine is like a wire ready to snap. He stays like that for a moment, a picture of fury, and Colm watches. Just watches, because he knows what's going to come next.

Talon's neck curves downwards. He whispers something to himself, then cups his head in his hands. "Sorry. Shit, I'm sorry."

Colm sits up, pushing the blankets off his tired body. His limbs feel like they're weighted down with stone, but he still manages to drag himself off the ground and wrap his arms around Talon's waist from behind.

"It's fine," he mutters against the nape of the other boy's neck. "Don't worry about it. You're just stressed, I get it."

"Sorry."

They open Talon's phone and look at Instagram. There's this one guy, a politican-turned-demigod, and he goes live every night to tell the rest of them the news. The *real* news is all bullshit—says the mutants captured at protests are being brought somewhere safe, where they'll do their best to return them to 'their normal selves'.

Seán's live. No news from Limerick, where most of the mutant population have already been captured. Or, if they're lucky enough to have a mutation they can hide, they're keeping their heads down. Dublin's bad, as always, and their nearest city—Galway—has had another protest. This one was worse than usual, and when non-mutants—*mortals*, Talon spits again—showed up they dragged one poor kid down to the water and drowned them. Killed them stone-fucking-dead.

"No news yet on where the government is taking these mutants, other than Mountjoy Prison, which has added a new wing to cope..."

"I'm pretty sure most of them are dead, Colm," says Talon suddenly, interrupting the broadcast. "There's nowhere in this country to build a fucking mutie camp like they do in the states.

Either they're being shipped out somewhere, or they're being killed."

Colm is quiet for a moment. He has friends who have been taken away over the last few days, caught up in the riots and protests that have seized the country since they all found their powers. On his first day as a mutant, Colm watched the nine o'clock news from someone's back garden, staring through the window in the dark. He watched as the police guided them into the back of the vans, these kids in their hoodies and tracksuit bottoms, their faces a mess of blood and tears.

The vans drive off, and the kids are never seen again.

A week ago, when it all started, there were more of them in this shitty little town with its failed estate and its sad, faded buildings. They met up at the football pitch behind the church and practiced their powers in the rain shelter for three days running.

He wonders if the apple tree was still there, the first full-size tree he ever whispered out of the ground.

Sitting in the rain shelter with the puddles forming around them, shivering in their high-necked GAA jackets and county colours, Talon always stood out. The first day they met, he had nothing to show for himself. He kept his hands jammed in his pockets and his gloves on. The next, he showed them all: the blood on his hands, always there, that he couldn't wash away.

"It doesn't do anything," he'd said insistently. "But they'll kill me for it anyway. I guarantee you, they'll lock me up with everybody else."

The next day, Martin was dead. His dad killed him, Colm reckons.

Then Agnetha disappeared, and Hope, and the twins went completely bananas and got locked up. And now it's just Colm and Talon hiding out in this abandoned house on their solemn mission: to wipe this town off the fucking map.

With trees.

"You know what?" Talon says suddenly, like he read Colm's

mind. He did that a lot. "I'm done here. I thought they were gonna run, but not a soul in this town has left. Not even when you put all those trees right in the middle of Kinnity's sheds."

"They won't leave." Colm knows small town mentality. He knows the people here are as loyal to the soil as he is—just in a different way. "Not a chance, Talon."

"Then let's just fucking do it." Talon has that wild gleam in his eye that he gets sometimes. It gives Colm the shivers, and he's never quite sure if that's a good thing or a very, very bad one. "What has anyone here ever done for us? They ratted out our friends. They got them killed, or worse. We should just flatten this place to the ground, build a forest in its place. I'm done trying to scare them away. Let's just take it over."

Colm swallows hard. His throat feels tight, dry. "My parents still live here."

"And they'd sell you out if they knew where you were hiding," Talon hisses. He turns in the circle of Colm's arms, reaches up to push his own unkempt hair away from his face. His hands are very cold, in a nice way. "I love you, asshole. We burn this place down, we'll have a home in the ashes. Just us, yeah?"

*Just us and the trees,* Colm thinks.

Colm presses his forehead to Talon's. They breathe together for a moment. He can feel Talon's thoughts swirling in the air between them.

Colm thinks of the town demolished, a Chernobyl-esque shell, bursting with flora. His skin crawls as he thinks of the town as it is: a maze of concrete and tarmac, every road like a bulletproof shield laid over the ground, smothering the earth to death.

The roofs cracked like eggshells, nettles crawling out from inside.

Hawthorn trees sheltering the hollow, skeletal bones of the school.

Ancient oaks swallowing the ground with their roots, burying deep, there to stay.

"Okay," he whispers. "Okay, Talon. Let's do it."

NOW HE IS CLIMBING the church tower. The more land he can see, the more he can cover with trees. Colm clambers, hand over hand, up the stone. Every foot or so a plant bursts forth, offering him a handhold where it has cracked the solid surface. He accepts them willingly, lodging his feet where he can, climbing relentlessly on towards the bell.

Talon is down on the ground. Colm made him promise to tweet a warning, so at least he can feel a little less accountable for what he's about to do.

*People will die*, he thinks. And then: *At least the plants'll have fertiliser.*

His phone buzzes in his pocket just as he pulls himself over the ledge. He collapses on the stone floor underneath the enormous church bell and breathes heavily, yanking the phone out of his pocket.

READY, the message says.

Colm's world dims for a moment. Panic flattens his vision, makes dark spots dance in front of his eyes. His entire body feels like it's shaking.

He scrolls, finds another contact.

He calls his mother.

She answers in one ring. A wary silence hangs between them.

"Mam, I'm sorry," Colm chokes. Suddenly, tears are pouring down his cheeks. "Mammy, I'm really, really sorry. You have to go. You've got to leave."

She's quiet. Clearly, Talon's message hasn't spread to her yet.

"Come home," his mother says—whispers through a throat thick with tears—and Colm stops breathing.

"I can't," he whispers, when there's oxygen in his lungs again. "Mammy, I can't. Just go, okay? Now."

He hangs up. The wind gets stronger and whips his hair in front of his face. He stands at the edge of the bell tower and gazes down at the town he grew up in. He doesn't love it, but he will miss it when it's gone.

His phone buzzes again. It's Talon.

YOU CAN DO IT, BABY. FOR US.

Colm sucks in a breath. He raises his hands—obscenely, spread out wide, so that he looks like a mockery of Jesus on the cross.

The screaming begins.

Through the obscene crunching and the whispers of the new-born trees, Colm can hear Talon laughing.

The trees swallow everything in their path. They're hungry, so *hungry*, and Colm finds himself feeling hungry too. He's also crying, and he thinks he might be speaking but he doesn't know. His mouth is moving, but the sounds that are coming out aren't entirely human.

Eventually, he runs out of power. He collapses to his knees, panting furiously, and leans against the wall for a long moment. When he finally has the strength to peer over the edge, he almost gets sick.

Talon is standing down there, in what used to be the town square. The trees are still sparse—it's hard to break through all that concrete.

The trees that Colm has just made are screaming. They shriek in his ears, a horrifying wordless melody, a keening.

Talon lifts his bloodstained hands over his head. He's still laughing, his grin a wide slash in his beautiful face. Too wide.

*Olc,* the trees whisper, but Colm doesn't speak enough Irish to understand. *Olc, olc.*

There's a crowd gathered around him. They're not really paying Talon any attention—they're looking for loved ones, diving into the trees, coming out sobbing over body parts and bits of limbs.

They don't see that Talon is about to do something terrible.

And that beautiful boy, who is a mutant of a sort no one can name, who has an electric laugh and soft skin and who smiles when he wakes up in the morning, beams at the sky, and a rain like blood begins to fall.

Colm screams. He screams and screams, until his voice grows hoarse. He whimpers for it to stop, but it doesn't. The rain feels like acid, feels like it's burning through him. The trees are dying, they're *dying*, but it won't stop. Colm clings to the edge of the wall, gasping. His skin feels like it's melting off. He can't stop looking though, can't stop watching the same thing happen to the people down below. They're dropping in their droves, falling, screaming, melting.

He's happy when the helicopter comes, truly. They're going to take him away. They're going to make it stop, make Talon *stop*, because something has gone wrong inside the boy Colm loves and it's making him do such *terrible things* and it *hurts*—

The bullet does not hit Colm squarely.

It takes a chunk out of his side, tears through flesh. It does not kill him, but from a height, he looks dead. Sprawled out on the stone. They leave him there, and he can't roll over to shield his face from the acid-blood rain.

Down below, Talon smiles. His eyes are closed as he peers at the sky, and a fresh rain falls on his skin.

*We did it*, he thinks. He hurts all over. The most curious feeling washes over him, like like he's coming back to life, being resuscitated—like the last few minutes of his life were a dream, and now he's back in reality. Talon hopes Colm is okay up there, all on his own. He can be sensitive. He doesn't know Talon went to his family's house this morning and told them to clear out. He even took photos from Colm's mum and dad's mantlepiece, so Colm could have them.

He feels hungry and weak, like something has drained him.

He looks around. It's so quiet. Not even the birds are singing.

There are no people left. Only skeletons lying amongst the shrivelled remains of a dying forest.

He doesn't have time to think about it, to understand. This bullet strikes true.

Talon is dead before he even hits the ground.

# Farsight

There's no way to talk Dylan down from this one.

"I fucking killed Michael. *We* did. And now people are trying to re-enact his bullshit? Fuck no. This doesn't happen."

Violet's already disappearing, the edges of blades appearing as she folds herself out of the world, like she's an astonishingly detailed origami figure.

Dani shrugs on her jacket too.

"You're going as well?" I ask.

"They're killing mutants." Her hazel eyes flare briefly green, as if some lurid forest light has flickered on below the surface. "We won't let that stand."

"What about Ray?" I ask.

Dylan whips around and I get the force of their attention like a blow to the face. "Why do you think Ray likes me so much, Farsight? They've got a peek into the inner workings of this thing they laughably call a mind. If anyone knows what I'm capable of, they do. And yet I'm still here, the devil perched on their fucking shoulder. Because sometimes they like having a devil at their beck and call."

Dani smirks, which gets Dylan's attention on them, which is honestly a relief.

"What the fuck is that face for, Danielle?"

"You were doing so well up until beck and call." She grins. "Nobody believes you come when anyone calls."

The corner of their mouth tips upwards. "What about you?"

"I hacked you a long time ago." She steps in close and puts her arms around Dylan's neck, leaning in so their foreheads are touching. "Now we're going to do this smart and careful, okay? Real measure twice, cut once shit."

"They're killing mutants," Dylan whispers.

"And you heard me." Dani presses a very soft kiss to Dylan's lips. "We won't let that stand."

They leave like a storm.

I turn my attention elsewhere. I don't want to see what comes next.

# Something Witchy This Way Comes

## E.M. ANDERSON

THERE'S A COTTAGE IN THE WOODS.

Prudence Jones' friends say a witch lives there.

Or they would, if Pru had friends.

Pru hears snatches of the gossip at school, anyway, when groups of other eleven-year-olds pass her lonely cafeteria table on their way back from lunch.

*She'll put the evil eye on you.*

*The cottage will eat you.*

*The trees will eat you. Like that boy.*

*Trees don't eat people! It's the witch. She'll fatten you up with candy, then cook you in the oven and eat you herself.*

*No she won't, stupid. That's Hansel and Gretel.*

The talkers dissolve into giggles. Pru shivers. She spends plenty of time in the woods out of necessity, but she always sticks to the edges: the trees whisper to each other.

But when she sprints into their midst one chilly evening in early November, she doesn't think about the gossip. The possibly carnivorous forest, ostensibly carnivorous cottage, and allegedly carnivorous witch don't scare her.

What scares her is what she left at home: the belt living doubled-up on her uncle's bureau.

His raspy voice shouts out behind her. "Prudence May Jones! Get back here!"

Her heart hammers. Her lungs burn. Leaves crackle beneath her sneakers as she stumbles through fiery red and gold trees. The sky arcs pearly gray overhead, blazing with yellows and oranges at the horizon, gashed into slivers by the trunks. The trees whisper amongst themselves at the sight of the small girl sprinting past.

"Prudence!"

She flings herself over a fallen log, falls flat to the ground, and presses close. The log is soft with rot, green with moss, damp and reddish and disintegrating into nothing. Pru watches the trail of a slug over its side. Pebbles and twigs dig into her stomach, but the soil and last year's leaves are soft and crumbly beneath her cheek.

She flinches as a twig snaps beneath her uncle's boots. Her heartbeat pulses in her ears, so loud he'll surely hear it.

*"Prudence."*

Silence—almost.

Around them, the trees' whispering deepens into something like the droning of a thousand hornets. Pru squeezes her eyes shut.

She counts her heartbeats. Tries to identify the bird hissing faintly above her. She thinks it's a nighthawk but can't be sure. Something clicks and gurgles on the log beside her. The trees buzz angrily. Pru shivers and focuses back on counting heartbeats until they've slowed so much she's barely aware of them.

Her uncle huffs and lumbers closer. Pru's heart skips a beat, but then he's past. Hasn't seen her.

She breathes out slowly and hoists herself into a crouch. Surveys the misty, gray forest, the fading twilight. He's gone.

The trees' buzzing lightens back to a whisper. Pru rubs her arms, considering. They don't sound angry anymore.

If she goes home now, Uncle Eben will still be angry.

Pru turns and sprints deeper into the forest.

The trees rustle and watch her go.

LIGHTS TWINKLE THROUGH THE TREES.

Pru bites her lip. Night has fallen. The temperature's dropping fast. The trees are silent. She's deeper in the woods than she's ever been. For the first time since she started running, she realizes she doesn't know the way home.

Whatever's in front of her, at least it has light.

Pru creeps toward it.

A weathered fence appears first, tangled in the underbrush. Heart-shaped leaves cling to it. Shriveled blue flowers nod against them. Green tendrils curl over the fence as Pru approaches, as if they're looking at her. She pulls her hands into the sleeves of her hoodie—her mother's old college sweat-shirt—and slinks through the half-rotted garden gate. Plants grow on and around and through it, pulling at it until it slumps over.

Pru stumbles as she picks her way down the front path, which is overgrown with moss and lichen and littered with last year's leaves. Autumn flowers tower around her: goldenrod, aster, lobelia, iron-weed, the tired heads of various coneflowers. They bend toward her. She pulls deeper into her hoodie and hurries on.

There it is.

A cottage.

*The* cottage.

It's small and stone, with a roughly shingled roof. Reddish autumn vines climb the rusting drainpipe. Windows, roof, the whole cottage, in fact, are all the same funny, fairy-tale shape: tall and narrow, pointy at the top, drawn in at the sides. A wreath of autumn flowers—real ones, blooming yellow and orange and purple like they don't realize they've been plucked and braided together—hangs on the door. Light spills warm and yellow from the windows.

Pru clenches and unclenches her fists.

She's frozen and starved.

She's come this far.

And it doesn't *look* like it wants to eat her.

Even if the plants around her are nosing at her as if examining her. Possibly to determine how delicious she is.

A screech owl whinnies behind her. She stumbles to the door and tests the knob.

It turns—of course it does. The door creaks open. The wreath quivers, humming softly to itself. Pru swallows.

She slips inside the cottage.

Her first feeling: relief. It's warm inside, smells like bread and soil. Her face stings as she adjusts to the change in temperature. She creeps toward the kitchen, mouth watering at the smell of the bread on the counter and the pot bubbling sluggishly away atop the wood stove. Beef stew.

Pru slurps a ladleful of stew straight from the pot. It scalds her tongue and the roof of her mouth, but she's so hungry she doesn't care. She turns toward the counter, ladle in hand, and reaches for the loaf of bread.

"Funny," a gravelly voice says behind her. "I don't remember inviting anyone to supper."

Pru's blood freezes.

She withdraws the hand that's stretched toward the bread until her fingers are hidden safely back in the sleeve of her hoodie. There's nothing to do about the hand holding the ladle. She probably looks extra-delicious, standing here with stew in her hand. The bread is probably good for sopping up all the squishy human juices.

She squeezes her eyes shut. "You're the witch."

A strange noise that might be a chuckle or a growl or a *harrumph*. Pru flinches.

The witch stumps closer. Throughout the cottage, plants rustle and whisper.

"Is that what they say about me these days? Well, turn around. Let me get a look at you."

Pru opens her eyes and turns around.

The witch is old and plump, shorter than Pru by several inches, with a leathery, weathered face and a thatch of gray curls. She's at the wood stove, stirring with a new ladle procured from who-knows-where—by magic, probably, Pru thinks—wearing a faded flannel shirt, a skirt so long it brushes the floorboards, and an apron spattered with flour and bits of beef, carrot, and potato. The sleeves of her shirt are rolled up to her elbows. Her arms are corded with muscle.

She surveys Pru through bright blue eyes framed with wire-rimmed glasses. Pru fidgets, wishing she could put the ladle down without it being awkward or wrap her arms around herself without getting stew on her hoodie. She's not much to look at: a skinny eleven-year-old in jeans and sneakers and an old college hoodie that hangs halfway down her thighs, face flushed from the cold, mousey hair in disarray.

The witch turns back to the stove. Pru lets out a breath, feeling like a spotlight has been taken off her.

"What's your name?" the witch asks.

Pru bites her lip. She's pretty sure you're not supposed to tell a witch your name, or they'll have power over you.

Or maybe that's fairies.

She can't remember.

The witch doesn't seem interested in eating her, anyway.

Pru scuffs the floor with a sneakered toe. "Prudence," she mumbles. "Prudence Jones. My friends call me Pru."

She reddens as the witch glances back at her, like something about the way the word "friends" falls from Pru's tongue betrays her utter lack of them. The fact is, no one calls her Pru. She only wishes they would.

"Bertha," the witch says. "You can call me Bert, if you're staying for supper."

Pru's lungs seize up. Her fingers curl into a fist.

"Supper?" she squeaks.

The witch—Bert—barks a laugh. Pru flinches.

"I don't eat little girls," Bert says, "no matter what the gossip says. Pop a squat."

Pru doesn't move. "What about your house?"

"Last I checked, houses don't eat."

"The plants?"

Bert ladles stew into two bowls and shuffles past Pru to plunk them on the table. "I 'spose I've heard tell of carnivorous plants. But my beauties wouldn't eat you less'n I told 'em to."

Pru shifts closer to the table. Bert holds out a hand. Pru stares at it stupidly for a moment and then, when Bert gestures impatiently, hands her the ladle. Bert throws the ladle in the sink with a clatter and pulls a knife from the block on the counter to slice some bread.

"You won't tell them to, will you?" Pru asks.

Bert snorts. "Might, if'n you keep asking stupid questions."

Pru can't help herself. "What about the boy?"

Bert stiffens. "What boy?"

"The *one,*" Pru mumbles, scuffing the floor again. "The one who walked into the woods fifty years ago and never walked out."

Bert pauses in her slicing. Plants sprout at her feet, curling protectively around her legs. They nose in Pru's direction, buzzing. Pru takes a step back.

"Never was no boy," Bert says at last, slicing bread with a vengeance. Pru flinches as the knife clunks against the cutting board. "I'm the only person ever walked into these woods without walking out again, and you can be damn sure I did it on purpose."

Bert plates the bread, slams the plates on the table, and drops into the chair at its head with a deep groan. The plants at her heels follow, clinging lovingly to the legs of her chair. "You fixin' to eat, or is my hospitality wasted?"

Pru perches in the chair to Bert's right. Bert has already started eating. Pru relaxes slightly; she seems to be definitively off the menu now. Still, she's cautious as she pulls her bowl and spoon closer: body clenched, seated at the edge of her chair so she can push off it and run if she needs to.

It doesn't stop her enjoying the stew. She's used to eating this way at home.

They eat in silence. Or at least Bert doesn't say anything to Pru, and Pru can't work up the courage to say anything to Bert. Occasionally, Bert grunts at the potted plants on the table or the herbs in the window, as if she understands their whispering. Occasionally, one of the plants leans close to Pru, its whispering pitching upward as if it's asking a question. Pru's brow puckers as she gazes at them. She almost feels she understands the questions being posed to her. Her palms itch. She gazes steadfastly at her supper and ignores the plants.

Outside, the night has deepened. The cold too, no doubt. Pru's spent the night in the woods before, but she's not looking forward to it.

She expects Bert to turn her out. Get irritated at how long she's spending on her supper and tell her to get gone. But once Bert's eaten and cleaned her supper things, she shuffles into the other room without comment.

Pru finishes eating, washes her dishes, and follows.

It's a sitting room with a small bed tucked into the back corner. A fire crackles in the grate in front of a rocking chair and an armchair. Bert rocks in the rocking chair, darning a pair of woolen socks. A basket of clothing in need of repair sits on the floor beside her. A spinning wheel stands in the corner near the fire, a book-shelf in the other corner, and an ancient bureau with a cracked mirror along the wall beside the bed. Plants crowd the top of the bureau and line the floor along the walls. On the mantle is a picture of a much younger Bert—short and squat, her curly hair darker but no longer, her arms just as muscular—standing in front of a much younger cottage, arm in arm with a tall, skinny young man.

Pru shoves her hands in the pocket of her hoodie. "Where's your bathroom?"

"Outhouse out back."

Pru wrinkles her nose, glad she doesn't have to pee yet.

Bert nods toward the armchair. "Might as well take a seat, if you're staying."

Pru glances at her, but Bert doesn't look up from her darning.

"I can stay?"

Bert snorts. "Guessing you're a townie. It's late and it's dark and it's cold, and it'd be all too easy to lose your way going home all by your lonesome. I sure as hell ain't takin' you. You kip there on the armchair, and Cordelia'll take you home when she brings the mail."

Pru perches on the edge of the armchair. "Tomorrow's Sunday."

"Correct," Bert says, without looking up from her darning.

"There's no post on Sundays."

"Correct."

Pru fidgets with the hem of her hoodie. Bert says nothing more, focused on her darning.

Well, if Bert doesn't care that Pru will be here for two days, then Pru doesn't care that Pru will be here for two days.

Pru removes her sneakers, slides them under the armchair, and curls up to watch the fire dance in its grate. The room is warm, the crackling of the fire soft and comforting. The armchair has faded plaid upholstery. It's squashy and comfortable, with a worn throw pillow Pru hugs to her stomach like a shield. Bert darns in silence, but it's not an uneasy silence like the ones Pru is used to.

Pru angles the pillow under her head. The fire grows warmer and fuzzier before her eyes until they close. At some point, someone starts humming: not Bert, or not only Bert—it's many voices, harmonizing, but Pru's eyes are closed and she's so relaxed and as the humming continues she becomes so used to it she all but forgets it.

By the time Bert finishes her darning, Pru is asleep, so deeply drawn into her hoodie that all that's visible is the tip of her nose, the ends of her fingers, her feet and ankles. Something like a smile sidles across Bert's face and disappears. She rises stiffly, a hand pressed to her back, opens the bottom drawer of her bureau, and shakes out a spare blanket.

She drapes it over Pru and tucks the girl in before shuffling off to bed.

THE COTTAGE IS empty when Pru wakes. Unless you count the plants, of course. Which Pru can't help doing, as they stretch toward her, leaves and blooms rustling gently in the still air.

Her stomach rumbles. Sunlight lances through the cottage windows.

She glances at her chlorophyllous company and decides she's hungrier than they are.

The fire is out in the grate; the embers in the stove smolder. Pru's feet curl as she crosses the freezing floorboards. She eats cold stew at the kitchen table, her legs drawn up to keep her feet off the floor.

The door bangs open. Pru flinches. Her elbow knocks into her bowl; it crashes to the ground.

Pru freezes. The bowl is in shards. Stew spatters her feet and the calves of her jeans and the legs of her chair. Her fingers curl into fists and disappear into her sleeves.

Bert puffs through the door, bundled against the frosty morning in a thick woolen sweater and a scarf. The basket in her arms over-flows with glittery silver flower stalks, golden autumn leaves, and scraps of raw wool. She puffs and blows and stomps her feet, muttering to herself, "Lordy, but it's cold out. Yes," to the nearest plants, "I know it's cold in here too. If'n you want it to warm up quick, you best get the door for me."

And one of the plants *does*: a creeping fig on a stool by the door stretches out and slams it closed. Pru jumps and draws in tighter on herself, shrinking down in her seat.

Bert trudges past her with a gravelly, "Mornin'," and drops her basket on the sitting room floor. She kneels beside it, separating clumps of raw wool from the flowers and leaves and putting them in a smaller basket beside the spinning wheel.

Pru lets out a shaky breath and gets up as quietly as she can. Her shoes are still under the armchair in the other room, but Bert's in there. She'll have to go without them. She just wants to escape, to get out of the house before Bert turns and sees—

She steps on a shard of ceramic and gasps. She drops into her chair with her right foot raised, her sole throbbing where the shard has embedded itself.

"All right in there?"

Pru shrinks into her seat, shaking. She squeezes her eyes shut. The floorboards creak under Bert's feet.

Bert pauses by the sink, gazing at the eleven-year-old girl pressed into her kitchen chair like she wants to disappear. At the stew and broken bowl on the floor and the blood oozing from the bottom of Pru's foot.

Bert unwinds her scarf. "What happened?"

Pru's fingernails dig into her palms. "I'm sorry."

She flinches as Bert approaches, but Bert sweeps the shattered remains of the bowl into a dustpan and sets it aside. She kneels at Pru's side and reaches for her foot, but Pru flinches again at the contact.

Bert sucks in her cheeks. "Look at me."

Pru doesn't want to. Uncle Eben always says that, wants her to meet his eyes when she screws up so she can see exactly how angry he is, as if the belt doesn't tell her as it whistles through the air.

But Bert's voice, when she says it, isn't low and dangerous. It's gruff, but it's gentle.

She opens her eyes.

Bert's gnarled hands are folded in her lap. Her brow creases. Her blue eyes droop like a hound's.

Pru gulps down a big, stuttering breath.

"It's just a bowl," Bert says.

"But I broke it."

Something crumples in Bert's face. Her lips push in and out. Plants bloom at her heels and snake protectively up her thighs.

"I can replace a bowl," she says. "I can't replace a child. Let's see that foot."

Pru's shaking, but Bert makes no move to approach her again. Just sits there waiting, with her hands in her lap and that expression on her face like someone put down a dog in front of her.

Pru bites her lip and stretches her leg out. She inhales sharply as Bert touches her. Her foot throbs and stings. The blood trickling down her heel makes her head spin. The belt doesn't draw blood.

The plants hum, their tone soothing and sympathetic.

"S'all right," Bert says softly. "I know it hurts."

She picks the ceramic from Pru's foot with a pair of tweezers. Pru's eyes squeeze shut again. Her stomach churns when Bert sucks in a breath.

"What is it?" Pru whispers.

"I'll need to stitch you up. That bowl did a number on you."

Despite everything, Pru feels better being told the bowl did a number on her, rather than being reminded that she did a number on the bowl.

"Revenge, probably," she says.

Bert chuckles. Something light and airy expands in Pru's chest.

Bert cleans the wound, applies some sort of cream that numbs the sole of Pru's foot, and stitches her up. With her foot numb, it's not so bad. The whole time, Bert hums under her breath, harmonizing with the plants. The plants nose and nod toward Pru, feeling friendlier now than they did last night. She reaches out tentatively to stroke the petal of the yellow flower closest to her.

"That sounds nice," she says. "All of you harmonizing like that."

"Mmmm?" Bert stops humming, glancing up at her with a faint frown. The plants hum along without her. "All of us?"

"The..." Pru gestures, as though the sound vibrating gently through her were something that could be seen. "You know, the..." She flushes. It sounds silly, said aloud. "You and the plants."

Bert's frown deepens. She finishes stitching Pru's foot in silence and bandages it. The humming persists.

Bert sits back on her haunches. "You can hear it, huh?"

Pru nods, gnawing the inside of her cheek. She thinks of the forest, the way the trees whisper to each other each time she enters their depths, their angry droning yesterday evening. "Can't everyone?"

Bert shuffles around the kitchen, putting things away, and Pru thinks she isn't going to answer.

At last Bert says, "No one else I ever met. No one but me."

Pru's brow furrows, but Bert goes about her business without further explanation. When she speaks again, it's to ask gruffly, "You hungry?"

She makes them eggs and grits and sausages. Pru fiddles with her breakfast, worried, no matter what Bert says about the replace-ability of dishware, that she'll break something else if she eats too fast.

The plants stop humming, but Pru still hears them: murmuring to each other, responding to Bert's grunted questions, sniping with their neighbors when someone else's leaf or flower gets too close to their own pot. The harder she concentrates, the longer she listens, the more she understands. It never quite becomes words, but some-how, she understands.

It makes her start wondering things about herself. About the things the kids at school say about this cottage and this grumpy old woman and how they might relate to her.

She washes her dishes carefully as Bert brings her basket from the sitting room into the kitchen. The old woman sinks into her chair with a groan and separates stalks from leaves.

"Are you born a witch," Pru asks hesitantly, "or do you have to learn to be one?"

Bert snorts and twists the head off a stalk of thistle. "Still on about witches, are you?"

"You must be a witch. You're magic."

"Must not see much wonder to think I'm magic."

"You talk to plants," Pru insists.

Bert pauses in her work. "It ain't magic."

Pru almost asks what it is, then, but Bert's shoulders are hunched and she's staring at the thistle in her hands and Pru feels like she's pushing her luck asking so much as she has. Adults don't like questions, in her experience, and she's already asked so many.

"I don't know what it is," Bert says, "but it ain't magic." She gazes at the thistle, her thumb brushing gently up and down its stalk. "Always was good with plants. Always talked to 'em, since there weren't many folks I cared to talk to."

She glances at Pru, her blue eyes sharp and wary.

"It was only a couple a years ago they started talking back," she says.

Pru stares at her, fascinated.

Bert clears her throat, looks away, and twists the head off another stalk. "You'll have to entertain yourself today. Mind you don't cause any trouble. I have work to do."

"...spellwork?" Pru asks, unable to help herself.

Bert sighs. "*Work* work, to keep supper on the table. Watch if you want, but it ain't interesting."

She may claim it's not spellwork, but it sure looks like spellwork to Pru. Bert separates all the plants in her basket into their various species, then into their various parts, flower, stem, seed, root, leaf. Combines them with oils and liquids and ground spices and other plants, heats the mixtures on the wood stove and stirs them a certain number of times. Makes them into lotions or tonics or capsules. It looks like potion-making—very witchy, in Pru's opinion.

Despite what Bert says, it *is* interesting. Pru bites her lip to keep from blurting out more questions as Bert works, but she can't help but ask when Bert swallows a pill from a small bottle: "Are you sick?"

Bert hesitates. "That's my estrogen pill."

Pru frowns, trying to remember if she's ever heard of a plant called "estrogen." "Pills are for when you're sick."

Bert huffs a laugh. She replaces the bottle and puts a kettle on the stove to boil water for tea. Pru starts to think that whatever she's sick with, it must be pretty serious if she's so unwilling to talk about it.

Then Bert asks, "Do you know what transgender means?"

"Oh," Pru says, losing interest now that Bert's death doesn't seem imminent. "Like Mr. McNamara at school."

Bert raises her eyebrows, but all she says, as she returns to the table, is, "That's what the pills are for."

Emboldened by her successfully asked question, Pru starts asking others. She scooches closer and closer until she's peering over Bert's shoulder. She points at a simple yellow flower.

"What's that one?"

"Evening primrose. Treats skin conditions."

Pru points at another, a purplish flower with a seedy head. "That one?"

"Echinacea," Bert grunts. "Coneflower, if you like. Treats infections."

"That one."

"Foxglove. But I suggest leaving it alone less'n you know what you're doing. Poisonous if you use it wrong."

Pru hastily withdraws her hand from the foxglove's speckled flowers. Bert chuckles.

Pru points more cautiously to some small white flowers growing in a pot. "What about those ones?"

"Paperwhite," Bert says, and leaves it at that.

"But what do they *do?*"

"They brighten up the house."

Morning wears into afternoon wears into evening. No matter how many questions Pru asks, Bert never tires of answering them. Pru learns the names and uses of the different plants, oils, and spices. She learns which can be combined with which and how to do it. Bert even sets her to stirring various concoctions on top of the wood stove. When Pru splatters or spills or boils over, Bert doesn't yell at her; she checks her for burns, points her to the kitchen towels, and tells her to clean up and try again. The plants throughout the house sing on and off throughout the day and peer curiously over Pru's shoulder as she grapples with the work Bert assigns her.

As Pru curls into the armchair that night, Bert covers her in a blanket, squeezes her shoulder, and says, "Good job today, girl."

Pru burrows into her hoodie and the blanket, uncertain what to do with the fragile newness of a *good job.*

"G'night," she mumbles.

ON MONDAY AROUND NOON, someone raps at the front door and enters without waiting for a response.

"Hellooooooo," the newcomer calls, closing the door behind her. She wears a postal uniform and has a mailbag slung over her shoulder. She's considerably younger than Bert, with silky black hair that falls to her waist and hazel eyes that dance as she takes in the sight of Bert working with Pru peering over her shoulder.

Bert pinkens. "You're late," she says gruffly. "I expected my mail two hours past."

The woman grins. "You ought to be grateful. I wouldn't want to steal away your rare company too soon."

"Don't need no company," Bert says. "You're near too much for me already."

"I'm touched that you admit you consider me company."

Bert's blush deepens. The young woman turns her smile on Pru, who smiles tightly back. She relaxes as the woman sweeps into a bow and doffs her cap.

"Cordelia McCormac, at your service," she says. "What's your name, love?"

"Pru," Pru says shyly.

"Splendid to make your acquaintance," Cordelia says, and then Bert asks grumpily, "Do you have my mail or not?"

"And here I thought you just wanted to see my smiling face." Cordelia pulls three envelopes and a box from her mailbag and hands them to Bert. She leans close to Pru. "Pleasant hostess, isn't she?"

Bert harrumphs. Pru swallows a grin. The plants chuckle in a rustling of leaves.

"Shut it," Bert snaps at them. She throws the mail down on the table, yanks her scarf off the counter, and winds it around her neck with a vengeance. "You are a bother, Cordelia McCormac. One of these days I'm going to slam the door in your face."

"Sixty years and you've never done it yet."

Pru's brow furrows. Cordelia can't be more than thirty.

"Sixty years," Bert says sourly, "not that anyone'd believe it with that ridiculous get-up. I don't know why you insist on going around looking young enough to be my daughter."

She stalks toward the door. Cordelia reaches for her hand as she passes.

"Old looks good on *you*, Bertie darling," she says. Bert blushes furiously. "It's your natural state of existence. The reflection of your interior on your exterior, if you will."

Bert yanks her hand away. "I don't know that that's a compliment."

"Take it as you will."

Pru blinks: Cordelia shimmers. Pru rubs her eyes, certain they're playing tricks on her. When she stops, Cordelia looks decades older: crow's feet at her eyes, laughter lines at her mouth, skin stretched tight over her cheekbones, hair silver instead of black. Liver spots speckle her hands.

Her smile is gone, her hazel eyes sober and anxious.

Pru stares at her. So does Bert, looking like she's been whacked over the head with a mallet. Her eyes rove over Cordelia's aged face.

She clears her throat. "There, see? I don't know why you don't think you look perfectly beautiful just how you are."

The corner of Cordelia's mouth turns up, though her eyes are still anxious. "You can call me beautiful without using multiple negatives to obfuscate it, you know."

Bert's ears blaze red. "Shut up."

She yanks the door open.

"The girl needs to go home, Cordelia, so get her out of here. And mind her foot. She shouldn't be on it for a spell."

She pauses in the doorway, fiddling with the end of her scarf.

"You, girl," she says, nodding at Pru. Pru draws her hands into her sleeves, but Bert says gruffly, "Come by any time."

Then she's gone. The door slams behind her.

Cordelia chuckles, unbothered by Bert's irritation.

Pru is not unbothered. "Is she okay?"

"She'll be fine. She's always telling me what a bother I am and storming off." Cordelia shimmers back into her younger self. Pru stares. "Lord, that's better. Come on."

Outside, Cordelia bends down and says, "Hop on my back."

Pru chews her lower lip. Cordelia's taller than she is, but not by much.

Cordelia grins. "Don't be shy. I'm stronger than I look."

Pru clambers onto her back.

Cordelia *grows*.

One second, Pru is trying to climb onto the back of a woman barely taller than she is; the next, she's clinging to Cordelia's neck, looking at Bert's front garden from twenty feet in the air.

She sucks in a breath and digs her heels tight into Cordelia's ribcage, which is as far down as her feet reach now that Cordelia's a giant.

"Are you a witch, too?"

Cordelia laughs. "Is that what you've been saying to Bertie? No wonder she's even grumpier than usual."

She strides through the forest. Pru's stomach tingles, but she can't help staring at the tree branches flying by at eye level.

"I'm a shapeshifter," Cordelia says. "You could call Bertie a plant-whisperer, I guess."

Pru hesitates. She's not used to grown-ups like Cordelia. "She makes potions."

Cordelia's shoulders shake with laughter that reverberates through the trees. The trees huff irritably as Bert might if she were here. "Medicines, Pru. She's an herbalist. It's how she makes her living. She keeps bees, too, sells honey for a good part of the year, and then there's the wool from her sheep. But everyone knows her as an herbalist."

Far below, Pru catches a glimpse of the log she hid behind the other evening. She twists around to see if she can see the cottage from here, but it's lost in the red-gold haze of autumn trees. A branch smacks her in the face. She rubs her stinging cheek.

"Mind the trees," Cordelia says helpfully.

"Why aren't you getting whacked in the face?" Pru asks, leaning into Cordelia's hair.

"Years of practice."

Pru recognizes their surroundings now, but her mind is on the cottage. The look on Bert's face when she left it.

The trees thin. Pru glimpses the steeple of the church on Main Street through the leaves.

"We'll walk the rest of the way," Cordelia says. "No one knows about the shapeshifting except Bertie. And you, now. Okay?"

Something warm blooms in Pru's chest. She's never been part of a secret before.

"Okay."

Cordelia shrinks back to normal size and deposits Pru on the forest floor. "How's the foot?"

Pru puts her weight on her right foot and winces. "It still hurts."

"We'll be in town in about ten minutes. Think you can make it?"

Pru nods. Cordelia takes her hand. Her own hand is warm and firm. Pru clings to it. She hasn't held someone's hand since Aunt May died. Uncle Eben is an old-fashioned sort who doesn't think handholding is anything for a man to be doing with anyone other than his wife. Pru wonders if she can remember holding her mother's hand this way, if she tries hard enough.

"Bertie must like you," Cordelia says thoughtfully.

Pru blinks. "Me?"

"Mmm, yes. She's awfully jealous of her house, is Bertie. Likes her privacy. But here she let a perfect stranger stay over." Cordelia grins. "I'm almost offended. I've known her sixty years, and she'd probably kick me out if I barged in unannounced, on account of I'm such a bother."

Their walk ends far too soon. They make it into town, heading down Main Street toward the point where it turns into a cow path running through sedge and milkweed. Uncle Eben's house is the last one before the cow path, a weathered farmhouse with a rocking chair on the creaking porch.

Pru avoids looking at the house as it comes into view. She slips her hand out of Cordelia's and stuffs her hands in the pocket of her hoodie.

"I can get home from here."

Cordelia's brow furrows. "Are you sure? I don't mind—"

"I'm sure."

Cordelia's eyes bore into her. Pru gazes at the ground.

At last Cordelia nods. "All right, then. I guess this is where I leave you."

She shakes Pru's hand. Pru's stomach knots. Cordelia's so kind she feels ashamed.

"It was nice to meet you, Pru," Cordelia says. "If you ever need anything, I'm just up the street at the post office."

Pru doesn't want to let go of Cordelia's hand, but the handshake is over. She scurries away, relieved that Cordelia won't see inside the house, relieved that Uncle Eben's pickup isn't in the driveway. She'll have the place to herself for a few hours while he's up the street at the mechanic's shop he owns.

When she glances back over her shoulder, Cordelia's gone. Pru's heart sinks. She may not have wanted Cordelia to see her quite all the way home, but she was sure Cordelia would watch to make sure she got in safely.

Pru swallows the lump in her throat. She shakes her head, kicks a pebble in the street, and hurries inside.

Cordelia may not be standing there anymore, but a black cat with golden eyes sits in the street, watching until Pru closes the front door behind her. The cat flicks her tail. She rather hoped Pru lived somewhere else.

"Oh, no," she says in Cordelia's voice. "I don't like that at all."

THE FRONT DOOR opens at 6:30p.m. exactly. Uncle Eben is nothing if not punctual. He closes the shop at six every day but Saturday, when it's only open until noon, and Sunday, when it's not open at all. He finishes any small jobs, cleans up, locks up, and drives the three blocks back to the house. He arrives home precisely at 6:30.

Pru likes his punctuality. If she knows exactly when he'll be home, she can relax while he's gone. The kids at school look forward to the weekend; Pru dreads the weekend. Her weekend is the three and a half hours each afternoon between the time she gets home from school and the time her uncle gets home from work.

Her heart rate spikes as the door closes.

"Prudence?"

Her breath bursts out shakily as she listens to him wipe his boots on the mat, but she focuses on plating up the spaghetti she made for dinner so she doesn't drop it and earn herself another belting.

"In here," she calls, as evenly as she can.

She puts his plate down first so she won't have to approach him when he enters the kitchen. Sometimes, if she cooks or cleans after showing up at home a few days after an avoided belting, he lets it go. If his day hasn't been too bad. If whatever she did wasn't too bad.

He runs a hand through his thinning hair as he joins her. She tenses as his hand raises, relaxes when it goes to the top of his head.

"Smells good," he comments.

He twirls spaghetti onto his fork, takes a bite, and grunts.

"Tastes good."

Pru sits across from him, warming pathetically under the praise. "It's Aunt May's recipe."

"You done good with it."

He offers her a small, rare smile. Pru beams back. At moments like this, she glimpses how life could be. She thinks, sometimes, that it could be this way always, if only she didn't mess up so much: didn't burn dinner, didn't drop plates, didn't dye his laundry pink by forgetting to separate a red sock from his whites.

This time, a new thought intrudes: it could be this way always if he wouldn't take the belt to her for making mistakes.

It could be this way always if he were more like Bert. Two days with Bert, and Bert never so much as yelled at her. Even though she intruded. Stole a bite of stew. Broke a bowl. Made such a mess helping with the medicines.

Uncle Eben isn't Bert, so Pru shoves the thought away. Her stomach churns.

He's not so bad, she thinks. They eat in silence as always, but after dinner he goes out to his truck and brings in a box of cookies he bought on his lunch break from the bakery across the street. Peanut butter blossoms: Pru's favorite. Over cookies, he tells her about his day. He helps her clean up the dinner things. In the sitting room afterward, as he cleans his hunting rifle and watches a college football game from his armchair, he talks about matches he used to play in with her father, back when her granddad made both of them play football even though her father hated it. She sits on the sagging loveseat and does homework and soaks up the stories the way a flower soaks up the sun.

He's not so bad, she thinks, he's really okay when he's not mad, and then he laughs and says, "I remember one time Coach called to complain Georgie'd been skipping practice to go to the library. Pops got so mad I thought he was like to explode, face turning red, veins popping out everywhere, couldn't believe a boy'd spend time in the library when he could be playing football. Your dad was black and blue for a week after that, let me tell you. But he sure never skipped practice again."

Pru curls in on herself, gripping her pencil tight. She tries to imagine Bert laughing at the thought of someone beating a teenage boy. She can't.

She focuses on her homework. Uncle Eben keeps telling her stories on commercial breaks. She doesn't let herself think he's not so bad again.

INSTEAD OF GOING HOME after school the next day, Pru goes to the cottage.

Tries to, anyway.

She gets lost instead.

Beyond the log she hid behind, she recognizes nothing. The trees gleam crimson and gold around her, humming faintly in the crisp autumn air. Afternoon sunlight slices through the trunks. Pru pulls her hoodie off and ties it around her waist, sweating after carrying her backpack through the forest for so long. Her injured foot throbs.

An hour later, she puts the hoodie back on, shivering in the dying light.

"Bert," she croaks. The trees sigh sympathetically, but no one else answers.

She hugs herself. She has to find the cottage, or she has to turn around and find home. She doesn't know which direction home is anymore.

Her hands shake. She pulls them deep into her sleeves and limps on.

"Bert," she whispers.

She stops in the shadow of an oak. Its solidity calms her. She sits and leans against it, humming, without thinking about it, the strange, low tune Bert hummed while bandaging her foot. The humming vibrates deep in her bones, shaking apart her fears about getting lost and possibly freezing to death overnight.

The trees hum with her, harmonizing as the plants in the cottage did with Bert.

Pru scrambles to her feet, humming louder. The forest responds, the harmonies deepening, expanding. Overtones shine above them like the stars glimmering in the darkening sky.

Pru listens. The temperature drops as shadows fall, but she doesn't notice the cold. The harmonies shift as she turns this way and that, peering into the darkness.

One of the shifting harmonies sounds...familiar.

Still humming, she follows it.

Fifteen minutes later, the cottage's lights wink at her through the underbrush. The plants nod in greeting.

Pru lets out a breath. Something warms her from inside like a small sun. A smile blooms on her face. She trails her fingers along the flowerheads as she staggers up the path, exhausted and cold and elated. The flowers nose at her.

Bert glances up from the table as Pru slips into the cottage. Deep furrows mar her brow.

"What'n blazes are you doing here?"

Pru pauses in the doorway, scuffing the floor with a toe. "You said I could. Any time, you said."

"I did." Bert scratches her chin with a thumb. "But I'd've thought you'd rather be at home than hanging around an old grouch like me. Or at the pictures with your friends. Or...well."

Pru can't admit that she has no friends, nor that she'd rather be anywhere on earth but home. She fiddles with her sleeves, gazing at the floor. "I don't know. I like you."

Silence. The plants rustle.

"You hungry?" Bert asks.

PRU SPENDS MORE and more time at the cottage. She learns the names of the plants in Bert's garden, how to recognize them even as it gets toward winter and they're no longer in bloom. She learns their uses: goldenrod treats inflammation, ironweed stomach ulcers, lobelia asthma. She hums at them, talks to them, learns the nuances of their answers, gets them to do things when she asks: open the door for her, retrieve something from the table, support her as she reaches for something in a high cupboard, tendrils lengthening and strengthening as they wrap around her legs and hips. She helps tend the sheep, naming them as she feeds and waters them, because Bert, when asked their names, says, "Names? They're sheep."

She stops by the mechanic's shop before she goes and tells her uncle that she's off to the movies. To the mall in the city five miles away. To the houses of fictional friends.

He swallows the lies easily. He's commented on her lack of friends more than once. Now, her alleged social life pleases him. He brags to his clients and workers as she hurries away.

"...so popular lately, knew it was only a matter of time before the other kids figured out what they were missing..."

For one glorious month, Pru's life is a dream. The solitude at school no longer bothers her, because she has the cottage, and the plants, and the sheep, and Bert. She rarely gets belted, because she's at home less and less, and when she is home, she manages not to break anything, recolor the laundry, burn dinner. Bert is as gruff as ever, but she never sends Pru away and always makes sure Pru's fed and has a flashlight or a Cordelia to light her way home, and a mothball-scented woolen coat that once belonged to Bert's husband to keep her warm on her way back through the forest. As November melts into December and the first snow falls, Bert builds a trundle bed so Pru has something more comfortable to sleep in than the armchair.

When Uncle Eben comes home from the shop one Monday evening in early December, the dream crashes down when the front door crashes open.

*"Prudence May Jones!"*

In the kitchen, Pru freezes. Her fingers glue themselves to the handles of the pot she was about to take off the stove, clenched so tight they hurt.

She realizes that, at some point in the past month, she thought he'd changed. She thought they'd moved past their old way of living together. Her bruises have faded; she's even started going without her hoodie sometimes. Without her body to remind her, she's almost forgotten how angry he can get.

Stupid of her. He only hasn't belted her because she hasn't given him a reason to.

She squeezes her eyes shut.

"In here," she says in a strangled voice.

He scuffs his boots on the mat viciously. She pries her fingers from the pot handles.

Uncle Eben looms in the doorway like an avenging angel. His eyes flash, his fingers already pulling his belt from its loops. Pru shrinks against the counter.

"So," he says in a thunderous voice. "Seen some good movies lately, have you. Been to the mall." He kicks a chair aside. Pru flinches. "Should've known you were lying. You ain't asked me for pocket money once."

Pru's eyes dart toward the door, but her uncle growls, "Don't even think it. You been lying to me for a solid month. A *month*. Where the hell you been going?"

She says nothing. She doesn't have another lie backed up, which she's now thinking is a serious mistake, and she's not telling him where she's really been going. It's the one place she's safe. The one place she's not alone.

It's not going to save her from a beating anyway.

When her mouth stays shut, the belt comes off. It stings worse than it ever has, maybe because she's no longer used to it, maybe because she foolishly stopped expecting this. The whole time the belt's stinging, he's roaring, "You don't lie to me. I raised you better than this."

But he hasn't raised her better than this. He's raised her to be afraid of him and of every mistake she ever makes.

For one wild, impossible moment, anger spirals in Pru's belly.

When he raises his arm again, she kicks him in the shin.

A gasp of surprise more than pain, a stumbled step back—Pru darts past him, scrambles around his chair, yoinks her backpack from the floor—then she's outside in the frigid night, with clouds overhead and snowflakes biting her face. He yells after her, but she doesn't turn around. She sprints into the woods without stopping as he crashes and roars behind her.

The trees mutter around her, swaying in the wind. The snap of branches grows louder as her uncle gains on her.

The ground slickens beneath her. She skids, slips, tumbles through the underbrush, so *loud*, he'll hear where she is and now she's scratched and muddy and tangled in shrubbery—

"Help me!" she yelps.

Her breath crystallizes in short bursts of cloud. Her heart hammers. At her whispered request, the trees' muttering changes, deepening into an angry buzzing like the day she met Bert.

The forest *shifts.*

She doesn't see it; she feels it. Roots upheaving, vines slithering down trunks and tangling together in dense curtains, the trees leaning in different directions than they did a minute ago.

"What the—" Uncle Eben mutters to himself.

Pru scrambles to her feet, listening. He curses, yanks at vines, whacks at branches, but the forest does not give in.

Pru backs away, slowly at first. As Uncle Eben's cursing fades in the distance, she runs.

She's out of breath by the time she reaches the cottage, but her frenzied heart calms at the light spilling through the front windows and the plants bending to greet her. The forest, too, bends over her, the trees keeping watch as their buzzing quiets to a soothing whisper.

"Thank you," she whispers back at them.

Cordelia is at the kitchen table when Pru slips inside, her face unlined, hair black and shining. She's in civilian clothing rather than her postal uniform, trousers and a sweater, with a long red coat hanging over the back of her chair. Her smile crooks quizzically as she takes in Pru's muddy hoodie, the flushed face. "Hey, Prudie. What happened to you?"

Pru shoves her hands in her hoodie pocket. "Nothing."

Bertie bustles in from the sitting room, carrying a scarf that looks freshly knitted. "Found it. Look here, if I catch you walking all this way in the cold without a scarf again—"

She breaks off and reddens as she sees Pru. She recovers quickly, clearing her throat and throwing the scarf at Cordelia. Cordelia snorts as she dons the scarf. Bert ignores her.

"What've you been about?" Bert asks Pru. "You're covered in mud."

"Fell," Pru mutters.

Bert harrumphs. "Well, let's fell that hoodie right into the laundry. You're not traipsing mud all through my house. It ain't big, but it's clean, and I'd like it to stay that way. Awful cold for you to be in damp clothes anyhow."

Pru hugs the hoodie tighter around herself, suddenly aware of every place the belt hit her, every welt, every bruise that will be purple by tomorrow. "I'm fine."

Bert trudges toward the sitting room, shaking her head. "I ain't asking. I'll not have you take cold."

She digs a worn flannel shirt from her bureau. It's red plaid and warm and far too big, which is all right since that's Pru's preference anyway, and it smells like Bert: like soil, like flowers, like fresh-baked bread and wood smoke and sheep.

Pru loves it, but she strips down to her tank top with dread.

Sure enough, when she emerges from her hoodie, they're both staring at her. Cordelia's smile is gone, her face brittle in a way that goes beyond expression, as if her shape has shifted on its own in response to the sight of Pru's welts and bruises. Bert's nostrils flare, her eyes wide and horrified. Plants spring up at her feet.

Pru hugs her hoodie to her chest. "It's not a big deal."

"It is so," Bert says at once.

"Uncle Eben doesn't mean anything by it," Pru says, unsure why she's defending him when a while ago she was kicking him in the shin. "It's how he was—"

"Don't you dare say it." Bert's voice simmers with anger. The plants snake up her legs to wrap around her waist. "Don't you dare say it's how he was raised. It's how I was raised too, and I'd never lay hands on any child. Never. Not for any reason."

Pru shrugs, her arms tight around herself. Bert tugs her close to examine the marks. Pru wants to sink into the floor.

"Bertie," Cordelia says softly, but Bert ignores her. Her eyes are stormy. The plants grow thicker around her.

"I will murder him." Her fingers tighten on Pru's hand. More plants sprout at her feet, cracking through the floorboards in their haste. "I will absolutely murder him."

"Bertie," Cordelia repeats sharply, and when Bert doesn't respond, she jolts from her chair. Bert's nostrils are flaring, her eyes wild, her fingers painful on Pru's arm. Cordelia puts a hand on her shoulder. "Bertie, go check on the sheep."

"The sheep're fine," Bert snaps. Plants wrap so far up her body she's all but clothed in them. Saplings bust through the kitchen wall with a crunch. A draft moans through the cottage. Pru shivers.

Cordelia's fingers tighten on Bert's shoulder, but her voice is calm. "Go check on the sheep. Getting upset isn't helping anything."

"I ain't—"

"Go on."

Bert releases Pru's hand, yanks her coat off its hook, and storms out of the cottage, leaving a trail of greenery in her wake. Cordelia sighs. Her brow furrows as she watches Bert's progress back toward the sheep pen.

Pru's eyes well up. She hugs her hoodie and tries not to cry. Plants sprout at her feet too, quiet little green things humming gently as they caress her ankles.

"Sorry," she whispers.

The furrow in Cordelia's brow deepens.

"My darling girl," she says, "you have absolutely nothing to be sorry for."

A tear slips out before Pru can stop it. She dashes her arm across her eyes. "I made her mad."

"It wasn't you, Prudie. Of course it wasn't you. It was..." Cordelia's fingers twitch. "May I take a look?"

203

Pru bites her lip, but she nods. Cordelia sits her down, folds Bert's flannel beside her, and puts Pru's hoodie in the sink. She takes Pru's hand, examining the welts and bruises on her arm.

"Why'd she get so mad?" Pru asks. "You didn't get mad."

Cordelia's face tightens. Her eyes flash like fire, so suddenly Pru's not sure if it's the light or her shapeshifting.

"I'm mad," Cordelia says, sounding utterly calm though her face is still tight. "I'm beyond mad. If I had him here with me..."

She clenches her fists, shimmering as if she's trying to shift but also trying not to shift. Her face blurs, lengthens. Pru glimpses something beaklike.

The shimmering dies away. Cordelia's hands unclench, and she looks like herself.

"Wolf's bane for bruises, yes?" she asks.

Pru nods.

Cordelia touches her shoulder and digs around in the cupboards until she finds a cream with wolf's bane in it. She applies it to all of Pru's bruises.

"I wasn't raised this way," she says. "My granddad raised me, lovely man, he was, and he never so much as raised his voice to me, even when I did wrong. Bert...seeing you like that, I think it dredged up some memories she'd rather leave buried. Her daddy was just like your uncle. Raised that way. Didn't see anything wrong with it. But he'd raise a hand to her for anything."

Pru winces as Cordelia's fingers brush over a welt on her back.

"Sorry," Cordelia says. "You see why she took it so hard, seeing you like this. It's like reliving what happened to her growing up." She caps the jar of cream. Drums her fingers on the table. "She shouldn't have gone off on you like that, though. I know it hurt her to see it, but you're the one living it right now."

"It's fine," Pru says. "I'm fine. It's not a big deal."

Cordelia touches her cheek. "Oh, Prudie."

Pru pulls Bert's flannel on. Although Bert is shorter than she is, her shirt is so massive Pru is swimming in it. It hangs down to her knees, the sleeves brushing past her fingertips. Not wearing her hoodie leaves her feeling oddly naked; she rarely takes it off, except to wash it on Sunday afternoons before snuggling back into it. But Bert's flannel is a pretty good substitute. Pru hugs it around her, inhaling deeply. Cordelia gives her a small smile and feeds her pasta from the stove. The plants shiver in the cold seeping in through the hole in the wall.

Bert stumps back inside. A gust of wind follows her, but she shuts the door on it. Her back is to the kitchen as she shuts the door, removes her coat, and hangs it back on its hook. Her shoulders are bowed. The plants nearest the door stretch and bend toward her.

Pru hugs herself tighter, biting her lip. When Bert turns around, her eyes are red and wet.

"'M sorry." Her voice is wet and raspy. She clears her throat. "If you want me to take care of this—"

"He's the only family I've got," Pru says softly.

Bert's face twists, but she nods. "All right, then."

She pulls a toolbox from under the sink to repair the busted floorboards and the holes in the wall. Cordelia squeezes her shoulder and takes Pru's things to wash up.

"Snow's flying. Hard to see out there." Bert clears her throat again. "Might want to stay here tonight."

Cordelia returns from the sink and puts a hand on Bert's shoulder. Bert closes her eyes, leaning against the wall with a weary sigh.

Pru fiddles with the placket of her shirt. "Thanks."

Bert cracks an eye open. "What for?"

For the shirt. For supper. For letting Pru into her home and caring for her, even though Pru burst in without invitation.

For looking out for her, even when Pru's not quite sure she wants looking out for.

She's not sure she doesn't want looking out for, either.

She doesn't know how to say any of that, so she creeps from her chair and wraps her arms around Bert's waist.

Shock radiates through Bert's body as Pru snuggles into her. After a moment, Bert drops her hammer and hugs her back. She's warm and solid, smells sharply of the cold night outside and a little like sheep. Her hug is ginger at first, like she's afraid she'll break Pru if she hugs her too hard. Then her arms tighten around Pru, and she rubs Pru's back, and Pru thinks she cries a little bit, but she can't be sure.

Pru's eyes prickle. She wants to cry, too: no one's hugged her like this since Aunt May died. Uncle Eben isn't a hugger.

If he were, she couldn't hug him this way. She'd be too tense. Too aware of his every movement.

They stand that way for a long time, while Cordelia cleans up the kitchen behind them and takes over the repairs. Bert's heart thuds evenly under Pru's ear.

At last Bert pats her back and says, "Getting late. Ought to get to bed."

She bustles to the sitting room to ready Pru's trundle. Pru clambers into bed and snuggles deep beneath her blanket.

"Where's Cordelia going to sleep?" she asks tiredly.

Cordelia winks at Bert. "I'll think of something."

"Shut up," Bert says. "You can sleep on the floor if you don't behave yourself."

"Give us a shirt, would you, Bertie? I don't fancy sleeping in my day clothes."

"I don't fancy you sleeping in my house," Bert grumbles, but she pulls another flannel from her drawers.

Pru falls asleep listening to them bicker.

PRU JERKS AWAKE, heart racing. The cottage is gray in the dim glow of the snow outside. The embers burn low in the wood stove and fireplace. The plants rustle sleepily. Pru gazes at the dark ceiling, gulping down deep breaths. She feels like she had a nightmare, but all that remains are the clinging, groping edges of horror.

Soft sounds come from the other corner of the room. Pru realizes they are kissing sounds and that Bert and Cordelia are kissing. They sit up in bed together, still kissing, and she squeezes her eyes shut. She knows what kissing sounds like. She used to hear Aunt May and Uncle Eben kissing through her bedroom wall on Sunday nights.

She used to hear other things, too.

She hopes Bert and Cordelia stop kissing before she hears that. Some of the kids at school like to go into graphic detail about *that* and all it entails. Pru is not one of them. She doesn't see the appeal of kissing, let alone the rest of it.

The sounds stop. The mattress creaks as one of the women shifts.

"Is everything all right?" Cordelia whispers.

Bert clears her throat. "The girl's right there."

Yes, Pru thinks. Yes, good. The girl is right there. Please do not subject the girl to any more kissing sounds.

"Pru," Cordelia says softly, and Pru almost answers.

Then she realizes Cordelia isn't talking to her. No one's noticed she's awake—why would they? She's silent, in bed, flat on her back beneath her quilt.

Bert lets out a breath. "Pru. Yes."

Pru turns over carefully so her mattress won't squeak and give her away. The light of the falling snow wavers over the two women like they're underwater. They sit with their foreheads pressed together.

Cordelia kisses Bert's hands, one at a time. "Why are you trying so hard to convince yourself you don't care about her?"

Something tightens in Pru's chest.

Bert sags against Cordelia. "I got no claim on her."

"You should."

"Should and do are worlds apart, Del. I ain't her kin."

Pru squeezes her eyes shut.

"You might as well be." Anger edges into Cordelia's voice. "You do everything for her that horrible uncle of hers does, and you don't beat her."

Pru flinches. In the other bed, Bert flinches, too.

"There must be something we can do," Cordelia insists. "We could report him."

"To who?"

"I don't know. The police, or—"

Bert snorts. "You don't know a damn thing, do you?"

They fall silent. When Pru looks, they're still sitting the same way, Bert sagging against Cordelia, Cordelia's arms around her. Cordelia kisses Bert's forehead.

"No one'd find anything," Bert says wearily. "Even if they investigated, they'd see a little girl living in a big, beautiful house with an uncle who feeds her and clothes her. If'n he hasn't hit her recent enough for her to show bruises, they won't have any reason to think it's true."

Pru pulls her quilt tighter around her. A pit digs into her stomach.

"We'd tell them," Cordelia says, but Bert snorts again.

"Who are they going to believe?" she asks. "The respected businessman selflessly raising the child his brother left behind, or the cranky old widow who lives in the woods and the woman who brings the mail?"

The pit in Pru's stomach widens. She buries her face in her pillow.

"Bertie—"

"You must know what they say about me, Cordelia. They say I'm a witch. They say I eat children. Or that my cottage does. Or that the forest does."

Pru's stomach twists. She said the same things. She's grown up hearing them. She said them right to Bert's face, the night they met.

"They wouldn't give her to me," Bert says bitterly. "Not even if they took her from him. No court in the world would give her to the old witch living alone in the cottage in the woods."

Pru's eyes prickle. She's never considered the possibility of living with Bert before, even with all the time she's spent here in the past month.

Now she's considering it a whole lot. But thinking about it now is like having something taken away from her before she knew she wanted it. Tears well up in her eyes.

Cordelia kisses the top of Bert's head. "Not alone," she whispers.

The tears spill over. Pru sniffles.

Silence. Then Cordelia says, "Prudie?"

Pru sniffles again. Her chest feels brittle, like it's about to shatter, and suddenly she's crying and she's not sure why. Bedsprings creak, then floorboards, and then Bert is there holding her. She picks Pru up and carries her over to the other bed, nestles her between Cordelia and herself. Pru clings to her, shaking and sobbing and getting snot all over her nightshirt. Bert holds her and cries too—not as wildly; silently, tears slipping down her cheeks no matter how tight she squeezes her eyes shut—and Cordelia holds both of them and whispers over and over, "It's all right. It'll be all right." The cottage smells of fading flowers.

Pru calms down and lies sniffling in their arms. Her chest still feels brittle. The plants hum soothingly.

"I want to live here with you," Pru whispers.

Bert's arms tighten around her. Cordelia sighs into her hair. She's old tonight, her face careworn and soft, her long hair silvery, liver spots on her hands and stretch marks on her thighs.

"Prudie," she says, "I wish it could be that way. But Bertie's right. No one's going to take you from a relative with a stable income and a nice house and give you to the witch living in the woods and the woman who brings her post."

Bert wipes her eyes on her nightshirt.

"Then let's not give them the chance," she says.

THEY WAIT until the snow has melted enough for them to get into town without relying on Cordelia's shifting to get them through three-foot-high snowdrifts: they don't want to draw attention to themselves. Pru is bundled in the old woolen coat Bert gave her, with a scarf piled high around her face. Bert is bundled similarly, a hat pulled low over her eyes. She's supposed to be wearing gloves, but she spends the journey twisting the gloves between her fingers.

"Are you okay?" Pru whispers.

Bert closes her eyes briefly.

"I ain't been back to town in near a decade. Cordelia brings me everything I need and takes my tonics to my clients." Her nostrils flare. "Never liked it here, growing up. Don't like thinking back on it."

Pru clings to her arm. "I don't like it here, either."

Cordelia leads the way, in the form of a black cat. She trots on before them, doubling back now and then to twist between Bert's legs.

The farmhouse is empty. Uncle Eben is at work. As planned: they'll have several hours to pack as many of Pru's things as will fit into the suitcase stowed under her bed, get out, and lock up.

Only they don't have several hours. Sometime over the course of the week since the blizzard, they lost track of the day. It's Saturday.

Instead of coming home at 6:30 as expected, Uncle Eben arrives half an hour after they do.

Pru is alone in the neglected sitting room, stealing a photograph of her parents from a dusty frame on the mantelpiece, when the front door scrapes open.

She freezes. Plants sprout furiously around her.

The door closes. He doesn't clomp through to the kitchen like he normally does. He pauses in the entryway, where melted snow from their shoes puddles on the floor.

"Prudence?"

She swallows, wondering if she can make it up the stairs to her bedroom, where Cordelia and Bert are packing her things, before he comes through and blocks her path. The plants at her feet twine up her legs. When she moves, they move with her.

Too late. Uncle Eben looms in the doorway of the sitting room, glowering down at her.

"Where the hell've you been?"

"It snowed," Pru says in a small voice. Her plants hug her legs and grow larger, rustling menacingly in Uncle Eben's direction.

"What the hell?" His eyebrows swoop low over his eyes. "What's going on?"

Pru doesn't answer, clutching the photo of her parents to her chest.

*"Prudence,"* Uncle Eben says, but she doesn't answer, and the belt comes off. He's so busy hitting her that he doesn't hear the footsteps in Pru's room overhead, or the voices as Cordelia and Bert come down the stairs, hears nothing until someone screeches behind him and he turns around with a "what the—" and finds himself face to face with a monster.

Cordelia has shifted into something like a raptor, if a raptor stood so tall her feathery head brushed the ceiling. If her eyes glittered fiery gold with rage. If she had a long, whiplike tail flicking side to side and scaled, taloned arms halfway between a human's and a reptile's.

Cordelia screeches again. The color drains from Uncle Eben's face. He backs away, shoving Pru along behind him. Cordelia advances, reaching for him with those taloned fingers while her wings beat a gust of wind throughout the room.

Bert shoves her way in between them, face pale and eyes wide.

"Don't, Del," she says softly.

Cordelia cocks her head at her, then hisses at Uncle Eben as he tries to slip past her with his hand on Pru's wrist. He stumbles back.

"Pru's right there." Bert puts her hands on either side of

Cordelia's feathery face. "Not in front of Pru. You can't do this in front of Pru."

Cordelia's face shimmers between bird and human. Uncle Eben squeezes past her this time, but Pru pulls her wrist from his grasp. She leans against the fireplace, her heart pounding.

Cordelia's face shivers from bird to human.

Bert lets out a breath. "There you are."

A gun goes off.

Cordelia crumples, shifting rapidly into her usual form and then into her true form, wrinkled, silver-haired, liver-spotted. She sags in Bert's arms, eyelids fluttering.

Pru's heart stops for a moment, then starts pounding so hard she feels sick.

Uncle Eben stands behind them with his hunting rifle in his hands.

"Get away from my niece," he says in a quivering voice.

Uncle Eben aims the rifle at Bert.

"Get away from my niece," he repeats.

Pru's mouth goes dry, waiting for Bert to do something. Anything. But Bert merely looks at him, her blue eyes wide and scared behind her spectacles, clutching Cordelia to her chest, plants springing up around her, she's going to get shot, so Pru shoves her uncle aside.

Rather, she tries to shove him aside. Uncle Eben is tall and broad, and Pru is a short, skinny eleven-year-old with no muscles to speak of.

It's enough. She grabs his rifle, hands smarting at the heat of the barrel.

"Prudence—get off—" he grunts, wrestling with her for the gun.

"Get out of here!" she says to Bert. Bert doesn't move. Pru elbows her uncle in the stomach, grabs Bert's arm and tugs her toward the door.

Uncle Eben yanks Pru away from the two women, hugs her close the way Bert's hugging Cordelia. Pru wriggles in his grasp, but his arms are iron around her. He backs away from Bert, taking Pru with him, and Bert looks more terrified than ever, but she's still rooted to the spot, plants twining up her legs and leaning toward Uncle Eben, nodding hungrily as Pru thought they did when she first saw them in Bert's garden.

"Help us!" she shrieks.

The plants drone like a swarm of hornets.

Then, as if they'd only been waiting for her to ask, they lunge at Uncle Eben.

They snake up his legs and torso, twining so tight that they cut into him. He drops Pru, yanking at the vines. She scrambles away from him. No matter how much he tears at the plants spiraling up his body, they regrow, twining tighter around him. They pull him to his knees, cut into his torso and arms as he writhes. He grabs for his gun, but a vine yanks it out of reach.

"Pru," Bert croaks.

The plants drag Uncle Eben to the ground, but at the sound of Bert's voice, Pru tears her eyes away. Bru's chest heaves, her eyes glisten, but she holds out a hand as best she can from under Cordelia's limp form.

"Prudence," Uncle Eben gasps behind her, clutching at the vines.

Pru grabs Bert's hand, squeezing her eyes shut. More plants sprout around them. She can't help shivering as they wrap around her legs, no matter how gently they do so.

"Get us out of here," Bert whispers.

The plants tighten around them. Pru flinches and squeezes Bert's hand, but instead of dragging them down as they're doing to Uncle Eben, the plants *move*. They thicken and lift Bert and Pru several inches off the floor and skate them toward the front door together.

*"Prudence!"* Uncle Eben roars, but they're out the door and off the porch.

A scream swallows his roaring.

Pru clings tight to Bert's hand as her uncle's screams ring in her ears.

"Don't look, Prudie," Bert says softly.

Cordelia stirs in her arms. She strokes Cordelia's hair, and Cordelia quiets again.

Pru feels sick. "What's happening?"

"It don't like that he's been hitting you."

Something cracks and creaks behind them. The screams cut off. "What?"

"The forest," Bert says.

A rumbling from deep underground. The slushy earth shakes around them, puddles of melting snow trembling. Up the street, car alarms sound. The farmhouse groans.

Pru can't help herself: she looks.

Trees burst out of the ground and snake over and through the farmhouse. Windows shatter, punched out by branches. Doors explode into splinters. Trunks, roots, and branches squeeze around the house like a constrictor crushing its prey between its coils.

"Don't look!" Bert says again, in a strained voice.

But Pru watches the farmhouse disappear in a crush of trunk and root and branch, until the forest swallows them up and the farmhouse is out of sight.

THERE'S a tree at the end of Main Street.

The kids say it used to be a farmhouse.

Now it's a misshapen tree, or maybe many trees twisted together, with a bulbous trunk big enough to swallow a house. Its roots rear out of the ground, so high a middle-schooler who's brave enough can slip between them.

Some of them do. Under cover of dusk, they crawl through the roots and branches to explore the splintered remains of the alleged house within.

The ones who get far enough say there's a tangle of roots inside in the shape of a body, a man curled in on himself.

The ones who don't get that far say they're full of shit.

Occasionally, they remember that a classmate named Prudence Jones once lived there.

*Do you think it's her?*

*The body? It's too big.*

*The tree probably sucked her up for nutrients or something. Like that boy.*

*Gross.*

Eventually, the talk turns back to the body-shaped tangle, the splintered possibly-floorboards, and the monstrous tree. The kids never thought of Prudence Jones much when she was in their midst; now that she's gone, they think of her even less.

Safely tucked away in a cottage in the woods, Pru neither knows nor cares.

She doesn't often venture beyond the garden. The day the trees destroyed the farmhouse, the forest closed behind them. The old paths changed, the growth and underbrush thicker the closer you get to town until it's all but impassible.

Pru doesn't mind. She never had anything in town but a house where she was belted and a school where she was ignored.

Here, she has sheep to feed. Here, she has plants to talk to. A Bert to teach her herbalism during the day and tuck her in at night. A Cordelia to kiss her forehead and cook her dinner, albeit more slowly and stiffly than she used to, because she's convalescing.

In town, the kids at school still say the forest eats children.

The kids are wrong.

The forest doesn't eat children. It eats their abusers.

# *Farsight*

"I love them all." Dylan wipes tears from their cheeks as I finish telling them what's happening. "I'm going to bring them the biggest fucking care package they ever saw, tell them they've got a home in Mutopia if they ever want or need it."

They've been moody since coming back from Ireland. The whole group has. Whatever they saw there unsettled them. It's been out of the news, which means they either dealt with it very gently or extra ruthlessly. None of them are talking about it, which makes me think it was probably the latter.

These are the times it's hard to square the different sides of Dylan Taylor. They've saved the world from monsters, but they're capable of terrible things. They've come back from Ireland with blood on their hands, and now they're a blubbering mess over a story about a girl being saved. To be fair, it also involves a hungry forest, and Dylan might be another limb of the mysterious sprawling greenwood that connects back to Cybele.

"I think they'd love a care package," I admit. "And the forest may well feel like home to you."

"Because it eats people? Is that your very subtle message?" They clack their teeth in my direction.

"It punishes people." My tone is darker than I intended, and it sours their mood instantly.

"Yes, I know." They slouch back in their chair, almost tumbling out of it. "We dance around this, you and I. We should've gotten better at it."

"Maybe it's what we need." I realise I'm sitting perfectly straight in my chair, hands resting flat on my knees, in complete contrast to their near-flawless inability to stay upright. "The two of us balance each other."

Dylan smirks. "Are you saying maybe Ray knew what they were doing, putting us in charge of this whole Awakenings project? Because that's giving that asshole a lot of credit. It's almost like we elected someone smart and competent as president. Wild shit."

I fix them with a glare. "I do realise you were elected first."

"Second." They wag a finger at me. "Alyse was first. But holy fuck, imagine if I was running the show. Instead of just sneaking around behind the scenes being a rebel and an asshat. Really not playing to my strengths."

"I never know how much of what you say is for dramatic effect."

They burst out laughing. "Really, Far? Neither do I." Then they have the audacity to roll out off the couch and slouch over to kiss my cheek. "Right. I'm off for dinner with the love of my life. I'll stop in later on and make sure you haven't sold us all out to the humans."

They give me a wave, and go jogging down the stairs, leaving me alone again. I sit for a moment in silence, before turning back to the window and gazing out across the world. My gaze watches Dylan as they leave my tower, the way their face lights up when they see Dani coming towards them.

The next thing I see is far less charming.

# Welcome to the Weirdlands

## HESTER STEEL

WHEN I WAKE UP, THE FIRST THING I REALISE IS THAT THIS is not a duvet.

The reason being, it's moving. Also, it's speaking.

It's hissing words, to be exact, soft sibilant words that blend into each other. I think they might be something poetic and dreamlike, and I get this feeling that if I stopped to listen to them they'd suck away my mind into their whispers. Luckily, I don't stop to listen to them. I'm too busy screaming.

Second advantage of being too busy screaming is that I don't have to remember, yet, exactly what's happening and why I'm here and what I think I might have become. Screaming is easier.

I kick my way out from under the thing that is not a duvet, which is not easy because it's all curled around me and it does not behave like duvets should. It *clings*. Even once I've wriggled out of it I'm *dripping*. Dripping. Slime.

I, Charlie Ives, star columnist for the *Daily Sentinel*, am standing in a strange room, dripping slime and screaming. Good morning!

Clarification, achieved in glimpses: this room isn't just strange as in unfamiliar. It's strange as in *bizarre*.

A normal bedroom gone very wrong. Flowers in a vase - apparently moving, possibly on fire - a set of antlers mounted on the wall, dripping something that hisses on the carpet - jars on tables, containing things with what could possibly be eyes - slabs of what looks like meat stacked like books on the shelves, bleeding titles -

I wish I hadn't looked at that lamp.

*This is a dream this is a dream this is a dream* -

But I'm awake and I have a horrible feeling creeping through my nerves and guts that I know exactly where I am.

And there is no time to think about that because something slick and silky and viscous, oscillating toxic shades of neon green and turquoise and violet, still whispering, is creeping across the room towards me.

*Michael save me*, but He won't, not me, not now, not any more. The only one here who can save me is me.

Waking up into a surreal panic adrenaline kick does not necessarily make for brain clarity, but I grasp the basics of escaping. Door. Open. Slam. Run.

I'm halfway across a chintzy wallpapered hallway when the brain catches up with two crucial thoughts. The first is that crawling neon sludge may not be stopped by doors. The second is that if I can't trust duvets or lamps or vases of flowers, I quite possibly can't trust houses in general, either.

The chintzy hallway pitches upside down just as the glimmering disco ooze comes writhing out through the cracks around the door.

I land on my belly on the ceiling-that-is-now-the-floor, winded in a punch to my belly. And the ooze lands right on top of me, glooping onto me like a glob of mayonnaise.

It flows over me again, seeping this feeling of *right, where were we, before you so rudely interrupted*. Now it's covering my mouth, smothering my screams, I hear its whispers. They're not language, but I understand them. It's telling me to relax. It's telling me that it won't hurt. It's promising me things I can't quite place, a scent of honeysuckle, the colour of light just before sunset, laughter too far away to pinpoint. It's telling me to surrender.

Ah yes, I remember how to surrender. I remember how to relax and let go.

This is all so familiar it numbs the terror and the agonising stupidity of me, after everything, dying in a pile of *multicoloured goop*.

I know how it feels when that tension goes out of you, that resistance dissolves away, and everything that is you becomes soft and moldable and submits before the hands that will shape you. I won't lie: it feels good.

And then there are footsteps, and voices, and I can breathe, and the slick suffocating substance is pulling away from me, and droplets of water are sprinkling themselves over my face.

A figure is standing over me, wielding what looks like a spray bottle and a rolled-up newspaper. "Shoo!" He's shouting. "Back off! Scat! Get back in your box!"

He's wearing a crisp suit and a polo neck. His head is - oh god -

I scramble up, catching a glimpse over my shoulder of the glittering goop crawling away abashedly. I shoulder past the abomination of a suit-wearer and there's a door, oh *Michael,* and I am throwing myself out of it, into a sunlit morning garden full of birdsong and flowers that look right, I think, unless you concentrate.

There's a man in a folding chair, in a t-shirt showing a nebula, his headful of braids held back by a thick pair of glasses. He's reading a newspaper; it looks like the *Sentinel,* but the headline appears to be UNTIMELY FRUIT ERUPTION CLAIMS -83 LIVES and I'm fairly sure we never published anything saying that.

In the other folding chair next to him, clutching a cup of tea - my heart constricts like it might be due an untimely eruption, too. Her freckles. Her curls. The little furrow between her eyebrows when things get awkward.

"Charlie," she says.

"Charlie?" The newspaper man nods. "Charlie. Well!" I know what he's going to say before he says it, because the words are already in my throat, they've been there since I woke up, in the form of a nausea that's spreading out through my whole body. "Welcome to the Weirdlands."

*I was someone else before it all started. We all mutate, when circumstances require. Into something broken, or into something new.*

*It doesn't matter what I was before. Who I was. I used to pray for forgiveness, every morning, kneeling in front of the television, staring into that golden eye on the screen. Forgive me for my transgressions, my lifetime of stubbornness and sin and pride. Until You came into our world to save us, I knew not what I did. Forgive me my nights of drinking, my indiscretions with an array of genders in club bathrooms, my arrogance. Forgive me my tattoos. I wear a thick cloth band around my wrist now, hiding the compass inked on my skin.*

*Michael watched me, from the screen, from the nanobots that flitted through the air like puffs of glitter around a makeup box. He forgave me.*

*I stopped praying for forgiveness, after a while, because those sins belonged to someone else, someone I'd forgotten so quickly.*

*The sky outside my bedroom was grey-green, heavy with what could have been clouds, but weren't, exactly. Pipes and wires curled over the road outside—Salvation Avenue, what used to be called West Green Road. The piles of fruit outside the Turkish grocery shops and the colourful posters in the windows of Caribbean restaurants were gone, replaced by "shortage, sorry" signs and golden crosses. The shouts in a spectrum of languages had gone quiet. Cities mutate, too. When circumstances require.*

*Walking through the smoky streets, screeching metal and scanning cameras, my eyes downcast, modest. I used to walk through different streets before, my head raised, arrogant. My eyes scanned the pavements now. They were swept clean, although when was the last time you saw a street cleaner?*

*I would commute through a world of smog and metal, murmuring prayers to the passing streets, listening to sermons on my headphones. There was no music any more.*

*My office building was still my office building, even surrounded by thick pipes, like veins, even buzzing with nanobots and circled with golden statues of angels, the only things in sight that weren't stained with the grime of pollution.*

*There were set words, when greeting the security guards, the receptionists, my colleagues. They would say "may you be cradled in His hands and golden heart" and I would reply "by His spirit and His wires," and bow my head.*

*When they first introduced these greetings people snorted and made comments about Handmaid's Tale bollocks and red not being our colour. The giggles went quiet when we realised He could hear them, the walls themselves cameras and bugs now.*

*Nobody was openly punished for laughing at Michael. Things just started happening to them until they didn't laugh any more.*

*The same thing happened when you said "no" to something that was evidently His will. When I was given an assignment, "no" was no longer an option. I used to whisper it to the mirror, just to feel my lips form around it again. I stopped doing that soon, too.*

*I didn't need to.*

*I was at peace.*

*Sometimes in the quiet moments, I allowed myself a little arrogance: I was good, I was doing this right, I was bending to His will, I was His living hand, a nerve of His body. In those moments the clashing, smoggy city felt like a halo arrayed around me.*

*Except when I saw her. Then the peace shattered into iridescent shards, sharp enough to scar.*

IT'S A VERY long time before I figure out how to make words again. The sounds that are coming from my mouth are, well, *sort of* language. Maybe a kind of proto-language. Some whimpers mixed in for extra spice.

I'm in the Weirdlands. It's as vertiginous and terrifying as being pitched into the Mariana Trench or onto the surface of Venus. Except there, doom is a simple thing like being crushed under tonnes of water or melted by sulphuric acid rain. Here, I'm guessing it's equally horrible but a lot more complicated.

She's not here. She's gone into the house, I guess. I think she said something about "restabilising" it, but she didn't look at me and I couldn't hear over the roaring in my ears anyway. Leaving me alone with braids and t-shirt guy and Big Head guy, who have introduced themselves as Dr Orrell GR Burke and Professor Bobosy Wolus, which I'm pretty sure is't even a real *name*.

Look at that *head*. A bulbous swell to the skull around the forehead, as if there's a brain four or five times the normal size in there. There's no denying what he is, he's not the kind who could hide it.

I look at him and it blares: *mutant, mutant, mutant.*

"We need you to tell us how you found us," he's saying, not looming over me now but sitting forward in his folding chair, fingers twitching under his beard. "We need to know if anyone else is coming. You were alone when we found what was left of your car at the edge of the Former Bog, but if you've got people looking for you..."

I look past him. The sky is blue. The sky is other things. The sky is moving - not the clouds, but the sky itself, and down where the horizon meets the pine-clad hills, it's bulging as if something might burst out.

I am here and this is real, and Michael is not coming, and

nobody is coming, not for someone like me. The word echoing around my head is *forsaken.*

"No," I shake my head, looking down, away from the hillsides and hedges and flowerbeds and the strange headachy neon auras that pulse around it all. "I'm alone. Nobody's going to save us."

That forehead can fit an uncanny amount of wrinkles. "*Save* us? My dear, no no no. Our concern is if anyone's coming to *stop* us."

"Stop..." I remembered how to make words, but now I think I've forgotten again.

"Studying the Weirdlands," Dr Burke says, in an accent that mixes up Manchester and Jamaica. "We're on the edge of where everything breaks down, so we're pretty sure Michael won't notice us tinkering. But if you've got a platoon of soldiers or an army of nanobots on your tail, we're probably going to need to pack up the specimen jars and the Boxes Of Living Nightmares."

"And the good china!" Professor Wolus reminds him sharply.

Dr Burke rolls his eyes. "We don't have any good china any more, remember? Remember *why*?"

"And *whose* calculations, pray, was I using when I *inadvertently* caused the temporal crystallisation incident -"

There's a cough, a gentle cough, from the doorway. I guess the house is *stabilising* again, although the walls are still rippling around her, the epicentre of everything, a tired-looking girl with messy curls and stains of red and indigo on her formerly crisp white blouse.

"Kasia." My voice strains like it might break. "You're really here."

Kasia still doesn't look at me. "Professor Wolus - can we have a word? In private?"

Dr Burke places a hand on Professor Wolus's knee as his eyes bulge. "Honey, why don't I show Charlie here around while you have a chat with Kasia?" His eyes glint. "We hardly want the dramas of young love distracting us from our work, do we?"

Professor Wolus looks like the dramas of young love are a lot more terrifying than a thousand boxes of nightmare creatures, which they probably are.

Kasia still won't look at me. Those shards that are all the feelings she stirs in me, they've concentrated themselves in my throat, and they're slicing it to ribbons.

I want to run to her. For the first time, courage flares up in me, and I want to stumble over to her, take her hands and say, look. This is me. *Me.*

I followed you here. Look, those flowers keep opening and opening in some impossible unfurling, and that hill is letting off a distant flutelike moaning, and that's the wrong number of wings for a starling pecking around the flowerbed for things that aren't worms. Look, this is actual hell, a place that could crush us in its fists, and I came here for you, and now I see you, I have no regrets. Look, isn't that what love is?

But Kasia is following Dr Wolus back into the house, her back turned to me.

*I FIRST SAW Kasia behind the coffee counter at the Sentinel building, back... before. Back when I was something else. Her name badge, her hair pinned back, her fingers deft, fluorescent fluorescent light making every freckle stand out like sparks rising from a bonfire. There was this wonderful awkwardness in the way we smiled at each other, the simple act of ordering a flat white becoming a complex ritual and we couldn't remember the steps and we didn't care.*

*When I sat down at my desk and sipped it, I imagined the warmth on my lips was a kiss, a caress over my tongue. Pooling in my belly and warming and energising me.*

*We didn't share that kiss on our first date; we only held hands on the second. There was this delicious slowness to it, something easing us both in so gradually and gently and we relished every instant of it, not wanting to rush because every moment of it should be allowed to stretch out luxuriantly.*

*Even though the world was getting weirder by the day, it was ours, and bursting with time, a billion instants we could shape around each other.*

*On our third date, we swam in the ponds at Hampstead Health, the water silky around us, the light playing through the silty water and dancing on her skin, my hands finding her waist. She tasted of water. Leaves danced above us. We wrapped ourselves in towels and trekked up to Parliament Hill to sit out on the grass and watch the sunset, lifting strawberries and wine to each other's lips, and then she looked out at the reddened skyline and said "what's that?"*

*I thought it was smoke at first, like maybe something was on fire. From up here, we couldn't see that it was a swarm.*

*We found videos - it was on one of those we heard the word "nanobots". Our hands were clasped together tight. Tightening, her thumb stroking mine even as it shook, as the internet cut out and the voice from our phones spoke a single word: "REJOICE."*

*That was what they called the Day of Glory. The day Michael came.*

*There was no more kissing, or strawberries, or leaves dancing above silty water. Over the next days, the nanobots settled in and began their work on the city, chewing it away, reshaping the streets and buildings, warping the trees, recolouring the sky. Over the next days, He began His sacred work on our bodies and minds.*

*After footage came out of what happened to that couple at that bar in Dalston, the ones He used as an example of what would happen to the promiscuous, Kasia and I swapped a few terse texts. We couldn't even say we'd miss each other. We'd see each other every day, after all. But our eyes wouldn't meet any more. That hurt too much. The temptation. The reminder of what we'd never have.*

*She was the splinter in me, the crack in my halo, all the broken things. Every day, the simple ritual of getting a coffee left me shattered, and I'd have to sit, quietly breathing, praying and praying for that splinter to slide out smoothly, before I sat down and got to work. Trying not to taste the memory of a strawberry-laced kiss in the caffeine on my tongue.*

*We never spoke. We kept our eyes downcast.*

*Still, I noticed on the days she wasn't there. I noticed, and fear gripped me, and I reminded myself that when people...* weren't around any more, *it was Michael's will, and He knew best.*

*And then there were the days she was gone, the ones that stretched out, and out, day after day, never her behind the counter, always the skinny boy, her friend, who filled in for her. And I was at peace and I didn't miss her and the splinter was easing out of my skin and I would rest in sweet surrender in Michael's golden hands, the last flaw smoothed away.*

*And then on the eighth day I asked her friend where she'd gone, and he played ignorant over and over until he caved and whispered a quick, panicked admission that she'd run.*

*And I got a pass to leave the city on some excuse about doing a firsthand report from the Badlands around Maidenhead, and I got in my car, and I drove out of the city, and I headed out into the unknown to find her, the shards and splinters glittering in me like they might show me the way.*

"WHAT DO you know about the Weirdlands?" Dr Burke asks me.

I look back over my shoulder at the house. A cottage, actually. A cute little cottage, thatch and apple trees and roses, set at the edge of a village where the road curves around between farmland and pine forests. A river burbles. Idyllic countryside scene, at a first glance. Then it's like a magic eye picture, a spot-the-difference game between reality and *this*.

Things move that shouldn't be moving. Things that should be

moving are still. The smell is chemical, the river giving off chiming sounds as soothing as they're alarming.

Those aren't sheep grazing in that pasture. You know how at a distance glance sheep look kinda like maggots feasting on a decaying hunk of land? Well. Uh.

"Nothing," I say.

"Correct." Dr Burke smiles at me. I don't remember the last time someone smiled at me like that, cheerfully approving, fully honest. My shoulders come up defensively, my body in some instinctive protective state. "Nobody knows anything about the Weirdlands except that they've sprouted in several places over the past year. Dorset, certain streets in Beijing, eastern Argentina, northern Senegal. Areas that grow more and more warped the closer you approach, and if you go in too deeply, you never come back. Is it the work of Michael?" He sees me frown at that blasphemy but says nothing. "Of mutants? Of whatever created the mutant phenomenon, or of something else entirely? Our working theory is that perhaps the same mutating agent that's been affecting people has... begun to change space, in some locations. We understand them as mutant *places*."

"Are we..." I try to find a way to put this. It feels kind of important. "Past the point. Where people. Don't come back?"

"According to our calculations, the point of no return is..." Dr Burke points. "Roughly around that tree. Where we are is the safe limit, to a given value of safe."

The tree is a few hundred metres away, and is giving off waves of heathaze and dropping what look like enormous gummy fruit sweets onto the grass, which swallows them.

I should feel relieved, but I don't. I guess... I guess I went past the point of no return a long time ago.

"And you're..." I rub my temples. I can't shake the feeling that this place is burrowing under my skin, doing its work. Moulding me, as Michael moulded me before. Little clay girl on a potter's wheel surrounded by revolving knives. "Researching it? What have you figured out?"

Dr Burke considers. His mouth's always twisted a little sideways, like a comedy-tragedy mask, one side smirking with amusement, the other full of harsh wonder. "Mostly that my husband should not be trusted with unknowable horrors *or* most household objects." He shakes his head. "We do our best with what crawls out of the Deep Weirdlands, but to be honest, our only conclusion so far is that it's designed to confuse us. We repeat tests over and over and get different results every time, and everything is impossible. And do not ask about what happens when we send technology in there." He shudders. "I still hear that drone *screaming* in my nightmares."

The grass is green and soft, but every step we walk it crunches and crackles like we're crushing autumn leaves and broken glass.

"The truth is," Dr Burke sighs, "there is probably only one way that we can know any fundamental truths about the Weirdlands, and that's to go all the way in. But from what we can tell, time and space starts to break once you're properly inside. We'd quite probably emerge from there last Tuesday in the middle of the Antarctic, with less knowledge than we went in there with."

His smile's reassuring. It smooths over what we both know: that they wouldn't come back out at all.

"But you're going to?" I ask quietly. "Go in?"

Dr Burke is quiet. I stare at the distant hills. Are they different, now, to when I looked at them earlier? I swear they were shorter. Or taller. Were they bare of trees before? Was I just looking at different hills? I don't trust my eyes any more.

The panic's died down, a little, now. I just feel exposed, confused, like someone's switched off the ground. I'm *forsaken*. I can't place all the things stirring in me at that. My mind's not ready for the scale of all this. Stunned. Hollow.

I want Kasia to hold my hand, stroke me with her shaking fingers, tell me she's happy I came all this way to find her. I can't find any solidity here, except her, and she's already slipping away like meltwater.

"Well, we've figured out a device to stabilise time and space inside the house, at least," Dr Burke says thoughtfully at last. "So, once we've worked out how to scale that down for transport... and if Bobosy doesn't insist on adding a million bells and whistles, some of them literal... we should be able to make a trip inside safely."

His smile's wobbly. I try to return it, the first time I think I've managed a smile since I left London. It's still quizzical. There's a question I really have to be asking here. "Why *would* you?"

"Charlie - is it OK if I call you Charlie? Charlie, there are two ways that human brains react to the unknown. One is denial, a desperate denial that kills and maims and suffocates. The other is utter captivation, the kind that pulls you into dark and wonderful places." He plucks a blackberry from the hedge, and it dissolves between his fingers into a clutch of beetles. They fly away in spirals. "Count me among the captivated every time, please."

I don't know what to say to that.

We stop for a second, at the edge of a slope running down to the river. Something that might once have been a deer peers out between the trees for a second. All antlers, all angles. It bounds out into the open, and vanishes.

"Oh, look. A normal thing," I observe drily, and I'm stunned by my voice. That's the kind of thing the old me would have said.

"You never answered us before," Dr Burke says, tucking a braid back behind his ear and looking directly at me, a sharpness in his stare. "What exactly are you doing here? And how, exactly, did you find us?"

I open my mouth, seeking a safe answer, an answer that won't deal the final shattering blow to everything I know about myself.

And that's when the sky attacks us.

*I REMEMBERED DRIVING out of London, before. Suburbs giving way to green hills, lakes, airports, motorways curving around towards broad horizons. I thought it would be like that still. It was not.*

*The badlands were blasted. Blackened trees disintegrated slowly on dusty hillsides; burned-out cars lay in ditches like bloated dead beasts. Rainbowy oil slicks. Smoke rising in columns, the ash drifting, reminding me of when I was little and a disease spread among cattle and they burned the culled bodies in great pyres that filled the air with foul fumes.*

*I kept urging myself to turn around, murmuring desperate prayers that were as much to myself as to Michael. I could still go back. I had a pass. I could still go back.*

*But I couldn't. Something had ruptured; this impulsive moment of betrayal had ripped something open, and I'd gone through, and even if I turned around and went home, something fundamental would be missing. The city had become my halo, and I'd ripped it away and thrown it into the dust. All that awaited me was judgement, Michael's and my own.*

*I don't know what I was expecting of the Badlands. A Mad Max hellscape, or a shaky civilisation trying to hold itself together as best it could. I found a bit of both. For every gang of raiders I had to outrace on the M5, I would find a struggling organic farm where friendly survivors would trade information and a few hours' work for food and fuel. Some people offered to let me stay; others grew suspicious of me. In one place, a shared human-mutant hideout in an old train yard, they recognised me and chased me out.*

*Parts of the country - most of the country, maybe - was still normal, I heard. I never found those places. It was like there were hidden walls, lost pathways, between me and them, like this was a detached world, a broken parallel place.*

*Everywhere I went, I showed them pictures of Kasia and asked if she'd passed through. This worked until someone decided my phone was more useful than me, snatched it, and ran me off with a pitchfork. Thinking about it, it's a miracle I kept hold of it as long as I did.*

*It wasn't just searching for a needle in a haystack. It was searching for a needle in a haystack where some of the pieces of hay would be quite happy to kill me.*

*And could, easily. Mutants didn't move freely here, exactly, but you saw them more openly than you ever did in London. Girls with tentacles lining their necks, old men massaging the soil to grow seeds into food in seconds, caped mock-superhero bandits sweeping down from the sky with hoots of excitement as I pressed the accelerator and screamed prayers.*

*I want you to think I was brave. I was not. It was weeks I was in the Badlands, and I spent most of those weeks running away from anything and everything, hyperventilating in my car on back roads among the blackened ruins of hedges.*

*There were days when I simply hid out in the quiescent corpses of woods and empty villages, shuddering, cursing myself for running, praying for forgiveness. On those days I believed that Kasia had to be dead, and that I would be, soon, too, and that this was His will for us. His punishment for rejecting the warm embrace of His arms.*

*Without his protection I felt unmoored, in freefall. There was a word for that feeling, but I couldn't find it.*

TO BE COMPLETELY EXACT, the sky spasms and twists, the fluffy cute clouds swelling like boils and twisting into new shapes, and a funnel of blue descends on us with the suddenness and *you're dead if this hits you* of a striking snake. It rips open. It has jaws.

The goddamn *sky* has *jaws* and inside them I see a vortex of stars.

I scream and at the same time I push Dr Burke aside into the protective shade of a tree. We press up against the rough bark, watching the sky's maw curling around, questing, seeking us. Dr Burke is digging in his pocket for something, going "fantastic, cool, it's never done this before!" like we're not about to die or something.

Just because this is exactly what we need now, the tree begins growling deep within its trunk. I say "um" in the second before one of its branches sweeps down and slaps us, sending us crashing back out into the open road.

The sky sees us.

It's drooling, dripping fragments of cloud and star onto the tarmac.

Dr Burke pulls himself to his feet, readjusting his glasses, peering up at the widening celestial jaws. "Well," he gives me a sidelong grin that looks more like a death mask, "I guess *this* is what we get for being among the captivated ones. This should be interesting."

And all I have in my mind is *no no no no no* but I'm straightening up in the swirling grip of my own terror and staring up into what's coming for us, adrenaline washing through me in a wild, final high -

And then there's a shout from behind us and Professor Wolus and Kasia are pelting down the road towards us, Professor Wolus struggling under the weight of a large wooden box.

"This should work!" He shouts, fiddling with the locks. "Hold on just a - moment -"

Dr Burke lets out a terrified giggle. "How d'you think we're going to *hold* on against that, honey?"

"Got - it -" Professor Wolus rips open the box and flings the contents up towards the descending sky, splattering it with -

The neon slime I had so tragically mistaken for a duvet this morning.

The sky sucks it in in seconds, and I watch it spiral away into that spinning cosmic vortex.

"Ah," Professor Wolus says, catching up to us now, standing with us in the path of the oncoming jaws, "that may have been the wrong box."

"I told you to label them," Dr Burke moans, wrapping his arms around his husband's shoulders, the six most profound final words I've ever heard.

I look at Kasia, and for the first time, she does meet my eyes. They spark with something I can't, or won't, name.

And then she raises her arms.

I double over, yelling, as a shriek of sound hits me like a force field, feeling like it's popping my ear drums right open.

Tears spring to my eyes, and through them, I see the sky-mouth recoil as if something has slapped it, rippling with shock waves.

"Run!" Kasia shouts.

We did not need anyone to tell us that. We scramble across the hot road, me screaming, Bobosy and Orrell clinging to each other's shoulders and almost tripping over each others' feet. We pass Kasia, who's still standing, I admit it, I see what she's doing, *emitting* goddamn *sound waves* at the sky-thing. It's only once we hit the garden gate and I stop, looking back, that she breaks into a run, too, joining us as we pile into the house and slam the door behind us, panting.

Four pairs of eyes, exhilarated and relieved and horrified and wary, flash around at each other. Outside, the sky is howling.

"You wasted some *perfectly good eldritch slime*, Bobosy," Orrell says at last, and the panic erupts from all of us in a wave of laughter.

*I'D BEEN out in the Badlands for weeks when it happened. It was one of those despairing nights, when tiredness and fear and the hostility of strangers had driven me deeper into the pit, and at the bottom was shame and guilt and horror and mourning.*

*I'd parked up by a lake somewhere, which must have been a nice tourist spot once, with terrace cafes and rowing boats roped up. It*

235

*wasn't nice now. I thought I'd probably be safe there, because the stench of chemicals and rot and the glowing rainbow slick on the surface would keep people away.*

*I'd pulled up by the water and cut the engine and sat in the driver's seat, sobbing and praying for forgiveness. I thought if I prayed hard enough, maybe, maybe He'd embrace me again. Maybe I could find that golden glow again, where my own goodness melded into His, and He shone out through my eyes and moved my fingers as I typed. Surely it was just there, just the other side of my shame and horror.*

I can be Your eyes and lips and voice again, *I begged Him.* Please, show me the way to You again.

*I prayed until I'd cried myself to sleep.*

*I was woken some time in the early hours. Not by any sound or movement, but by a sudden jolt of emotion slamming inside my chest, spreading out through my body in volts and volts. I couldn't name it. There was pain, a deep rupturing pain of loss, and beside it, an unnameable elation.*

*It was not like anything I had ever felt before, and it was not Him.*

*I opened my eyes, and blinked at the outside, clearing the tears that had sprung up.*

*The slick of rubbish and chemicals staining the lake was disappearing, inch by inch, as if something was drinking it away. The moon shone now on a crisp clear surface, the water rippling against - blink, blink, against reeds that burst from the soil, growing in seconds, spearing up towards the sky.*

*The skeletal trees lining the horizon were shifting and waking, broken branches growing back, leaves sprouting. It was like watching spring sped up, the land reawakening, the bare dry soil rippling with new grass and wildflowers. Vines crawled across the terraces of the abandoned cafes, blooming with jasmine and honeysuckle.*

*My breath held, I opened the car door and stepped out onto the newborn grass, taking cautious steps down to the water's edge. A part of me was screaming* wrong, wrong, how, *but that part was distant and indistinct, an echo of something dying. Most of me was just over-*

*whelmed, sweet energy coursing through me like my own veins were awakening and blossoming, too.*

*So raw, so blissful, so bittersweet. I couldn't name what had been lost, but at the same time, something had been* given.

*Was this the Weirdlands, somehow? No. It didn't feel weird. It felt like the most natural thing in the world, like the earth remembering itself.*

*An egret moved ghostly among the reeds, turning its head to look at me before flapping away into a sky that was clearing, moment by moment, of its smoke and dust. For the first time in a long time, I saw the stars. A breeze danced across my skin. Was it summer? It felt like summer.*

*I suddenly realised what it was I'd been feeling, out here in the Badlands all this time, that terrifying vertiginous sensation. Alive. I felt alive out here.*

*I had no time to process that thought because a sudden sharp pain cracked awake. Bright, hard and superficial, and familiar - coming from my wrist. My tattoo. The little compass tattoo on my wrist, the one I'd had done after coming back from backpacking when I was a teenager. It was the same pain I'd felt when it was done - needles prickling at my skin.*

*I pulled away the wristband I wore to cover it up, and almost fell over in shock. It was glowing. Giving off shimmering waves of amethyst and amber light.*

*The pain redoubled, so intense that it kicked off a cracking agony in my bones, and I couldn't breathe from it, so dizzying that my brain just said* nope *and I fell to my knees and passed out on the new, still-growing grass.*

OUR LAUGHTER DIES DOWN PRETTY QUICKLY when we start peering out of the windows and realise that the sky is angry. Experimenting with shades of blue closer to neon turquoise and violent indigo, it's writhing and spasming. Cheated. Occasional tendrils sink down like tornadoes gone wrong, searching for us.

"We should probably..." Orrell's still breathless, from running and from laughter. "Investigate this."

"Maybe reinforce the defences on the house as well, hmm?" Bobosy suggests. "I do not believe we wrote *violent sky* into our list of situations requiring contingency plans. The *oversight*."

"Can I help?" Kasia asks.

I wish I'd thought to ask that. I'm just too busy shaking at this point. I know where that yawning sky would have delivered me to. That vortex simply led deeper and deeper into the strangest corners of the Weirdlands. I've been feeling ever since I got here that they wanted to swallow me whole; I just didn't expect it to be that *literal*.

It's reaching out for me. It's trying to pull me in. Us, or just me, I don't know. But now I've seen into that grasping void, I feel it viscerally, a new tug at my nerves. I don't really want to say that out loud.

"Why don't you take a moment with your friend here," Orrell twinkles at Kasia, who stays stony faced, "and we'll give you a shout if we need a hand, okay? Good. Let's go."

They disappear through a door labelled "ABSOLUTELY NOT" in permanent marker. Something behind it is whirring, and something else is squawking.

Kasia and I are alone at last in a room of dusty glass animals and lace curtains and undead flowers in vases. The silence grips us as our eyes meet.

Behind the door I hear Bobosy shouting something about "the crustacean formula," and a corner of Kasia's mouth twitches.

"They're pretty wild, aren't they?" I say, my voice coming out much more strangled than I planned.

Kasia breaks eye contact and peers out between the lace curtains. I don't want to know what those patterns of shadow, like clouds or low planes passing over the sun, might be. Whatever they are, they settle something in her mind. I hope it isn't the conclusion, *well, we're dead anyway, might as well talk it out first.* Those sounds and lights coming from outside: they colour every word with the awareness that it might be the last thing we ever say.

"They're wonderful," she says. "Absolutely bonkers. They have *wacky adventures.* We're having a wacky adventure, you know? The kind that's so silly you just have to laugh sometimes and you might die horribly but you'll go down wisecracking. The kind you get when you're curious and hungry and alive and aware of how ridiculous everything is, and it's a farce but it's terrifying but it's *fun.* It takes a while to get your head around it, but once you do... you think, we could have lived like this. On the edge, laughing at the madness of it, always two steps away from danger and three away from discoveries that blow *everything* open. We were meant to live like this."

I inhale deeply, as if I'm pulling her words deep into my lungs where they could take root and bloom. "When you say *we.* Do you mean mutants?"

"Oh yeah. You want to get into that, do you?" Kasia sighs, raises her hands, and the hum and buzz of electricity in the house ripples around me, tingling my skin, warping in my ears into distant snatches of music. "Fuck's sake. *Humans* and *mutants.* I mean *we.* I mean whatever. I mean *people.* People were meant to live like this, life was meant to be this *discovery,* and the whole reason we can't is because of people like you."

Those final words kick my gut. There's no disguising that look in her eyes now, fixed on me. Rage. Rage crystallising into hate at the edges.

I open my mouth. I close it.

"Do you want to know why I ran away?" Kasia asks, her voice saccharine. She leans back against the wall, arms folded, regarding me. "If you're wondering, by the way, yes, I was always a mutant, all the time you knew me. I don't spill that kind of thing on the first date. I can manipulate the hum. You know the hum? The sound that some people can constantly hear, the background buzz of electricity or distant traffic or things nobody can quite place? I can play with it. I can make it play me music, or I can concentrate it into sound waves that could *maybe* smash a window if I *really tried*, or I can get it to carry me conversations from just out of earshot. Dangerous, huh? I should probably be locked up." She twists her lips. "Bullet to the head would be cheaper, though, right?"

I swallow. "You know I don't think that. I -"

"Funny," she says, her head to one side. "My neighbour knew about it, a bit. I got the hum to play him music when we got high on the roof one night, Before. I trusted him with it. He knew I was basically harmless, so the whole of last year, he looked out for me. Until one night the hum carried me the sound of his voice reporting me to an anonymous Mutant Watch tip line. What do you think could have changed his mind?"

The sky hisses and roars into the silence, and the silence curls up and sits stony and toxic in my belly and chest.

"*The Myth of the Harmless Mutant: The Insidious Threat That Could be the Death Knell for Humanity,*" she says brightly. "Came out a day or two before I had to run, didn't it?"

I sit down hard on an armchair that's far too soft.

"Not your best piece, I have to admit." Her cheerful tone doesn't flag. "I liked your one on the internment camps. *Sun, Sea, Sand and Supervillains: The Mutant Holiday Camp Funded by YOUR Taxes.* It wasn't even inaccurate! They did imprison those people in an abandoned hotel, didn't they? I'm sure they moved them somewhere much nicer when they closed it down after the article came out! And oooh, your piece on, what was it, the mutant threat to women's honour? Loved that one! Really enjoyed the crackdown the week after, too!"

In the quiet that falls down between us, twice as heavy as before, Bobosy and Orrell's voices echo through the door, bickering about what ate the wrench this time.

"They told me what to write," I say, gazing at the swirls on the carpet. They're only moving a little.

"Yeah," Kasia says. "Those articles *definitely* read like someone who was just doing what they were told. Zealous? You? Didn't come across a *bit*." She sighs. "And I had to see you every day, and I had to keep my mouth shut and make you your damn coffee, all the time knowing you'd go up there to your desk and type your little words and help bring on the day when I'd be..." She shrugs, the words too heavy to say.

I force myself to look up at her. All those shards. They're dancing in my nerves. "I did what I had to do to survive, Kasia! We all did!"

"Bull*shit*." Kasia snaps. "Plenty of us managed to survive just fine without turning into Michael's golden girl hate propagandist. You did it because you liked it. You enjoyed the power. You enjoyed the glory."

I want to rewind the world. Upend it. Rewire it. I want to take every single molecule and remake it over a billion years until I create a universe where what she just said wasn't true.

I don't dare to break eye contact. But my voice is the softest whisper. "I did. Yeah."

Kasia nods once. Not understanding, not empathy, just like I've proved her right.

"I've been scared all my life," I say, my voice still small. "Of things I couldn't understand. Of things changing, of those big ruptures where everything falls away under you. Right from the first day that the mutants started appearing, I was... I was terrified, okay? It was too seismic. And when Michael came it was like... He understood. If I just made myself into what He wanted me to be, that change wouldn't be too bad. I'd fit that world around myself, and I'd be safe. Everything was horrible, but... for the first time ever I wasn't afraid, because I knew the rules."

"And how many people had to die or suffer so you could feel like that?" Kasia asks bitterly.

241

The broken pieces of what we held when I kissed her in the ponds lie scattered between us, too sharp to walk over.

Fuck it. The roaring of the sky is getting louder.

I'm going to say it. Admit it. To her, and to myself.

"I'm paying the price now," I say, finding some force in my voice too as I finally let my tongue shape the words and make them real. "You want to know how I found this place? How I found you?"

I stand up, pull the wristband down my arm and hold up my wrist, so she can see my tattoo. See the wisps of light rising from it, wavering. See what I've become.

WHEN I WOKE UP, I was lying face-down in the grass, splayed, my legs twisted uncomfortably under me. Grass. I smelt it, crushed under my nose. I couldn't remember the last time I'd smelt grass. It felt uncanny, something I hadn't even known was gone.

I climbed up carefully. This was not the place where I parked my car last night. It was lush and verdant, even more than it would have been back Before. Vines dripped towards the lake's surface, and were starting to crawl across the road. The scent of soil and flowers hung heady in the air.

It was like something had been released, and was stretching out.

I stretched myself out, too - it is not comfortable sleeping through intense pain while faceplanted. My muscles ached, my neck cricked. My wrist -

No pain there, not any more. But whatever happened last night wasn't a dream or a hallucination. It was still glowing softly, the colours of fire and sunsets and jewels rising off it in luminous waves.

And the needle was still moving, swinging here and there like it was seeking true north.

You can think about this, *my brain informed me.* You can say what this means. You can admit it. You can say what you are now.

*But I couldn't say it. Not even in my mind. There wasn't horror, and there wasn't wonder or joy, either. There was just an emptiness and if I stepped into it I'd fall forever. No. I wouldn't say it.*

*I stared at the needle, letting my mind be empty. Birds were singing in the branches. Everything was wide open, and because I didn't know if I should be excited or afraid, I was just nothing. A blank canvas. Maybe somewhere on it there was the faintest sketch of Kasia's face.*

*The needle settled. I knew what it meant. The instinct was inscribed on my skin and way down deep in my gut.*

*I stood up, walked to the car, and set off, following the road it had drawn out for me.*

"YOU'RE A MUTANT," Kasia says evenly, as I finish the story. "I see."

The quiet spins out. I hear Bobosy's voice behind the door saying something about how "these readings appear to be, um, *backwards.*"

"You're backwards."

"My gosh. So I am. *Fascinating.*"

I smile halfway at Kasia. "Sounds like they're having their wacky adventure."

She doesn't return the smile, but she doesn't glare, either. "Sounds like it."

"I want this," I say, speaking it into being. "I want to live like this. I'm not scared any more, Kasia. Not now that I'm here with you. If we survive..." I gesture at the window. "If we survive *that...* I'll learn. To live that way, to let it be absurd and maybe dangerous but... but *open.* You know? Maybe you can show me."

Kasia steps forward, the swirling and howling of the world

243

outside the net curtains illuminating an inscrutable expression. A scrutinising expression. She's just a few feet away from me when she bursts out laughing.

"Fuck that, Charlie," she says. "Wow. You spend your life screwing us over so you can *feel good* in a nightmare dystopia, and now you're one of us for two days and suddenly you want, what, a crash course in how to mutant? You want a manic pixie dream mutant to teach you to be alive again? I'm sorry, but that died the day you chose your career over our, goddamn, lives."

She's not laughing any more. She's heaving with fury.

The last pieces of anything we shared crunch into dust under her feet. The last gleaming doorway through to somewhere where I might have found a new ground under my own feet creaks closed, and some lock somewhere clicks shut.

"I... I came all this way for you," I say, pathetically.

I expect her to snap even further, to boil up to a point of rage. I kind of expect her to be shouting at me as the furious sky swoops down and takes us. But instead, she softens.

"Of course you didn't," she says, looking at me with something that's almost sympathy; it's sad, at least. "Charlie, you don't even *know* me. We went on *three dates* like a year ago. You buy coffee off me and our eyes don't meet. You know *nothing* about me. You know so little about me that you didn't even notice I spent this past year hating you. Of course you didn't drive for weeks across a post-apocalyptic wasteland then dive into some kind of altered reality for *me*." She shakes her head. The way her curls bounce. "Whatever you came here for, it's not me."

I don't know what to say to that, those soft, firm words sliding into me and curling up there, dissolving through my neurons. A response stirs, but there's no time for it, because there's a murmur and a clatter and the whole house shakes under a hammer blow.

"It found -" Kasia begins, her eyes wide with terror, but she's interrupted by screams from behind the ABSOLUTELY NOT door.

"Fire extinguisher! NOW!"

"That's not fire!"

"My god, you're right!"

It's followed by a loud robotic voice in what I think is Russian.

The house shudders again. I hear cracks.

"What's going on in there?" Kasia shouts.

Bobosy pokes his enormous head out of the door. "Well, hmmm, it seems the house stabiliser has either achieved sentience, or become, well, *possessed.* We also appear to have discovered an entirely new form of chemical combustion, which..."

"Bobosy!"

"Oh yes, and, well. Apparently we have around, um, four minutes before the entire house disintegrates."

"And the... sky thing gets us?"

Bobosy's eyebrows draw down, and his lips purse, a tiny face disguising terror under a bulging skull. "Yes. It would seem so. Yes."

"Let me take a look," Kasia says, that tension in her voice where she's holding together by a thread and it will snap if she stops moving. "The stabiliser and me had a good talk last night, I think it likes me."

The door opens for her, and I peer through and I see her, Bobosy and Orrell, surrounded by wires and metal and screens and electric flashes and uncanny light. And I stand there like a god damn lemon. The useless one. I can't exactly write a convincing propaganda piece to get us out of this.

Or.

I look down at my wrist. I look at the light swirling up from it, the needle swinging here and there, an intangible caress on my skin.

My mind chooses this moment to deliver a response to Kasia, and it comes with a spike of those splinters of feeling. *She's right.*

The shards lodged in me over the past year had nothing to do with her, really; they were the shards of me. The pieces of me that wouldn't die, no matter how I tried to kill them. The guilt and the hope and the curiosity and the tenderness that were shattered under the hammer blows of life in Michael's London. I saw her reflection in them; I didn't know what else to see there. But they were always mine.

And now they've brought me here: a doubly outcast girl at the edge of the world with countless lives on her conscience, glowing ink on her skin, and curiosity reborn in her soul. Trapped in a house with two mad scientists and the girl she thought she loved, watching them scramble to save themselves as the clock counts down to disaster.

Kasia's eyebrows tight behind her glasses as she whispers to the machine. Bobosy staring in fascination at something that isn't exactly fire. Orrell's hands pressed against his temples.

I ask the compass, *which direction do I go, if I want to save them?*

The needle swings. It points towards the three of them, the machine.

The needle swings. It points towards the front door, the outside, the hungry sky.

It swings back and forward. Two paths.

And if this were the kind of story that was easy, it would be a clear choice. I could go in there, I could help them, I could have some answer they'd missed, and I could fix this. And I'd stay here, grudgingly tolerated by Kasia, welcomed by Wolus and Burke, new lab assistant with a workspace with broken horizons. And I'd work, I'd work every day, I'd learn to be something else. A mutant, having wacky adventures. Struggling each day to deserve to be a part of some strange family on the edge of everything and one day, maybe, earning it.

Or I could take the other way out. Step out through the door. Let the sky snatch me up and destroy me, hoping that would pacify it and buy them their chance.

A single bright moment of sacrifice. A sad, pretty little redemption story.

But this story isn't that. Stories mutate, too, when circumstances require.

Because it's not destruction waiting for me out there. If I stay here, maybe the sky would stay mad and destroy all of us, but if I go out there, if I step into it willingly, somehow I know, I would persist. Transformed, maybe. Absorbed in some way, perhaps. But I'd still be me. Far more me than I ever was in Michael's London.

Nothing buys back lives, no narrative structure stitches together broken people again. It's not redemption I came here for. It's something else.

I look back at the friends I might have had.

I don't say goodbye. I open the front door, and I step out. I plant my feet firmly on the ground, among wildly blossoming flowers and twisted hedges and new colours.

The outcast girl on the edge of everything, carrying light on her skin that might make her the only person who could find their way through a place where time and matter and space warp into new shapes. The girl who's going to learn to be captivated by the unfamiliar instead of helping to crush it.

This is not surrender.

And the sky descends, and swallows me into the unknown.

# Farsight

These Weirdlands make me very uncomfortable. I'm going to have to write up a report on this and submit it to the Mutopian government. Someone will need to investigate, because whatever's going on there could be an enormous problem. I can't even comprehend it, even on the scale of the things I've seen. A research rabbithole shows me that the new government in the United Kingdom is planning on building an enormous wall around it. I've no idea if that's enough to keep something like that contained. Is it possible for the land itself to mutate, or is there something else going on here?

I don't ask Dylan about it, because their curiosity will get the better of them. And even though we don't always agree on the best course of action, they're definitely a cat I'd like to keep around. It's partly in case of emergency, but I've also come to enjoy their company. Despite my frequent misgivings about the way they operate, I do think we make a good team. Going into the Weirdlands seems like a terrible idea, and those scientists should probably be locked up somewhere.

I'm closing my laptop and starting to think about sleep when a flash of light catches my eye. Something out there, calling for my attention. Like a part of my brain has always been watching for this. An angel, coming back to life.

Nausea twists my stomach. This shouldn't be happening.

This can't happen.

I was one of the last mutants to be put under in the Dark Year, before it was Emma and Alyse alone who fought Michael to a gruelling stalemate. I saw more than most about the changes, and was a witness to what the angels did. Their sculpted golden bodies, their many glowing eyes. I still sometimes dream about the way they killed people. Light lancing from their faces, so bright it would blind you. Struck down by the glory of the Lord, and his holy servant. All networked together, eerily synchronised. The way they would all turn their heads to look at a target, a pack of them glowing like they'd been spat out of the heart of the sun.

This cannot be.

They cannot be *back*.

I clutch at my throat and stare into the distance, willing all this to be wrong.

# Moth, Flash, Flame

MONICA GRIBOUSKI

It was 2:23am and Moth was going to kill an angel.

Not that she knew how. Not that she had any semblance of a plan. But she had confirmation from the bugs that could split out of her skin that a big metal thing was lying in wait in the machine room ahead. Behind her in the HVAC vent they'd been crawling through, her ex-best-friend stabbed a flaming hole into one of the angel's defense drones. And Moth knew her other best friend had to be somewhere ahead of her, trapped.

No one else would've sent those codes to her. No one else could've found Nate besides Moth and Jaya working together again.

So now they just had to wreck a garden-variety servitor. One that might be dead-set on obliterating mutants. With its laser eyes.

The drone fell steaming from the flame jets at the back of Jaya's fists.

"Thanks," Moth said.

Jaya brushed her hair out of her eyes, leaving a smear of dust along her forehead. "You said around the next corner?"

"Yeah," Moth said, loathing the way Jaya was cautious with her, even now. "We should probably be quiet."

"I'll go first," Jaya said.

A lot of things had happened to lead to this point.

BEFORE SHE WAS MOTH, she was Ellerie Jacobsen, high school sophomore, living a very ordinary life in a Boston suburb. Her greatest goal in life was to get into MIT with her two best friends, a dream they had shared since middle school, and she had organized her life around doing just that.

Robotics club, Tuesdays and Thursdays. Cybersecurity competitions whenever she had time. Cramming to get perfect grades, to nail the SATs.

Jaya joked once that Ellerie didn't have a social life, but it was just that her social life was the same as her school life. Cheering with the robotics club jumping around her as their programmed bot landed a ball in the target. Chugging Red Bull at a Friday night cybersecurity competition, fingers shaking as she typed on her teammate's laptop. Long study sessions with her two best friends, Jaya's neat handwriting filling out perfect flash cards, Nate's endless ability to explain any concept the two of them couldn't grasp, even though he was two years ahead of them and the information should have gone cold in his brain.

Ellerie loved it. She didn't want anything else. She sometimes had a hard time saying what she meant, but she'd had the same friends since forever, so they always understood her anyway.

"Mutant vigilantes were again attributed to the latest in a chain of robberies, this time from a cash-loaded armored vehicle," said a newscaster on the video Jaya was playing. "We're going now to a witness who claims Marvelous hand-delivered a parcel of cash to his door—"

"She's hot," said the witness, a hoodie-wearing teenager, and Ellerie realized the video was a fancam as the music kicked up into a driving pop beat and the video cut to slo-mo shots of famous mutant Marvelous flinging debris, flipping her hair, walking down the street sipping iced coffee. Ellerie wondered how anyone could look that cool.

"Dani Kim could telekinetically throw me across the room and I would thank her," Jaya said, in the middle of reapplying nail polish after it had gotten chipped at field hockey practice. Ellerie felt much the same, but thinking about it— and thinking about Jaya thinking about it— made her face go hot. The video started to loop and Ellerie hit pause.

"I kind of feel bad for them all, honestly," Nate said. "It seems like a lot to deal with."

The fact that mutant clusters had been springing up worldwide felt like a movie, like it was happening to another world. Ellerie thought that it might be cool to be in a superhero team with her friends, but not if it interfered with her robotics schedule.

Jaya recapped the nail polish and flapped her hand around. "What, becoming vigilante heroes? It seems pretty fun to me."

"A couple of them died, I think," Nate said, grimacing. "That's a lot more pressure than we have— ahh!" Nate's phone vibrated in his hand and he jolted so hard he threw it. Ellerie tried to grab it and it bounced off her palm, but Jaya snatched it and handed it back to Nate.

"Agh," Jaya said, "smeared my nails again."

"Oh my god," Nate said. "My mom says my letter from MIT got here. No mom I do not want you to open it!" He was tapping wildly on his phone.

Jaya and Ellerie sucked in breaths and exchanged a glance.

This was it: the first step of their collective future. Ellerie felt shaky.

Nate looked worse, pulling his glasses off to run a hand down his face. "I'm gonna puke."

Jaya put a hand on his shoulder. "Nate. Kumquat. Breathe."

Kumquat was their code word: to listen no matter what, to tell the truth. "It's going to be fine," Jaya continued. "No matter what it says."

"I can drive us all to your place," Ellerie said, quickly downloading their robot's code back to her laptop from the school machines. She unplugged it all and shoved it in her backpack.

"Okay," Nate said, "okay."

And of course he'd gotten in: brilliant, sweet Nate who volunteered at the senior center because he genuinely liked it, who had finished the SAT faster than anyone else in the room. He cried when he got the acceptance, his mom wailing in the background, Ellerie and Jaya dancing in the kitchen.

Junior year was stranger without him. Jaya was throwing herself into her own college applications, and between that and Jaya's varsity field hockey schedule, Ellerie felt like the brief oases of robotics club were their only time together. But they made the time last: bingewatching anime when they were too stuck on coding errors, late enough that the school janitor had to regularly kick them out.

"I'm tired," Jaya said one night when the janitor had not yet found them. She was leaning her head against Ellerie's shoulder as the outro song of My Hero Academia played on Ellerie's laptop. Ellerie felt like there were a thousand fluttering wings inside her ribs flowing from Jaya's warmth.

"We can go home," Ellerie said, even though she didn't want to.

"Not that kind of tired." Jaya straightened. "Like, in my heart."

"Oh." Ellerie straightened.

"Like, what am I doing this all for?" Jaya leaned back against the wall, leaving Ellerie's skin cold at the places she'd been. "MIT's just a place. Any college is just a place. I'm gonna pay a bunch of money and get a piece of paper. What if I went to Alaska and learned to be a forest ranger instead?"

The fluttering wings in her suddenly felt more like fear. She didn't know what to say: they'd all wanted the same thing for so long, or so she'd thought.

Jaya must've seen the dread on her face. Her mouth thinned to a line. "Don't be upset, I'm just saying it. My parents would kill me if I moved to Alaska."

"Right," said Ellerie.

"You've got to have thought about it too, though, right? Like those mutant kids. They can do whatever they want." Jaya stared out through the classroom windows into the dark fields outside. "Go wherever they want."

Ellerie had never thought about it.

ELLERIE HAD ALWAYS HAD A SECRET, and it was that she was in love with both of her best friends.

Thirteen, watching Nate dance with Amber Brown at middle school semiformal, fighting the urge to go over there and shove her. Jaya had appeared, even though she'd kissed two separate boys that night, to swing her around in a circle. "El," she sang, "slow dance with me instead!" Jaya's lips sending a thrill up her spine when she leaned into whisper, "I heard Amber's breath is godawful. Wonder if that's why Nate can't look at her straight."

Ellerie was pretty sure Nate couldn't meet her eyes because he was nervous. She didn't know if that was because he genuinely liked Amber, or if he was trying to figure out how to escape her. "He looks kind of cute in a suit though," Jaya said, staring over there. "Who knew?"

Fifteen, watching Jaya sprint over grass at a field hockey tournament, shouldering another girl onto the dirt and sprinting for the goal.

"She's amazing," Nate said next to her, voice full of awe, and Ellerie wondered if she wasn't the only one with a crush.

Even now, with Nate in his first semester at MIT, Ellerie only felt it more. He was home for the weekend and the three of them had gotten together to sail on Upper Mystic Lake with Nate's dad's boat club pass. Nate rolled his sleeves up to tack the sail while she and Jaya sat in the back of the little boat with a bluetooth speaker and a bagful of fresh grapes.

The sunlight lit Nate's brown hair copper. Jaya's tan legs rested over Ellerie's pale ones.

Jaya had to leave early for a field hockey game, so Nate ended up driving Ellerie around, picking up ice cream to eat in Nate's backyard.

"What's the best part?" Ellerie asked, deep into grilling him about his semester so far.

"Obviously the classes are really cool," Nate said, "But I think my favorite thing is all the new people."

That same fear again. A thousand wings beating around her lungs.

"The first few weeks were this weird alchemy where like, you could just ask to be anyone's friend, because we were all in the same boat of a new life," Nate continued. "The person you sit next to at a club social could end up being your best friend for the next four years, or you could forget them a week later."

Ellerie stuffed a massive spoonful of rocky road into her mouth so the brainfreeze could distract her from her worrying. Nate was allowed to make new friends.

"I figure this next year might be pretty hard for you, being the youngest of us," he said, turning to her. "I hope you don't feel alone. I'm not going to forget about you."

The brainfreeze was what was hurting her— that was all. She looked up at the moon rising over the yellowing oaks in Nate's backyard to avoid meeting his eyes.

"But it's also okay if things change a little, El." He bumped her with an elbow. "It's exciting, to see how we'll all grow up."

HALFWAY THROUGH ELLERIE'S junior year, the greater Boston area began to change.

The Cute Mutants had fallen, and angels were moving in to improve the world.

The first thing the AI angel overlord Michael did was landing a contract to make the subway run smoothly. The newer college students all seemed impressed, but Ellerie had lived here all her life, and saw the same wariness she felt on others' faces: no one could fix the T this quickly. It was eerie.

Then the skyline of the Financial District started to grow even higher. Ellerie saw it from across the river, standing outside the Museum of Science— glass and steel skyscrapers spreading out into downtown, running over the old packed brownstones of the North End and Back Bay like a postmodern architectural virus. "We used to have fackin zonin' laws fuh this," said a construction worker to his buddy while they stood smoking outside another new development that Ellerie passed on her way to an art supply store in Fenway. "Whatevah," said the other, "least we're gettin' paid."

The changes were almost good and then they were suddenly bad: the city's new infrastructure was well-working, but all weaponized to ensure there were no mutants around. Once while Ellerie and Nate were thrift shopping in Cambridge, they saw a kid with a nose ring get tackled to the ground next to the vintage overalls. Their eyes lit bright silver and ice spewed from them, crusting the arms of the officers in black with eye-shaped logos that held them to the ground.

Nate grabbed her hand and dragged her towards the changing rooms, where they hid in a stall together. Nate didn't let go of her hand— for some reason, it made her feel more safe than anything. Finally, Ellerie heard a van door slamming outside— she peeked out to see the kid being dragged into a van with a big eye logo.

The subway became a method to check for mutant DNA— a scan as you went through the gates. Boston and its suburbs were getting locked down.

And still, life went on.

Jaya got her acceptance letter. Ellerie found out via a picture message in their group chat with Nate, a single shot of the letter with no other context.

Like a splinter, Ellerie remembered Jaya's confession about wanting something else. Was she happy? Did she not care at all?

Panic rising, Ellerie bailed out of dinner with her mom to drive to Jaya's house, parking half on the curb. She mashed the doorbell repeatedly. Jaya hadn't answered her or Nate's congrats message—

But then Jaya's mom threw the door open and hugged her and dragged her inside, and Jaya was celebrating in the living room with her younger sister. "El!" Jaya yelled, "can you believe it? Come here, have some cake—"

It was all fine, she thought, of course that had just been a stressful night for Jaya, of course she'd just been so excited now that she hadn't thought to say anything more.

Ellerie would still have the future she'd dreamed of with her friends.

ELLERIE DIDN'T GO to parties on principle, but at the end of Ellerie's junior year and Jaya's senior year, Jaya demanded it, her last big high school party. Ellerie felt like she was careening towards a cliff— Nate back after finishing finals and indescribably older after a year of college, Jaya about to head for the same, Ellerie alone for another year. She chugged disgusting-tasting jungle juice as she watched Nate explain something animatedly to a senior from their robotics team.

She was feeling the future press down on her like a foot on her throat. Jaya had ripped through three short-term boyfriends this year, and Nate kept talking about someone named Kai from school like they were the hottest thing. She had to do something, she thought, staring at group of people playing spin the bottle across the room, a girl from her year crawling across the floor to kiss another girl.

But how could she ever choose between her friends? How would she ever confess when it could ruin everything?

What did it matter anyway when they were both leaving her?

Ellerie found herself drunk. She'd only been drunk once before, off champagne they'd snitched in Jaya's basement, playing tipsy Mario Kart the three of them. She'd fallen asleep on Nate's chest with Jaya on her hip.

The party felt nothing like that cozy comfort: music blasting, people she didn't care about trying to yell conversions over their cups. But Jaya looked like she was having fun, playing beer pong with some of her field hockey friends, and at one point Jaya pulled her into the game, laughing delightedly.

"Come on, El," Jaya said, "me versus you, let's go."

Ellerie couldn't help but smile when Jaya smiled at her. Maybe it would be better to just have fun. Keep her secret for a little while longer.

Ellerie ended up winning, somehow, and her pong partner Alice picked her up on her shoulders and charged around the room chanting her name. Jaya was applauding, glossed out.

Ellerie could be cool, she supposed. She could like parties.

A freshman from the robotics team— here because he was someone's little brother— cornered her at the snack table afterwards.

"It was just so smooth what you did at the competition to fix that misaligned axle," Benny said. "Like, you're basically a genius, *and* you can hang out with those field hockey girls?" He laughed nervously and overpoured his soda, hurrying to mop it with a pile of napkins.

"It helps that I have cool friends," she said, feeling herself realize it as she spoke it, "but really, you just have to try stuff."

"I wish I had friends like you," Benny said.

She talked to Benny for a while longer. It was easy, and by the time Benny awkwardly announced he had to pee and hurried off, Ellerie felt high off of her newfound capability. She stumbled into a table and then set off, wondering where Jaya and Nate had gone.

She wandered down a hallway, and as if thoughts could summon, Jaya swung out of a room and almost into her. "Oh!" Said Jaya, who looked flushed. Maybe she was drunk too. "Hey. El." Jaya put her hands on Ellerie's shoulders, her eyes danced between Ellerie's. She seemed like she was chewing something over.

Ellerie felt suddenly flooded with purpose. She could be the kind of person that won pong games and impressed freshmen. She could be the kind of person that, instead of quietly steering towards the future she'd set for herself years ago, could just reach forward and take it. At least a part of it— one she'd never let herself articulate aloud.

Ellerie leaned forward and kissed Jaya.

For about three seconds, it was perfect. Jaya's hands tightened around her shoulders, then her lips parted and she leaned against Ellerie. Jaya felt like her vanilla shampoo, like the acrylic nails she stuck on in between field hockey and robotics, like endless evenings working and laughing.

Then Jaya pulled back.

"I have something I need to tell you," Jaya said.

Ellerie swayed. Jaya's dark eyes were the prettiest thing she'd ever seen— like she could fall into them, and keep falling, and still always feel safe.

"El," Jaya said. "I just kissed Nate."

"Oh," she'd said, trying to read the way Jaya's brows had pulled together and failing. Her heart flip-flopped. "Congrats?"

"No, I mean—" Jaya's eyes flitted down to her lips again, and Ellerie felt herself swaying forward. Jaya stopped her, gentle, but it had the emotional force of a slap. "We need to talk about this! All of us!"

"Sure," she said. Had she messed up? All Ellerie wanted was to curl into the warmth of her again.

Instead she ended up puking in the bathroom moments after Jaya went off to gather Nate. Bad, this was bad. Ellerie chugged water from the sink with her hands and stared at herself in the mirror. She'd just kissed Jaya! Who'd just kissed Nate! And now they wanted to talk! She staggered down the hall like it was a nightmare.

Jaya had commandeered one of the mansion's many bedrooms for this talk, and the atmosphere when Ellerie walked in was as palpably bad as her nauseous headache. Nate was sitting on the bed head in hands in full existential crisis mode; Jaya was pacing, her heels off and clutched in her hand.

"I'm sorry," Nate blurted off the bat, before Ellerie had sat down. "I didn't realize you two were—"

"We're not," said Jaya, and Ellerie's heart wrenched. "I mean, I didn't know we were until now."

"Just never mind," Ellerie said. "I'm happy for you two." She wasn't. "Forget what I did."

"It's just that I'm leaving after this summer," Jaya said. "And Nate's already in college."

"Leaving," Ellerie repeated. "You're going a fifteen minute drive away."

"It's going to be different," Jaya said. Ellerie realized she had tears in her eyes.

"I said forget it then!" Ellerie snapped, and stood up so abruptly the world tilted and she stumbled into the nightstand.

"El," Nate said, standing up to catch her elbow, "are you okay?"

"Sure," she forced out. All she wanted to do was leave.

"Kumquat," Nate said.

"No!" She felt herself knock the light off the stand as she tore her arm from Nate. "Fuck off." Maybe she was starting to cry too. "I mean, I'm sure you guys will be happy together. Bye."

She flung herself out of the room before either could stop her. It was a long, cold walk home, but Ellerie could barely feel it between the tears and her half-drunk state. She wasn't good at anything after all.

> N8: el i dont want to leave things like this
> N8: i am physically incapable of living with the thought
>    of you not talking to me :face_vomiting:
> N8: talk to me? please.

Nate bombarded her with messages; Jaya sent her nothing. She took that as disapproval enough, and ignored them both, too searing with rejection to contemplate a reply.

But it was like her personal life was a reflection of the rest of the world: just after the party, it all began to burn down.

The most powerful mutant on the planet wanted Michael out, and Goddess seemed willing to do anything to achieve it.

Mutant versus angel fighting carved holes through the suburbs, blasting entire streets into ash. Evacuations started, clogging up the highways worse than a holiday weekend. All of central Medford was wiped into a wash of desert; the Fells became a twisted wilderness that was rumored to harbor mutant rebels.

Ellerie hid in the basement, clutching her mom and her childhood radio. "We should've driven to Maine," Ellerie's mom kept saying as explosions rippled in like thunder.

It had been weeks without talking to her friends, but she needed to know Jaya and Nate were okay. "Status check," she said into the radio, tuned to their special frequency.

A long pause. "Status check," she repeated. "Kumquat."

They could be dead, or not remember the radios, or not care to answer her. Any number of horrible reasons.

"Here," Nate's voice warbled, breathless. "I'm here."

Ellerie pressed the radio to her forehead like it was Nate's clammy hands. "Good," she said.

Three minutes later, there was a burst of static. "Hi." Jaya's voice, thin. "I'm okay. I was trying to get my dog downstairs too."

"Is Cooper alright?" Ellerie pictured the neurotic lab mix drooling his anxiety onto Jaya's finished basement's faux-hardwoods.

"He'll live," Jaya said.

She wanted to say more, but she didn't know what. So instead, she waited, and Nate and then Jaya took up asking for status checks, each of them pinging once an hour as the fighting lasted the night. At two in the morning, Nate came back on.

"I have to go," he said, sounding thin. In the brief space between his words and his finger on the call button, a sound like a jet passing by roared and cut out. "I'm okay, I just have to check on something."

Ellerie didn't sleep the rest of the night.

OVER THE NEXT FEW WEEKS, the fighting centered back on the city, and school began, stubbornly in person despite the chaos still happening a few towns away. Without Jaya and Nate there on top of the state of the world it all felt fake. She slept through morning classes and programmed games on her calculator in others, checking her phone every chance she could sneak it to see if either of them had messaged her or if there was any news out of the city.

Nate, trapped on the other side of the checkpoints because of early-move-in, had made them all a groupchat on a messaging service that hadn't yet been cracked by Michael. Since the radio night, they'd been talking again. But it was always tense and weird, mostly updates.

*n8: things are getting intense here. multiple profs gone*

> *because they were mutants. school's trying to push*
> *back but hard to fight against killer robots*
> *J: at least they let you on campus. my classes are all*
> *online*
> *n8: haha jaya i dont think you want to be here*

Ellerie didn't have anything to add, so she mostly stayed quiet. The pauses between messages grew longer. Finally she couldn't stand it any longer and sent one herself.

> *El: guys, the admissions site keeps going down*
> *El: do you think i should still apply the regular way or*
> *is there some special apocalypse alternate app*

Neither of them answered for days. The day before the early action application was due, Jaya sent: *just try it anyway.*

So she did. The form submission spat back a 404. She emailed her full application to the admissions office too just in case.

That night, Ellerie dreamed of a sword punching down into earth, a great gush of energy flowing back into the world. It dug vines up into her and caught the fluttering wings inside her chest.

When she woke up, she was coughing. She jackknifed to sitting in her bed, hacking into a hand. When she finally caught her breath, a cluster of little grey moths sat on her palm, trying to flick the spit off their wings.

She ran to the bathroom, horrified. In the mirror she watched as a moth fluttered out of the skin on her cheek. It took off and landed on the mirror, and she could feel the coolness of the glass under its feet in some new section of her brain, could see her own shocked face staring back at her in reflection and moth-eye both.

She was a mutant.

She gave herself a new name, and didn't tell it to anyone. Who was left to tell it to?

MOTH WAS SITTING on her bed upside-down, ignoring her calculus homework, when she heard the static.

She jerked backwards so fast to roll off the bed that she almost tore her kpop goth girl group poster with her bare heels. She landed awkwardly on hands and knees and fished underneath her bed past socks and a C++ textbook to latch onto her radio.

It was the first time it had sounded in at least a month. She knew those beeps anywhere: morse code. She and Jaya and Nate had been using it since middle school to talk to one another in late hours, a stubborn habit from before they were allowed cell phones and also pretended to be spies.

This felt more like a spy game than anything: a month without talking to her friends, Nate mysteriously silent, Jaya still stubbornly quiet. Boston was recently ousted from its mutant-hating AI overlords, but still a mess in the aftermath. She transcribed the message on a thrift shop receipt on her floor.

*dig where the sandwich fell*

Properly cryptic.

Moth, though, knew exactly what it meant. Even though it was 10:34pm on a school night, she found herself throwing on a hoodie and sneaking down to the basement to grab a shovel.

Moth wasn't sure if one was allowed to park in front of a mutant-twisted forest. There were no signs, just trees curling up into the sky, impossibly fractal. She cranked the parking brake on her shitty Ford Taurus and got out, fetching the shovel from her trunk.

Back when she was a freshman, she'd flung an entire chicken parm sub off the top of an old spraypainted watchtower in the Fells by mistake when the three of them were hanging out. Moth had no

265

clue if the watchtower still existed in this version of the Fells, and she was a little freaked out at the idea of going into a mutant forest. But she was a mutant now too, and she'd do anything for Nate.

She sent bugs out ahead of her, whatever little good that would do. She'd know if some scary mutant was coming to eat her ahead of time to have a moment of fear before she died. Cool.

Her moths didn't land on anything but trees, and even though the trails were overgrown and horrorshow-like in the glow of her flashlight, Moth recognized them. It was a twenty minute walk to the tower and she was excruciatingly aware of her own breathing the whole way. The radio sputtered its morse code message in whisper-talk on repeat in her pocket.

The tower finally loomed above, a concrete affair now repainted with mutant-flavored murals. She recognized the Cute Mutants logo in neon purple, the vigilantes who'd made a mutant nation. As a mutant, now, herself, should she be contemplating running away to the moon or their rumored mutant island paradise, or joining a superhero squad?

She just wanted to get into college.

Though, what did it mean anymore? It was a goal leftover from a different version of herself, one who knew a lot less about how the world worked.

Moth looked up, as if amidst the dark trees hanging over the concrete tower's top she could see the three of them in the past. Jaya laughing and shoving her, Nate diving for her dropping chicken parm like it was a precious object as it toppled over the edge.

She amended her thought. She just wanted her friends back.

Moth glared at the exact spot where her sandwich had fallen and started to dig.

After a ridiculous amount of digging— so long that she'd almost given up twice— the shovel hit metal. Moth dropped to her knees and scrabbled in the dirt. Her stubby fingernails uncovered a shining bronze helm, a screen, an indentation she recognized.

She jumped back. It was an angel, one of the giant golden servitor robots that had roamed Boston as an AI enforcer. Decommissioned, screen dark. The eye logo she knew now belonged to Quietus, the anti-mutant coalition that had driven Boston into the ground, was lined with dirt in its forehead.

Why the fuck would Nate have sent her here?

Moth cast around for a second as if the trees would give her answers. When nothing came, she picked up her shovel again and dug deeper, under its neck.

The screen on its face lit up.

Moth screamed and smacked it with her shovel. This did less than nothing: it lifted a shining arm out of the dirt and latched it around her ankle. These things had laser eyes, didn't they?! She tripped immediately, kicking at it, ready to die.

There was a flash of bright light. The hand around her ankle went limp. Moth opened her eyes to find a searing beam of fire coming out of the fist of her best friend like a reverse-grip dagger.

Jaya straightened up, the fire by her hand quenching out.

Jaya was a mutant. Jaya was here. Jaya was staring at her like Moth was the one that had broken her heart, not the other way around.

Moth stumbled to her feet.

She wasn't sure if she wanted to scream at Jaya or hug her or cry. Instead, she said, "the radio," and pointed at the matching one hanging off Jaya's belt, whisper-beeping. "You came too."

"Of course I did, dumbass," Jaya said. Her voice was broken glass. "I don't—"

"Hey," said a voice, and she and Jaya spun around. "What are you doing digging up the angel graveyard?"

The person addressing them was dressed in a puffy winter jacket and had way too many eyes by human standards. "I'm Oracle."

"Moth," she said.

"Flame," Jaya said.

Moth glanced over at her. Jaya was frowning at her in surprise— probably that Moth was a mutant too, and she hadn't told Jaya. But then Moth couldn't help it— she snorted in laughter, genuine, bittersweet joy hitting her.

They matched. Even though they'd broken apart. Their powers matched, a silly little thing.

Jaya's frown wavered at the edges looking at Moth.

"Hi," said Oracle again, "the graveyard?"

Moth startled away from Jaya's searching eyes. Right. "Our friend told us to come here." She lifted the soft-speaking radio in her hand.

"Ohhh," said Oracle. "Sweet boy. A real shame, hm?"

Her stomach dropped. "What do you mean?"

They flinched. "Oh, it's not— right, okay, you've wrecked that body." They gestured behind Moth at the smoking guardian in the ground. "So we're in this timeline now."

"What happened to Nate?" Jaya pushed, angry.

Oracle raised their hands, stepping back. "I don't make a habit of changing the future, just reading it." Some of their many eyes blinked. "Badly."

"Okay," said Jaya, "but you clearly know something. Where is he?"

Oracle pointed. At first Moth thought it was at her, but then she realized it was specifically towards her pocket.

The radio had changed beats.

Instantly, Jaya was pulling out a notebook to transcribe, Moth crouching to train her light onto the pages. They murmured the letters in sync as they happened. Moth could smell Jaya's shampoo with how close she was, warm vanilla, and it made Moth think of kissing her.

> bldg 9 follow secret path. bring angel screen to
> angel here

Jaya finished transcribing the message; it began to repeat. She stared at it, her face lit from the reflection of Moth's flashlight off the notebook.

"We were fighting servitors," said Oracle. "There's one still there, it sounds like. A bunch of the mutants in this forest are from Nate's group."

"What do you mean, his group?" Jaya asked.

"The dorm house we all lived in— we got caught near a Goddess versus Michael fight. Almost got torched by lasers, instead we all got powers, like some kind of Goddess backwash."

It took a moment for this to sink in, and when it did, Jaya and Moth looked at each other again.

Nate was a mutant too. It felt illegal that both of her best friends were mutants and she'd found out months after the fact.

"We probably would've died over the next couple of months without his help," Oracle continued. "It's rough, suddenly going mutant in the middle of a Quietus hotbed halfway through the Dark Year. Nate organized us into a team, found ways for us to sneak past the checkpoint in little groups." Oracle shivered. "I hope I never have to walk on subway tracks again."

Moth tried to picture it: their nervous Nate, taking the helm in the middle of an active warzone. Of course, though, of course— Nate's quiet calm in moments of group panic, taking the wheel so no one else had to suffer. The way he'd pulled her into that changing room and held her hand.

"What's his power?" Moth asked.

"The most Goddess-y power of the bunch of us," Oracle said. "He'd been good with tech before, but now he could crack complex systems in seconds. We called him Flash, like how you rewrite a drive."

Moth's first thought was how great that would be for acing programming classes. Then she felt like a shithead for thinking it.

"He went back in again," Oracle said. "Most of us stayed here."

"But it's been two months since Michael fell," Jaya said. "None of you have bothered to find him?"

"Our house is gone," Oracle said, and some of their eyes were watery. "Blasted to dust. Some of us tried poking around, but there was still a rogue angel cluster over east campus."

"Isn't the school going to do something about it?" Jaya was furious. "Look for missing people?"

Oracle shrugged. "A lot of people went missing, including staff. Some got hurt, some got taken, some left. It's a mess. They're working through it slowly, and I don't blame them. And mutant relations are weird still— I take classes online, leave my camera off." Oracle frowned. "We were able to take down some of the servitors in the Dark Year, but." Oracle swallowed. "I just know there's now a pack of golden drones that haven't been letting anyone into the biometrics robotics building, no matter who you are. That's what Nate was going back in for."

They leaned in to Jaya's notebook and pointed at *angel here.* "Sounds like he's still fighting them."

"You said you were his friend," Moth said. "I can't believe you stopped trying to find him."

"Not all of us have fire fists or morse code clues," Oracle said, glancing between Jaya and Moth. "Good luck though, if you're going."

Why had Nate chosen to spend time with this person in school, who wouldn't go back for him? But Moth clamped down on meaner words. "Thanks for the info."

Jaya was already drilling the screen out of the dead angel to slip into her backpack. When Moth looked up from helping her pry it free, Oracle was gone.

"I've got the Range Rover," Jaya said, her mother's shining car, "but the Taurus might be better?"

"Yeah," Moth said. "Won't matter if the Taurus gets blown up by a rogue cluster."

As Jaya turned down the path back, Moth swore she saw another hint of a smile.

She wanted so badly to say something that would mend the gulf between them, or for Jaya to do the same. She didn't know what would encompass all of her messy feelings: the way Jaya felt unknowable now, the way Moth's lips still burned at the memory of the party. She'd give it up for a chance at what they'd been before, even though in retrospect she'd been ready to burst even then.

Instead she drove into the city in silence.

"Moth, huh?" Jaya said finally. "What, can you fly?"

"I wish," she said. She flipped a hand on the steering wheel rim as they paused at a red light, and a moth fluttered out of her skin as if emerging from a cocoon. She had it flutter over to Jaya's outstretched palm. Under the moth's feet, Jaya was warm.

"Gross," Jaya said, but she held it up close until all Moth could see was her wide dark eyes.

THE JOURNEY into Building 9 was filled with that same still-out-of-place feeling: Jaya knew where they were going, Moth didn't. Moth watched as Jaya pulled out a screwdriver to unhinge a metal panel from the wall next to a vending machine in the school building's basement, the fluorescents bright overhead even this late at night. Jaya seemed incredibly cool; Moth just felt nervous.

"Nate took me through this with him once, after I got in." Jaya said as she shone her phone's light into the guts of the building she'd revealed. "You go in first, so I can put the panel back after you."

Twinging with jealousy and her own inexperience, Moth crawled inside. She set her sneakers on the rings around a steam pipe, and, without waiting for Jaya, began to shimmy up it.

After minutes of crawling over pipes and vents, Jaya led her into a vent that opened out into the night sky. They both hauled themselves up onto a concrete roof, finding themselves in the center of campus on top of a big dome. The Charles river stretched like a lazy cat below them, and closer by, the bright lights of a construction crew worked to raise new walls around a gouge through three school buildings and a lawn.

The two of them sat on the edge of the domed roof for just a moment, looking out over the Charles. The rotting skyscrapers of Michael's mark on the skyline were stark blocks against the lights of a Fenway game in the distance, the ever-glowing Citgo sign closer by. The Charles river siren— a mutant who Quietus never managed to dislodge, and who was quickly becoming an elusive city mascot— was singing, voice clear over the water. Moth recognized it suddenly as a minor-key rendition of *Sweet Caroline*.

There was a different world where Jaya and Ellerie were sitting on Little Dome as themselves a year from now, all in regular classes, all scampering around the machine rooms of the school at night like regular felonious college kids with Nate leading them. Instead they were venturing into a construction zone harried by killer drones to save him, and Moth still didn't know if she'd have to move across the country for school after.

"I can't remember," Jaya said.

Moth looked over; there was a set in her jaw that Moth had interpreted as still being pissed with her. "I know after this we go back into a big vent," Jaya continued, "but I can't remember where to go after that."

Moth realized Jaya was close to tears, and suddenly felt horrible for missing it. She put her hand on Jaya's arm. "You said he just showed you one time. That's okay to not remember."

Jaya snatched her hand away. "It's not. El— what if he's hurt?"

"I have an idea," Moth said. "Show me to the vent, and I can find him."

MOTH SAT IN THE VENT, eyes closed, Jaya standing guard ahead of her. She sent a thousand little moths into a thousand rooms. One flapped towards the moon outside, buffeted by breeze. One crawled along a vent in between floors. One landed on the arm of a patrolling security guard.

And one landed on cold, smooth metal.

*Bring angel screen to angel here,* Nate's second message had said. She couldn't find flesh in that room, but maybe the angel here was all they needed to trigger the next step.

"I found it," she said, blinking her eyes open, "but there's a lot of little drones moving around still, and a big room with a human guard patrol."

"I can take care of that," Jaya said, standing. Her eyes lingered on Moth and the way her bugs were landing on her cheeks and arm, melding back into her skin. Was it weird?

But Jaya offered a hand. Moth thought about the way fire leapt from them now, then took it anyway. They were both weird now.

They paced along the line of the dome, then dropped down to another rooftop and skirted over to an access door. Moth pulled out a beat-up old plastic froyo loyalty card and used it to jimmy the plastic into the latchbolt until it could slide open. They slipped inside into a machine room humming with HVAC. This was what adventure felt like, Moth thought— this was what she'd been dreaming of for years, and it hadn't taken a stupid college admission to find.

Right as they reached a door across the way, the handle of it rattled. With a gasp Jaya pulled her away and into a narrow locker. Jaya had just gotten the locker closed when the room's door swung open and a security guard wandered in, her flashlight striping light through the locker slats onto Jaya's face.

They both held their breath. Moth was maybe imagining it, but she thought she could feel Jaya's heart thundering through her chest, pressed up against her own. Against her will she thought of kissing her again, how for a second the world was better than right.

The guard's footsteps were receding.

"Jaya," Moth whispered. "I missed you. I'm sorry I didn't text you for a month. My brain just stopped working after we didn't hear from Nate and after delayed admissions and after that— that party. But I did miss you—"

"Shut up," Jaya hissed, and Moth stared up at the ceiling of the locker in furious shame. She realized then that a light was playing through the slats again, that maybe Jaya had stopped her because the guard was on her way back. Seconds ticked by and Moth tried to make even her breathing as silent as possible.

Jaya reached over and found her hand. Jaya squeezed it.

Tears sprung to her eyes. There was no light shining through the slats anymore. They should keep going to find Nate.

"Go ahead, El," Jaya murmured after a moment, and creaked the locker door open. Then, to her back: "I missed you too."

TWO DRONES FRIED by Jaya's fists and many vent turns later, they finally made it to the little room her bug had found. Moth paused Jaya around the corner.

"We don't know if the angel there is online," she whispered. "If it's still controlling those drones. So we have to be ready."

"You mean me," Jaya said, but she was smiling. "Moths won't stop a servitor. I'll go first."

Moth didn't like that— didn't want two of her friends hurt by angels— but she didn't have a better idea. So Jaya took the lead.

What they found in the room instead was a golden servitor slumped against a table, tools spread everywhere. The room itself looked like a forgotten bathroom that had been half-demolished and swallowed by later construction; the dirty table was clearly a later addition, dragged in by whatever enterprising student had decided to turn it into a hidden workshop. The angel was missing its face screen, a cracked one lying on the ground, its glass shards shimmering in Moth's flashlight.

"Okay," Jaya said to the empty room. "What now, Nate?"

Nothing answered.

"Maybe we should attach the screen to this one?" Moth asked.

They set about doing so. It was simple, and working together with Jaya made it fast. As soon as they attached the video connectors the screen flickered to life in their hands and they both flinched.

The angel did not move.

Moth squinted down to find the screen displaying a command prompt. The background of it was the Quietus logo, but with a sharp line drawn through the eye. Fingers shaking, Moth typed a command to display the contents of the folder. There was a single movie file called *watchme*.

Jaya, looking at her, nodded. She hit play.

A light slivered out of the angel.

Not a laser— a projector. On the opposite concrete wall, half blocked by some of the dangling electrical wires, a recording began to play.

It was from the perspective of the angel, a camera zooming in flight over the Charles, skimming low over the campus. An active fight— a mutant on the ground was slugging glowing bubbles at the angel; the audio was peppered with the *dingdingding* of them bouncing off the angel's armor. A light flashed out from just below the camera and seared along the ground to hit the bubble-mutant. Bubbles shot no more.

Something else hit the angel from the side— there was a sound of motors whirring in overdrive even as the angel tilted and fell, crashing to the ground.

Shoes sprinted into view, a pair of beat black Converse Moth knew. "Nice aim," Nate said, and crouched down into view, familiar messy curls and bespectacled blue eyes like a shot to her heart. He peered into the camera, hands on either side. "I need ten seconds."

"Flash," said someone out of view breathlessly. "It's getting back up—"

The angel reached out through a sticky web coating it, grappling with Nate. The laser shot from the angel again and Nate dove so it only seared dirt, but fire was racing along the angel's body, burning off the web that had trapped it. "My leg!" screamed the other person. "It got my leg, I can't focus—"

The angel was on its feet again, turning towards the other person: a pale kid with great gobs of webs on their hands, clutching their left shin, now a smoking mess. They scrambled backwards along the ground as the angel advanced.

There was a thump from behind the camera and the angel tilted forward. Moth could see Nate's arm smushing over the camera, rumpled noises as the angel flipped him over its back. Nate landed on the ground, grimacing, but reaching up for the angel again.

The laser flashed bright enough to block out the screen. When it cleared, there was half a second of footage of a body falling to the ground, a close up on black Converse.

The footage flickered and went out.

Moth felt a tear roll down her cheek.

That— that wasn't possible. They'd come here to find Nate because he'd sent them a clue, one only he could've sent. This video made it look like he'd— *died. Months* ago.

Jaya's eyes were wide in the dark glow of Moth's phone. She swiveled to face the angel, then leapt toward it.

"This thing killed Nate!" She wailed, fire catching out her palms. "I'm gonna burn out its fucking guts!"

"Wait!" Yelled Moth— the light was pouring from the angel again, a second video. Tears streaming down both their faces, clutching each other, they watched.

Static across the screen, diagnostic lines of code blazing. The angel was crawling in a dark hallway. Words played across the screen, maybe internal to the angel's system: CODE MISMATCH DETECTED, UPDATE TO LATEST? Y/N?

The prompts vanished. Moth couldn't tell what had been selected.

The angel reached a metal access panel on the wall, peeled it off, and climbed inside.

Time skipped in a wave of static. Moth recognized this room, its distinctive giant fan blades only lit by some glow on the angel. AUTOMATIC UPDATES REQUIRED, flashed an alert again. A code prompt appeared and the user controlling it tried to disable automatic updates. They failed to enter a correct admin password, trying again.

AUTOMATIC UPDATES BEGINNING IN 5:59. The angel paused its crawling, then suddenly reached for a discarded metal pipe on the ground. The camera flailed wildly to the sound of scraping metal— Moth realized it was dragging the pipe over its own back.

Sweating, Moth leaned to look at the back of the angel in front of them. Sure enough: deep rusted gouges lay along the back of its neck, wires poking out as if something had been ripped out.

CONNECTION OFFLINE, the screen read, and the angel crunched computer chips in its hand. SWITCHING TO ALTER-NATE PROTOCOL FOR UPDATES...

In the video, the angel punched the ground. Quickly, in the dirt, it wrote with a finger.

*disable updates zigbee in chest*

The screen went dark.

Zigbee was a communication protocol like wifi and bluetooth— maybe the alternate one that the angel had been trying to access. Why would an angel try to disable its own updates? Moth shone her flashlight on the ground, and sure enough, the words were still outlined there in the dust, though smudged.

And there were more below it. Each line fresher than the last.

"Look," she said, and crouched down, Jaya's hand still in hers.

*10s after boot b4 connection attempts again*
*Trying to patch self*
*Kumquat kumquat kumquat*
*DO NOT CONNECT!*

How would the angel know their code word? Oracle had said Nate's power was being good with technology. *Give me ten seconds*, he'd said on the video. What had Nate been doing to it?

Moth stared at the prompt screen again. Below the edited Quietus logo, she realized there was dim text.

*Nathaniel Cluster v0.0.1*

A jolt ran through her like the angel had shocked her.

"Do you think he's..." Jaya said.

"We have to get the other connection devices out," Moth said, already running her fingers along the angel's chassis looking for how to get in. "There were some servitor blueprints posted on the Instructabot forums a couple weeks ago, can you pull them up?"

"I downloaded them when they dropped," Jaya said, shining her phone screen at Moth. "They use a fucking weird screwslot, but I 3D printed one." She fished a little torque wrench out of her pocket to pass to Moth, pointing at the joints with hidden screws.

With some amount of work, they had the angel's chest disassembled. It was a glittering forest of parts inside, densely packed chips and fans and pieces Moth had never seen before. She felt like a doctor, like this was the weirdest game of operation, like they were back in a long night up in the robotics lab at school before a competition.

"Do you remember," Jaya said, "when Benny spilled an entire glass of soda on our main bot the Thursday before the nationals?"

Moth smiled as she unscrewed another board. "The sound of it as it hit the inner fans. Splurt. Nyoooom. Our hopes and dreams dying."

"But Nate fixed it," Jaya said, voice thick. "He didn't even get mad, just got to work swapping out literally every piece we'd built that semester."

"We just can't mess this up," Moth said. "If we can take the transmitter out without messing anything else up— he wanted us to come here."

Jaya nodded. A tear from her face fell onto Moth's forearm.

After some time in the dark, they found the zigbee transmitter. Using Moth's utility knife heated to glow with Jaya's flames, Moth did the jankiest soldering job she'd ever done to take out the transmitter. In silence, they replaced the boards they'd moved to access the zigbee, then sat staring at the angel with its chest chassis still open.

"What do you think," Jaya said, "should we try to boot it?"

Moth nodded. Jaya pulled the keyboard onto her lap again and woke up the sleeping screen. It took them some time to figure out a command to boot in this unfamiliar system, but they eventually got to a dialogue. Moth hit the enter button.

The angel jerked.

They both jumped back, Jaya shifting ahead of Moth, flames springing to her fists.

"You," said the servitor, in a flat mechanical voice.

A light flicked on from the dome of its head, blinding Moth. It shone over them both.

"Mutants," it said.

Jaya stepped further in front of Moth and lifted her fists, fire crackling. "Is that a problem?"

"You," it said again. "You came."

Moth's heart twisted. "Nate?"

"Can't connect," it said.

"We took out the zigbee," Moth said, and stepped around Jaya and her twin flames. She reached a hand out to touch the cool metal of the servitor's head. "Nate, is that you?"

"Kumquat," Jaya said, with a thick, angry voice, "tell us what's going on."

The servitor lifted its golden hands up in front of it's screen. "Is this... all I am now?"

"Nate," said Moth again, now horribly sure, and moved forward to wrap her arms around the angel. "It's okay. We'll figure it out from here."

The angel's arms flew around Moth faster than she could respond, crushing her ribs. She gasped and threw herself backwards in a panic, worried she'd gotten it wrong. She couldn't free herself— but oh, it wasn't squeezing further.

The angel was making a noise. A single tone robotic wail.

If she thought hard, she could picture the sound Nate made when he cried, a prolonged whine. She went limp and leaned her head against him. Seconds later, Moth felt Jaya wrap arms around them both.

IT WAS 3:30pm on a Tuesday when Moth got her letter. *We apologize for the delay in processing applications,* she read, and flung her gaze to the next paragraph—

*We are excited to congratulate you on your acceptance...*

If it had been earlier this year, she would've sobbed with relief. Moth waited for tears to come, for anything— but no, she was just standing here. She set the letter down.

Moth drove over to Nate's place like she'd planned. It had been a few months since she and Jaya had dragged his new servitor body out of the guts of Building 9, and his family was adjusting. His parents weren't home when she pulled into the driveway— they'd been attending a "parents of mutants" support group. Moth figured it was hard to process when your son uploaded his consciousness into the machine that killed him.

It was proving hard to process for Nate too, in fits and starts. Instead of the warm shy kid he'd been, or the brave leader he'd become when Moth wasn't looking, he was now distant, uncertain, sharp.

"Before when I used my powers, it felt like the computers I hacked were parts of me," Nate said. He'd been working on a voice that sounded more like him; Moth had helped him find a bunch of his old videos to feed into a program for it. "I never told anyone that — it felt too much like cheating already to be that good at tech, never mind that I felt like I was making new extensions of myself every time I took over a system."

She and Jaya and Nate were laying on his bedroom floor like they'd used to. But now Nate had to fold his big golden legs up onto the side of his bed to fit, and Jaya had to lift her hands into the air when she got too sad or mad to avoid burning his rug. Moth kept her bugs to herself.

"So I thought when I was fighting that servitor, I had a chance of taking control of it. I'd been afraid before of pouring myself into something that big. And I'm still afraid, living inside it. Feeling out what it— what I— can do." Nate reached up to adjust his nonexistent glasses, an old habit; his golden fingers clinked into the screen over his face and then fell back to his side. "If I think about it too much— if I'm really myself, or if the real me died and I'm just a copy who *feels* like him— then I wanna throw up."

"I don't think you can throw up anymore," said Moth.

Nate made a noise that she thought was a little snort.

They'd spent a lot of time lying around like this at first after the rescue, both Jaya and Moth trying to put in the work to make sure Nate felt like himself as much as he could. But MIT had reinstated some in-person classes and Jaya was around less and less; Nate was being dragged to a mutant-specialized therapist by his parents. Moth was almost failing a couple classes, so the breaks were probably a good thing.

It felt nice to be all together again now, but as they neared spring finals season, it also felt like approaching a bigger ending. At one point Moth offered to walk to the corner store to pick up ice creams for her and Jaya, and when she got back, Jaya was hurrying downstairs into the kitchen.

"Oh," Moth said, "are you leaving? You said you wanted one."

"I know," Jaya said, "I don't really want one— it was an excuse to talk to Nate alone." She smiled, sad. "Sorry."

Moth felt suddenly uncomfortable, extremely aware of the two Choco Tacos melting in her hands. "I can put this in the freezer." For who? Nate wouldn't eat it.

"I wanted to talk to you alone too," Jaya said.

"I got into MIT," Moth blurted.

Jaya's eyebrows went up. "Hey," she said, "congrats."

"Yeah." This was nothing like it was supposed to have gone. The Choco Tacos were searing her hands with cold, getting mushy inside their plastic wraps. "Sorry, what were you going to say?"

Jaya sighed. "I kinda figured you were holding out. What I'm about to say stands even more though."

She took a step forward and put her hand on Moth's arm. "I care about you a lot," she started, but the tone of it was already *goodbye*. "I'm really glad we're talking again. I was an ass, ignoring you, but you didn't reach out to me either. And I've realized in the break that I just need a little space."

"What does that mean?"

"It's not that I don't want to be friends, or even that I don't like you... like that." Jaya swallowed. "I just want to know what else I can do. Who else I can be. I want that for you, too."

They both stood there, Nate's kitchen clock ticking overhead. Melted ice cream dripped from a hole in a wrapper onto Moth's sock.

The thing was, Moth had known this was coming. Pain, and understanding. Everything had changed around Moth's feet no matter how she'd fought to prevent that, and it would keep changing.

Months ago that would've crushed her. Now she thought she could chart a path through it, even though it hurt.

"I understand," she said. Maybe the tides of change would wrap around and bring Jaya back to her. Moth, Flash, Flame— they were all linked.

"Okay," said Jaya. She leaned forward, hesitated a second, then pressed her lips to Moth's.

Warm vanilla sugar, now with an aftertaste of smoke.

Moth kept her eyes closed when Jaya pulled away so she wouldn't have to see the look in her eyes as she left. Time passed in clear seconds, the kitchen clock tocking. Moth heard Jaya's car start up outside and pull away.

"You got the same speech too, huh?"

Moth opened her eyes to find Nate's golden armor filling the doorframe. "At least you got a goodbye kiss," he added, and lumbered over to sit next to Moth on a stool.

Moth's ears burned. It was harder to read Nate's new form, harder to know what to say when so many things hurt him.

"Did you know I always liked you too?" Moth said.

"You're using the past tense," Nate said.

Agh. Just because she was trying it more often, it didn't mean she was suddenly good with words. "I still— you're still Nate. I just don't know anything anymore. About our whole lives." The fact of her acceptance letter pressed up against the back of her teeth— but would telling Nate just remind him what he'd gone through?

It was hard to tell from Nate's screen where he was looking, but Moth thought it was at the floor. "I liked you too," he said. "Why would I keep coming back to visit on weekends if not? But sure, everything's different."

He didn't sound happy, and Moth felt like she'd bungled it.

Hurting him and Jaya before had only been patched through by an elaborate rescue mission, and Moth never wanted to go through something like that again. How could she say all the mess she felt?

Nate had always known what to say. She reached back in time, to a girl that hadn't known how to spew bugs or to scale a building for her friends, to a boy that hadn't sacrificed warm blood to save others.

"I hope you don't feel alone," Moth said. "I'm not going to forget about you."

Nate didn't say anything for a little while. But then he moved his cold, heavy fingers to rest over Moth's.

MOTH STILL HADN'T RESPONDED to her letter. She found herself driving to the twisting trees of the Fells, parking under a poplar that was still bright orange fall colors even though it was almost May. She sent moths out through the leaves until they landed on a many-eyed person deep in the woods.

"We found him," Moth said when she approached.

"I knew you would," said Oracle, smiling in a sweaty way.

Annoyance flashed in her. If Oracle could read the future, why hadn't they told her what would happen? And further— why had Moth gotten a stupid little bug power, rather than reading the future?

With future sight she would have gone to Nate before he'd gotten laser-fried and uploaded. With future sight she would've known not to mold her entire life around a goal that was never going to happen the way she thought it would. With future sight she would be able to pick a new goal now, one that was the *right* one, and not feel like she'd been set out to sea with no land in sight.

Moth took a shuddering breath.

"I came to ask about your remote classes," she said. "I think

Nate would like to go back to learning, but he's so used to helping other people that he can't ask for help himself. Can you meet back up with him and explain how you're doing it?"

Oracle's many eyes blinked. "I can do that."

Moth thought about asking them about herself. If she should go to MIT after all, if Jaya was going to leave her, if Nate was going to end up okay. Instead she traded numbers with Oracle to text them Nate's address.

Oracle handed Moth's phone back. "I'm glad we ended up in this timeline now," they said. "I've been looking forward to having you as a friend."

Unbidden, Moth recalled that freshman kid from the robotics team, how she'd drunkenly advised him to just try to be cool until you were, how he'd wanted a friend like her.

What was the future Moth like in Oracle's head? If Moth pictured it herself, maybe she could become it. Since the last time she'd seen Oracle, she'd done a lot herself: become her own mutant vigilante, rescued her friend. Caught a dream and held it in her hand, ready to let go.

"Well, cool," Moth said. "We can hang out sometime. I'm free tomorrow afternoon, if you want to have a picnic here."

"I haven't had a picnic in a while," Oracle said. "That'd be fun. I'll have you meet some of the other mutants here if you want."

After waving bye to Oracle, Moth found her feet taking her towards the tower, over the now re-buried dead servitor, up the circular concrete staircase. She ran her fingers over fresh graffiti and rounded onto the top.

The moon shone bright over the wild forest. Far in the distance, Moth could see the domes of the campus lit at night.

She flung her arms out, sending moths peeling from her skin. Their wings churned the cool night air and Moth felt it in herself, like leaning out a car window, the wind moving through her. Again she was a thousand wings in a thousand places: landing on the shoulder of a mutant in the forest below, touching the cool glass of

Nate's bedroom window, winging high over the dome where she and Jaya had sat on the roof.

She had never tried to fly a moth so far from herself. She felt the dome moth falter, alighting on the concrete edge of the building. But Moth knew now she had more in her— that maybe, if she tried, she could keep flying forever.

The moth lifted off again.

# Farsight

Another crisis averted, and now my tower is full of people. I'm not sure how it became a spot for congregation, rather than my lonely perch to look out on the world, but I find myself liking this. They remind me of a litter of puppies, constantly making noise and tangling themselves up with each other. How do you get to be so comfortable with a group of people? Do you have to go through terrible things to bond you all together, or is this something you can generate through desire for connection alone?

I've always been too prickly, too stand-offish, overly concerned with what others think of me, and judging their behaviour in turn. I've had colleagues and associates and acquaintances, but never someone I'd truly call a friend. Would that make me pitiful in the eyes of this group? I can't imagine they'd truly want to include me, but they've still chosen to all come *here*, and now Feral is handing me a beer.

"Thank you." I feel stiff and awkward, especially when she bats at me with her tail.

"Show us something pretty, Far." Dylan lounges in the window, staring out at the island.

"Really?" I shuffle towards the group, sipping at my beer. They're all clustered at the window, completely blocking my view.

"Yeah, we're always looking for problems and crises. There have to be good things."

"Excuse me." I nudge my way through the group until I'm

standing in the middle of them. Below me, the island looks impossibly beautiful, unreal blues and greens painted by nature herself. It is a jewel, sparkling with life. I want to tell them that they'll never see anything more beautiful than this place—or even each other. That they should treasure what they have, because it's impossibly precious.

But they know this. They're looking outwards, because they want a better world.

All they want is a sign, and I'll show them one.

Mutants, living in the world. Thriving and looking after each other.

They must be somewhere out there.

# *Vibe Check*

## CHARLOTTE HAYWARD

IT'S WHAT PEOPLE SAY ABOUT ANY LIFE-SHATTERING disaster – you hear about it on the news, but you never expect it to happen to you.

My personal disaster wasn't cancer, or a car accident, or a freak flood that washed away everything I loved. No, the thing that broke my life beyond repair was sodding superpowers.

I'm past the worst of it, though. I've had the meetings with supervisors, counsellors, even the university dean. I've had the tearful 2am arguments outside the Student Union with friends who couldn't understand why I was dropping out, even as the weight of their feeling made my head feel ready to burst. I've torn down the photo collage I spent a whole afternoon painstakingly tacking up, and boxed up all the bedding and saucepans I unpacked with so much hope six short months ago.

I've even had the breakup.

And I've only had this bloody mutation a week.

Things have to get better from here, right?

I lean against the window, the cool glass soothing my headache as I watch the blurry outlines of fir trees slide by. The same five

291

mournful love songs as always are playing on repeat on *Magic Radio*, and Mum's in the driver's seat beside me, nattering away about how excited everyone is to have me back.

It feels like any other weekend drive home, if I stay facing forwards so I don't see the cardboard boxes heaped on the back seat – my entire life, all my dreams of a fresh start, neatly wrapped in newspaper. I might be able to ignore the boxes, but no matter how high I crank the volume on *Total Eclipse of the Heart*, I can't blot out the *other* reminder of the hellscape my life's become.

I know exactly what Mum's feeling.

The waves of anxiety coming off her are jarringly at odds with the relentless tide of enthusiasm bubbling from her lips. She glances over at me, mouth pinched into a too-tight smile, and turns the radio down a notch.

"Oh, Melly. I know you're disappointed with how things worked out, but it's not all bad! Try to look on the bright side."

*Disappointed* doesn't begin to cover it.

How would you feel if you woke one morning to a maelstrom of excitement, stress, exhaustion and ennui, so overpowering you couldn't tell where your own feelings ended and your flatmates' began? How would you feel if your fresh start, everything you'd spent your entire school career working to achieve, was shattered overnight because some quirk of fate transformed you into a radio receiver tuned to the emotions of everyone in a hundred-metre radius?

How would you feel if you knew with *absolute certainty* that your girlfriend of three years didn't love you any more?

Mum's still chattering away, eyes back on the road, but it's hard to focus on her cheery words when I'm being buffeted by her tiredness and trepidation. Her new wariness around me coaxes out my own worries about returning home, until I lose track of where my fears end and hers begin – a feedback loop that quickly becomes too much to bear.

"Mum, *please*," I snap, making her jump. "Can you... I don't know, worry a little more quietly? You're giving me a headache."

That's all it takes for her background-level fretting to spiral into painful, flustered panic.

I flinch, turning back to the window and peering into the darkness. "Ugh, Mum, you're making it worse. Just focus on the road."

She's silent as we turn off the motorway, but her guilt crashes over me in relentless waves. I risk a glance at her as we pass under a streetlight, and immediately wish I hadn't. Her cheeks are flushed, her eyes teary.

"Sorry, honey," she whispers. "This is going to take some getting used to."

I lean against the window and close my eyes. "Yeah. For you and me both."

WHEN I WAKE the next morning, my mind's quiet, and for one brief, wondrous moment I think I dreamt the whole thing – that I'll open my eyes and find myself back in my cluttered dorm room in Nottingham, a "good morning" text from Amy waiting on my phone. But instead of the discoloured magnolia paint, Artex swirls and slow-blinking fire alarm that have come to feel like home, I find myself facing the blu-tack-speckled ceiling of my childhood bedroom, and it all comes back to me in one horrible, breathless rush.

There's no more Amy. No more Nottingham. And the green and pleasant patch of suburban hell I spent the last four years plotting my escape from is, once again, "home".

Yeah, things really can't get much worse.

On the plus side, my bedroom's far enough away from the rest of the house that I'm alone with my own feelings for the first time in a week. Small mercies.

My respite from this curse of a mutation doesn't last long. The moment I leave the sanctuary of my attic bedroom, I'm bombarded with a heady cocktail of excitement and worry, tinged with a hint of sorrow. The nervous component builds as I descend the stairs – from me or my family, I'm not sure. Maybe both. I wince as I hit the creaky spot on the fourth step down, because apparently being away for six months means I've forgotten how my own house works, and wince even harder as the anxiety in the kitchen flares in response.

The kitchen's filled with noise and chatter, but the moment I step through the door the room falls silent. Two sets of nervous brown eyes – and one wide, thrilled pair of blue ones – turn in my direction.

"Melanie!" my youngest sister – she of the blue eyes – squeals, leaping up from her seat and barrelling across the tiled floor to greet me. She throws her arms round my waist with a force that almost knocks me off balance. Or perhaps it's the joy bursting out of her that sends me reeling – a sense of delight, of *rightness* so strong it overpowers every other feeling in the room, including my own trepidation. She squeezes me tight, enveloping us both in a cosy, happy bubble, and I feel a small smile creeping onto my face.

She pulls back, still beaming, her happiness crashing over me – but what she says next makes my grin falter.

"Is it true? Are you a mutant now? What's your power? Does this mean we're gonna go live with the Cute Mutants?"

A dismissive scoff cuts through her barrage of questions, and there's a flare of irritation at the breakfast table. I don't need to look up to know who it came from – there's only one person I know who exists in such a perpetual, seething state of simultaneous jealousy and overinflated self-worth.

"Don't be stupid, Olivia," my middle sister drawls. I can't help wincing. Lucinda and I are less than two years apart in age and we've fought like cats from the moment she could walk, but I'd hoped that given the circumstances, she'd show me some sympathy. Apparently she had other ideas.

"There's no way Melly would pass the Cute Mutants vibe check," she says. "They're badasses who aren't afraid of anything, and Melly... well, she's scared of everything."

My heart stutters, and I'm not sure if it's a reaction of my own or a secondary response to the sudden spike of tension in the room. Nobody says anything to contradict Lucinda, though.

"I am *not* scared of everything," I mumble, glaring defiantly at my fluffy socks.

A waft of smugness. "Keep telling yourself that. I'm not the one who got one of the most basic, entry-level powers, and got so freaked out I had to quit uni." She glances up from her phone to give me a nose-wrinkled once-over, then narrows her eyes like she's found me lacking. "I mean, look at you! You got off *so* lightly – no weird horns, no extra limbs, nothing! Just the same sad Melly." She smiles to herself, as if remembering something. "Pity, really. There's this mutie boy at school who's got these spines down his back, and he curls up in a spiky ball when he's startled, exactly like a hedgehog, it's *hilarious* –"

"Lucinda, don't use that word," Mum interrupts. Both her voice and the emotions crackling around her are deadly serious.

"Why not? Everyone at school says –"

"I don't care what everyone at school says." She sets a bowl down firmly on the table, its clink punctuating her words. "You are not to use that word under this roof. Melanie's been through enough as it is."

I shuffle numbly across the kitchen and take my seat, too caught up in the internal whirlwind of self-deprecation Lucinda's kicked off to pay much attention as Mum pours me some granola and hands me a tub of yoghurt.

It's stupid, really. It's not like I'd even want to be a member of the Cute Mutants.

Well, okay, maybe in the darker, lonelier moments of the last week, I've thought about it. Perhaps, as I tore the grinning photos of Amy and I down from my pinboard, I imagined Chatterbox emerging from some glowing portal and holding a hand out to me. Perhaps I grumbled *that'd show her* as I tossed the long-distance train tickets I'd been saving for an anniversary scrapbook into the bin. But they were only fleeting thoughts, I swear. It's not like I've come up with a mutant codename or anything.

Mum's sharp voice and barely-holding-it-together patience cut through my thoughts, jolting me out of my brooding.

"Hurry up and *eat*, Melanie, we've got places to be," she says, pushing the untouched bowl of granola towards me. "I've got you a trial shift at Oak House, and they want you there for ten."

I frown at her. "Oak House? The old people's home on the hill?"

"*Yes*, the care home. I got chatting to Kirsty's mum at the PTA meeting last Thursday and mentioned you were coming back, and when she heard about your power she got *very* excited. They're desperate for staff, and it'll do you good to get out and about rather than moping around here all day, so we agreed we'd get you started as soon as!"

"Mum, I –" I don't know where to start. She obviously knows she's messed up, because the moment I open my mouth, the relentless enthusiasm she's spent the last thirty seconds battering me with fades into the background, superseded by a fresh wave of guilt-flavoured worry. I fight through her tornado of concern and find my words. "You can't just go around telling people I'm a mutant! What if she'd been a follower of one of the extremist groups that splintered off Michael's rotting corpse? Hell, how do you know she *isn't* in one of those groups? Or had you forgotten the vast majority of the world *still don't like us?*"

She jerks back, her guilt and her voice rising ever higher. "Don't be ridiculous. It's the Shermans, we've known them for almost a decade! I hardly think they'd associate with... with those types. Things like that don't happen round here."

"Are we talking about the same town? The place where Amy

and I couldn't walk down the High Street holding hands without being glared at? Of course there are people like that here. Why do you think I've spent the last four years trying to get *out* of this dump?"

Her expression hasn't changed, but the guilt's subsiding, giving way to irritation. I've pushed it too far.

"I don't have time to have this argument with you, Melanie," she says, turning away. "Finish your breakfast and get dressed. You're going to Oak House."

AN HOUR later and I'm wedged into a broom closet, wedging *myself* into a stiff blue uniform and wondering why the hell I agreed to this. Well, no, I know exactly why I agreed to this – because the alternative was being stuck at home with a bored, irritable Lucinda.

It takes me longer to get changed than it probably should, thanks to the uniform being both too tight and starched to within an inch of its life. At least my mutation means I feel the approaching cloud of apprehension before its owner reaches me, giving me a few seconds' warning to finish squeezing into the navy trousers.

The knock's soft and hesitant, the voice that follows even more so. "Everything alright in there?"

"Yep, sorry, just coming!" I wedge my trainers back on, give the tunic one last half-hearted tug downwards, and open the door to reveal –

Well.

A girl in a matching blue uniform stands before me, fist raised and far too close, as if she was about to knock again. She's a few inches shorter than me, with silver-grey curls pulled back off her face in some kind of intricate French plait. She looks about my age, so I'd think it was an e-girl-esque dye job, if not for the fact that her skin's a dark blue-grey, like the evening sky just before a squall hits. Her cheeks are spattered with raindrop-like freckles, and miniature stormclouds dance in her eyes.

There's also the slight complicating factor that as I swing the door open to meet her, I sense a flicker of… *interest*. Attraction-type interest.

What I couldn't say for certain is whether it came from her or from me.

We stare at each other, a blush the colour of thunderclouds rising to her cheeks.

"Hi," she says, and bites her lip. Which gets me thinking about her lips, how they've got this faint shimmer on them like rainwater, and – *goddamnit, Mel, the cute girl's talking to you, focus.* "I'm Tempest. They asked me to, um, show you to the new unit?"

"Oh, yeah, of course," I say. She finally steps back, leaving behind an earthy scent like fresh air after a storm, and I awkwardly scramble out of the cupboard and into the laundry room. I hold out a hand to her like some goddamn Tory fresher on orientation day, before coming to my senses and stuffing it in the pocket of my tunic with an awkward nod. "I'm Mel. Melanie."

There's a spike in anxiety from the storm-skinned girl, and she smooths back her already perfect braid. "Right. Melanie. My name's not really Tempest, of course, it's Jess, I just thought –"

"Hey, it's cool, don't worry about it," I say, offering a reassuring smile – and only partly because I want to snap her out of her anxiety-spiral before it starts giving me a headache. There's something about this girl that makes me want to soothe her nerves, to reassure and befriend her. Maybe it's because she's the first mutant I've met in person. Maybe it's just that she's very, very pretty.

I clear my throat. "So Tempest's, like, your mutant name?"

The flush on her cheeks deepens, and the awkwardness creeping towards me makes my skin crawl. "Yeah," she says. "It's silly, I know. I'm probably being really cringe, but... they told me you were a mutant too."

Jesus. Is there *no* sense of privacy in this town?

"You're the first mutant I've met who's my age," Tempest continues, fiddling with the star-shaped charm on her necklace. "I've been wanting to try out the codename thing for ages, and I thought... I don't know. It was a stupid idea."

"It isn't stupid at all! I think Tempest's an awesome name."

She looks up at me, eyes brightening. She's smiling shyly, and beneath her embarrassment, beneath her anxiety, there's a glimmer of what feels like hope. "Really?"

"Yeah, it's cool. Like the Shakespeare play, right? *What's past is prologue.*" My inner literature geek jumps out before I can stop it – god, she's going to think I'm such a nerd.

But she just beams at me. "You got it!"

I find myself smiling back. "So I'm guessing your power's something to do with storms?"

She nods enthusiastically. "Yep! I can do this –" She waves a hand in the air, and suddenly there's a loaf-sized cloud floating in the middle of the laundry room, hissing tiny sparks of lightning. There's a momentary downpour concentrated over a small square of tiles, and then the cloud dissipates with a tinny boom of thunder.

"It's not much," Tempest says, with another surge of embarrassment, "but it comes in handy. I use them to clean up spillages, mop the floors – and I've been trying to work out how to make tropical stormclouds, so I can give the residents warm showers."

I stare at the patch of air where the cloud used to be. I can still smell the rain. "Are you kidding? That was incredible!"

Her embarrassment rises again, but this time it's tinged with pride. "You really think so?"

"Yeah. Seriously. It's *so* much cooler than mine."

I realise it's the wrong thing to say before her eyes widen, before I feel the flare of curiosity. "I'm sure yours is great too! What is it?"

This time, I'm certain the sickly embarrassment in the pit of my stomach is all mine. "It's really not," I mumble, staring at the floor. The tiles are polished to a shine that makes my once-white trainers look ridiculously tattered and grubby. "I'd rather not talk about it, if that's okay. I'm... still adjusting."

The pang of guilt that hits me is so strong it almost knocks me back. I look up to see a cluster of black clouds gathering over Tempest's head, these ones darker and far less friendly-looking than the first.

"I'm sorry," she stammers. "I didn't mean to push you."

I offer her a shrug. "Hey, how were you supposed to know?"

A couple of the stormclouds drift away from her, and the guilt-barrage softens a little.

"We're all good, I promise," I say, coaxing my voice into something encouraging. With every word, the sadness around her fades back into that low-level hope, so I know I'm on the right track. I keep chattering, and once the clouds have all but vanished, I step back and give her a smile. "Come on. Let's get this trial shift over with."

TEMPEST LEADS me into a small new-build unit off the side of the main building, and through to a brightly-lit sitting room. Squashy green armchairs are dotted around the room, and French doors open out onto a garden bordered by fat, leafy hedges. Two white-haired ladies are locked in a battle of wits over the chess table, while a bald man dozes in an armchair in front of the television.

There's also an old man bumping against the ceiling, giggling as he bobs towards the open window. With his neat white beard and burgundy dressing gown, he looks like he's stepped – or should that be floated? – straight out of *Mary Poppins*. And when I look closer at the ladies playing chess, I realise neither of them are picking up their pieces – they're walking across the board by themselves.

"That's Doris' illusion power," Tempest says, pointing to the table. "She sets up a different game every day – it's saved us a fortune in board games. Keeps Brenda from getting bored and shifting into her bear-form, too. The last time she did that she ate all the Fish Friday suppers and destroyed Doris' favourite quilt, so we do our best to keep her occupied." She tilts her head towards the ceiling. "And that's Frank," she adds, with an indulgent smile. "Don't mind him. He's just vibing."

I don't know where to look. My eyes dart between the man on the ceiling, the bickering ladies at the chess table, and the woman with a greenish tint to her leathery skin who's just wandered in from the garden, carrying a radish the size of my head.

I feel like I've stepped into a parallel universe.

"Morning, Jessie!" the woman with the mega-radish says cheerily, plonking it down in an empty armchair. "This must be the new recruit."

Tempest nods. "Winifred, this is Mel. Mel, welcome to Oak House's very own mutant squad."

"I –" I shake my head. "I don't understand. What is this place?"

There's a gentle waft of amusement from both Tempest and Radish Lady Winifred. "Why did you think Mrs Sherman was so keen to recruit you? Mutants are springing up across the world, powers manifesting in people of all different ages, and some of them are frailer than others."

"Frail?" Winifred scoffs. "Speak for yourself, dear."

There's a flare of affection from Tempest. "Either way, some people's families or existing care placements couldn't cope once their powers manifested," she continues. "Oak House saw a gap in the market, both for temporary accommodation while our residents get used to their mutations, and for more permanent placements. And, well, here we are. The UK's first care home for mutants."

I don't need my power to detect the flush of pride Tempest feels as she tells me all about Oak House's latest venture. It's written across every inch of her body. She loves her work – she cares about what she does, about the residents here, and spending time with them makes her happy.

And as Winifred winks at me and I hear Frank chuckle from the ceiling, I catch myself wondering if it might make me happy, too.

TEMPEST and I laugh almost non-stop all shift – even in the more chaotic moments, like when I drop a soup bowl at lunch and startle the bald man, Norman, from his snooze. The moment his eyes snap open, every metal object in the room rockets over to orbit around his shiny head, making him look like a much smaller, grumpier Saturn. We get my keys, Tempest's bobby pins and various paper-clips and spoons unstuck easily enough once Norman's recovered from his rude awakening, and he forgives me before I've even given him my special emotion-guided grovelling apology. Still, I make a mental note never to wear metal jewellery to work.

By the time 8pm rolls round, I'm exhausted, but my cheeks hurt from smiling. It's not that I've forgotten my mutation – its spectre has hovered over me all day, both in the bittersweet, faintly amused emotions of the residents and in the fog of guilty curiosity that flared up around Tempest each time we started a new task, like she was certain this was the moment I'd reveal my power. I felt a little bad about the inevitable surge of disappointment that followed, but that's just guilt-overspill from her, right? I mean, I barely know the girl, and it's not like I'm *lying* to her. I'm just… choosing to withhold information.

Either way, minor guilt-feedback-loops aside, I'm the happiest I've felt all week. My shoulders and knees ache from all the bending and lifting I've been doing, but it's a *good* kind of ache, a reminder that I've spent the day doing something useful instead of sulking in my room and avoiding the world.

I find my way back to the laundry and wrestle out of the starchy uniform, and am heading along the wide, blue-carpeted corridor towards the exit when Mrs Sherman emerges from her office. Tempest stands a few steps behind her, beaming and awash with excitement.

"It's good to have you back in town, Melanie," Mrs Sherman says, with a tired smile that comes nowhere close to her eyes. I'm not getting much from her emotion-wise – just hunger and exhaustion, which I could've figured out without the help of my supposed *superpower*. "We've been so short-staffed, and Jess tells me you did a brilliant job today. You've passed your trial shift."

"With flying colours!" Tempest pipes up from inside the office, her entire form glowing with pride. I smile back at her. It's not like I expected to fail, with the world's softest stormcloud as my supervisor, but it's nice to hear some praise after spending the last week feeling like I can't get anything right.

Mrs Sherman notices my smile, and claps her hands together. "Wonderful. So, when can you start?"

I WIND up going back the very next day.

Only because I need to escape Lucinda's Easter-holiday-boredom wrath, of course. It's nothing to do with how, after I got the news from Mrs Sherman, I couldn't wipe the smile off my face the entire blustery forty-minute walk home (I could've got the bus, but I didn't fancy being shrouded in a claustrophobic fug of boredom and frustration and goodness only knows what else after I'd actually had a nice day). It's *certainly* nothing to do with a silver-haired, storm-skinned girl.

Still, I can't deny how my heart soars as I step into Oak House's kitchen, dressed in my slightly roomier but still terribly starchy uniform, and see her break into a delighted grin. Happiness blooms out of her like crocuses bursting from the ground after a cold winter.

It's just the aftershocks of her happiness making my heart flutter an excited beat of its own, nothing more. Still, I have to admit it feels nice.

The day passes in much the same way as the previous one. Once everyone's up and dressed and breakfasted, Tempest and I clear the plates and retreat to the kitchen together, so she can fill me in on all the Oak House gossip while we're washing up.

I dump my handful of plates in the sink and reach for the tap, but she bats my hand away before I can turn it on. My skin tingles a little as the side of her hand brushes mine, which must be another part of her mutation, right? A little jolt of lightning jumping from her skin to mine?

"Hang on," she says. "There's something I've been wanting to try for ages."

She waves her hand, and two swirling grey clouds appear inside the industrial steel sink. They rumble gently, flickering with sparks, and then they both erupt with rain. Freezing droplets of water spatter onto my palms.

I smile at Tempest, at the thrill of satisfaction radiating out from her, and pick up the sponge. My hands are trembling with cold by the time I've finished rinsing the plates, but I press on, buoyed up by Tempest's excitement.

I pick up a butter knife, and a tiny fork of lightning jumps from the right-hand cloud and grounds itself on the back of my hand.

I drop the knife in shock, snatching my hand back as it clatters into the sink. The clouds vanish in an instant, Tempest's pride warping into panic.

"Oh god, I'm so sorry!" she says, and I can *feel* her flapping even before I turn round to look at her. Her face is stricken, guilty tears welling in those thunderous grey eyes as she takes my hand in hers to inspect the damage.

"It's fine," I say. And it *is*. The shock of it was far worse than the actual pain – there was a momentary twinge, like burning your fingers on a candle flame, but that sensation's already fading.

"Sorry," Tempest murmurs, turning my hand over like she's searching for evidence of her own wrongdoing. "I should've realised – I've tried it a few times by myself, but the lightning never hurts me. I didn't think…"

"Tempest, seriously, it's fine. It didn't even hurt, I was just surprised!"

Tempest shakes her head and turns away, her sadness swelling outwards as a dark cloud bubbles up above her head. "Let's stick to the normal way of doing things from now on. It's safer for everyone that way."

She floats anxiously in my periphery for the rest of the morning, shrouded in a cloud of self-accusation so thick that none of her usual sunbeams break through, no matter how many times I reassure her that I'm okay. She's still trapped in her self-loathing spiral when the lunch trolley arrives, and I'm trying not to snap at her, but the neverending guilt-storm is starting to give me a headache.

"Stop worrying about me, I'm fine," I grumble as we dish up the lunches. "Look, it hasn't even left a mark! I've had beestings that hurt worse."

She shrugs as she scoops an extra dollop of mash onto Frank's plate. "I'm not worrying. I'm totally over it," she mumbles, avoiding my gaze.

The sulky guilt-fug shrouding her says she most definitely has not.

I roll my eyes as I slop beef stew onto the next plate, then turn to her with a scowl.

"Why are you lying to me?" Maybe it's a side-effect of the mopiness that's been seeping out of her all morning, but the words come out far snappier than I intended, and my stomach twists as she winces. I sigh, and soften my voice. "Come on, you're obviously still upset about it –"

Her eyes flash with lightning. There's a thunderclap of anger, followed by a splatter of mashed potato as she dumps her ladle in the metal tray with trembling, furious hands.

"Why are *you* still pushing this?" she snaps, dark clouds rising from her shoulders. "I told you, I'm fine. Why can't you drop it?"

I open my mouth to respond, then realise I can't. Not in the way I want to, at least. I want to say I know she's not over it, that her misery's been seeping into my bones all morning, leaving me with stomach-churning guilt and a throbbing headache. But that would involve telling her about my power, and I *can't*. I can't bring myself to ruin this burgeoning friendship, or whatever it is that's growing here. I can't bear the thought of her looking at me the way Amy looked when I told her, of feeling the panic, the fear, the *oh-shit* horror of scrolling back through the last 24 hours and realising exactly how much I knew.

So instead, I shrug, mutter "If you say so," and ladle some more stew onto Winifred's plate.

It's only when she hunches her shoulders and stomps off towards the kitchen that I realise that maybe, in *not* telling her the truth, I've wound up spoiling our friendship anyway.

Tempest and I barely speak for the rest of the shift. I spend the afternoon in the garden with Winifred, marvelling as she harvests metre-long sticks of rhubarb and hefts them into the sitting room without breaking a sweat. She tells me she's always loved gardening, but when her power manifested she got overexcited and grew a marrow so big it knocked down the back wall of her kitchen. She was the first resident to move into Oak House's new mutant wing, a few months back, but she's learned to temper her power since then. She was only meant to be here until they finished fixing her kitchen, but she liked it so much she decided to stay for good. These days, she busies herself with tending the garden, and grows enough fruit and veg to keep the entire town in rhubarb crumble.

I enjoy sinking into the feeling of rain on my face and dirt beneath my fingers as I help Winifred gather her latest crop, but I also have an ulterior motive for weathering the on-off April showers all afternoon - the bottom of the garden's the only place in the new wing that's out of range of Tempest's seething emotions.

Even as Winifred and I dig through the dirt, I can't stop myself looking up at the French doors every few minutes. Tempest bustles back and forth inside, carrying mugs of tea and freshly-laundered towels, a grumbly grey cloud floating in her wake. She casts occasional glances out the window, watching Winifred and I work, but whenever I catch her eye she turns away, shoulders hunching. The pangs of worry from Winifred let me know I'm not the only one who's realised something's amiss.

"She started it," I grumble after Tempest gives me a particularly pained look through the rain-spattered glass. "If she'd just *admitted* she was still upset, this would never have happened."

A flare of sadness from Winifred. "I've known Jessie for almost four months now, and if there's one thing I've learned about that girl, it's that she's proud. She reminds me of my daughter in that way. She's worked hard to master her powers, and I'll bet she didn't want you to know how anxious her little accident earlier made her feel." She pauses to tug rhubarb from the earth. "And yet, despite her attempts to brush it off, you refused to be fooled by her unconvincing little act." Winifred smiles. "She's not annoyed at you, not really. She's annoyed at herself for not doing a better job of hiding her fears."

I sigh, and sink down on my knees into the wet grass. "I can't help it. I don't *want* to know all her inner anxieties, but..." The words slip from my mouth before I've fully realised what I'm saying. "It's my mutation. I can sense the emotions of people close to me – no, more than that, I feel them like they're my own, and the stronger the feelings are, the more overwhelming it gets. They give me headaches and make me all shaky, but I can't figure out how to switch it off." I shrug, and meet her olive-green eyes. "Trust me, if I knew how to temper my power like you have, I absolutely would've done it by now."

307

There's a sudden burst of affection, tinged with a slight sadness. Winifred's warm, callused hand caresses my shoulder.

"Oh, sweetheart," she says. "Why don't you tell her? She wouldn't want to cause you any hurt."

I shake my head briskly, blinking back tears at the wave of compassion that just washed over me. "I can't," I mumble. "My ex, my family, everyone else I've told… they don't understand. It freaks them out, the idea that I'm constantly aware of what they're feeling."

A spark of amusement twists through her empathy. "And these people you told, were any of them mutants?"

I bite my lip, but shake my head again.

"Well then, don't you think maybe it'll be different this time?" She chuckles softly. "Trust me, if there's anyone who's going to understand that these mutations can be both blessing and curse, and that we all have to come to terms with them in our own time, it's the people in that room. Give her a chance."

The warm, comforting pull of her compassion is too strong to resist. I relax into it, letting the calming feeling spread through me. *Maybe she's right. Maybe everything will turn out okay, if Tempest only allows me time to explain…*

"Tomorrow," I say, with a firm nod. "I'll let her cool off this afternoon, spend tonight figuring out how best to explain everything, and I'll tell her tomorrow."

Winifred's callused thumb rubs against my shoulder. "Wise girl," she says. "Things always look better in the morning."

THE NEXT MORNING, I rise half an hour earlier than normal, smudge some lipgloss and eyeliner onto my face, and attempt to twist my hair into a French plait rather than its usual scraggly ponytail.

None of that's for Tempest, though. I just fancied a change. As a matter of fact, I've barely thought about Tempest since our argument yesterday lunchtime. I definitely didn't stay up until 2am drafting believable-but-suitably-grovelling excuses in my notes app.

Besides, like I said, I barely know the girl. If I give my big speech and she recoils like Amy did, it'll probably bounce right off me.

Probably.

I walk into the Oak House Mutant Squad sitting room with an overly-jovial spring in my step and a smile plastered on my face, and find the place in utter turmoil.

The dining table's upended, chairs scattered around it. Winifred, Doris and Norman are hurrying back and forth along the corridor where the residents' rooms are, waving their arms around in front of them. Frank zooms across the ceiling, shouting "Come out, it's okay, we're not going to hurt you!"

Tempest and Brenda are nowhere to be seen.

Just as I'm about to call up to Frank and ask what on earth is going on, a brown bear bursts through the French doors.

I yelp and jump backwards, my panic only amplified by the seething anxiety coming off the residents. None of them seem to be remotely startled by the bear that's leapt into their midst, though – or maybe they can't see it? They're still shuffling up and down the far corridor, holding their arms out like they're worried they're going to bump into something.

The brown bear cocks its head to one side and makes a soft rumbling noise. A gust of gentle concern washes over me, and as my terror settles into the new feeling, I notice the long string of pearls hanging around the bear's neck.

"*Brenda?*" I whisper. The bear makes a strange coughing sound that sounds almost like a laugh, but before I can ask whether her bear-ness is what's got everyone so worked up, a tidal wave of apprehension crashes over me from behind – followed moments later by a cautious tap on my shoulder.

I whirl round to find Tempest, wringing her hands and awash with anxiety. A black cloud trails in her wake, bigger than any she's summoned before and seething with unspent lightning.

"Have you seen Ernie?" she asks, desperation shining in those stormy eyes.

I frown. "Ernie?" The name sounds vaguely familiar, but I can't place it. "Who's Ernie?"

Tempest chews her lip, shuddering as the downpour from her angry little cloud strengthens. "He's the new resident." Of course. In all the angst of yesterday afternoon, I'd completely forgotten about our planned new arrival. "He arrived late last night, and I thought everything was okay, but this morning, I was laying out breakfast, and he just vanished! We've been searching for the last half-hour, and I thought bear-Brenda's sense of smell might help, but we still can't find him and now his son's on the phone and..." She sags, and the cloud hanging over her head rumbles darkly as I'm hit with a wave of despair.

I rush to her side and lay a hand on her shoulder, squeezing tight. I'm just about able to suppress my shudder as a drop of freezing rain spatters against my exposed skin.

"Hey, it's alright," I say, and relax into the tiny glow of comfort that began weaving through her panic the moment I touched her arm. I squeeze her shoulder again, coaxing the feeling out of her like I'm cupping my hands around a tiny flame. "He can't have gone far. What's his power again?"

She sniffs. "Invisibility."

"Right." Invisibility. I can work with that. I force a smile for Tempest, a plan already taking shape in my mind. "Leave it to me. I think I know how we can find him."

She shakes her head, her guilty sorrow redoubling its efforts to stamp out any trace of hope. "We've searched the whole place, Mel, he's not here. He could be anywhere in town by now."

Her black cloud fizzles ominously, and I drop my hand from her shoulder. The last thing we need is another mini-lightning strike sending her into even more of a panic.

"Just let me try this," I say. "If I can't find him, we'll take the search out into town."

She nods and wipes her eyes, a momentary glimmer of hope peeking through the gloom. "Okay. Do what you have to do."

I step away from her writhing vortex of panic, moving towards the centre of the room, and close my eyes.

I feel Brenda's concern, twisted with curiosity, a few short steps away. I feel Norman's growing restlessness and Doris' ever-expanding worry as they search the bedrooms down their end of the complex. I catch a brief flash of Frank's excitement as he whizzes over my head, and then it fades away, trailing along to the opposite end of the long corridor.

And there's something else. Something desperately, painfully sad.

I open my eyes.

"He's outside," I say. "Round the side of the building, near the bins, I think."

Tempest's gaping at me. Her cloud vanishes with a pop, which I suppose is progress, but she's still not *happy*. She's baffled, her bewilderment flavoured with a hint of sadness that does nothing to put my mind at ease about what's to come.

"How did you –" she starts.

I shake my head, already moving to the exit. "I'll explain later," I mutter. I grab her hand without thinking as I pass, and we rush down the corridor together, the slight thrill Tempest feels at my hand in hers enough to settle both our nerves. For now.

We dash past Mrs Sherman's office, not even stopping to address the flare of confusion that hits me as we hurry past our boss. As we race through the automatic doors, the despair I briefly lost track of as we ran towards the exit fades back in again, pulling me towards our missing man.

And as we step round the side of the building, still hand in clammy hand, I realise exactly why Ernie came out here.

A lush green hill rolls gently downwards, descending into a small orchard at the boundary of the Oak House grounds. If you look beyond that cluster of trees, there's a clear view across the south end of town – row upon row of neat suburban streets, interspersed with primary schools, corner shops and cafés.

There's an aching homesickness from somewhere off to my right.

I release my grip on Tempest's hand. "He's here," I whisper. "I'm going to go talk to him."

Worry swells and bursts from her like a firework, sadness trailing in its wake. Grey clouds are swirling around her head again, and I pat her arm, giving her the most confident smile I can muster.

"It'll be okay," I whisper, as I anchor myself to the shivering mass of despair looking out over the hillside. "I've got this."

I really hope I've got this.

Slowly, oh so slowly, I step deeper into the cloud of sorrow, wincing as it creeps across my skin.

"Hi, Ernie," I call out, looking towards the centre of the storm, to where I hope Ernie's eyes are. "I'm Melanie, I'm one of the other care assistants. Why don't you come inside? It's freezing out here."

The sadness twists, irritation flaring through it.

Okay. Time to try a different tack.

I sit down on the grass beside his grump-sad maelstrom, and turn to look out at the view.

"That's where you live, isn't it?" I ask, nodding towards the neat lines of terraced houses. The sadness around me deepens, and I think back to the case notes Tempest and I skimmed yesterday – something about him being his wife's main carer, but needing a brief stay here until he got a handle on his mutation, because his constant disappearances were scaring her. Poor guy. "Must be quite a change, being here," I say, stretching my legs out. "I'm sure your wife's in good hands, but that doesn't stop you missing her, right?"

There's a painful wobble in the air, a pang of such strong yearning it launches me straight into a highlight reel of my most treasured memories with Amy – the memories I sobbed over for hours in the first few days after we broke up.

Strangely, they don't sting as much now as they did a week ago.

"I know what it's like to have to leave somewhere you love," I say, still staring out over the hill and hoping Tempest and Ernie won't notice the tears in my eyes – tears that are *definitely* just a side-effect of Ernie's homesick-fog, nothing more. "It happened to me when I first got my power, too. I tried to hold on, to pretend everything was normal so I wouldn't have to leave the people I cared about, and I managed it for a few days – but if I'm honest, they were pretty miserable days. You can't live like that, you know? It felt like I was constantly playing catch-up with myself, keeping track of all the lies, all the awkwardness..." It's all flooding out now, all the guilt I've kept inside over the last week, and with Ernie's sorrow washing over me like this, I'm not sure I could stop it if I wanted to. I tug a few strands of grass from the ground and twist them between my fingers, but Ernie's sadness is settling at my words, twisting into something closer to relief – relief at finding someone who understands. I clear my throat. "My mutation got the better of me eventually, and I wound up here, but you know what? I think that spending some time here, meeting other mutants and learning from them, is going to be exactly what I need. It'll take a while, but things are going to get better. I can already feel it." I shrug, and smile out at the view. "You're not here as a punishment. You're here because it's the best place for you right now. Took me a little while to realise that, but trust me – it's true. You're among friends."

There's a shiver of excitement from Tempest, tinged with blessed relief. I look down at my lap and see a wizened, sun-spotted hand resting on the grass beside me, a gold wedding band gleaming in the morning light.

I glance up, and my eyes meet a pair of sparkling brown ones, sunk deep in a kindly, age-worn face. Ernie smiles a watery smile, and a fresh wave of sadness hits me, but it's somehow warmer than the ones that went before.

"I miss her," he whispers. "It's not even been a day, and I miss her so much. I thought I was coping with it, but then the breakfast eggs came out, and –" He sniffs. "I made her eggs every morning for fifty years. I know exactly how she likes them, and now I'm not there to make them for her and I can't stop thinking that it's my fault for not getting a handle on this thing quick enough –" His sorrow crests again, rising to a peak, and I lay my hand over his and squeeze gently as his shoulders tremble.

"It's not," I whisper. "I promise it's not. These powers are unpredictable, especially at first. Nothing about you being here is your fault." The wave of guilt recedes, and the easing-up means I'm able to press my smile into something more genuine. "See? That feels better, doesn't it?" I squeeze his hand again, and am graced with a small surge of comfort. "Now, how about we get you back inside? I'll make you a nice cup of tea, and we'll see if we can track down a spare ipad to set up a video call with your wife, if you'd like."

Ernie nods. "That would be nice," he says, a dimple forming in one whiskery cheek. The sadness is still there, but it's settled now, more of a background-level homesickness than the spiky, over-whelming thing it had been when we first found him. He pushes himself to his feet and dusts his trousers down. "Thank you. For coming out here, and talking some sense into me."

"Any time," I say. "I wish I'd had someone to do the same for me, when my mutation kicked in."

I straighten back up and turn towards Oak House, coming face to face with a stunned-looking Tempest.

"How did you do that?" she hisses, eyes wide, a dark grey blush skimming her cheeks. She's feeling so many different feelings it's hard to pinpoint just one – awe, pride and relief are all in the mix, but so are suspicion and fear.

"I'll explain everything once he's settled," I whisper, and lead her and Ernie back inside.

Once he's sitting at the dining table, chatting happily to his wife and son and munching his way through a packet of Custard Creams, I lead Tempest over to the kitchen, out of range of the watchful, curious eyes of the other residents.

This isn't how I expected my big confession to go, but judging by the fog of wonder hanging around Tempest, now might be a good time to broach the subject.

"So, I suppose I have a confession to make," I say, leaning against the wall and looking deep into those stormy eyes. "You know how I didn't want to talk about my mutation?"

She nods, chewing her lip. Nervousness writhes around her, but she's trying her best to force it down and give me her full attention, bless her.

"Well, I can feel people's emotions," I blurt out, before I have the chance to overthink it. So much for all my notes-app speech plans. "All the time. Not everyone, just the people who are nearby, but it can still get really overwhelming. That much feedback, all those competing feelings? It's a lot to process, especially when I'm somewhere crowded. That's... a big part of why I came home from uni."

Tempest's brows furrow as curiosity ripples through her nervous fretting. "So, what, it's like you're performing a constant vibe check on everyone who comes near you?"

I smile at the phrasing, despite the mingled worry of my own nerves and the overspill from Tempest's. "Yeah. A vibe check. You could look at it like that."

And then something strange happens.

Her low-level anxiety doesn't flare into panic, like Amy's did, or Mum's, or the few friends at uni I tried to tell before realising it was easier if I gave up and bailed on them without explanation. She doesn't yell at me for invading her privacy, like Lucinda, or make falsely cheery remarks that clash horribly with her inner turmoil, like Mum.

No, Tempest does something entirely different.

Her curiosity grows, drowning out the worry entirely, and along with it twists a faint thread of happiness.

"Thank you for trusting me enough to tell me," she says, smiling that brilliant smile. "It means a lot."

I blink at her, not quite believing what my eyes, my ears and my goddamn superpower are all screaming at me.

"You're not annoyed?"

She shakes her head. "Why would I be annoyed? I mean, yeah, I wish you'd told me earlier, as it would've saved me from awkwardly trying to pretend like I was fine when you could *tell* how not-fine I was. But I get it. You think I told everyone straight away when I got my power?"

I frown. "But you're –" I gesture to her grey-blue, raindrop-freckled skin, not quite sure how to say what I want to say without sounding like a complete arsehole.

"Well, yeah, I couldn't hide it from *everyone*, but I clung to normality where I could. Dad doesn't live with us, and some of my best friends are at uni, and you wouldn't believe the excuses I came up with to avoid Facetiming them." She gazes up at me with those gentle grey eyes, a soft smile playing on her lips. "Vibe check. You know, that would make a pretty sweet mutant codename, if you ever felt like trying one out."

I find myself smiling back, and though I can feel her joy washing over me, the spark of delight in my heart is entirely mine.

I take her hand, both our smiles growing in tandem as I gaze down at her, our combined happiness so bright it feels like I'm about to burst.

"Tempest and Vibe Check," I say. "I like the sound of that."

"Tempest and Vibe Check and the Oak House Mutant Squad!" Frank calls from somewhere above us, making all three of us burst into laughter.

"Yeah," Tempest whispers through her giggles, squeezing my hand. "I like the sound of that too."

# Farsight

"They're fine, right?" Dylan frowns at me. "We don't need to perform a rescue mission?"

"We're not invading a care facility," I snap. "And it's very frustrating to have you breathing down my neck wanting to attack everything."

Dylan paces in circles around me, as if they're creating a psychic whirlpool of frustration to drown me in. "The UK is fucked though. A bunch of them still love Michael, there are goddamn hate crimes every other day. I just want to make sure everyone's okay. If anyone comes near the Oak House Mutant Squad, I'll tear them apart."

"Are we killing things?" Feral prowls into the room. She's very beautiful with soft fur and a tail twitching around behind her head. She bats at Dylan affectionately with her claws. "Who did something bad?"

"Nobody." Dylan glowers. "Yet."

"Is Farsight making us sit on our hands again?" Feral narrows golden eyes at me.

"I'm taking precautions!" Sometimes having to answer to a bunch of bloodthirsty Gen-Z people makes me want to scream. I remind myself I'm dealing with a grieving, fragile, and actually quite dangerous group, so taking a breath or two is not the worst idea. "The political situation is not exactly stable, and very notorious mutants preemptively stabbing people for possibly threatening the elderly is not helpful in the least."

"Don't worry." Feral pats my head like I'm the furry animal in this scenario. "We won't hit anyone without permission."

"Keep an eye on them," Dylan says intently. "They need to be looked after."

"It's all very sweet," I insist. "Everyone's looking after each other. This is how things should be, and you don't need to jump at monsters under every bed."

Feral and Dylan exchange glances, like they've seen enough monsters under enough beds to draw some pretty concrete conclusions.

"You wanted something beautiful," I protest. "I found something for you. It wasn't supposed to be an opportunity for you to go growling at shadows again."

"Double-edged sword." Dylan scowls at the window, as if they can see directly into Oak House. "Now I know there's something beautiful, I'm waiting for something to step out of the shadows and devour it."

"Not everything devours." I feel the urge to hug them again. They seem to need it.

"No." Dylan leans into Feral, both of them holding each other up. "But a lot of things do. The world needs a lot of goddamn heroes, or at least people who'll stand up and do the right thing more often than they look away."

And here's that obscure need to please them. "Fine. I'll find you some heroes. Now go and find something fun to do, and stop annoying me."

"You're a gem, Farsight." They wink at me. "Nobody believes me when I tell them how sweet you are."

"And yet everyone believes me when I tell them how annoying *you* are." I blow them a kiss, pleased to have gotten one over on them for once.

Feral gives a yelp of laughter, and Dylan swats at her, the two of them chasing each other down the stairs. Honestly, they might be in their twenties but they're practically still children. The weight of the world on their shoulders and all.

# California Dreaming

### AMANDA M. PIERCE

I FLICK OPEN THE TOP OF MY ZIPPO AND ROLL THE FLINT wheel two times before the flame catches. It dances anemically over the wick, reminding me that I still haven't replaced the lighter fluid.

The tip of my eyeliner smokes as it rolls over the heat. I douse the flame, toss the lighter into the cup holder of my truck, and press my eyelid down. The kohl is still hot as I draw a line along my lashes.

The engine in my piece-of-shit Durango rumbles so loud that it rattles the rearview mirror. My reflection vibrates as I inspect my reddish blonde hair. It's pulled into a ponytail today, with a strawberry-patterned scrunchie that smells like actual strawberry. My barely-there blonde eyebrows are gelled in place, and my freckles are completely hidden under the new MAC concealer I just got. The only things I can't cover up are the puffy bags hanging under my hazel eyes.

I need to start sleeping again, but finals start tomorrow. There aren't enough hours in the day to help my dad with the farm, plan my graduation rager, *and* study for the Latin AP test. So, instead of resting, I've spent the last four nights translating Classical poetry and pounding Red Bull til I reach an out-of-body experience. I'm basically a Salem witch.

The clock flips over to 7:02 AM. On cue, the truck engine settles to a sated hum. The dumb beast is so old that it needs to idle for four minutes before I can drive. If I pull away after three minutes and forty seconds, it will stall at every stop sign. The skeezy guy selling it gave me a good deal, and now I know why. The truck is a lemon, and not the cute kind growing on our farm.

I pull the gear shift into drive and gun it over the driveway, sending gravel spraying. Mom's already at work, and Dad's tractor is a plume of dust on the horizon. There isn't anyone to scold me for driving irresponsibly; as if they don't do the same thing when they're late for church every single Sunday.

The truck lumbers to the end of the driveway, which is sheltered by a copse of sequoia trees. Their trunks are so wide they're nearly impossible to see around, so I crane my neck, looking for any oncoming traffic. People drive like comic book villains around the back roads of rural California. It's not enough to look both ways— you have to roll down the window, listen for ten seconds, then consult with the Fates on whether you'll be crushed like a grape by an El Camino.

Luckily, today's not my day to die.

My brain switches to autopilot once I'm cruising. The county roads out here aren't even named—just numbered. They're actually kind of pretty, when you're not cursing them for being so narrow. The crumbling pavement is lined with eucalyptus trees wrapped in a bathrobe of morning fog. Green thistles crown the ditches, decorated with spiky, purple flowers. A wild peacock picks through the dead grass, squalling for attention.

It's all peaceful until I reach the burn scar.

Then, it's not so pretty at all.

Blackened tree trunks push through the ground like rotten teeth. The grass is gone, leaving the hillsides blanketed in grey ash.

The melted remains of a white, plastic fence are drizzled like icing along the edge of my neighbors' property.

A burned-out horse trailer still stands at the end of the road—a grave marker for the Murphys' oldest mare, Chiclet. I used to feed her apples while my dad hayed their field. In exchange for his work, the Murphy's offered me riding lessons, but I was never brave enough to get in the saddle.

Ever since the fire, I spend my nights wondering what Chiclet felt before she died.

I'm so fucking emo lately.

I punch the radio on, letting a trap beat chase away my grim thoughts. I don't need that shit infecting my daylight hours, too.

The county road wraps around the rolling hills and drops into the valley, rejoining civilization. Clusters of McMansions dot the golden rangeland like acne. Next to the Catholic church, a food truck is slinging vegan breakfast burritos. The customers are smothered in carnitas steam and diesel exhaust while they wait.

There's a girl built like a redwood standing at the front of the line. Ali Gray: the asshole who used to be my best friend.

My eyes stick to her like a roach trap. She's wearing pleather combat boots and a vintage Woodstock t-shirt—her dad's, from when he actually went.

Creamy, long legs peek out of her green, canvas shorts. *I* was the one who told her she should burn everything in her closet that didn't show off her calves. Now, it's a kick in the face every time I see them.

I'm so distracted I almost miss the stoplight turning red. I jam the brakes too hard, making the tires screech before jerking to a stop. Ali cocks her head, ear suddenly pricked toward the road.

*No no no.*

She tucks her short, black hair behind her ear and fixes her green eyes on me. Her brows are so thick that I can see their arch from here.

She lifts two fingers to her forehead in a sarcastic salute.

I push my palms against the steering wheel until my shoulders disappear into the seat. Underneath all the concealer, my face is hot. Thankfully, she can only see the blush I painted on, not the one that's boiling up my neck.

The car behind me beeps, furious that the light is green and I haven't moved. I mash the gas pedal, but nothing happens. The truck is stalled.

"Unbelievable." I slap the steering wheel.

The car behind me beeps again. It's a classic Impala, restored and repainted matte black. The windshield is tinted so dark I can't see the driver, but I know it's Drew Kemp laying on the horn without letting up. Nobody is anonymous in a town this small.

"Go around!" I screech, waving my hand out the window. Drew peels out just wide enough to avoid side-swiping my mirror, then barrels through the light.

Ali Gray is still staring at me with that fucking smirk on her face. She turns around to accept a silver-wrapped burrito from the food truck, then marches toward a mint green bicycle balancing against the light post. She swans her leg so high over the seat that her shorts ride up her ass.

My throat tightens in response.

I restart my engine, letting it growl at top volume. Even though I should let it idle for another four minutes, I rev the gas and drive right through the stale red light.

Ali Gray pedals away in my rearview mirror until her marble legs shrink to a pale dot.

THE ONLY PARKING spot in the Senior lot is the one next to Drew's Impala, which is blasting death metal so loud his gold rims are vibrating.

Reluctantly, I slide into the space, giving his drivers' side door a wide berth. He's one of those guys who's always angry. His Instagram is all hunting photos of dead animals, and his Twitter is full of vaguely threatening song lyrics from his SoundCloud. He got cancelled last year for a track titled "Skull Fuck," and he's been a ticking clock ever since.

Right now, he's charging himself up for the day, and I don't want to be around when his battery reaches full.

I sling my giant messenger bag over my shoulder, then ease the door open and slip out. Drew's window rolls down, surrounding me in a tinny wall of shrieking music. The singer is screaming about burying the world in a shallow grave. Real nice.

"Yo," Drew barks over the cacophony. I pretend like I can't hear him, gently closing my door and hurrying off. "Nice trunk."

My face warps into the barf emoji, but I'm halfway to the entrance so he can't see it.

The school is broken into two main sections—old and new. The old building is a stuccoed rectangle from the sixties. The school's name is soldered to the front in silver metallic lettering, but the words were too big for the space, so some dumbass chose to put one word on each line.

Springer

Unified...

School

District.

Nobody knows why there's an ellipsis in the middle of the name. It's a bad sign to have a grammar error on the front of a school like that, but it hasn't been fixed in thirty years.

The old building houses the auto lab, where students take vocational classes on how to fix (*cough* steal) cars. The new building is all poured concrete and computer labs, where they teach future IT jerks to fix (*cough* hack) computers.

All the movies would suggest there should be some macho divide between the vocational and college-bound students, but after last year's wildfire burned down half the town, most of us are just happy to be alive.

I file into the old building behind Minu Robarge and Janessa Montero, two-thirds of the Gay Straight Alliance Club. Although, it could just be called the Gay Club. There's not much straight alliance in a town as conservative as Springer. Last Sunday, Mom and I sat through a forty-five-minute sermon where the priest cobbled together some unrelated quotes as evidence that God hates gay people. Trust me when I tell you: that sermon would get a zero on an AP English test. Too much extrapolation.

Despite the priest's *obvious* misinterpretations, the crowd didn't whisper a word of objection. Even my mom, who's cool about most things, sat there staring blankly.

So I did the same.

"Hi, Gemma!" Janessa Montero gives me a mega-watt smile, showing her perfect, post-braces teeth. Her brown, spiral curls are done up in a ballerina bun. She self-consciously readjusts her t-shirt. It's sheer yellow, which looks really nice against her olive skin, except there's a huge brand name across the front. And the back. She looks like a billboard.

"Hey, Janessa."

She pulls a sheet of paper from her blue trapper-keeper, waving it at me with a French-tip manicure. "Get in loser, we're having a GSA social this weekend. Just kidding. About the loser part. Not the social."

I snatch the flyer and tuck it into my messenger bag before anyone sees. "Thanks, but I'm still too busy."

"Cool cool cool." She smiles, but her eyes pinch like she's staring at the sun. "*Love* your lipstick, by the way. I've been searching for a red like that."

"Mhm." I offer her a tight smile. Janessa hasn't worn anything other than cherry Chapstick her entire life. She probably thinks Nars is the new NASA rover. She's always pretending to like the same things as people, even when it's clear she doesn't.

I get it—other humans are impossible to figure out. But a fish could tell Janessa that air is stupid, and she would rather suffocate than disagree. She's nice and all, but she's too afraid to speak her mind.

"You don't need makeup, Janessa." I blow her a Ruby-Woo colored kiss. "You're perfect the way you are."

"Oh-em-gee, Gemma." She mimics an air kiss back at me. "*You're* perfect the way you are."

Ali Gray saunters up, and now the entire GSA is standing in front of me. "Eh. She's cute and all, but...*perfect?*"

I give her a red-lipped sneer. It's the one color she hated on me, and I've worn it every day since we stopped being friends.

"So judgmental, Alison." I drag my fingers through my hair and flick the ends at her. "You really need to work on that."

"Hey ladiiies," Janessa cups her hand around her mouth, smiling nervously. "Why can't we be friends?"

"Because," I insist. "We can't."

Ali takes a step toward me. The perfume of her almond soap makes my mouth water. She's so tall I have to tilt my head back to maintain her withering stare.

"And why can't we be friends, exactly?" she whispers.

I snort, trying to force her scent out of my head. "You know why."

"Come on, Gemma." She makes a coaxing motion. "Use your words."

It's the same thing she said to me during our last night together —her lips stained with cheap wine, confessing something that should have stayed locked inside. It nearly killed me to push her away. Every morning for six weeks, I dragged myself into the shower and cried. I cannot feel those feelings again.

I won't survive.

Ali purses her shell-pink lips, looking at me like a bug she wants to crush. "That's what I thought. Still lying to yourself."

I surge forward and bite the air in front of her face. She rears her head, stepping back like a startled colt. Her green eyes are round with dismay, a red flush creeping up her jaw.

"Now kiss," someone says from behind me.

I whip around to find Drew Kemp with his hand rustling around in his front pocket. His blonde hair is so greasy the roots are sticking together in wide ribbons. The headphones around his neck are spewing a white-noise version of the same shrieking music.

"Oh, please." Ali's face hardens. Her cheekbones are sharp as broken glass. "I'd sooner kiss you, Drew."

I snort in disgust, head crooked as if she slapped me. With a prim shrug, she wraps her arm around Janessa's shoulder and steers her down the hallway, leaving me alone with Drew, who's still rummaging in his pants.

"Did you hear that?" He gives me a smarmy look, staring through me with his water blue eyes. "I think she likes me."

"She does not."

"One thing's for sure." He shrugs one shoulder, pulling his hand out of his pocket to put his headphones back in. "She really doesn't like you."

*False.*

Instead of answering, I march off toward my first class, refusing to make eye contact with anyone else. They can't see how pissed off I am, or they'll know something is wrong. And there's never anything wrong with me.

Gemma Lamont does not get flustered.

I am a stone wall.

A cold piece of glass.

A deep, dark well.

BY THE END of the school day, my eyes have shriveled to raisins from focusing. When I step into the sunlight, the wind whips grit under my eyelids. I blink it away before the tears can fuck with my makeup.

I need to drink some water, for once.

The vending machine is located across campus in the new building, forcing me to drag my white Jordans through the dusty courtyard. Janessa spots me from across the sidewalk and I make a quick adjustment toward the unisex bathroom, hoping to avoid her. When I grab the handle and yank, the door doesn't budge.

"Occupied, dumbass!" someone yells from inside.

Damn it. I'm trapped.

"Gemma." Janessa leans against the bathroom door. "Sorry about earlier. Ali was way out of line. I was like, 'I don't know her.'"

"It's fine." I shrug. "We just grew apart."

In reality, Ali deserves to drop kick me into the moon's orbit for the way I ghosted her. I guess she hasn't told Janessa what really happened.

Janessa presses her elbow against the door and rests her head against her fist. "You two used to be friendship goals. Y'all had your own language. It was kind of annoying to have lunch with you—" Her face blanches and she covers her mouth with her hands. "I'm so sorry."

"It's fine," I chuckle. "I get it."

The toilet flushes inside the bathroom and Janessa jumps away from the door one second before it slams open. Inside is Drew Fucking Kemp, exiting way too fast to have washed his grody hands.

He flicks his fingers under his chin. "What are you looking at?"

"Not you," I snap.

He opens his mouth to retort when the ground suddenly lurches beneath my feet.

"Oh shit." A wave rocks my knees, and I steady myself against the bathroom doorframe. "Earthquake!"

"What?" Janessa looks up at the ceiling, confused.

I bend my legs like I'm on a paddle board riding out a wake.

Drew snickers and pulls out his phone to record me. The quake is so strong, I can't get my footing to swat his camera away. All I can do is hold onto the doorframe and pray.

The earthquake abruptly ends. The concrete, which felt like liquid underfoot, is solid again. It's the shortest one I've ever felt. There isn't even an aftershock.

"Um...Gemma?" Janessa waves her hand in front of my face. "Are you...feeling okay?"

"Yeah. I think it's over." I let out a sigh and sag onto the floor. "That was a big one."

Drew watches me through his phone screen, a look of toxic glee on his marsupial face. "Are you having a stroke?"

"What do you mean?" I flip off his camera. "There was a damn earthquake."

He lets out a high-pitched laugh. "No, there wasn't."

"Yeah, there was." My voice is infected with doubt. The heat of embarrassment creeps up my neck. Did I just act like a total space case in front of Drew's camera? "Janessa, you felt that. Didn't you?"

Drew whips his camera toward Janessa. Instead of answering, she lets out a strangled noise. She stares down quizzically, touching her throat.

Great, now she's acting weird, too. What is happening to us?

Drew zooms in on her reddening face. "What a couple of spazzes."

"Get out of here!" She flails her hand at him, accidentally knocking his phone out of his hands. It skitters across the pavement, landing face up to reveal a spiderwebbed screen. She and Drew stare at it like they're stuck on pause.

Oh shit. He's going to freak the fuck out.

Slowly, Janessa's vibrant face drains of color. Drew's eyebrows turn down into the shape of a v, and his hands clench into fists. Grey, acrid smog spews from between his fingers.

I pull my collar over my nose. None of this makes any sense, and it just keeps getting stranger. It's like reality took a smoke break and let chaos take over.

"Dude...what's wrong with your hands?" I ask.

"Holy shit." He stares down at his fists. Smoke wafts on the breeze as if he's holding a coal in each palm. His face breaks into a delighted smile, opening his fists and holding them up for us to see. They're empty except for a pink circle scalded into each palm. "This is so metal."

And then it hits me. The stories of people waking up one morning being able spit acid, or read minds. The mania that swept social media and news outlets. The police marching through the streets with militarized weapons.

Drew is a mutant, and him being able to spontaneously sizzle is decidedly *not* metal. It's...probably very bad.

"You're one of those," I whisper.

"I am," he says in a hushed voice. "And I'm going to haunt everyone's dreams."

He squats down, snatches his phone, and runs off toward the parking lot.

"Well, shit." I squint after him. "How did that happen?"

Janessa clutches her throat and makes a horrible gagging noise. The whites of her eyes are streaked with red. Suddenly, she bolts for the nearest trashcan and full-body heaves into the garbage, groaning like a cow trapped in barbed wire.

Ali appears across the courtyard, eyes locked on her new best friend.

"Janessa!" She darts toward her, already freeing a water bottle from her bag. "Here, take a sip."

She eases the bottle to Janessa's lips and lets her take a greedy gulp. The water bursts back out of her mouth and wets her shirt. It's like her body is rejecting everything inside it. She can't keep anything down.

People are gathering around now, pulling out their phones to capture it. Ali turns her furious gaze on them, marching forward and knocking the cameras out of our classmates' hands. She looks feral, and I can't even imagine how embarrassed she'll be when someone on the internet edits these clips together from eighty-five different camera angles.

She and Janessa are making such a scene, they're going to draw suspicion. Someone is going to mistake her for a mutant and call the police. When they show up at her house, she won't behave. I know her. She'll get herself sent to jail, or one of those black site experimental stations.

More and more people pull out their phones, and Ali finally realizes she's outnumbered. She wraps her arms around herself, panting and heaving. There's a line of dewy sweat along her forehead.

"You should be ashamed of yourselves." She points her finger accusingly, making eye contact with every single camera.

I have to stop her before she becomes a viral video. There's no hope for Janessa—we'll be seeing gifs of her yarfing for the next six years—but I might be able to save Ali from becoming Shaming Shannon. Or worse.

"And...scene!" I clap my hands, trying to make it seem like we're just clout-chasers staging a fake video. "Good job everyone, I hope the internet thinks it's real!" I yoke Ali around the neck and start dragging her toward the parking lot. "Let's go."

"Wait, I need to tell them they can't share that video—" She bucks away from my arm, but I hold tighter.

"Are you *new* here?" I mutter out of the corner of my mouth. "You're not going to convince them to do anything. Now grab Janessa so we can escape."

"Fine." Ali bats my arm away with a hollow thump.

"Ow!" I have to grit my teeth to stop from hissing. "What was that for?"

"Oh please, I barely touched you." She kneels down to scoop Janessa into a fireman's carry. The poor girl has spit and vomit all down her front, and from the look of the trashcan, she ejected everything left in her stomach. It even looks like there's a chunk of flesh, but if I stare any longer, I'm going to add to the pile.

Geez, maybe Janessa is mutating too.

"Take me home," she keens. "Please, take me home."

Ali bites her lip and gives me a sideways glance. "Can you, um—"

"Yeah. We can take my truck."

She stares stoically ahead, nodding her chin once. Janessa buries her face in Ali's shoulder, and that's when I notice something off about her Woodstock t-shirt. Oddly, there are a bunch of little slits in the fabric, like a bunch of tiny blades punched through. Surrounding each slit are a handful of reddish fibers, almost like cat hair.

But Ali is allergic to cats.

She follows my gaze suspiciously, shifting Janessa into her left arm and pinching two of the fibers. They're attached to her skin like hair.

My eyes stretch wide. "Uh...Alison?"

"I don't know what they are" she says.

"It's not that." I point to Janessa, cradled in Ali's left arm like an infant. "Have you always been able to lift an entire person, one-handed?"

"Ohmygod!" She slides her other arm beneath Janessa like she could drop her at any second. Then, tentatively, she pulls the hand away again. Janessa doesn't even jostle. "It must be the adrenaline."

"Or human growth hormone." I point to Ali's legs, which are covered in the same wiry, red fuzz. With two fingers, I tweeze one off of her thigh.

"Ow!" She flinches away. "What are you doing?"

"Sorry." I pull my hand back sheepishly. "I wanted to test something."

"Save the experiments for later."

"Right, of course." Panic trills in my ears. Alison is changing, too, but maybe if I ignore it, it will go away.

My keys are buried in my messenger bag, but I feel around until my finger finds the unlock button. Across the parking lot, the Durango honks open.

Ali wrinkles her nose. "I can't believe I'm getting into that global warming machine."

"You have filaments growing out of your skin, and *that's* what you can't believe?" I scoff. "Would you rather take Janessa home on your handlebars?"

She stops on her heel and looks toward the teachers parking lot. "Mr. Rose has a bike trailer for his kids. He would totally let me borrow it."

"Don't. You. Dare." Janessa's eyes pop open, bloodshot and bleary. "I have suffered enough humiliation. Put me in the truck."

I pull the back door open and wave Janessa in. "You heard her."

Ali performs a theatrical shudder before sliding Janessa into the backseat. "I'll have to plant three trees just for getting into this gas guzzler."

"The planet thanks you for your sacrifice."

In the parking lot, Drew's car is noticeably missing. In its place is a sooty outline on the pavement, like a cartoon bomb went off. This is all bad. How many people at this school are going to go home and never be seen again?

It's like there was some cataclysmic shift in the universe. *Oops, all mutants!*

I want to investigate the smoke ring around his parking spot, but, with Human Geyser and Fuzzy Captain Planet in my truck, I don't have time to deal with Drew Kemp's shit.

I toss my messenger bag in the backseat and vault myself up.

Ali yelps the moment her ass hits the seat. She jumps up and hovers like it's a dirty toilet. "Are these *leather*?"

"Alison." I squeeze the steering wheel until pink lines appear all over my knuckles. "Please stay focused on the issue at hand."

She blows a stream of air that ruffles her long, swoopy bangs.

Like a deflating balloon, she sinks into the seat. "At the very least, you could stop idling."

"We've got two minutes and forty-five seconds left."

"What—?"

"Hey, what's that smell?" Janessa lifts her head from the seat. She hangs over the glove compartment, using her nose like a metal detector.

"Dead animal." Ali glides her hand over the back of her chair like a game show host.

"No. Something different." Janessa rifles through my cup holders, tossing the lighter onto the ground. She runs her fingers over the loose change, selecting a sticky quarter out of the console and staring at it like a macaron.

"What are you doing?" Ali stares in horror as Janessa shoves the quarter in her mouth and moans, sagging against the backseat in relief. A hum starts in her throat to the tune of the newest Ariana Grande song.

"I think..." Janessa sings breathily. "Something is really wrong."

"Um yeah!" Ali shouts. "You just ate a quarter!"

Janessa lurches for the cup holder and grabs the rest of the coins, leaving only lint and the burnt end of an old french fry behind. She shoves the whole handful of change into her mouth. The coins clink against her teeth as she sucks on them.

"That is so filthy!" Ali covers her mouth in horror. The sunlight catches the red fibers growing out of her arms. "What are you doing?"

Janessa presses her hand against her chest and squeezes her eyes shut.

"I can't stop," she sings, exactly like that EDM song by the same name.

"We need to take you somewhere safe." I slide the gear shaft into drive. We *should* be taking her to a doctor, but ever since they became mandatory reporters to the police, it hasn't been safe for anyone to go. Even if all they have is a rare disease that's hard to diagnose. "What's your mom's phone number?"

She opens her mouth to answer and immediately horks up a pair of pennies. She snaps them up and stuffs them back in her mouth. "We can't! Call! My mom. Because she doesn't! Have! Paid sick leave."

"Are you—"

"Stop!" Janessa claps a hand over my mouth. Her eyes are wild. "Stop asking me questions. Can't you see what's happening?"

Ali chews her lip and runs her hand up and down her arm. The red fibers are getting thicker, and somehow her head is brushing against the roof of the truck. "It's impossible. We woke up totally normal. We can't be...*that.*"

My eyes swivel toward her. "I think you might be mut—"

"Don't say that word." Ali presses her finger against my mouth. She smells like crushed pine needles.

"There's no other explanation," Janessa hisses.

"But, mut—*those people*—have powers," Ali says. "Like, super-hero shit."

"Not all of them." I tap the steering wheel, trying to remember. "There was that girl on the news whose teeth turned into piano keys."

Janessa gulps. "The x-rays revealed metal strings in her brain."

Ali folds her arms and flops against the seat. Her lip trembles. "So, the doctors are going to find loose change in your gut, and... weird tendrils growing out of me. We'll be pariahs." Her face pales. "They might send us to one of those labs and peel us apart."

"Hey. It's going to be okay." I run the back of my hand down Ali's shoulder. "Your secret is safe with me."

Both of their heads swivel toward me.

"Gemma." Janessa shakes her head. "It happened to you, too."

"What do you mean?"

"There was no earthquake. Nobody else felt anything, it was just you."

I hold my hands up in front of my face. Nothing feels any different. I'm not stuffing dirty change in my mouth, or growing fibers all over my body. I'm still the same, they're the ones acting strange.

I tilt my head sympathetically. "Maybe you just missed the earthquake because you were...mutating?"

Janessa stomps her foot against the floor mat, pointing to her throat. She's all out of change, and she can't answer me without it.

"Of course. You're in denial." Ali shakes her hair. "Do you hear this girl?"

Janessa punches the back of Ali's seat. I feel suddenly guilty, I never realized how many questions we ask in a day.

"Whatever," I say. "Let's just get the hell out of here."

"Yes!" Janessa gasps, her voice finally released by a statement. "Go."

WHEN WE PULL into Janessa's driveway, there are two disheveled-looking figures standing on her porch. There's a girl wearing a pair of three-inch platform boots straight out of 1998. Her legs are wrapped in fishnet stockings, and she's wearing a lime-green PVC dress.

The second person is wearing an oversized Jack Skellington sweatshirt. The hood is pulled tight around their green-tinged face, haloed by purple-dyed hair. There's a ring of pale, pink petals around their feet, like they hosted a summoning circle. They're holding a frayed wicker basket in one hand and a bag of In N' Out in the other.

"Greetings, earthlings." They have a soft-spoken accent that's hard to place. England? "We come in peace."

The rubber-clad girl holds up a peace sign. "I'm so excited to be here! I *love* American fashion."

"And it loves you." I don't have the heart to explain that her outfit expired thirty years ago. "Whoever you are."

"Sourpatch." She offers me a hand still greasy from french fries. "And this is Chatterbox."

Janessa narrows her eyes, sharing a suspicious look with Ali. Those sound like mutant codenames. "What brings you here?"

"The infamous fast food." Chatterbox shakes the In N' Out bag. "Which is...I have to say..."

"A fucking travesty." Sourpatch horks a sticky wad of spit onto the ground. The dirt sizzles. "The fries are so starchy they turned my acid into goo."

"It's totally overhyped," Ali says. "There's barely anything vegan."

"Oh, are you vegan?" I ask, feigning ignorance. Ali glares at me, and I ignore it. "I didn't know, you've never mentioned it."

"Knock it off, Gemma." She flicks my arm, and it feels like I got hit by a softball.

"Ow!" I swing around and punch her in the arm, but her flesh doesn't even move. My fist crunches against her like I hit a tree. "Fuck!"

Chatterbox tilts their head quizzically. "That's enough, children—"

The cup in their hand flies forward, spilling soda all over us. It dampens my shirt and drips from Ali's hair.

Chatterbox stares open-mouthed at the fallen cup, leaking sugary ooze into the dirt. "I told you, I had it under control."

"I guess that's my cue to reveal the real reason why we're here." Sourpatch drums on the hem of her lime dress. "Chatty?"

"We got an alert that four new mutants were just awakened." Chatterbox winks at us. "And here they are! Well...three of them."

"No...no no no." Janessa sinks onto her knees, closing her eyes so tight her eyelashes disappear. "My parents *just* got used to me being gay."

"You don't have to be afraid," Chatterbox says in their warbling accent. Australian, maybe? "Anytime you need, you can come to Mutopia. It's safe there, for everyone."

"I am *two weeks* from graduating and going to college. I was going to be free." Janessa slaps her hands against the ground. "I can't take this right now."

"Awww." Sourpatch kneels down to her level. "It's okay...we brought you a welcome basket. Nobody can be sad around a welcome basket. Right?"

Chatterbox slouches toward Janessa and offers her the basket. The whole thing is mummified in wrinkled plastic wrap. Inside is a bed of paper towels cushioning a handful of small objects.

It's mostly empty space in there.

"See!" Sourpatch points to the objects. "There's some Cute Mutants wristbands...a bag of wasabi Doritos...and my favorite. Keychains!" She tears into the basket, freeing one of the tiny wooden baseball bats hanging from a metal ring.

"Are you a sports team, or something?" Janessa asks.

"Ew," Chatterbox says.

"No." Sourpatch sticks her tongue out. "We're, like, superheroes."

Oh fuck. These are *the* mutants. The cute ones, who practically unraveled the universe and then put it back together again. They don't fuck around, and they're here, telling us we're one of them.

This isn't a joke. It's real.

"We're really mutants?" I gently pat my stomach, then my neck, searching for something different about me. "You know for sure?"

"Well, she's clearly got something going on." Chatterbox points to Ali, who—since I looked at her thirty seconds ago—has grown taller than my truck. Those red fibers are growing out of her knuckles.

"How about you?" Sourpatch asks Janessa.

She snorts, giving us all a furious look.

"She has trouble with questions." I reach into my messenger bag and rummage around. There's one dime left. "Janessa, what happened to you?"

I feed the coin into her mouth and a showtune melody bursts from her throat. "I threw up *allllll* my lunch, and now I have a hunch!" Pause for jazz hands. "That I can't answer questions without eating a bunch of spare change."

Sourpatch breaks into applause. "The pipes on this girl!"

Chatterbox inclines their head toward me. "Does she sing all the answers?"

"Only if you feed her change."

"At least choosing a codename will be easy." They shake their head. "You're going to need a lot of quarters for Jukebox, over here."

Janessa groans. "I'm going to have to work at the laundromat just so I can eat."

Sourpatch sizes Ali up. "Can we call you Maine Coon?"

"I don't think it's cat fur." I squint at the whorl pattern forming beneath the red fibers on her skin and snap my fingers. "She looks like a redwood."

Ali holds her arms up to the light and her face scrunches into a horrified mask. "You're right."

"Oh my gosh." I press my fist to my mouth to stop from cracking up. "You're becoming your favorite thing."

Her brows curve up and her eyes pinch like she's going to cry.

It drains the humor right into my feet. "Hey, it's going to be okay."

"Easy for you to say, *Gemma*." She flares her nostrils and tosses her hair—a bull ready to fight. "What's your mutation, being heartless?"

Chatterbox stuffs their hands in their pockets and backs up. "I am sensing some unresolved tension."

Sourpatch hunches toward their ear. "Angry girls are angry."

"Seriously. What's her mutation?" Ali turns her burning gaze toward the Cute Mutants. "Why does she always get to hide, but Janessa and I can't?"

Sourpatch makes a little o face, pinning me with her gaze. All the soap opera story lines are coming together in her mind.

I roll my eyes and toe the ground. It's nobody's business but my own whether I'm a mutant or not. If I'm not ready to jump on the parade float, that's my choice.

"Well...um..." Chatterbox's charming accent manages to diffuse a bit of the awkwardness. Now I remember, they're from New Zealand. "We've found that most mutations stem from a part of your personality."

"Genetic artistic license." Sourpatch nods emphatically.

"So, your vegan friend is becoming a tree." Chatterbox makes finger guns at Ali. "And Jukebox...really liked showtunes."

"No." Janessa shakes her head. "I have a deep-rooted inability to verbalize my thoughts, so I use pop culture references as a crutch."

All four of us—me, Ali, Chatterbox, and Sourpatch—squint at her.

She shrugs. "I've been working on it with my therapist."

"Damn, girl." Sourpatch gives her a fist bump. "Good for you."

"So that leaves Gemma," Ali says.

"Maybe I'm not really a mutant."

Her shoulders sag, eyelids drooping with exhaustion, and for a moment I wonder if my power is sucking the joy out of people I love—I mean, hate.

"I can't do this with you again." She curls her long, fibrous arm around Janessa's shoulder. "When you're ready to be yourself, come find us."

Her redwood fibers catch on Janessa's shirt, dragging it up her back as they walk toward the front porch. Janessa unlocks the door and Ali hunches down to fit through it. They close it firmly behind themselves, without looking back.

"Can you believe they just left without saying goodbye?" Sourpatch stomps her platform boot in the dust. "Do they *know* who we *are*?"

"Americans," Chatterbox mutters. Their ear tilts toward the basketball hoop hanging above Janessa's garage. It's vibrating, and the screws holding it up start twisting in their anchors. "No, that's okay. Revenge isn't necessary."

"Well, it was nice to meet you." Sourpatch hands me the sagging welcome basket. "We tried contacting the fourth mutant, but he didn't show up for his shift at In N' Out. So, if you see Drew Kemp, make sure to share the Doritos."

"Wait, *Drew*?!" I clutch the basket to my chest, but the Cute Mutants disappear before my eyes. One minute they were standing in front of me, the next, they're nothing but two sets of footprints in the dirt. A trail of dust rises from the imprints, like they got snatched out of the air.

I'm alone.

Janessa's house is silent. I *could* ring the doorbell, apologize, and try to figure this thing out with the only people who will understand. But I don't want to deal with Ali right now, and there's no way in hell I'm going to hang out with Drew and make nice about being mutants together.

The thing is, I don't *have* to change anything. Whatever my mutation is, it's small enough to hide. I can carry on as if nothing has changed, pass through society like a plain old white girl from rural California. My head aches with ambivalent relief. I know there are people who can't hide, but at least my secrets can stay mine.

The most I can hope for is that Ali and Janessa go back to leaving me alone, Drew joins a league of super villains far away from here, and I finish out the last week of senior year with my untarnished reputation intact.

SATURDAYS BELONG TO MY PARENTS. Every weekend I trade off working the cash register in Mom's thrift shop or helping dad with whatever scheme he's cooked up for the farm.

The last few weeks, Mom relinquished her time so Dad can get more help with planting season. She claims it's because he needs me more than she does, but I think she's tired of me rummaging through the new donations and taking the best clothes for myself.

What can I say? I have an image to maintain.

There's haze on the horizon when I step out onto the field. Dad's blue tractor is trundling along the rows, carrying an old-fashioned seed drill behind it. It looks like a giant metal bear paw dragging its claws through the dirt.

It's late in the year to be planting anything—we normally get crops in the ground much earlier—but the day we were supposed to start, our water allotment was cut down by half. After a rainless winter, the entire state of California is under strict drought regulations. Small farms are low priority, so our water allowance was the first to get slashed.

Which is why there's a roped-off section of fallow land being prepped for a well. It's expensive as fuck to drill a new well, and it takes forever to finish. Three months ago, Dad hired a professional company to identify an underground water table, but they haven't returned to drill, since every other farm is trying to do the same thing.

From the seat of his tractor, Dad waves me over. He shifts the machine into park and the thunderous engine drops to a rumbling hum.

"Hey, kid." He tips the bill of his frayed Aggies baseball hat at me. "Saw your lights were still on in the middle of the night. You okay?"

My eye bags are so big they look like pillows at the bottom of my vision. They're swollen from the hour and a half I spent sobbing into my pillow, which I *thought* was a private moment.

"Yeah, just studying."

"Does pre-calc usually make you cry like that?"

"Have you seen those equations?"

He chuckles, leaning against the steering wheel. "Well then, I'll give you something easy to start with. The wind scattered the well markers. Put them back up, and then you can start weeding."

I give him a salute. "You got it."

The tractor snarls to life and lurches forward, heaving its claw behind. I pat the giant wheel and let it pass before marching across the field toward the well markers. The wind blew so hard it dragged the little blue flags across the field and deposited them by the grain silo.

I gather up the metal posts until I'm carrying a bouquet of flags toward the well barrier. The wind rattles them, sending a vibration through my hands. Goosebumps crop up over my arms as the rumble gets worse, jostling my elbows until the joints creak. It feels like another earthquake.

Chatterbox's voice echoes in my head. They were certain I had mutated, but they hadn't come to any conclusions about my power.

I was really hoping the mutation was buried so deep nobody would ever know about it. Not even me.

The ground beneath me heaves like a wave, and suddenly my hands seize up, sending the flags fluttering to the ground.

My arms shake uncontrollably.

A deep rumble groans through my head, followed by the sound of water boiling inside a kettle. One moment I can see the ground beneath my feet, then everything turns the color of wet compost plowed into the soil.

I'm sinking.

Insects skitter through the dirt around me, their squirming legs sending chills down my neck. The sound of rushing water gets stronger, beckoning like an underground ocean. My legs feel icy, as if I've plunged into a winter pond. Water laps against my lips, then my eyes, sucking me under. It forces its way into my nose and down my throat. The roots of my hair tingle with cold, and my curls float around my head like a drowned girl.

A shudder wracks my lungs. I can't breathe.

"Gmmmm..." A disembodied voice groans overhead. "Mmmma."

Somehow, I've sunk into the dirt. My hands are the only thing I can still control, so I claw at the soil packed above my head. My body breaks apart and surges right through the clay like rivulets of rain on a window.

"Gmmmma!"

My fingers break through the top layer. I dig my nails into the sunbaked soil and wrench my body out of the pit, coughing dirt and water out of my lungs.

"Gems!" Dad grabs me under the shoulders and pulls me to my feet. "Are you hurt?"

I spit a clump of red clay into my hands. I don't know the answer to his question, so I ask my own. "What happened?"

"You got sucked underground. Like quicksand." He hurries me away from the well markers.

"It's a water table." I cast a glance over my shoulder. The ground is solid—no sign of the sink hole I just clawed my way out of. The only clue as to what just happened is a small patch of wet dirt already evaporating in the brutal sun. "The markers were in the wrong place."

Dad looks at me quizzically, a stack of wrinkles forming on his forehead. Other than the clay I coughed up, my skin and clothes are spotless. He reaches for my hand, hesitating before he touches my skin. There's a tremor in his fingers that I've never seen, and a wave of shame crashes against the rocks of my heart. He's afraid of me.

Honestly, I'm a little afraid of me, too.

"Are you...one of those...?"

"People who fell down a sinkhole?" I snatch my hand away. "Yes, I am."

"Christ, I'm sorry, kid. I don't know what I was thinking." Dad scrubs his hands over his face, smearing a line of dirt across his forehead. "C'mon, let's get you to the doctor's office, make sure everything's alright—"

"I feel fine." The flags are scattered around the wet spot where I came up for air. If I focus on those, I don't have to look into his eyes.

"Gems...you were under there for a while. We should get an x-ray, make sure there's no damage to your lungs."

What he's forgetting is the blood test the doctors will do if they think there's a chance I'm a mutant.

"I'm not even coughing." I stick the flags down in a circle around the water table, making sure the well diggers know where to drill. "I was scared, but I'm not anymore. Besides, who will do the weeding?"

"As your father—"

"Hold that thought." I cock my head toward the driveway, where a Prius is speeding over the gravel, spraying stones behind it. Mrs. Gray skids to a stop in front of our house and throws her door open.

She cups her hands around her mouth. "Have you seen Alison!?"

"Shit." I comb my fingernails across my scalp and grab the base of my ponytail. If she mentions Ali's mutation, Dad will know what's going on. And once again, Ali will be forcing me into a conversation I'm not ready to have. "Be right back."

I jog toward Ali's mom, trying to give myself enough time to talk her out of spilling the secret before Dad catches up. "Misses Gray, please, it's going to be okay—"

"She never came home last night, and she won't answer her phone." She shows me her blank cellphone screen. "I tried her father, her grandparents, Janessa..." She rattles off more names, but my brain has disconnected. Ali's mom tried calling *Janessa* before me. The realization slices through my heart. "Please, Gemma. You're my last hope before I call the police."

*Last hope.*

"I saw her yesterday after school. She and Janessa were having a sleepover."

"Janessa's mom hasn't seen them either. Where would they have gone?"

*Last.*

If Ali and Janessa took off, their parents don't know what's going on. My secret is safe until we find them.

"Maybe they went camping," I say. "Ali has a spot up on Blue Ridge."

It used to be our spot.

"I just have this feeling like something is wrong." Mrs. Gray tucks her bottom lip between her teeth. "I know things have been difficult between the two of you, but I need your help. Can you show me her spot?"

"I'll go, don't worry about it." If Ali ran away to the woods, it's safe to assume she needed to finish mutating in peace. "Why don't you keep looking around town?"

"Thank you." Mrs. Gray sags in relief, letting her head fall back. "Here, let me pay for your gas."

I hold my hand up, refusing the twenty-dollar bill she fished out of her wallet. "The first rescue is on me."

Mrs. Gray tilts her head and gives me a sympathetic smile. "You were always my favorite, Gems."

*Were.*

Dad bustles up behind us, mopping his brow with a red bandana, catching his breath for a litany of questions.

I don't want to get trapped in their parental anxiety spiral, so I head inside for my car keys. "I'll call you when I get to the spot. Let you know what I find."

ALI'S SPOT is this open meadow in the middle of the redwoods. For a while, it was our spot, but, last time I was here, we burned our friendship to the ground. The only thing left here are memories covered by the ash.

I was perfectly happy leaving Ali with the scorched earth. In return, she left me with the community pool—not that it's worth going without her to swim with.

When I arrive at the trailhead, my truck is the only car in the parking lot. The trail lost its popularity since the creek running through it dried up.

I slam my door and head for the rickety wooden bridge suspended over the dry creek bed. My phone buzzes with two new texts from Mrs. Gray, both asking if I've arrived yet. I shoot off a quick answer and head into the woods.

Ali and I liked this spot because it was the only mountaintop with cell service, so we could post thirst traps on IG. When the creek still existed, we would strip down and swim naked like wood nymphs, splashing around till our lips turned blue. Then we'd cuddle under a blanket and warm up at the foot of the giant sequoias. Real Greek mythology shit.

Now the creek is dead, and so are the chances of us ever doing that again.

The forest is quiet as I hike up the hillside. The only birdsong is the cry of turkey vultures looking for carrion. This place used to be overrun with mouthy magpies chasing hawks from their nests, but they haven't returned since the fire.

Things don't live here anymore.

"Alison?" My voice spreads in every direction, bounding through the tree trunks. "It's m—it's Gemma."

I hoist myself onto a massive log obstructing the trail and shimmy to the other side. A plump black widow skitters away from my hand, taking refuge under a broken bough.

I dismount onto a crunchy pile of leaves and cup my hands around my mouth. "Your mom is really worried about you."

A crow jumps from a thicket of poison oak and disappears deeper into the woods. My gaze slides back to the trail and I notice a set of mint green handlebars poking out of a holly bush.

Ali's bike.

I rush over, nearly tripping on a wild cucumber vine that leaves a trail of itchy spines along my ankle. In the basket of her bike is Ali's phone, backpack, and a grocery bag stuffed to the brim with weird organic snacks. I push the contents around and wrinkle my nose. This girl loves fruit leather.

Her phone is dead, but that's normal. She always forgets to charge it. When I bought her a portable battery, she reamed me out about lithium mines.

What scares me most about this scene is the untouched food. Ali demolishes snacks. One time she had a stomach flu and kept shoving ginger snaps down her throat between every puke session. If she'd been out here all night, there would be nothing but empty wrappers in this bag.

My heart twists into a knot. Something is really wrong.

The ground around her bike looks normal—no sign of dragging or fighting. But then I see something that sends a chill skimming down my back. Her green shorts and Woodstock t-shirt are laying on a rock beside the dry creek.

"Alison!" I march toward the creek bed, building a story in my head that gets scarier with every step. Someone must have followed her here. Waited until she was alone. "Ali—"

My leg slides into the ground up to the knee. Wet clay cakes my ankle, and my calf stretches like taffy toward the undulating water deep beneath the forest floor. I brace my hands against the surface, but they sink right into the soil until my elbows disappear.

The creek isn't gone; it moved underground. And it's sucking me in.

"Not now!" I flail through shallow mud. The more I struggle, the deeper I go, until I'm up to my neck in silt. Earthy water tickles the back of my throat and I splutter, craning my neck to keep it from filling my mouth.

I grab onto the nearest thing I can reach—a tangled pile of roots —and hold on like a buoy in the ocean.

The roots shudder, releasing a guttural groan. They come alive under my hands, slithering out of my grip. Suddenly, the trunk bends in half like a broken matchstick.

Then, some invisible force rips the tree right out of the ground. It pulls free as easy as a weed, the roots dangling in the air like severed veins. The tree hovers in the air, inching forward until it's positioned right over my head. If it falls, it'll crush me.

Frantically, I push off the shore and sink deeper into the ground, trying to swim through the dirt. The tree follows me, bark splintering as a branch crashes down so fast the only thing I can do is close my eyes and brace for impact.

Five spindly boughs close in a cage above my head. The points penetrate the ground and close around me like an arcade claw.

The tree lifts me up and deposits me onto solid ground in a heap. It looks just like a hand as it hovers in the air. The whorl patterns even look like fingerprints.

A throaty, guttural moan rumbles from the tree. "Gemmmma."

I don't fucking believe it. It looks like a hand because it *is* a hand.

"Alison!?"

The wooden palm tilts up at the wrist and the fingertips wave coquettishly. They're so big they send a breeze that ruffles my hair. Horror and relief war in the pit of my stomach. There's no more denying her transformation.

Her legs—twin redwood trunks—are wide as telephone poles. Her feet are writhing balls of roots that slide and slither over the soil. Two knotty growths make up her kneecaps, smoothing out into a vast body built of bark and bough.

Her knees creak, the trunks bending and squeaking as she

kneels down between the other trees. She crouches onto all fours, bringing her face closer to mine.

Her green eyes are still human-looking, set in two shadowed sockets. Red fibers fringe them like eyelashes. Her aquiline nose has been re-constructed from slices of bark, like one of those 3D wooden puzzles. A wreath of charred pine needles hang around her face, shuddering like locks of black hair. Two darkened shadows form her eyebrows, which are raised in fear. She presses her ligneous lips together in a frightened look that is so Alison, it makes me want to cry.

I approach her slowly, placing my hand against her rough cheek. Her head alone is taller than me. I could nestle my entire body into the seam of her lips, or fall into her mouth like some biblical giant.

She could devour me.

"Are you okay?" I slide my hand along her jaw, searching for body heat. Her bark is bloodless, chilled.

Her lips part slowly, moving like an ancient forest spirit. "I'm scared."

My hair blows back from the force of her breath. It smells like crushed pine needles and sun-warmed sap. A golden drop of syrup forms in her eye and drizzles down her cheek.

She's crying.

My shoulders curl inward, heavy with the weight of her sadness. I want to take her fear inside myself and bury it at the bottom of my well.

"I know." My eyes drop to the ground between us. It's blanketed with brittle, orange pine needles that haven't been disturbed by human feet in a long time. They still won't be, even after we leave. Because our feet are no longer human. "I'm a mutant, too."

She sucks in a breath, and her gasp drags me across the dirt toward her mouth. I'm at her whim, caught like a bird in a storm. I have to brace myself against her lips to avoid being swallowed.

"What's your power?" she asks.

"I'm not exactly sure, but I keep dissolving into the dirt whenever there's water around."

Her giant eyes slide toward the puddle at my feet. My sneakers are sopping wet, little rivulets pouring out of the perforations like a dripping shower head.

Ali frowns. "You're leaking."

This must be my mutant power—becoming water, absorbing it. But the only place it exists in this drought-gutted wasteland is underground.

"I can feel it vibrating. It pulls me down, and by the time I know what's happening, it's too late."

Ali squints her enormous green eyes. Her pupils have a constellation of silver flecks. "You need a stick. Like a dowser."

"A what?"

"A water witch. They use forked rods to find wells." Her giant, woody arms hover over my head and she snaps a thin branch off.

"Doesn't that hurt?"

"It's kind of satisfying, actually. Like pulling a loose tooth." She hands me the Y-shaped branch. "Hold that out and walk toward the creek bed."

I wave it around limply. "This is silly."

She rolls her galaxy eyes. "Humor me."

"Fine." I hold the forked ends in each hand and point the long end in front of me. "Wait. What part of you am I holding?"

"Focus."

"Is it, like, a finger? Will it grow back?"

"It's a branch." She makes a fist and new growth bursts from her hand. "I have branches, now."

I cast a cheeky glance over my shoulder. "Geez, you don't have to *bark* at me."

"Oh my god." She drags her hand over her face, scattering chips of herself onto the forest floor.

The branch in my hands suddenly jiggles, right before I reach the dark spot where I fell through.

"Hey. It's working." I toe the ground and my foot sinks into the shallows. "You were right."

I take another timid step and she pinches the back of my shirt between two red fingers. With her tethering me, I can test my new power.

"Speaking of being right..." Her fingers slacken around my shirt. I peer over my shoulder to see her roots shrinking. Her body is mutating again, getting smaller. "I had a lot of time to think last night, and...I shouldn't have pushed you into coming out."

My shoulders stiffen. Whether it's from her words, or the water soaking into my legs like a sponge, I don't know. "What makes you say that?"

"I spent all night hiding from my parents because I didn't want them to see me this way. And it made me realize what you must have felt." Her arm shrivels into a more human shape, the bark breaking off in sheafs to reveal her pale flesh. "I'm sorry."

Tears fill my eyes, filled with all the grit and clay I've sucked up from the ground. The dirt scratches behind my eyelids, burning my sinuses. Muddy tears pour down my face like a fountain.

I didn't realize how badly I wanted to hear those words, but she did.

And she gave them to me.

"Damn it, Alison." I rub the back of my hand over my face, smearing my concealer. "You're fucking with my makeup."

"Sorry."

I dab the corners of my eyes, but it's hopeless. The layers of concealer wash away until there's nothing to hide behind.

"I missed you so bad," I say.

She exhales in disbelief. "You did?"

"Every day." I rub my runny nose on my arm. "You went missing, and I was the last person your mom asked for help. She called your asshole dad before she called me. Fucking broke my heart."

Her face transforms, shedding layers of bark. Her ivory cheeks are still streaked with golden lines of sap. She's herself again, glowing and naked in the filtered sun.

"Even after everything we did to each other..." Her voice is breathy like the wind through the trees. "You were the only one who knew where to find me."

After everything we did. The weeks of silence, dirty looks, whispered epithets. We tried to wound each other with our absence, but all we were doing was wasting time. All because I wanted to keep lying to myself. To deny what I've known since I first laid my greedy eyes on her.

"Because you're *mine*, Alison." I knuckle the tears from my face. "Obviously."

She runs her small hands across my neck, sliding her fingers into my hair. Her nails scratch my scalp as she pulls my mouth to hers.

The dam inside me breaks. I drag her body against me, gripping her jaw and kissing her hard. Water spills from my fingertips and drips down her collarbones. Her tongue slides against my lips and I let her in, savoring the bitter taste of pine.

She breaks for air, staring at me with a ferocity I've never seen. "I knew it."

"Knew what?"

"You love me." She runs her finger over my lip, wiping away one of her syrupy tears.

"Maybe I do." I pinch the tip of her finger between my teeth, and she gasps. "Maybe I always have."

"Uhhhh..." Janessa is standing behind us with her phone up to her ear, staring open-mouthed. "I found them, Mrs. Gray."

Ali's eyebrows knit together and she draws a line across her throat, mouthing the words, "Don't tell her anything!"

Mrs. Gray's voice squawks on the other line. Before answering, Janessa reaches for an antique change dispenser fastened to her belt. She tosses a quarter into her mouth and swallows.

"Yeah," she answers, sounding like the Usher song. "Ali says she'll call you back in a minute." She slams her finger on the end button. "Would either of you like to explain what's going on?"

Ali puckers her mouth sheepishly. "How did you find us?"

Janessa shoves another quarter in her mouth.

"Gemma!" She sings my name like the beginning notes of Thriller. "Left Find My Friend on. Why are you naked?"

"Oh shit." Ali blushes, and bark blooms over her skin like scales. It covers her from nape to knees. "I got so big, my shirt was starting to rip."

"She turned into an actual tree," I add. "Branches and everything." Reluctantly, I grab her clothes off the rock and toss them to her, noticing a delicate patch of roots still shuddering around her toes like a sea anemone. "How did you change back?"

She pulls her shirt over her head and the bark scales disappear. Her heavy-lidded eyes drop to my lips. "I really wanted to be small again so I could kiss you."

My heart rises like a bird on a swell. I dip my feet into the groundwater and send a flirtatious stream toward Ali's feet.

Her roots undulate and she squirms. "That tickles."

Janessa watches the woody tentacles writhe around Ali's feet. "What is going on?"

Ali lifts her damp foot into the air. "Gemma's watering my roots."

"Excuse me?" Janessa's face pinches in disgust. "Is this some kind of entwife foreplay?"

I suck water into my finger and spray it like a hose at her. She shrieks and jumps back. "You are a mutant!"

"My name is Dowser." I wave my drippy fingers at her. "I can control groundwater."

"Great. Really happy for you." Janessa claps sarcastically. "A power you can hide. Meanwhile, I had a pile of nickels for dinner, and everyone thinks I'm losing my mind."

Ali's face falls into a guilt-ridden scowl. We've been playing around while Janessa was all alone.

"I'm sorry, hon. We're going to figure this out," she says. "Maybe we can spend some time in Mutopia. Learn to use our powers. It'll be a gap year to travel and see the world, like rich people do."

"You don't get it. The Cute Mutants can help you two." Janessa folds her arms over her chest. "What are they going to do for me—teach the world to only speak in statements?" Her hands curl into fists and her face turns bright red. I've never seen her so upset. "I can't go to *college* now. Do you know what professors do in lectures? They ask questions. People are going to notice me stuffing dirty quarters in my mouth just to pass my classes. We may be out of the dark years, but this country has been divided for a lot longer. The world is not going to change for me—"

"Sweetie." Ali pulls her into her arms, which grow twice the size. Janessa is locked in her embrace, nearly eclipsed by Ali's trunks. The pressure of her embrace seems to be draining Janessa's anxiety. "The people who love us will change. We don't have to convince the whole world."

"One step a time." I join the hug, resting my head in the crook of Janessa's neck. "We'll do it together. The three of us."

"Really?" Janessa peers down at me. "You're ready for that?"

Over Janessa's head, Ali meets my eyes. The same question is etched in the downward curve of her brows. I wasn't ready before, and it smashed our friendship into pieces. I know she's wondering if one kiss was enough to glue it back together.

"I'm ready now."

Ali clears her gravely throat. "Does that mean what I think it means?"

I give her a curt nod, because I'm not sure I can form the words *I'm gay.*

A small smile curls the edges of Ali's lips, but her eyes are still wary. She's offered me her heart before, and I broke it. Neither of us is sure I deserve a second chance.

Janessa's phone rings again and she smacks her forehead.

"Shoot. Your mom." She hands her phone to Ali, who stares at the number on the screen nervously.

The moment of truth.

She presses the phone to her ear. "Hey ma, I'm fine. Sorry—" Her expression falls into a frown. Then her eyebrows jump up her face. "We have to go."

"What's going on?" Janessa and I ask at the same time.

"There's a wildfire." She snaps her fingers and herds us toward the trail. "It's headed this way."

MY TRUCK RACES down the mountain, slamming into potholes and sending our heads crashing into the ceiling. Janessa is scrolling Twitter and rattling off updates as they come.

"CalFire is calling it a four alarm."

"That's bad." Ali watches smoke gathering on the horizon. It's probably a mile down the road from us, but distance means nothing. The entire state is a tinderbox. We're at the will of the wind. The flames could bear down on us in minutes.

"Someone got a drone picture. It looks like a bunch of letters burned into the mountain," Janessa says.

My hands tighten on the steering wheel. "That means it's intentional."

"What kind of monster would do that?" Ali asks.

I can't imagine. We've all seen the aftermath of the last fire: white skeletons burned clean of flesh, sitting upright in their bombed-out cars.

Right now, the girl I love is biting her fingernails in the passenger seat, and it's my job to make sure she doesn't burn alive the way Chiclet did in her horse trailer: trapped in the thing that was supposed to keep her safe.

"Oh my god, look." Janessa holds her phone over the console, but I can't break my eyes away from the road. We made it back to the main intersection, but all the other neighbors are fleeing. I have to wait for five trucks to pass before I can keep moving.

The moment I do, another truck bears down on my bumper. It honks like mad even though I'm going as fast as I can. My heart is slamming against my chest so hard I can feel it in my teeth.

The truck behind me peels out and passes even though there's barely enough room. His mirror almost scrapes mine.

"I'm assuming the fire spells out a message," I say.

"Shit, sorry." Janessa holds it closer to her face. "It says, 'You'll all pay.' And it's signed with some weird symbol. WildFire?"

"Sounds like a mutant name." Ali's voice is whisper thin.

"Sounds like Drew Kemp. He had that smoke coming out of his hands." I slam on my brakes as a second truck races around me. All the rules go out the window in an emergency like this. "Pull up his Twitter."

"Ugh, listen to this." Janessa scoffs. "'Despite all my rage, I'll trap all you rats in a cage.'"

"It's gotta be him." Ali grips the oh-shit-handle above her window as the Durango bobs in and out of another pothole. "I can't believe the universe would put that kind of power in his hands."

"Drew loves vague tweeting. It must be a clue." The edge of the forest melts away as I drive toward downtown. Open fields unroll like a patchwork quilt. Behind us, a tower of smoke crawls over the mountain. It's white now, from quick-burning fuel. Soon, it will turn black: the color of burning houses, melting plastic, boiling bleach. The flames will eat through summer dresses and beach blankets, belching soot and ash until the town is coated in dirty snow.

"He started the fire outside city limits..." Ali mutters.

"Trapped in a cage. Trapped in a cage." Janessa drums her fingers against the back of my seat. Her phone beeps with an emergency alert. "Evacuation notice for Springer. First Responders are setting up at the University football stadium."

"There will be a huge crowd at the stadium." Ali snaps her fingers. "What if he's smoking us out? If everyone is gathered in one place, they're an easier target."

"Trap all you rats in a cage." Janessa stares at her phone screen. "I think you're right."

"Call the police," I hiss. "Tell them!"

Janessa dials 911. It rings and rings. She hangs up and tries again, but there are so many people doing the same thing, she can't get through.

"See." Ali points at us for emphasis. "Chaos. We can't communicate with each other. Everyone's confused. Nobody will see him coming."

"I'll send a warning out on Twitter, but I only have, like, fifty followers." Janessa frantically types out a message. "We have to get over to the evacuation center and tell someone."

I make a split-second decision and take a hard right, flying down a country road that spits us out a few miles from the football stadium.

The streets are clogged with overpacked cars, their trunks unlatched, displaying the contents like half-chewed food. Between the gridlocked cars are people running on foot, carrying babies, dogs, shopping bags stuffed with valuables. On the sidewalk, an old man with a parrot on his shoulder lugs a cello case behind him.

"Park it." Ali points to an abandoned parking space. Her eyes are pleading. "We can run to the stadium from here."

I want to blow through the entire town and keep driving until we can't see smoke. But Ali hates it when a butterfly hits a windshield. Her heart won't be able to bear a town full of innocent people trapped in the burning cauldron of the stadium. Especially when there's something we can do about it.

"Fine." I jam on the brakes to let someone pull in front of me, then pull into the parking space they just abandoned. It's not like the Durango is so reliable, anyway. "But if shit goes sideways, you have to promise me you will save yourself."

"Gem—"

"Promise me." I grab both sides of her face, my eyes boring into hers. She purses her lips, and I wonder if she's feeling the weight of our responsibility to each other. I have her heart to protect, and she has mine. And that complicates everything.

She nods weakly. "I promise."

My hands tremble against her jaw. I don't believe her.

"Let's go." Janessa pushes her door open, magnifying the sounds of panic around us. Kids are crying, mothers are shrieking, dogs are barking. In the distance are endless sirens. They never get louder or quieter.

We comb through the crowds, trying to find openings to run through. There are so many bodies moving in so many directions, it's hard to keep pace.

"Should we warn them?" Ali asks, huffing beside me.

"We don't know for sure if he's going to attack the evacuation center. If we send them away, we could make things worse."

Janessa nods behind us, covering her ears with her hands. "I'm scared."

Ali touches her back. "We'll take care of you."

"We're a team." I give her a double thumbs up. "And good job being honest about your feelings."

She rolls her eyes, but a small smile creeps over her face. "My therapist would be so proud."

As we approach the stadium, the crowds condense into an orderly line. The queue snakes all the way across the parking lot.

Ali stops short, her heel dragging in the dust. "The line is too long. We need to tell someone what's going on."

"He might already be in there." Janessa's hands fall away from her ears. "Oh my gosh, do we have to *fight* him?"

"We don't...I can't..." Ali bites her lip, giving me a surreptitious glance. I already know what she's going to say. She's the type of girl who scoops caterpillars off the sidewalk with her bare hands.

"It's okay. You can be on rescue detail," I say.

"Are you sure?" she asks.

"You'd be terrible in a fight," Janessa says.

"Right." She nods, relieved. "I'm going up to the front to ask if Drew checked in."

"Good," I say. "Janessa and I will try the side doors, see if we can sneak in."

I march off, but Ali grabs my elbow and swings me around. She plants a firm kiss on my lips, tasting like birch syrup. People are watching, but I can't focus on anything other than her soft mouth.

She breaks away with a wet smack. "Be safe, Gems."

"O-okay." I stare after her, dumbstruck. There's no way of knowing what we're about to face, or if we'll survive. An intrusive thought beats against my brain like a dying moth. This could be the last time we ever see each other. The thought makes my throat constrict. "I will."

She winks and strides off, but her lips and face look pale. Like she's already fading away.

"LET'S GO." Janessa yanks my wrist in the other direction.

"Sorry," I mumble, following her across the dusty parking lot.

"Holy shit, look at this." She walks up to the first set of double doors leading into the stadium. There's a chain around the handles, and a Master lock hanging like a pendant from the center. A wet line of rainbow-colored fluid paints the doorstep. "The doors are locked from the outside. And...it smells like gasoline. He's already here."

"Let's try the next set." I point her farther around the open-air building and pull my phone up, dialing 911 again. The line doesn't even ring this time. The cell towers must be overburdened.

The second set of double doors are locked the same way, and the third. Finally, on our last-ditch effort, we find the boiler room left unlocked. Just inside the door frame, we find a stack of breeze blocks.

"I bet this is his escape route." Janessa kneels to inspect the tower of concrete.

"Where did you...?" I cut my question short. "I don't know where you learned all this."

"I watch a lot of true crime." She picks up a cinderblock and flings it outside. It falls heavily, only a foot away from her. "The perp always makes a mistake, you just have to find it."

The air suddenly stings my nose, sending a cold shiver down my spine.

Smoke.

"We have to go."

Janessa and I head into the open-air hallways, following the arrows pointing toward the field. The smoke is getting heavier. Drew must have started already. We're too late to stop him.

But Ali would want us to try.

"Here, field access." Janessa speeds out of the dark hallway and into the sunlight of the open stadium.

I take a tentative step onto the field, feeling vibrations all around. The grass is bright green and soaked from the sprinklers. I can sense the system of pipes radiating with contained water, and that keeps my feet from dissolving right into the ground.

The field is packed tight with people waiting for bottled water and first aid. Nurses parade back and forth, carrying rolls of bandages and tubes of ointment. Emergency cots are set up in a circle around the outside ring, empty gurneys awaiting their victims.

They'll be holding corpses if we don't figure out how to stop this.

"There." Janessa points to a figure dressed in a red, leather duster. He looks like a cheesy video game villain. Smoke pours from his open palms. "It's Drew."

The people around him are sniffing the air, trying to find where the smoke is coming from. One woman turns to him and screams.

"This boy needs help!" She races over and throws her sweater on his hands to smother blaze. The polyester melts, fusing to Drew's sleeve. His knuckles pulse with fire.

"No." A cruel smile mars his face. Plumes of thick, acrid smoke surround him. "You need help."

He winds his fist up and punches the ground. A fireball explodes around him, burning the wet grass to cinders. He's completely unharmed in the center of an orange ball. Only the tips of his feathered, blonde hair are smoking.

Tentacles burst from the fireball and spread toward the door. They carve the field up into sections, trapping groups of people in a labyrinth of seven-foot flames. Screaming crowds scatter toward the exits, but the fire jumps up over their heads.

Smoke falls over the field like a curtain, forcing the fresh air into a narrow window at our feet. Janessa and I drop to our knees in the grass, army crawling toward Drew. We pass a woman ripping a piece of her own shirt and covering her daughter's mouth and nose with it.

Sweat breaks out over my body, and my stomach twists in fear. There's so much water in the pipes underground but I can't access it. There must be a way to touch it—a hose or something.

The walls of flame surge higher and wider, fueled by Drew's power. He smashes his knuckles together and two new fireballs sprout from his hands. He launches the twin suns toward the distant emergency exits. The orange globes burn a hole through the crowds, leaving nothing in their wake but a smoking pile of ash. The scent of burned hair and charred flesh fills the stadium.

All of those lives, ended in the blink of an eye. Ripped from the earth as if they never existed. My body goes numb with shock. A scream is locked inside my chest, but I can hear it thundering in my own head.

The fireballs smash against the exit doors, igniting the puddles of gasoline. Drew has trapped everyone in the stadium so he can burn them alive. It's so violently planned—so disgustingly precise —that my mind goes blank with rage.

In this moment I can only think of stopping him. Forever. No matter what it costs me.

"What are we going to do?" Janessa asks, cowering beneath the thickening smoke.

"I need to access the water."

"What about the sprinklers? There's a head right over there." She points to the chalk lines painted on the grass. In the far corner is a circular hole punched into the turf.

"Yes!" I crawl toward it, scrabbling to pull the plastic sprinkler head up. It's jammed tight, but I manage to pry it open, ignoring how my nails bend back.

The spout is pointed, perfect for me to fit my mouth to the end, suck in a deep breath, and blow. Water gurgles through the pipes, and the sprinklers around me dribble, but nothing comes out.

"Try harder!" Janessa shrieks.

Gulping down another breath, I blow through the spout, focusing all my attention on the strange network of vibrations under my control. Water bursts from the spouts at full force, drenching the stadium and everyone still trapped in it.

"You're doing it," Janessa cries, holding her hands out. Water patters against her open palms and dampens the back of my shirt, soaking me until I've sponged up enough to leak out of my shoes. My limbs are heavy with it.

The flames sputter as sprinklers douse the field. In the center of the stadium, Drew stands with his hands outstretched in the mist. Little flecks of steam roll off his cheeks. He scowls at the hoard of people running toward the bleachers, climbing for fresh air.

A shadow passes over him and he squints at the sky. A canopy of branches reach across the horizon, followed by a pair of god-sized green eyes.

My heart clenches like a fist. Alison is here.

Her wooden hand grips the side of the stadium like a salad bowl and she reaches in to scoop up a handful of people.

"What the fuck is this?" Drew knocks his knuckles together, forming more fireballs that lick up his arms. He aims one at Ali, and my world narrows to a pinprick.

Drew Kemp is threatening my girl. I won't let him.

A jet of water surges from my arm like a firehose, knocking Drew to his knees. His hands fly out to break his fall, and the fireballs wink out in a wall of steam.

Ali's hand disappears on the other side of the stadium, but I know her. She'll keep coming back until everyone is ferried to the other side. I have to keep Drew focused on me.

"Hey, asshole!" I scream.

"You're going to regret that." He jumps to his feet, staring daggers at me. His irises are a strange, flat red.

He flares the hem of his red duster, winds his arm back, and slams his fist into the ground. A comet zips across the field and buries itself in my gut, sending me sailing backward. My skin puckers, the excess water boiling through my veins. I cough out a plume of steam, laying in a helpless heap. There are people who need me, but I can't get up. The exhaustion is too much. Drew is too strong, driven by his endless well of anger. I'll never be able to compete.

A blurry orange ball flares to life and I brace myself for the end. It'll incinerate me just like his other victims. The only thing I can hope for is that it's as quick as it looks, and I won't really feel anything when I evaporate.

Instead of coming toward me, though, the fireball streaks like a sparkler toward the sky.

Toward Ali.

He's going to hurt her. He needs to be stopped.

Condensation fogs my eyes as I roll onto my knees, summoning every last drop of boiling water inside me. I aim my hands at him. Hot water spouts from my hands in a violent stream, fueled by all my fear. Heat drains from my limbs like a thermometer.

The boiling water pummels Drew, searing his face. White blisters bloom like mushrooms over his cheeks, and a melted piece of plastic droops out of his bloodshot eye. It's a red contact lens, curled up like a red Fortune Fish, revealing his plain blue iris underneath. His other eye is swollen shut.

"Give it up, Drew!" Janessa stuffs a handful of quarters into her mouth and purses her lips. One by one, she shoots them like little bullets, slicing his coat open and lodging in his chest. One of them hits a blister in his cheek, breaking it open and sending pus oozing down his jaw.

Seeing him like that, flayed and in pain, makes my knees wobble. I press them together and brace my hands on my thighs to keep from collapsing. I'm not cut out for this violence. The sheer brutality makes me ill.

Grief for this world burrows like a worm into my chest. Mutants may be a different species, but it is human sickness that makes us spill the blood of others to save our own.

The sound of screaming brings me back. The crowds have gathered in the far corners of the stadium. There's nowhere left for them to run. The exits are chained, the bleachers are cloaked in smog. At any moment, Drew could summon another blaze and incinerate them. The only thing they have left to do is wait for his next attack, and hope they're fast enough to dodge it.

Ali scoops another handful of screaming children, but it's not fast enough. The smoke is putting the youngest ones to sleep, their parents dragging their comatose bodies toward the few pockets of fresh air they can find. It's hopeless. It won't be enough to save them in time. But I don't know if I have what it takes to end this.

Someone has to make sure Drew can't hurt anyone ever again. I'm afraid it has to be me.

"Alison, the doors!" Janessa cries.

A giant tree trunk swoops over the stadium, but the moment it approaches the blaze, it's engulfed in flame. Ali yanks her arm back, shaking her combustible fingers until the sparks die out. I can hear the sap fizzing inside them.

It's too dangerous for her to break open the doors. We need to work together.

I fit my lips over the sprinkler and drink my fill. My body swells against my clothes, water leaking like sweat from my armpits and wetting my shirt. Taking a deep breath, I plug my nose and aim my fist at the fire.

Water shoots out of me with so much force it rattles the doors against their chains. A wave surges through the narrow slit, soaking the flames until there's nothing left but a trail of steam on the concrete.

Ali fits her wooden finger underneath the chain, and with one grimace of her ligneous mouth, she yanks it open.

Captives throw themselves toward the new exit, desperate for freedom. They barge past each other, forming a clot around the doors. Drew eyes the traffic jam greedily, cracking his smoking knuckles. He's going to send a fireball to incinerate them.

I don't know if there's enough water in me to stop him, and I don't have time to refill. It will only take a second for him to create a blistering meteor.

I'll have to stop him with the only thing I have left—myself.

I jog toward him, trying to figure out what the fuck I'm going to do. There's not enough water inside me. "Janessa, fire away."

Janessa fires another round of quarters at him, slicing shallow wounds in his arms. A lock of hair flutters to the ground as a dime thunks into the back of his skull.

He snaps his fingers, creating a solar flare that scorches the last coins into orange raindrops that smear across the grass. But the distraction did its job. He's not looking at me.

I lower my shoulder and lunge. My body connects with Drew's chest and we're falling to the ground in a jarring crash. My neck snaps backward and my jaw feels like a drawer sliding off its track.

Drew is beneath and on top of me at once, his leather coat stinking of burned flesh. It's enough to make a girl go vegan.

Before I can catch my breath, Drew grabs my shirt and wrestles me into the grass, pinning me with his weight. I only have time to throw my hands up before he raises his fist and slams it into my face.

Fire sears my cheek, so acutely hot that my hair sizzles against my skull. The cushion of water between my skin and bones is the only reason my brain didn't fry, but the damage to my body is undeniable. I can taste bitter smoke rolling off my charred skin.

This burn will leave me irreversibly marked. For the rest of my short life, there will be no more hiding. I'll bear the scars, and the world will remember I'm a mutant.

Drew winds up to hit me again, and I'm so afraid of the pain that I find the strength to roll away from it, cowering with my head in my hands. Drew's fist smashes into the ground, forming a halo of flame around us.

Janessa fires another wave of coins, but they transform into useless molten lumps, spattering his sleeve like bird shit.

A sob bursts out of my throat like bile. Nothing is working.

"Dumb bitches." Drew's puffy eyes find mine, and his mouth twists into a swollen smirk. "You really thought you could beat me?"

Behind his shoulder, Ali curls her fibrous hand into a fist. Her fingers squeak against each other as a crop of three seedlings burst from between her knuckles like a sylvan Wolverine. Baby roots snake over the sides of her hand, reaching tentatively for solid ground.

"We haven't lost yet," I say, drawing his attention away as Ali aims her spindly claws at his back. I have no idea what she's planning, but I hope it's enough to end this fight. My body is aching from wounds and water, and I'm afraid this whole plan was a fatal mistake. "Heads up."

Ali slams her fist into Drew's back, forcing her seedlings

through his stomach. His face crumples in a mask of pain as the sharp end of a baby redwood pokes through his belly button.

The seedlings detach from Ali's hand with a snap, their roots slithering over Drew's back. He beats his hands against them, drawing lines of fire that shrivel their weak boughs.

One seedling withers on contact, shrinking into a mummified arrow. Drew slides it out of his stomach in a spray of blood that spatters my clothes. He scrapes his nail over his skin to cauterize the puncture wound.

"Gemma," Ali groans in her ent voice. "Now."

At once, I understand her gruesome plan. Without question, I summon the last dregs of water into my hands, focusing so hard that the grass around me shrivels into a brown patch. I've pulled the moisture from every green blade.

I press my swollen hands against Drew's chest and release a fountain of water that blasts the blood from his shirt and soaks the seedlings' roots.

The baby trees shudder, their roots flailing like a terrible sea monster. Drew's bloodshot eyes widen in horror as the twin trunks begin expanding inside his chest. He locks onto the saplings with frantic eyes—one red, one blue.

"You fucking bit—"

The trees burst through his chest, splitting his ribcage open with a creak. His flesh stretches like plastic wrap, tearing into uneven chunks. The redwoods wet their roots in his blood and grow even bigger.

Within seconds, they've grown at least six feet tall, fertilized by Drew's innards. The only thing left of him is a dismembered leg, with its knee still buried in my gut. I toss it aside and scamper away from the roots writhing over each other like a ball of eels, puncturing the football field and digging for more water.

Drew is dead. Growing from his wet corpse are two ravenous sequoias, their fibrous trunks knit so tight they look fused. At once, his labyrinth of fire dissipates in a cloud of steam.

We won.

CHATTERBOX CAN'T HOLD their booze. That's the first thing I notice as they grab the pink bedazzled microphone and clumsily vault themselves onto the coffee table.

My graduation party is suddenly quiet as a wild synth melody starts up. Two hundred eyes flit over to my TV screen, lit up with lyrics for some bizarre anime song I've never heard before.

Chatterbox starts singing in their cute kiwi accent, closing their eyes as the frenetic music builds. The title plays on the screen, *Yuri on Ice*? Who knows.

Sourpatch snatches the microphone and pulls it close to her latex-red lips. Everyone at the party is watching the Cute Mutants, but nobody else knows the lyrics.

For two weeks I absolutely refused to consider karaoke at my graduation rager, but Ali wouldn't give it up. She tried every which way to convince me, and finally found one that worked.

Turns out she's a very convincing orator.

"See, I told you everyone would like it." Ali sidles up to me, red solo cup in hand. Her green t-shirt is riding up, revealing skin so pale it looks like cream ready to spill over her waistband.

"I can't believe people actually like having that much attention focused on them."

She whips out her phone and starts recording me. "Observe the Gemma in her natural habitat. Reclusive. Mysterious."

I cover the camera with my hand. "I do not wish to be perceived."

After everyone was safely evacuated from the stadium, videos popped up all over the internet of Janessa and I fighting with Drew. In a matter of days, I went from anonymous high schooler to small-town anti-hero.

When the police dubbed Drew's attack an act of domestic terrorism, his family launched a PR campaign to clear his name. They called him a lost boy, a victim of PC culture, and when none of that worked, they sued the school for a bevy of unenforceable crimes and tried to get me expelled.

Some people agreed with them, including the priest at my parents' church. That first Sunday after the attack, while we were still grieving the deaths in our community, his sermon veered into the sin of mutation.

While I sat there, wishing I could evaporate, my mother slammed her hymn book down, called the priest a fucking blowhard, and marched our whole family into the parking lot.

None of us have been back.

Ali tucks her phone in her pocket, a coy little smile curling her lips. "You look like you're having fun."

I narrow my eyes at her. "You look pleased with yourself."

She shrugs, tilting her head coquettishly. "Your dad stopped me on his way out."

I take a gulp from my cup, trying to hide my face. It had taken me an entire hour of hemming and hawing before I admitted I was both gay *and* dating my childhood best friend, who'd been sleeping over at our house for seven years.

"And?"

"He said he was happy for us." Ali wiggles her nose like a bunny. "And that I better not break your heart."

"Oh my god, Dad..." I press my cold cup to my forehead, combatting the blush prickling over my face.

"It was sweet." She boops my nose. "He's a good dude."

"My parents were actually kind of psyched when I told them about my powers. I'm pretty sure Dad's jury-rigging some mobile sprinkler so I can water the farm for him."

"It's hard, you know. Being so extremely right," Ali says.

I roll my eyes, but I can't help the smile blooming over my face.

She leans close, her lips brushing the shell of my ear. "Say it."

I look up through my lashes and draw my tongue over my lips. "You were right."

She bites the rim of her cup, staring uncertainly at my mouth. She's still not used to me being flirtatious, and it throws her off in the cutest way. Years from now, when we've been dating for eternity, I hope her lips will still tremble when I turn it on for her.

"Happy graduation, ladies!" Janessa marches up to the kitchen counter carrying two white bags. "I got us matching presents."

She hands each of us a bag, but before we even open them, I notice what she's wearing. It's a black sweatsuit with a belt loop to hold her change dispenser filled with quarters. White lettering trails down the sleeve, spelling out JUKEBOX.

"No way." Ali tears her bag open to find a matching top. Her sleeve says SEQUOIA. "This is the coolest thing ever."

"Don't worry, Gems. I made sure Ali got sweat shorts so you can stare at her legs all day."

I yoke Janessa around the neck and kiss the top of her head. "You're a pervert's best friend."

She punches my arm. "Literally."

"These are awesome." Ali pulls her sweatshirt over her head and inspects it. "But where's the Cute Mutants logo?"

Janessa slips a coin from her dispenser, pops it in her mouth, and grimaces. She's not answering.

I crook my head. "Something is wrong."

Janessa pulls her shirt up to reveal an arcade token stuck inside her belly button like a coin return. She fishes it out and tosses it in the trash, then shoves a real quarter in her mouth. She hums the tune of a Celine Dion song and starts singing. "The guy at the print shop said he can't put trademarked logos on anything. Take it up with Chatterbox."

I free my own sweatshirt from the bag and pull it on. From upside down, it says RESWOD. "How do I look?"

"So hot." Ali grabs my hoodie strings and pulls me into a kiss, drawing a few catcalls from our drunk classmates lounging around the kitchen. Even though Ali's in her human form, she still tastes like pine resin.

"Ugh, come on you two." Janessa hangs over the counter and makes an exaggerated gagging noise. "There are, like, two hundred other people in the room."

"Sorry." Ali releases me, looking like the cat who got the cream. Whatever the fuck that means.

I offer Janessa a sheepish bow, but I don't apologize. Because I'm not sorry.

Not one bit.

# Farsight

"They're cute," Alyse says. "Maddy reckons they're like we were back in the day."

I open my mouth to speak, but Dylan gets there first.

"They *are* cute, and don't give me that look, Farsight. I know we can't have a million rogue mutant superteams roaming around out there. But if you won't let me stop humans from doing bad shit, I can't stop mutants from doing reckless shit. Do you want me to lock them up and drag them back to Mutopia so we can keep an eye on them?"

That is precisely what I think we should be doing, but I can't say that because it's not fair. I have an abundance of caution, and every mutant who appears dangerous to the eyes of humanity puts us at risk.

"We've got all the socials," Dani says. "And a newsletter. That girl with the data powers from Ray's office runs all the accounts. We should use them more. Put out, like, bulletins and shit."

"Bulletins," Dylan smirks.

"Yes, public service advisories. Don't use your powers in a way that makes people scared. Otherwise Dragon and Feral will pay you a visit."

"Maybe." Dylan sighs elaborately. "It's just nice seeing kids do it on their own. Old school shit. Starting gangs, saving the day. Makes me feel nostalgic, makes me feel old."

"Simpler times, darling." Alyse smiles, but it stutters and turns into something more shaky, because those times came with other people. "We should do a mission, for old times' sake. The gang back together. Dress up, find someone to punch."

Dylan's eyes brighten, and I clear my throat.

"Goddamn it, I hate being notorious." They scowl right at me, and I try not to quail. "Ray's already made it very clear that I should only leave the island if it's totally necessary and vital for matters of security. I'm the queer in the chair now. Waggling my fingers behind the scenes. It sucks."

I'm about to talk about the importance of Dylan's role on the island, but Dani can't stop laughing about the queer in the chair until Dylan stops her mouth with a kiss.

"We'll send someone to talk to them," Dylan says, once that finishes. "Tell them to be careful. The world will stay on its axis, Far, don't you worry."

# Gary

EMMA JUN

"SASH? WHAT ARE YOU DOING?"

This is the first clue I'm not in bed. That and the ache of weight on my feet. My consciousness fights through a layer of sleep fog, the panic that I might be late for class again and the general confusion before I think about replying. Is everything even working? Oh god... Sleep paralysis!

The hall of our shared house certainly isn't my bed, but I'm wearing my sleepy time t-shirt and pants. Half right. It's darker than the royal family's history yet I can see the thankfully familiar silhouette of June, clutching herself in surprise at my presence.

"Toilet," I say, debunking the paralysis theory. Pretty sure I hadn't been there and no urge to go, but apparently my first instinct is to make excuses. Always trying to be normal.

I check my pulse: normal. Why do my fingers ache like I've trapped them in a door?

"Looked like you were just standing there. Scared the crap out of me," she says and pads towards the bathroom. "The breakup with Scott was my trauma for the semester. I don't want to add stalkery housemate."

"June," I speak again, without the thinking that makes people respectable.

She stops, facing into a sliver of moonlight. Her blonde hair is scruffy from bed, a rock band t-shirt on over baggy striped pants. She's practically a model of glamorous uni life, but I bet that she has no idea who the band is.

"That was probably you banging about the last half hour too," she says, all softness gone from her voice.

I don't think so, but apparently I'm not a reliable source anymore. Probably should delay my essay another day then.

"Tea," I say. My first consciously chosen words are pretty familiar in this shared house. "Can't sleep now."

From the kitchen, I time the filling of the kettle to mask June's business in the room above. Chamomile tea it is then. I never liked the stuff, but articles say not to have caffeine at night even if it does seem to focus me and relax me. I'd also read that was a sign of neuro-divergence which sent me into a panic spiral for a few weeks until I had reasoned that it was a crappy pop-science article anyway. What do they know? A similar shite blog had published that a giant acid death cloud would dissolve the Earth in 2018 and despite me being terrified to the point where I refused to form any new long term relationships, it had not happened … yet.

I check my pulse again. Damn, why is it racing? Fuck it. I throw the camomile back and grab the regular. Yeah, calming down now.

THE BENEFIT of having my sleep disturbed is that I'm awake for uni. Not that the anxiety of showing up to an early morning lecture I've hardly attended all semester isn't already killing me.

The campus is like a botanical garden and bustling. It actually looks like the promo pics on the prospectus today, so they could have saved money on photoshop, but go inside any building and the photo opportunities end. There's cramped halls and decor that was last revamped in the 70s. Not sure which century though. I get lost in a corridor of caffeinated people until I remember that I'm supposed to be in lecture hall B, not A. Then I pace outside the door as my nerve endings and stomach revolt. The only thing that ends it is another student arriving. I duck in to avoid their judgement.

The door has T.A.R.D.I.S. qualities, opening into a space larger than it implies, but it's packed nevertheless. I'm not so late that the lecture has already started. I'm just late enough to have no choice in seats. The lecturer is bound to notice me as a troublesome fresh face (and ergo, a slacker) among the hundred or so students. Logic fails me like an undernourished knight facing a dragon. Still got energy to shake like a leaf though. Always enough energy for that...

My pulse peaks as I commit to an end row seat and hope the red haired girl in a tank top doesn't bite my head off for invading her space. When it's clear that this isn't going to be the thing to kill me, I imagine what it's like to talk to her as she chats to whoever is on the other side. I'm not turning far enough to identify the target of my green eyes. She'll notice. They'll make awkward eye contact. I'd have to move or die of shame.

I get out my notebook, three pencils and an eraser, scribble the date in the corner of the paper and wish I had more to do to distract myself. My doodles always look like triangles of light lost in darkness and again I wish I had any drawing talent. If wishes were fishes I'd open an aquarium. Is that a thing or did I make it up?

"Good morning," the professor announces. I hadn't even noticed him come in, or walk on his tiny stage. I panic to get pencil to paper.

He launches into the basics of social psychology and I scrawl down what I can. Why does no one teach how to write notes? That would be valuable at school, right? That thought makes me miss the reason why goths are nicer than basketcases.

My hand stiffens. Cramp? RSI is a bitch. My whole arm is struck rigid. I've experienced some strange anxiety symptoms, but this...

"Chicken soup," I say as loud as I can without being heard, but it's not loud enough for me to recognise the words I heard you can't say during a stroke, so the compulsion makes me say it again. My latest crush looks over at me. I'm gonna be trapped in my stupid flesh cage dying of embarrassment.

Everything in me tightens like I just dropped a full drink and I'm waiting for the glass to shatter on the floor. The adrenaline kicks in with a thump. Before eternity can take me into its paralytic nightmare, I jump up so hard my butt slams on the back of the chair.

Eyes stare now. The lecturer freezes. I want to run, but instead, I leap up onto my section of the long desk, wondering W.T.F. because I didn't do that.

My heart is hammering. The room is buzzing with cries of "she's crazy?", "prank..... stupid," and I hear "mutie" in there somewhere.

I'm on fire and my head is thumping. Not a stroke. Something seriously wr —!

My body takes off along the desk, kicking up papers and crushing fingers. The whiplash is metaphysical. In a flurry of shoe squeaks and paper, I crash into the aisle, and someone's bag. My ass, elbow and I can't tell how many other places are scraped.

Students jump trying to get a clearer look at me.

"I think you should get out of my class," the lecturer booms.

What happened? Like seriously, I've never heard of anything where... oh god. The heat is all over me, spreading like downed Tabasco. It can't just be embarrassment. My whole body feels like it's on fire, or tearing itself to atoms in a nuclear blast. My vision blurs, the lights, shapes, swimming in a ripple of sparkling grey.

"...OK?"

Someone in blue puts a hand on my arm. Then, snap. Everything's back in crystal 8K and a stream of vomit ejects my meagre breakfast. It took me hours to eat that...

The professor isn't calm now. There are too many voices. Out,

out, out. I pull hands and clothing to get to my feet, push through the swarming figures and out the door.

AFTER I GET HOME and hide in the dark for a couple of hours, I try to research what clearly isn't cancer or epilepsy as Google seems to think. It was too precise. Like control. I resign my research to failure at about 2 am, after falling down a sleep experiment / demonic possession rabbit hole.

Should I go to school tomorrow? Social embarrassment is usually a two day minimum for me, with jumping on desks and puking being pretty high on that scale. I'm so lucky none of my housemates are in that class. I'd become a real allegory of the cave.

I change into a baggier t-shirt and collapse into bed not expecting sleep to take me, but next thing I know I'm dreaming about running on swimming pool tiles, terrified I'm going to slip and bust my head open. Only I know I'm not. Somehow. None of which helps the fear go away, because that's as encoded as my pale skin and black hair.

It's an outdoor pool, because it's really windy and cold. I'm not wet so I haven't been in the pool yet. There are hundreds of others packed in the water and I'm just running around the edge endlessly. I want to swim. That's why I'm here, right? But it's not like I'm gonna ask someone for my turn.

I reach the far edge. There's no wall or barrier of any kind. There's not even ground because, and this is the only certainty in the dream, it's on top of an impossibly tall building, one that's probably made of Jenga and held together with desperation. I don't have time to count the dozens of floors below but that doesn't stop me leaping like that scene in the Matrix. Woah. I eat air like it's candy floss. Then I land on an identical skyscraper with another packed swimming pool I can't get into. Everyone is having fun.

Splash! Water hits my face, right between the nose and the eye. It's such a visceral experience that the dream fades. Water actually hit me. In the really real world. And in the prolonged instant it takes my mind to rise to the surface, many more drops hit me.

It's raining.

I'm outside. Victorian tiled roof. Red brick chimneys all down the street. Tiny front garden two floors down. A few lights on in the windows and me, standing in the stormy night like Batgirl with bad concussion.

"Sleep."

A voice. I don't exactly hear it and it has no gender, or presence either. Pure meaning forming in my brain.

I've watched lots of movies about strange events. Hell, I've seen lots of *real* strange events with all the mutant things, the robot stuff, asteroid bases in New Zealand on TV. Weird was bound to find me sooner or later, and there's some tiny relief that I'm not seriously ill after all, but it's drowning in the deluge of stimuli. I've become some puppet to a mutant, and what can a puppet do to stop the puppeteer sticking his hand up its ass? The fact he's controlling me is the only thing stopping me from collapsing into a shaky puddle on the rooftop. Itsy bitsy Fuki washed out by the rain.

He must hear all this.

"Why are you doing this?" I direct the thought.

"Opportunity."

Seriously?

"Wouldn't you make a lesser being your slave if you could?"

"Get out!"

If TV has taught me one thing.... I try to picture this mysterious figure, this alien virus in my brain, and visualise it blown away into the dark void, by waves of blue energy.

"I'm not there. You're not here." The words coalesce in my mind like an urge.

My body crumples under the weight of an unseen force. I was foolish to think I could fight it. Just pointless, hopeful pictures.

382

The rain lashes my face like the spittle of my oppressor. Flashes of a demonic figure arcing over me at an impossible angle. I can't even close my eyes. What's real?

"Get off me," I almost weep, disgusted at how pathetic I sound.

"Don't ruin this for me, vertebrate," it says. "You and me, we're.... Shit! Returned."

Nothing changes, but everything does. I lie in the rain, gasping like a goblin is sitting on my chest, only, it becomes apparent, the goblin has gone. I cry this time.

And the reality of my ridiculous position seeps through to me with the rain through my clothes. What's more uncomfortable, the hard slate tiles under my bare feet or the rain? No, it's probably my free will dying like South American democracy.

I pick myself up, but I doubt I'll ever put myself back together, my arms holding back the shivers in a poor attempt.

How to get the hell off this roof? After checking all sides, I dangle over the kitchen extension and drop down, and from there to the plastic wheelybin in the backyard, the grassy lawn, and then I leave by a gate almost blocked by kid's toys. Lucky bastards. That family has each other.

So, what? I'm mentally bound to another person now? Which would be great if it was Irene from Red Velvet or Tom Hiddleston, but in the lottery of mutant shit I get the psycho. There should be a police department for this. "Help, I'm a victim of a mutant powered crime." And then they gear up with psychic powers and catch this sick fuckberry. There's not even any mutant team to help. Those British heroes.... There was the guy who could manipulate milk. Like, what a rubbish power. Stupid misfit. They wouldn't be able to help me even if they were still alive.

I find the street name at the next corner, Richmond Road. That's only two over, but I'm already soaked. So it's not like there's a rush.

Would my housemates believe me if I said something? Neither of them have had a mutant experience, but after the Dark Year...

I weigh the advantages and disadvantages of appearing (more) crazy to my friends until I make it home, push in the front door and notice I'm dripping all over people's shoes. It's quiet, and it's just us girls anyway. I take off my sopping clothes in the hall, shivering, and carry them like a soiled nappy.

I'm passing the living room door, the first room in the house, and the 20th Century Fox title music blares through the door ajar. I jump in my skin, because I don't have anything else. Inside, a guy on the sofa looks directly at me. He smiles, but he's kind of embarrassed too. Then I hear Winona, my other housemate.

"What are you laughing at? Johnny? Hey!"

I run up the stairs, ready to absolutely die.

My clothes? Dumped outside the bathroom. Me? Locked inside it for almost an hour. What the fuck are they doing watching movies at - I check my classic looking smartwatch - almost 4 am? They'll ask stupid questions in the morning and what will I say? That's if.... if I have any choice in the matter. The mutant won't stop next time. He'll make me do whatever twisted, perverted shit, he has in his mind forever. My fucking life...

There's shouting downstairs. Winona isn't taking the interruption so well. The walls feel like they are falling in slow motion and I'm gonna be crushed. If I could just have some part of my life to find peace in, but it's all fucked.

"WHAT THE FUCK were you doing last night?"

Winona is in my room, leaning over my bed, in fact, and somehow doing a better job than my alarm clock. Oh wait, I switched that off. She's not like June. More like a raccoon caught in a garbage raid.

I don't answer her, far more concerned with the vice crushing my stomach, which is set to burst. My jaw aches from an epic clenching session. I think my little toe is okay though. Yay. Plus side. Of course, Win takes my silence as a personal slight.

"You realise he has a thing for you now? I'm not fucking him while you're in his head."

She yanks my duvet off. I get a whiff of her drugstore fragrance. I'm curled in a ball, hands clutched between my legs, but she thinks it's "gross," and she stomps far, far away.

"I don't even... I like girls!" I scream after her and instantly regret it because my head rings. I stretch my neck this way and that, eliciting cracks and crunches. Then wiggle my jaw to the same effect. Great. I just need a migraine and this will be my dream last day on Earth.

Either way, that yelling has used up all my energy for the hour. Nothing left to do but lie here and worry about how to stop a mutant taking over my body. They *should* have a police squad for this. And then I latch on to the mental image of Leslie Nielsen deadpanning through a catastrophe to distract me into something that resembles sleep.

My phone beeps a few times with crappy subscriber emails and someone liking an attempt at humour I made on social media months ago, but otherwise the various aches are the only constant. Like background symphony to my life.

Who was I kidding last night? I couldn't turn to friends. Winona barely tolerates me at the best of times and June is only interested in me filling gaps in her social calendar...and the police? Even if they listened to me about the mutant, how could they detect it, let alone catch him? He might even have an army of remote controlled flesh puppets to protect him. I'm alone in this — like always.

I eventually have to get up to use the toilet. Some things you can't argue with. That's right. Some things you can't argue with.... The swirl of toilet water drills this into my brain. I have to find something this mutant can't control.

From the middle floor landing, the house seems quiet, so I brave downstairs; extra careful this time because the thought of last night's impromptu peepshow has me folding in on myself like a collapsing star.

Gravity is too strong.

That was it. He couldn't control me if I was uncontrollable. And I don't mean rebellious, because he totally could. Last night, I hated him, wanted him off me with all my being but I couldn't do a thing. I needed to be paralysed, drugged or drunk. And I'd have a chance, maybe, to talk to him. A lot of slurred variables there, but drunk me cares not for fear. Drunk me laughs in the face of fear and then she runs away to the toilet because she literally has a girl's bladder.

In the fridge I find Winona's usual stash of lager. She already hates me, so I pull out a six pack and get started. I settle in the living room, on the opposite end of the sofa to you-know-what. On goes the TV. *South Park*, the pilot. Wow. I wasn't even alive for this one.

Drink is generally a bad idea. Hangovers make my anxiety worse. Worrying about hangovers makes my anxiety intolerable. Yet, so does having my body be someone else's ... What would I be then?

The first can is gone in three minutes. By 11am I'm drunk enough to be hungry and start making more cheese toasties. The entertainment moves onto episodes of *Invincible*. He takes a lot of shit, but he doesn't go down. I gotta be like him. Stick to my goals.

By 2pm it's my fourth can and I'm onto movies. *Total Recall* is the G.O.A.T. Arnie fighting against another version of him. He's got my back. I yell my fan girl cheers at the screen.

As I'm loading up *Memento* on TV, I hear the door click and the exasperated sigh of June as she drops keys in her purse.

"Juney!" I shout, and I'm hit with a wave of nostalgia for the freshman days when we clung to each other, and giggled through nights out at clubs we felt obligated to go to. I totally had a crush on her for... ever.

She's in the room without me actually seeing her come in, like she melted in from my memory, but she probably breezed in like a ghost. A glamorous ghost. They are everywhere.

"Hey... Sash? Good to see you up, you're..."

She's more together than me if I had superglue. An outfit that is casual piece by piece, but somehow says she's a tiktok queen with several brand deals. Her hair is clipped up at the back, but bangs swishing around her face like a natural highlight. She looks like Buffy le vampyr slayer when she does that. Oh my god, she totally looks like Buffy. Fucking dream.

I kick the empty cans under the table, the movement triggering a burp.

"You're drunk! What the shit!"

"Don't worry. Issa plan," I say, waving like from a cruise ship. "Goodbye!"

"Sabotaging your studies is a plan? Oh nevermind.... You've gotta stop this shit."

I nod. "You use big words. That's why I like you."

"Wheen told me what happened last night," she continues, but as soon as she says Wheen I start making cries like I'm going down a series of waterslides. Attention span: squirrel!

She gives a judgemental stare before storming out. And then I remember why my crush never went anywhere. She got totally obsessed with studying and we never hung out anymore. I pined. I didn't deal. And it was possibly made worse by her still being around in my course and dorms, but I'd be homeless now if I didn't have her to move in with for our third year.

"Bye then, bitch."

So grateful.

I get through more drinks and one more movie, though don't ask me what it was, plus a brief glaring session with Winona when she comes home, but she doesn't say anything, so that's a win 'cos arguing is effort.

Higher brain is trying to cry, but she's under so many beers it's more of a gargle. I need more money. And cheese. Why is cheese the greatest invention cows ever gave us?

That thought is interrupted by a tide of disgust rising within myself. Cheese is not disgusting. *He* must be back.

"Bad time?"

I hoped the alcohol might drown out the voice. It comes through as sharp as ever. My skin tightens on a rack of anticipated shame, even while the spike of adrenaline pushes me upright, knocking the slime off my neurons. I end up flailing for the edge of the seat. Funk as druck here. My half empty can plummets before I realise it was me that hit it.

"Fuck you. I'm on you!"

Kind of.

"You don't know anything. And now your own body betrays you. You're pathetic."

"So glad to dis'point you," I hiss.

It's working. He can't do shit with me. I might even have ruined his plans completely. Yeah, I'm also aware I'm shouting about it.

"Amuse, perhaps. Your people poison themselves like this? It's pathetic."

I'm filled with a bubbling sensation of joy. I stretch out on the sofa amongst my mess of cans and snack wrappers, laughing my head off, or my abuser is laughing at me, or... or... He's laughing! The psychic fucking mutant with a mental link to my drunk brain is as fucked up as I am. Maybe it works both ways. Then I realise he probably heard that - and that. I hope the alcohol blurred it out. How do I use it? It didn't work on the rooftop. I can't fucking think.

"We would... we never do something like that," he continues. "Not harmful, but this is.. this is fun."

He's not noticed yet.

I jump up on my feet and almost go through the glass coffee table. "I command you to leave me alone," I shout at him... but mostly at the ceiling.

"What's got into you?" the voice asks.

"You mean, wos gottin' you?" I reply, and can't help a smile even though I don't think he can see it. Maybe he can feel it.

There's a pause quickly flooded with panic. For a second, I look for a local explanation. I'm not worried about housemates hearing me. I totally don't give a shit at this stage. No, it's not my feeling. It's his. It really does go both ways.

I hear colorful words in my head and he's gone again.

I wait until I'm sure, like a statue commemorating how not to live your life.

A little while into the night, another toilet trip, terrified to open my brain to the possibility of an early hangover. My only conscious thought is a continuation. Who am I kidding? He's not beat. He's probably going to come back even stronger, with a plan and force me to submit. I've bought myself time at most. I'm too useless to actually succeed.

At least when I return to sleep it's dreamless.

I WAKE up keenly aware that something is different. A soft warmth has enveloped my whole body. I'm a plant in the sun. No sore or achy limbs. I don't think he took me sleepwalking last night. That's a win, right?

It's only when I move to check my clothes that the hangover hits: a sharp, full ache in my head and a taste in my mouth like I ate roadkill. OK, now I know I'm not dreaming. I reach for my clothes anyway. I have to know if they are wet. A few failed and frustrated grabs later, and yesterday's hoodie, leggings and frilly doughnut nightmare that I use as a skirt are confirmed dry by shaky hands. My pyjama t-shirt and underpants too. Success. That's enough to get me out of bed, but my yammering heart protests. I'm pretty sure it's edging towards a breakdown. Fuck, fuck, fuck. No pain though. I wait for it to calm a bit before making a snaky path downstairs.

It'd be peak me to defeat a mutant attack only to be killed by incidental binge drinking. Today is gonna suck.

In the kitchen, June is mumbling about a box of missing crackers as she checks cupboard after cupboard. A hot flush runs through me. Head down. I'm just here for some water.

"Did you eat them?" she snaps as a greeting.

My glass clanks against the tap. Then, I give myself some thinking time by failing to turn the tap twice.

"Eat what?" I say and slink away. Wait. Some bravery chimes in, which is odd; who gave that emotion a megaphone today? Maybe my anxiety is hungover too. If I can't stand up to my roommate, the mutant is gonna walk all over me for sure. Fuck this. I turn back to her.

"Probably," I add.

"That was all I had for breakfast. I don't have time to..." She checks her watch and then lets out an exasperated groan. The song of her people.

"Why are you so strung up, B? The crackers don't matter."

I sip my water to stop me bleating anymore. If I throw in another obscure quote she'll know I actually can't do conversations.

"Oh yeah? I should take advice from you when you've been flashing visitors and daytime drinking for stress management? God, Sash. You've never been such a mess."

She has no fucking idea. Fuck her. The crackers were fucking delicious. Probably. I walk out giving her the finger under my t-shirt, then hide upstairs 'til she's gone.

House free, I dash to claim the TV. The rush throws my head out of sync with my body, and my foot hesitates on the stairs. There's a feeling like someone is watching me.

"I didn't want to do this," it says. "but you've shown you won't submit."

I stumble down the last few steps into the wall as if ejected from my crowded headspace.

"Do what? Just leave me alone!" I scream.

"Too late for that. You're dangerous to my plans. It would have been so much easier to conquer your planet from within."

Planet? What was he talking about?

"Once your DNA entirely matches mine you will work with me peacefully."

"What? The fuck?"

He's an alien? It's not a fucking mutant. It's an alien! Is this real? I need a breath.

"The change will be slow. Probably painful, but you can't fight it."

"Wait!" I plead. "What...? I don't ... what's this got to do with me?" The whole world is swimming. Only the wall catches me.

"I'll come back when you're more compliant," he says.

Floods of tears make me so fucking hate myself.

I had thought it would be a heart attack. Or stroke. But I'm gonna turn into an alien? Some grey headed, ass prodding idiot?

That's probably racist.

C'mon, brain, at least let me grieve in peace.

For god knows how long I'm convinced every twinge and ache is a sign my body is beginning the metamorphosis. Will I change before anyone even comes home? Maybe they'll find a grey wrinkled alien wandering around their house.

Maybe an hour later, maybe two, but before I've even moved from the wall he returns. I can feel it now, when he's here, a presence behind my head, someone invisible watching over my shoulder.

"How are you doing?"

The voice is softer now, which just makes me feel more sick. This maniac has compassion, which just confirms the punishment.

I can't answer.

"It's not all bad," he says. "You will have purpose. My people have no concept of alienation."

Ha, good one. I actually chuckle.

"Your people..." soon to be my people I guess. "Tell me, are you really an alien?"

The sunlight dances on the wall opposite in watery patterns.

"Yes, I'm from a planet quite different from yours. Mostly submerged. Not that you would recognise it as water. We live in colonies of billions. We have travelled the stars."

"Have you visited Earth?" I ask, finding his story comforting now if only as a distraction.

"Hell no. I believe our entire civilisation is exterior to your observable universe. Short of a wormhole we could never meet."

Even this rejection hurts me like a blade.

I can feel a buzzing in my skin, like a layer of energy is enveloping me.

"Why are you talking to me about anything?"

A pause.

"It doesn't matter what you know. You'll be one of us soon."

"Then why not tell me how you control a life form beyond the observable universe?"

"Quantum entanglement," he says.

I've heard of that. I'm not big on science but I watch a lot of YouTube videos about weird and wonderful things. Plus there was that episode of *Red Dwarf* where Cat and Kryten get quantum entangled and start doing the same things at the same time.

My tongue feels swollen and my limbs are oddly both heavy and disconnected. I stretch my legs up the opposite wall.

"As I remember Einstein called it spooky action at a distance because entangled particles affect each other instantly no matter the space between them."

"Exactly," he confirms. "We are entangled. Anything I do, you can do too, instantly. To change your DNA I just crank up the power so you're *exactly* the same as me."

That's the phrase that summons tears. It's like he's teleporting into the space I occupy with all the resulting mess.

"How long have I got?"

"A day. Before it gets really bad."

I look at the circle of front door light and smirk despite it all. "Is that your day or mine?"

"Clever. Our days are 19 times as long as yours. I'm sorry, but it's yours."

"Alright, Gary. I'm gonna call you Gary now. Is that ok? Actually, I don't care. There was a really annoying boy called Gary in my junior school. Well, more than the others... "

"Your designations are meaningless to me. And temporary. Though your resolution is frustrating."

"Ah just wait. I wouldn't be surprised if your DNA got fed up with me and left too."

"I don't understand... Oh. Humour. Ha. Ha."

I find myself almost laughing too, with real mirth, unlike him.

There's a click at the front door to my right. The blurred shape of June is visible through the frosted glass. I'm not even sure how to explain a fraction of the situation so I dive up to my feet, straighten my clothes and wipe away any sign of tears. June and Winona enter our lovely alien petri dish.

"Sash," June says. Toneless. "Have you been out?"

She could only be more mad at me if she used my real name, but she's the one who named me Sash anyway.

"I-I met someone..." I mumble not wanting to seem like a total loser even now. Then I remember they know I have no friends. She doesn't seem to acknowledge this.

Winona gives me a stare that could grill turkeys and something riles in me. Like what did I ever do to her. I give their wide berths a wider berth and decide to take over the lounge after all. If I die tomorrow I'm dying watching Buffy season 5 one more time.

"Are these people really your friends?" Gary asks.

"They're the people who hate me the least," I reply, digging out the DVD set from the precarious stack by the fireplace.

The briefest of pauses from him.

"That's a cynical description of friends," he says.

I shrug. "But accurate. You have cynicism on your planet?"

"Since we are communicating on a quantum level direct meaning is communicated rather than hollow words and so your mind is just manifesting my thoughts in a way you can understand." And then he adds: "like two networked computers running different operating systems."

The D.V.D. plays the way-too-loud, way-too-long intro animation. I hate them, but it's comforting to experience it.

"Oh, sure. So did I come up with that O.S. analogy or was that you?"

"It doesn't matter. I think you should get new friends."

I hit play.

"I would if I wasn't dying tomorrow."

I let my dumb butt fall on the sofa and as soon as it hits the cushions anxiety eats me up from the inside, powered by the inexorable march of time. I know how this ends. Damn Gary is right.

"You know what?" I stand, hitting stop on the remote. "I'm going out."

OUT IS ANOTHER INSIDE, a half hour walk away through that sunshine and fresh air stuff they have on TV. And it's full of other people. The student bar is a rustic structure living inside a glass and steel building as if a lumberjack got lost in an airport and just decided to build his home in the middle of it. There's a good spread of clientele. Two boys sit over by the big windows, legs spread out from the bench, mouths guffawing loudly while a willowy brunette perches next to them, dragging on a cigarette. A spectacled girl whispers secrets to her redhead friend at the other end of the bar. There's pool tables through that way, usually busy at all times of day. The bar counter is empty.

My pulse is racing. Gary has been chattering interestedly about human social patterns all the way here. His people tend to keep away from each other else one absorbs the other and then follows a host of legal battles for property and family rights.

"So this is it? A meeting place? And there's no murder at all? No adsorption."

"Only of alcohol," I send back while checking my pulse again. When I'm convinced I'm not walking into a heart attack, I approach the bar and sit at one of the inappropriately giant stools.

I know if I don't order something straight away I'm gonna get the 'weird girl' looks so I ask for a pint of bitter from the shaved head, football type on duty.

Well, I'm here. Scratch that off my bucket list.

My drink arrives and I start sipping like I'll be seen as a fake if I don't. It tastes of yesterday but I force another bit down.

"You should tell me of these buckets," says Gary.

"Not now, I—"

"Hey," I hear outside my head. Wasn't expecting that.

A boy, stocky with gold jewellery like he's in *Sopranos: the Next Generation* hovers around my stool.

"Fuki, right? I've seen you in the lectures."

I stutter.

"Well, are you?" he says, a big smile on his face.

I'm deathly afraid to express anything.

"Fuck-y," he says, emphasising to make his attempt at Earth humour clear. "because I'm down if—"

I turn away. It'll take me months to dissect these layers of embarrassment. Obviously, I don't seem gay enough.

"And that's why I don't use my real name," I tell Gary.

"Ha, you people are obsessed with reproduction and excrement. It's hilarious."

The boy has had his laugh — probably thought he was original too — so he wanders towards his mates by the pool tables. Without thinking about it my leg shoots down and kicks the stool next to me. It skids across the floor and under his feet as he's walking. He trips and almost goes face first into the lilo.

"Hilarious," Gary repeats.

Seems it doesn't matter who Gary makes miserable, but that made me feel better. Like, why do I have that guy's attention anyway? Geez. A pain shoots up my back and I have to struggle not to look like a freak as it forces me to lean against the bar until it passes. And fuck this ticking clock.

I pick up my glass and storm over to the least asshole looking girls and introduce myself, before I can change my mind. Amazingly, they don't mean-girl me out the door. Even so, for the first ten minutes, I'm all about running my hair behind my ears and hugging myself, but it turns out, beyond the cliche of "what are you studying?" we have TV shows in common and they like philosophy and out-there science ideas. Gary even throws a few stunning facts of the universe into my brain and I try to control my own amazement as I relate it. Before I know it, there are tunes on the jukebox and the day is more of a blur than when I got plastered drunk.

This is quite nice. Just this. I try to ignore the knowledge that it will end soon. I never really enjoy happiness because I'm always aware it's going to end while it's still happening. I try to let the conversation drown that out.

In my head I share a thought with Gary. "Why take over one world and get rid of me when we can work together and take over two?"

"Explain." He's there immediately proving that he was lurking.

"You must have knowledge that would be extremely useful to my people. Astrophysics and star charts, advanced physics, right? We could control the flow of that information, for a price, and I'm sure, as primitive as we are, we must have knowledge that would benefit your species. Even if it's just the map of the local area."

This is the moment years of watching TV has prepared me for. I can tell he's thinking about it.

"You propose an alliance?"

His interest gives me hope. I sneak the crowbar in a bit further.

"What are you gonna do with this planet anyway? It's so far from your home world you can't mine it or enslave us in any effective way. And that goes to your ruler. We can work in secret together. Keep all the benefit to ourselves."

"You lack knowledge of politics."

I nod along to my companions' conversation.

"That was always my weakness. Maybe if leaders weren't such dicks we'd look up to them and learn more."

"They *are* always keeping the mitochondria to themselves and boosting their own productivity."

Sure, Gary. Strange answer, but it makes me realise I don't know much about him. Like what kind of alien he is. Surely they aren't just world conquerors. He's probably some kind of a person too. With wants.

I've gone all quiet but I'm on to something.

I return to the other conversation for a bit, but it's strange. I can see a future. Where has that been all my life? I need more time to think about it and I can't plan anything with Gary watching my every thought so I throw myself into the conversation with these girls, hoping he will lose interest in me. It's hard. Words don't come easily and I'm sure I'm saying stupid things, but all the time I'm thinking about how to beat Gary at his own game. In pieces. A little bit here. A little bit there. Nothing that on its own won't look like random speculation (I hope), but pieced together over many hours of random human chatter it makes a plan. I mustn't hold it in my mind all at once. I have to trust my memory.

Eventually, we exchange messenger IDs and say goodbye. There's talk of an engineer's party and me being invited. They're engineers. So clever and useful. I try not to have crushes, but who am I kidding? Meanwhile, what am I? Alien food. It would be fun to shock them with more alien technological facts.

"Might be amusing," Gary replies as we walk out.

He's teasing. I don't have long left. Despite the fun I've had today, my back is painful all the way up and my ears have been buzzing intermittently.

The bus pulls up at the bus stop and I get on to see an old lady who wishes she had gone grocery shopping at a quieter hour.

The bus isn't very full. I take a seat two rows down on the left like always. There's a lad sat at the back that spikes my senses. I can hear the buzz of his ridiculously loud dance music from his headphones and he's blathering to himself. I'm not surprised that he has a can in a plastic bag. I sink into my seat. Gary picks up on the threat.

"Eat him," he says.

"That's ... not how we do things," I reply. "Anyway I don't want to deal. Just tell me how long I've left. I feel like I'm dying here. Will I wake up if I go to sleep?"

"What? Yes. Certainly. I said a day, didn't I?"

"I guess," I say, and stare out the window.

It's turning into another rainy evening. The dark of the residential streets is perforated by the occasional streetlight glowing orange. They zoom by too quickly to see any detail of the street.

The lad behind me is talking to others and fidgeting in his seat. I snap forward in mine, the pain again. The fingers tapping on the bus leather stop. I've caught the eye of the lad at the back of the bus. Shit. Maybe he'll leave it.

"You can give me more time," I continue with Gary. "It's not like a bomb. It's a biological process."

"You're not going to give this up are you? You can't just let me have this?"

"What do you mean?"

"You're the same as everyone here. I can't..."

A pause, in which I notice out of the corner of my eye, the drunk guy is staggering over while the bus is moving. Burberry cap. Sports jumpsuit. I can't deal with more.

"It's a lie, OK? I can't change your DNA any more than I can change my own stupid future."

"What are you saying? I've been thinking I'm going to die!"

"That time you were in the lecture? You felt sick?"

"Sick! I thought I was being torn apart."

I'm struggling to stay still, tearing the skin on my fingers to shreds.

"That was me testing how much you could change. I was trying to go gaseous, like we do for long transport."

"It didn't work..."

I feel like all the land has dropped away and two mighty seas have collided in the space that was me. Relief and anger. Can I admit...? Yes, anger. But still fear of this, whatever it is.

The drunk lad is right behind me now, saying something about me being rude.

"I needed some advantage. It's your .... Shit.... Ah, my big mouth."

"My what?"

Nothing.

"My shit?"

I maybe said that out loud. There's silence on the bus.

He was scaring me. How was this more scary than death?

The lad is jabbing me with a finger from his can hand.

"You're not listening to me. Hey."

I freeze. If this alien doesn't get my brain, this drunk idiot will probably kill me. I tense so hard my neck cracks.

Still, Gary's voice coalesces in my mind, continuing my panic. "I don't have to tell you anything."

Fuck. He's like my little cousin. Am I dying or not?

My hands start to tingle like a nerve is trapped somewhere in my elbow and I'm shaking. He's hiding something. Which is a ridiculous thing to think because of course he's hiding something: he's a malicious alien entity invading my mind and trying to erase me so he can take over the world. It sounds ridiculous even in my head.

The drunk keeps shouting for my attention. I can't ignore him. Stares are coming from the few others here.

Odd that Gary is doing nothing.

"What is this you're feeling? It's horrible," he says, as if by explanation.

"Anxiety," I say. "I'm gonna die and this guy behind me is gonna make my last moments miserable. I just want to be left alone. And *you* won't tell me what's going on."

Gary is reeling. I can feel the stomach sickness in him too, spreading like the effects of the alcohol did.

"I feel my biological function will cease any moment. You... you live like this? Feeling *this*?"

"Every day," I tell him.

"I underestimated you. All this time you were holding back to spare me. How powerful to function despite this. You control the link, you control the flow. I was stupid to try, but ... my life is so useless!"

He didn't mean for me to hear that last part, but lucky for him it's not the most interesting part of his lament.

"What do you mean 'I control the link'?" I ask.

"Do you not? You initiated it."

"What do you...?"

Holy shit.

I initially thought it was a mutant controlling me. I was cata-strophising so hard I would have believed anything, like an alien race had technology to control a person light years away. It distracted me from what was really happening. My changes. *I'm* the mutant!

The lad behind me is tapping me like a broken TV remote and he wants his misogynistic porn.

I stand up and shout "I'm a fucking mutant!" to the whole bus. Then the lad has second thoughts because I bet he saw on his T.V. several reasons why.

Relief, a flood of it. This changes everything. I'd felt so lost, alone, maybe now I could find people who cared. I could find the other mutants.

I spin round and face the goon, but the bus driver suddenly slams the brakes.

"Mutant life form detected," the bus driver says in an awfully mechanical voice. "Use of lethal force authorised."

We all lurch as the bus comes to a stop haphazardly across the road, chaos and horns around us. I clearly hear that voice repeating its status update. Not liking it either.

Everyone is frozen.

The bus driver unfolds from his seat. He transforms before our eyes. The well cushioned middle aged man dissolves into a leaner, muscled form, his skin is as green as his uniform was.

"What the fuck?" I whisper.

It marches towards us. Towards me. The newsflashes of the last few years sprint through my brain towards one conclusion.

"Mutant death squad," I mutter. "Welcome to the fam., Sash."

"Seems your planet has some racial issues," says Gary.

"Understatement." I snap back. "I don't even know my power. He can't..."

The happiness I felt a moment ago already seems like a dream. I'm gonna die quicker than I thought.

"Your power is me," Gary says. "We are one on the quantum level."

"Whatever that means. Just do something 'cos..." I'm whimpering in my head and for all I know outside as well. I'm stuck between violent chaos and violent efficiency.

"Gary!"

"I can see him. Focus. Let me in." I feel a blue line. That's what springs to my mind as our connection. "Duck!"

I do and the massive green arm swipes over me.

"Now jump!"

I push, and my legs feel strange. My stomach lurches with how high I go. Not superhero levels, which thanks, because of the ceil-

401

ing, but I zoom above his swing and in a panic I grasp the monster's shoulder and ear. Gravity must be less or Gary has more strength than me.

Whatever Gary had planned I messed it up and my stomach becomes lead again. How can I focus when danger is literally here? I drop, yanking the monster's ear.

He swipes and grasps randomly. A wild arm bats me aside. It's effective. I have mental time to prepare for the pain, yet even as I smack into glass and metal, hear the glass splinter under me, I'm barely winded.

"Gary is jelly, remember," he tells me. I'd be thankful if I could tell which way was up.

The death squaddie winds down, and I have time to roll across the seat and around him. No one is going to stop me. They're all pressing as far back into the bus as they can. I'm even very pleased to see the drunk lad.

A few steps from the front doors, claws scratch my legs. The damn doors are shut. Where's the button?

The monster is stronger and pulling me back.

It's on all fours in a pounce, then he's on me and the world races for the finish, splintering around me. I feel like I'm in a bubble until after we're through the windscreen and smacking into the tarmac.

"Sorry. I couldn't... that anxiety stuff has thrown me off," Gary says.

"I know," I flash back. "I need to get away from this thing!"

It loosens its grip. The tumble hurt it more than it expected. Or maybe it doesn't think. It's a robot animal. If I ran, it would hunt, and I'm probably bleeding track marks now.

I'm fucked.

I'm fucker than fucked.

I try to get to my feet, but my legs have taken Gary's jelly nature seriously. I don't notice any cuts though.

Maybe jelly can help.

"How high can we jump?" I ask Gary, feeling like I couldn't ride an escalator. "Can I get on top of that house?"

"On three," he chimes.

I sink down as low as I can. It feels at once totally ridiculous but also cool. Is this me? I'm still jittery as shit but on the signal, we push off simultaneously and I'm suddenly on a rollercoaster speeding to a peak. Before I realise we've passed the first floor, a glimpse of some kid's room in darkness through the window, my brain catches up to our ascent. Then we're descending and my feet madly scramble, my entire being begging for footing. The call is answered by rooftiles.

"Shit, shit…" I feel like someone has just shoved a mountain under my feet.

And have to catch my breath. This mutant shit is….

"No problem," Gary says.

"That's gonna take some getting used to. I never even did PE class."

The monster is blinking up at us. It runs at the house. The crunch of claws on brick tells me he can climb.

"What's the plan?" Gary asks.

"Gravity," I say. "Do you think we can unbalance that thing?"

"When you're made of cytoplasm you need considerable force to even make a tap. The equivalent manifested in a solid form should be considerable."

"I feel like I'm gonna puke."

The monster crunches closer. I daren't lean too far to look. Its back muscles ripple.

I stand back, try to get a solid stance. What the fuck am I doing? I've never even squashed a fly and moths make me run for the far side of the room.

"We won't miss this one," Gary reassures me.

The monster is up before I can change my mind. Its head is a pointed cousin of a human skull, not a round edge on him. His eyes tell me he wants to crush me against it.

"Now!" Gary screams.

I can't move. This monster is here to kill me and who am I to fight?

He screams again.

I snap out of a bad daydream. No thinking. Only action. Take my quaking limbs and all that energy and fuck this monster off the goddamn roof!

"Now!" I scream back at Gary.

All my anger, all my disgust into this pathetic attempt at a fist. I have an image of Monkey D. Luffy screaming "Gomu Gomu Pistol!!" but I daren't even. There's a real monster, still rising to its full height.

It catches my fist.

I fucked it up.

I'm trapped in its lazy one handed grip. It didn't even take any effort.

"Shit." Gary exclaims, "I missed it. Sorry. Don't worry. I got you."

The monster twists my arm back, but instead of snapping it bends at an impossible angle which makes me feel sick. Honestly, I don't know what's worse because I don't feel like I'm in my body anymore. This isn't me. It's against everything I've ever learned.

The monster leans into me. So close its rancid breathing is inescapable.

"Mutant extinction is authorised," it growls like a primitive Cyberman.

My whole head could fit in that jaw.

No, I'm not going to let anything choose my future, but me.

"Kick!"

I get a flash of panic from Gary. "I don't have legs."

"Whatever you got. Now!"

I'm falling backwards to avoid the monster and that gives me more weight to our kick as I abandon supporting myself at all.

The monster hops bounces with the force of the blow, and its

404

growl collapses into a groan. From the floor, I flash an image of instructions to Gary and pray his brain works as fast as mine.

The monster straightens. I push myself up and forward with Gary's tentacles as hard as I can. Arms out again. The monster topples backwards, and I almost can't believe it when it stumbles back and drops with a howl off the roof. There's all sorts of crunches, thuds and bangs.

My heart is racing as I steel myself to look over the edge. The bay window broke his fall half way down, but the monster is bent over the steel railings of the front yard's fence. He ain't moving, which is enough for me.

"Now what?" Gary says "I've seen enough of your memories of horror movies to know…"

"Now we run," I interrupt.

Someone across the street has already flicked their light on and soon they'll be calling the police. I don't know how people deal with things like that, but I won't be here for it.

With Gary's help, I'm half a mile away on another rooftop before you can say 999. I'd call it safe but I don't think I will ever know that anymore.

I pause, looking up at the stars. It's not exactly clear in the city. The evening has a yellow haze, but some stars make it through.

"Where are you?" I ask.

"No way to know. Technically, we're in separate universes."

And I can't help feeling that's the worst news I've gotten recently. I'm always alone.

"Don't worry. You've got your mutant kind now."

I laugh. "Are you kidding? The first mutant I met was trying to kill other mutants. They're probably as bad. No different from humans anyway, which is bad enough. It's me and you, you idiot. As long as you promise not to try and screw me over again."

Can you hear mental sighs? I think I just did.

"No, ma'm," he jokes.

We decide to walk the rest of the way home on the street like a normal person. And that's how I decide I'm gonna have to be: *like* a normal person.

"So what are you going to do now?" he asks.

"You mean 'we'. We are gonna take over the worlds."

"*You* can," he snaps back. "Some of us have work in the morning,"

"What? You're a pencil pusher?" No response but I was starting to get used to fishing around his brain for answers. "Oh my god, you are, aren't you? Figures."

We pass a house with a steel white gate. A cat meows and squeezes under the lowest bar.

"What's that? Looks tasty. We should eat it."

"No!"

I reach down to pet it.

"Sorry. My people absorb other lifeforms and add their biological distinctiveness to our own."

"Don't even change the subject, loser."

The cathead bumps me a couple of times for pats and then slinks off.

So what am I going to do, really?

WHEN I GET HOME, June is asleep like a congealed puddle on her notes at the kitchen table and when I leave in the morning Wheen is just coming in the front door, ending her latest walk of shame. Her clothes and her face are a mess. Streaks of black on red track tears down her cheeks. Her eyes meet mine for the briefest second and then look any which way. I bite down the urge to make a comment. Lucky for her I've got some place to be.

The science building is more modern than the humanities building. Wide windows, glass everything, no concrete in sight. I check the office chart in the entrance to make sure where this professor's room is. The Internet had the room number, but not where it was. 3rd floor.

I walk through the lobby. It's quiet. Most students are nursing a hangover, but the professor I want to see keeps early office hours.

The lobby is an open space with cross crossing balconies and walkways all the way to a large glass ceiling.

I leap up to the first balcony, bounce up to the middle walkway and then up to the third like I'm just taking two steps at once on the stairs. Still no one around, better that way. I don't want to give Gary excuses to see if his absorption trick works.

The office has a frosted glass door.

I knock and wait.

There's some shuffling and a gruff voice beckons me in.

He's behind his desk. A sweatered gentleman with the luck of going white haired not grey.

"I don't recognise you," he says. "What can I do for you?"

Gary has filled me in with what I need to know for this meeting to work the way I want it to.

I walk over to his desk and I try to imagine how this might look. A meek Japanese girl, dressed like a mess, wandering into the den of male academics at large with a big claim about a long standing problem in the scientific community. I remain standing until he invites me to sit. He's gonna invite me to sit.

"I've solved the three body problem," I say.

He smiles, a little bit of a scoff there. However, that's the last time any of them do.

# Farsight

There's something odd blocking me from seeing everything around the Japanese girl in England. It's like my eyes water when I look at her. I make a note in the file, and flag it for further investigation. One more file among hundreds, a host of possibilities. The sheer number of them is starting to feel overwhelming, and I turn over vague ideas for a new classification system in my head.

I reach for my mug of tea to find that it's cold. Lost track of time looking at that last case. One more slight oddity about it. I glance towards the kettle to find there are a whole bunch of faces in the doorway, all looking in my direction.

"We've come to drag you away," Dylan says dramatically.

My first instinct is to panic.

"For your birthday," Dani adds with a laugh.

Alyse is standing behind her, holding an enormous chocolate cake. She looks tired and has dark circles under her eyes, but she's in coherent human form and there's something like a smile sketched on her face.

"How did you know it was my birthday?" For some reason, that's my first question.

"Emma knew." Alyse holds out the cake. "She always remembered everyone's birthday. So I suppose it's a happy birthday from her as well."

Dylan comes alongside me and slings an arm around my neck. "Are you mad we spoiled your peace and quiet, dearest Farsight?"

"No." I lean my head briefly against theirs. "This means a lot."

"I told you!" They punch the air. "Far is a secret soft."

Everyone's laughing, but none of it feels malicious at all. "I don't even know what that means," I protest.

"It means we like you," Dani says. "Even if you're bossy and disapproving."

"And always telling me no." Dylan sighs. "Like you think you're our parent. Our real ones were all smart enough to stop telling us what to do."

I shake my head. "This feels like a very backhanded compliment."

"I don't like many people," Dylan declares. "But I find myself inordinately fond of you, Far. How's that?"

Dani nudges them. "You always say shit about being a misanthrope, but you seem to constantly accumulate friends wherever you go."

"I blame Alyse for that," Dylan says.

Alyse presses her hand to her chest, eyes wide with faux shock. "Or maybe you're more adorable than you think. If you can win even Farsight over..."

"Did I really win you over?" Dylan spins in their chair, almost tumbling out.

"Perhaps." My smile is too wide to be enigmatic.

They burst out laughing. "Well there we go. A glowing review. Five stars. A great perhaps. Now come on, you dreamy old-tower dweller. We're going out to dance and to party."

I'm standing by the window, and I turn to look out over the island again, its beaches and forests drenched by the setting sun. There is a vast world out there, new mutants being awakened every day. New stories of hope and terror and love and pain. I'll watch them all, and I'll help as many as I can.

We'll do it together.

Mutants rising.

# contributors

**SJ Whitby** possibly doesn't exist. They're what passes for a mind behind the Cute Mutants series, from which this anthology sprung. You can find them on Twitter at @sjwhitbywrites, but enough about them. There are far more interesting people to meet.

**Shelly Page** is a writer, attorney, and homeless youth advocate. She lives in Los Angeles where she dreams up grand adventures for queer characters. She draws inspiration from the hundreds of books in her home and from her own experiences as a Black queer woman. You can find her on Twitter at @shelly_p_writes.

**Elle Tesch** lives just east of Vancouver, Canada. Forever surrounded by forests and mountains, it was inevitable that she would daydream about what might lurk in those trees. She writes what she knows best: hungry monsters, casually cruel villains, and ace-spec girls one step down from ruthless. You can find her on Twitter at @zipitelle.

**Andy Perez** is a native New Yorker, a part-time writer, and a full-time bitch. When she's not worrying about writing, she can be found worrying about her cute demon mutant dog Bingsu in her definitely-haunted house in Austin, TX. She likes to fill up her online cart with sales items and X out of the tab once she checks her total. You can find her on Twitter and Instagram at @ohdee-andy. Please don't send her messages and expect a prompt response. You'll receive a reply in approximately 2-3 business years.

**Hsinju Chen** grew up in Taiwan and currently resides in central Illinois, where they are pursuing a PhD in Electrical & Computer Engineering. She holds an MS in Communication Engineering with a focus on electromagnetic waves. When they are not busy writing academic papers or dreaming up stories, they are reading queer literature and deciding what book to add to their massive TBR. You can find her on Twitter at @hsinjulit.

**Shannon Ives** graduated with honors from the University of Iowa with a B.A. in Anthropology and a minor in Latin with a focus on myth, religion, and magic, and the roles women play in each. Her writing explores how traditional power structures perpetuate violence, and her characters seek to tear them down. She is represented by John Baker at Bell Lomax Moreton. You can find her on Twitter at @thestickwitch.

**Melody Robinette** is a YA Gothic Fantasy author who grew up living in a daydream. She is a lover of all things macabre and fantastical. Aching love, longing glances, and enemies who fall for each other are her bread and butter. She also has an unhealthy obsession with the grim reaper and traipsing through cemeteries. Melody now teaches highschool in Austin, Texas with her bartender husband and their three ridiculous felines. You can find her on Twitter at @MelodyRobinette.

**Astra Daye** is an author of speculative fiction entwined with nihilism and unconventional perspectives of the eventual. She speaks a number of languages badly, but the one she prefers is mathematics. These days, she's trying to write without giving herself neck problems.

**Yves Donlon** has a degree in English Studies from Trinity College Dublin and an obsession with all things medieval. When they're not writing books with tragic endings, they're traipsing around the museums of their new home in York, England, visiting coffee shops, and collecting oddly-shaped rocks. You can find them on Twitter at @yveshwinter.

**E.M. Anderson** (she/her) is an alleged person but more likely three trees in a trenchcoat. Her work has appeared in *Wizards in Space Literary Magazine* and GutSlut Press's anthology *Suicidaliens*. It is her doom to one day vanish in the depths of a forest, never to be seen again, after ignoring the repeated warnings of the locals to stay out of the woods. Until that fateful day comes, you can follow her on Twitter at @elizmanderson.

**Hester Steel** is a cosmic mistake but we're trying to make the best of it. She's currently based in London, but doing her best to find a solution to that, and in the meantime tidies up news articles for money and writes horror and fantasy for less money. You can find her on Twitter at @SteelHester.

**Monica Gribouski** is a writer, lapsed programmer, and larper from New England. She likes short video games, long books, ludonarrative assonance, electronica, and bulk boxes of rooibos tea. You can find her on Twitter at @oneiroboros.

**Charlotte Hayward** (she/her) is a writer of contemporary fantasy stories about queer teens with anxiety and uncontrollable magic. She's based in Edinburgh, and spends her spare time living vicariously through her D&D character. You can find her on Twitter at @thatchazza.

**Amanda M. Pierce** lives in the golden hills of Northern California. She grew up on the East Coast, where she spent all her free time with her feet in the water. Her love of fantasy started in the mudflats of Cape Cod, where the changing tide reveals strange wildlife and lost artifacts. She works in a plant science lab and will talk your ear off about mutations gone wrong. You can find her on Twitter at @amanda_m_pierce.

**Emma Jun** is just another universe generating brain in a squishy, meat jar who thinks far too little of herself. When she's not generating a reality to complain about she's writing about other realities which are slightly more appealing if only for all the cute girls, or playing video games, or watching movies, or waiting for a tentacle beast invasion. Y'know, girl stuff. You can find her on Twitter at @EmmaJuned.